TALES FROM THE FOREST
Fairytale Anthology 4

www.YeOldeDragonBooks.com

Ye Olde Dragon Books
P.O. Box 30802
Middleburg Hts., OH 44130

www.YeOldeDragonBooks.com

2OldeDragons@gmail.com

ISBN 13: 978-1-961129-63-4

Published in the United States of America
Publication Date: May 1, 2024

TABLE OF CONTENTS

FOREWORD

Four years! Wow. Can you believe that? We are entering our fourth year of these amazing stories and anthologies. And I have to tell you, we have the best authors in the world! I love these men and women who *do* come to us, literally from around the world, thanks to the marvels of the internet. Most of our writers have been with us for multiple editions now. You'll find such familiar names as Stoney M. Setzer (who has not missed a volume yet!), Pam Halter, Rosemary DiCristo, Lindsi McIntyre, Jim Doran, and Michelle Houston. We've also entertained visits from Kathleen Bird, Jessica Noelle, and Angela Watts in previous editions. But this time we have two—yes, *two*!—new authors to introduce to you. Rachel Greco brings us a tale of magic deep in the woods. Yvonne McArthur gives us a light-hearted story of a motorcycle-riding grandmother with a prickly exterior that covers some pretty serious wounds beneath. This was such a different twist, I was immediately in love with this "Grandma"!

Not all of our stories fall into the fantasy genre this time. You'll see a wide cross section of science-fiction and fantasy, mixed in with some serious mainstream fiction that covers domestic violence and even child abduction and slavery. (and yes, a prickly little Grandma!) We also have one story by Michelle Houston that is about family and difficult decisions. Quite the departure for Michelle, since we've had both science fiction and fantasy from her in the past, but this story is truly a pull on the heartstrings.

We received more stories this year than we've ever gotten before, and we had some very hard choices to make. These were the best of the best, and we are so grateful for the wonderful authors who took their time to write their stories and get them sent to us through a busy holiday season. We continue to be overwhelmed by our amazing authors and their gift for storytelling.
And I continue to be blessed by the best business partner I could ever ask for. God has been good to me. Michelle Levigne has truly been my encouragement, my cheerleading section, and yes, even the mighty wielder of the cattle prod when necessary. (It's been necessary quite often on this particular edition!) I am so thankful God sent her to me at this stage in my life. I would probably be sitting in a rocker knitting without her to keep me going. Writing and publishing is a grand adventure, the last one in my

lifetime, and I'm going to make it last as long as God gives me breath.

We had a wonderful time putting this book together. It is our fervent hope that these stories will bless you, challenge you, and entertain you.

Deborah Cullins Smith
March 2024

And now a word from Dragon Two …

What she said! This is an amazing collection, pushing the envelope even more, and yeah, requiring some really hard decisions from us. There were several stories that we both loved, but … *sigh* didn't have strong enough ties to Red Riding Hood to make the cut. We strongly encourage those authors to submit those stories elsewhere, and try again, because their imaginations and writing chops came through big-time … just not in the direction we needed.

(Side note: It ain't easy being on this side of the editing desk. Have some sympathy for the editor who says no, and keep in mind that you're a good writer even when they say no if they add: But try again!)

Start brainstorming for the next anthology, which will be Classic Monsters Anthology 4, this fall, featuring (drumroll!) …

The Invisible Man.

Doesn't have to be the old black-and-white movie version. It can be all the TV shows, from the David McCallum version, onward. Or the original HG Wells book. Or … well, you know the drill by now.

Have fun and see you in the fall!!

Michelle L. Levigne
March 2024

THE CASE OF THE MISSING LEGS
Rosemarie DiCristo and Pam Halter

"ALL RISE! Hear ye! Hear ye! The Honorable Owl-iver Wendell Holmes presiding. Draw near and ye shall be heard!"

Judge Holmes, a huge, forbidding Great Horned Owl, took his seat. The courtroom clerk, Donald Dormouse, continued, "This morning's case is The Forest Wolf Pack Versus Granny Lovett." He turned to address the courtroom. "You may be seated."

"I'll hear opening statements now," Judge Holmes said. "Prosecutor Tucker Lupin?"

Tucker, a large gray wolf with steely blue eyes, stood and tugged on his suitcoat. "Thank you, Your Honor. Good morning, ladies and gentlemen of the jury. As you are aware, the maiming of wolves all over the woods has been concerning to all. For approximately the last five weeks, wolves from different packs have been found with their left hind leg chopped off! And right after this began, Granny Lovett just happened to offer a new selection: Forest Fry Bread, some of which is stuffed with meat. Coincidence? I think not."

"Objection! Speculation!" defense lawyer Izzy Fox called.

"Sustained," the judge said.

And so it went. Izzy called objection four more times before Tucker was done with his opening statement. Finally, it was her turn. She stood and faced the jury.

"Your Honor, esteemed members of the jury, thank you for your time. My opponent would like you to think my client has done and is doing a heinous crime simply because she introduced a new menu item for her well-established food truck. This is not a new business, but one that has been going on for years. She has no motive or opportunity, as owning your own business is a very time-consuming endeavor."

Izzy finished her opening statement without any objections from Tucker. She sat down next to Granny and gave her an encouraging smile.

The judge called for witnesses for the prosecution. Tucker stood and shot Izzy and Granny a smug smile. "I'd like to call as my first witness … Mrs. Wolfington."

A murmur ran through the courtroom as the wife of the latest victim approached the bench and stepped up into the witness seat. She sat, wiping her eyes with a handkerchief.

Tucker walked up to her and took her paw. "It's okay, it's okay. We just want to hear what happened."

Mrs. Wolfington sniffed. "Well, I was just getting ready for bed. Lonan was out on the nightly hunt. I had a bad feeling about it, though."

"What kind of feeling?" Tucker asked.

"Objection!" Izzy called. "Irrelevant. Feelings don't prove anything!"

"Sustained," Judge Homes said.

"Go on," Tucker urged Mrs. Wolfington.

"Well, I had just eaten a meat pie for a snack when I heard a knock at the cave door." She paused and shuddered. "It was Officer Benedict. He had terrible news. My Lonan had been attacked!" With that, she burst into tears. "His leg had been chopped off!" she cried. "There was blood! Blood! Blood everywhere!"

"Objection!" Izzy shouted over the howling of the wolves in the court audience. "How does she know this? Did the officer bring Mr. Wolfington to the door?"

"Sustained," the judge said. "The witness will not embellish her testimony."

By then, though, Mrs. Wolfington was sobbing uncontrollably, so she was excused.

The next three witnesses went the same way. Izzy couldn't even cross-examine because of the hysterics of the wives.

"Mr. Lupin, I have to ask you to cease with these witnesses," the judge said wearily. "Do you have anyone who actually saw something?"

Tucker pulled himself up to his full height. "Your Honor, I must say I am shocked at your attitude. Wolves are being maimed but you seem surprisingly blasé about it. Is it because wolves are thought to be Big and Bad?"

The wolves in the courtroom audience growled.

"We don't appreciate the stereotype."

The judge leaned forward until he was practically beak to snout with Tucker. "Any more of that, Mr. Lupin, and you will be in contempt of court."

Tucker stepped back, made a sweeping bow, and said in a silky voice, "I apologize, Your Honor, but the wolf attacks are traumatic experiences, and of course the wolf wives are doubly traumatized."

When Judge Holmes opened his mouth to speak, Tucker quickly said, "I'd like to call as my next witness, Sydney Squirrel."

There was mumbling in the audience as Sydney took his seat. He had a toothpick in his mouth that he pushed back and forth with his tongue.

Izzy whispered to Granny, "What's Tucker up to?"

Granny whispered back, "No idea."

Tucker sauntered to the witness stand. "Mr. Squirrel, please tell the jury what you saw the night before last."

Sydney pulled the toothpick out and stuck it in his shirt pocket. "Wells, as ya know, I'm new here in da forest. Heard it wuz a nice place ta live. But I ain't never expected ta see wut I saw."

Again, the court audience mumbled.

"What did you see?" Tucker prompted.

"Wells, I seen the wolves on da hunt. And whilst I wuz gettin' ready ta bed down for the night, I heard dis sound, like a snake in da grass. So's I looked outta my nest and there wuz dis shadow thing followin' da wolves. Quiet an' sneaky-like."

"What happened next?"

"There was dis thumpin' and bumpin' and howlin'." Sydney gave a shudder. "An' I curled up in my nest, pulled leaves over meself, and hoped I wasn't next!" He gave another shudder. "I likes me legs."

"No more questions," Tucker quickly said.

The judge, still looking weary, asked Izzy, "Would you like to cross examine?"

"Yes, thank you, your Honor." She walked to the witness stand. "You heard thumping and bumping and howling, is that right?"

"That's wut I said."

"Did you actually see a wolf being attacked?"

Sydney shifted in his seat. "Wells, it wuz dark-like."

"So, you didn't see anyone or anything attack the wolves," Izzy pressed. "The thumping and bumping and howling could have easily been part of the hunt."

"Objection!" Tucker cried. "Speculation!"

Izzy walked back to her table. "No more questions."

Judge Holmes asked, "Any more witnesses for the prosecution?"

"Uh, yes," Tucker said. He turned to scan the audience. "But I don't see her. Might I request a recess so I can go and look for her?"

"Granted." Judge Holmes banged the gavel. "Court adjourned until tomorrow morning at 9 o'clock."

Izzy and Granny stood. "You go straight home," Izzy said. "I'm going to talk to Chukhpelek. He knows all the squirrels in the forest. If there's anything to know about this Sydney Squirrel, the Squirrel Network will find out."

Granny lifted her eyebrows. "The Squirrel Network? Is that necessary?"

"Yeah," Izzy said. "Squirrels are everywhere! If anything at all is going on in the forest, they'll know."

"Hmmmm." Granny paused a moment. "Well, if you think that's best."

~~~~~

"Sydney Squirrel? Nah, never heard of him," Chukhpelek said. "But then, Squirrel's a common last name for us. Let me ask around."

"Great. Thanks, Chuck," Izzy said. "And I'd appreciate any
~~~~~

information you can find out about who's attacking the wolves. Someone must have seen something. The forest isn't that big."

"I'll do what I can to help. But you might want to think about contacting Sam Hill."

"What the – Sam Hill? Who's that?" Izzy asked.

Chukhpelek gave a short laugh. "He's the best detective in this forest."

Izzy wrote his name and location down, wondering why she had never heard of him. She tucked the tablet into her rucksack. "Thanks, I'll check him out."

~~~~~

"You're back early," Red commented. "How did it go?"

Granny went to the cabinet and poured herself a small glass of whiskey. "Eh, it went." She took a sip and sat down at the kitchen table. "That wolf lawyer had some of the hysterical wives as witnesses. Trying to get sympathy. And some podunk squirrel who didn't see a thing." She took another sip. "A different witness didn't show up, so the wolf lawyer asked for a recess. I don't know. Doesn't seem like he has much of a case to me."

"Where's Izzy?"

Granny shrugged. "Gone to see some squirrel about the squirrel witness and a squirrel network thing. Too many squirrels for my liking."

Red smiled. "Well, you have to admit, they're everywhere."

"That they are."

~~~~~

Izzy gave a tentative knock on the door of the tree trunk that had the name *Sam Hill, Detective,* carved on it. She wished she had talked to Chuck before the trial started. If she had known about this detective, there might have been evidence to clear Granny right away.

She knocked again, harder this time. After a few seconds, the door opened. A slender, gray female mink stuck her head out.

"Yes, can I help you?"

Izzy nodded. "I'd like to talk to Mr. Hill. If he's in."

The mink looked Izzy up and down. "Do you have an appointment, honey?"

"No, sorry."

The mink sighed. "Mr. Hill is a very busy raccoon. You need an appointment."

Izzy felt frustration rising. Her tail gave a twitch. "How do I make one?"

"You have to talk to his assistant."

"And who is that?"

The mink winked. "Me. Come on in, honey."

Izzy's anger melted. She followed the mink into the tree office. It was a small, but efficient-looking place. There were bookshelves on one wall, not quite full. A desk sat to the left of the shelves. On the walls were pictures of Sam Hill (Izzy assumed) with clients (she guessed). They must have been happy with his services since they were all smiling. Izzy hoped that was a good sign.

"Now, what can we do for you, Miss?" the mink said from behind the desk.

Izzy turned from the pictures. "My name is Izzy Fox. I'm a defense lawyer. Chukhpelek from the Squirrel Network recommended Mr. Hill. For any information."

The mink gave Izzy a calculating look, as if she wasn't sure Izzy was on the up-and-up. "I'm Pepper. Pepper Mink." She gestured to a chair in front of the desk. "Tell me what you're working on and how you think Mr. Hill can help."

As briefly as she could, Izzy explained the case so far against Granny. "My client is innocent, Ms. Mink. The evidence against her is purely circumstantial." Here, Izzy leaned forward so she could beam an earnest look into the mink's still-wary eyes. "But I need proof of that... or at least proof of someone else's guilt."

Pepper nodded slowly, then reached for her desk phone and pressed a button. There was a brief burst of static, then she said, "I think you'll want to see this potential client, Mr. Hill. Ms. Izzy Fox."

A tinny voice responded, "Send her in."

Pepper gestured toward a smooth, flat door that seemed almost concealed in what Izzy had assumed was the back wall of the tree. "You can go in now."

Izzy stood, and as if that would give her confidence, straightened to her full height and strode through the door.

Once inside, she stopped short in surprise. Sam Hill was the largest raccoon she'd ever seen. Could a raccoon weigh a seventh of a ton? Well, that was just an estimate, of course, but she wondered briefly if it was a successful business that had him nearly double his weight since he'd posed for those photos on his wall. And paid for what was obviously a very expensive navy-blue pinstriped suit and vest, lemon-yellow silk shirt, and pink paisley tie.

Hill leaned forward. "Are you indeed Ms. Izzy Fox?"

"Yes, and I need—"

Hill held up a paw. "I've been following the case, Ms. Fox. I know Granny Lovett well. Good food. And I know much about you. This is your first trial, you graduated second in your class from Forest Law, you're known to be thorough, efficient, and honest."

Whether it was the intensity of Sam Hill's gaze or the fact that he knew so much about her, Izzy said, "W-well, I'm sorry to say I know very little about you. Except for what Chukhpelek told me, and he only—"

Again, Hill held up a paw. "I am also thorough, efficient, and honest. I get results."

"Y-yes, that's what Chuck—Chukhpelek—implied when he, um, we…" Rats, now she was downright stammering. She swallowed. "I suppose you can guess what I want you to do."

His nod was so slight, Izzy barely saw it. "Find evidence that will clear your client."

Her nod was swift and eager.

"It may take time, Ms. Fox, but before we proceed, I must inform you: my fee is considerable, and not contingent on success."

Izzy licked at suddenly dry lips. "Well, I suppose you'll want a retainer?" Rats again, she *was* thorough and efficient, so why was she making that sound like a question?

Hill nodded. "As an advance for expenses. And I'll need all the information you have."

An hour later, Izzy was ready to leave, but before she could, Hill stopped her. "Ms. Fox?"

Izzy turned.

"Keep in mind. It's extremely hard to find a black cat in a dark room." He smiled. "Particularly when there is no cat."

~~~~~

Day two of the trial began with buzzing whispers as Emily Evans-Smythe took the stand.

"Mrs. Evans-Smythe," Tucker Lupin intoned. "Will you please tell the court what you saw the night of January 23rd?"

Emily was the widow of one of the wealthiest landowners in the county, and she wore her clothes, put on her make-up, and styled her shiny-blond hair as if trying to prove that. "Jessica—um, Granny Lovett, entering her home at 2am."

"And this was the night of the attack on Peter Wolferian."

"Yes. The very night." Although Emily's voice was smoothly patrician, her ice-blue eyes narrowed as she glared at Granny.

"What was Mrs. Lovett doing as she entered her home?"

"Carrying a wrapped package, the size and shape of a wolf's leg—"

"Objection!" shouted Izzy Fox. "The witness couldn't possibly—"

But Emily continued, "—and I shouldn't have said 'entering' because Granny Lovett was *skulking* into her house—"

"Objection!"

"—as if she had something to hide!"

The court audience gasped. A small wolf howled.

"Objection," cried Izzy for the third time as Judge Holmes said sharply, "Mr. Lupin, will you please control your witness? Objection sustained."

"My apologies, your Honor." To Emily, Tucker said, "So, Mrs. Lovett was seen entering her house at 2am with a large package."

Emily continued to glare at Granny. "Yes, sir. And soon after, I smelled what could only be grilled wolf coming from her kitchen."
~~~~~

A female wolf gagged as the court audience growled painfully.

Izzy came to her feet. "Objection! Again, the witness has no way of knowing—"

Emily retorted, "I happen to be a grade-A chef—"

Meanwhile, Judge Holmes was saying, "Mr. Lupin, please—"

Tucker once again made a sweeping bow. "I apologize, your Honor." To Emily, he said, "Is there anything else you'd like to tell the court?"

"Naturally, with the spate of wolf attacks and the suspicion surrounding Mrs. Lovett..." Here Emily tried to smile at Granny. "...I asked around. No butcher in the tri-state area has provided meat to Mrs. Lovett for over four months—"

"Your Honor." Izzy thunked her head onto the table. "Objection."

"Sustained, Ms. Fox. The jury will ignore Mrs. Evans-Smythe's last statement."

It went on like this for a bit, with Emily Evans-Smythe providing no further usable testimony.

When it was Izzy Fox's turn to cross-examine, she leaned toward the woman with a small smile. "Is it true you own the largest cattle ranch in our county?"

"Yes, ma'am."

"And is it true that cattle ranchers have an adversarial relationship with wolves?"

Emily chewed at her lip while the court room rang with hoots and grumbles.

"Mrs. Evans-Smythe?"

She chewed at her lip a bit more before responding carefully, "They kill our livestock."

"Might you yourself," asked Izzy, "have a reason for wanting the wolves eliminated?"

"Objection," shouted Tucker Lupin.

"Your Honor," Izzy shot back. "It's a matter of public record what Emily Evans-Smythe's opinions of wolves are. She's blogged about it, as well as written countless articles stating that ranches and wolves cannot co-exist."

"Objection overruled. Proceed."

"Where is your ranch, Mrs. Evans-Smythe?"

"I'm sorry?"

"Where is it? Close to Granny Lovett's home?"

Emily looked down at her perfectly manicured hands.

"Mrs. Evans-Smythe," Judge Holmes said, "you will answer the question."

"Five miles out of town," she whispered.

"Can you repeat that?" Izzy asked.

"Five miles out of town."

Again, Izzy gave a small smile. "Then what were you doing outside of Granny Lovett's at 2am?"

"I..."

"Isn't it true that you are known to frequent The Last Chance Saloon, which is down the block from Granny Lovett's house?"

"Objection. Really, your Honor, this is beyond..."

But apparently Emily Evans-Smythe had had enough because she stood abruptly and tossed her head so quickly, Izzy had to back away or be head-butted. "Yes, I was at the saloon, but it's not like I went staggering out the door into the snow. And just what are you implying?"

"Mr. Lupin," Judge Holmes cried. "Will you please...?"

Either no one heard, or no one was listening.

Emily continued, "That I attacked those wolves? Oh, yeah, I hate them." Suddenly her voice was less patrician and more like the local gal she was before marrying the now-deceased Edmund Evans-Smythe, whose mega-ranch she'd inherited. "Hate! But I wouldn't maim them."

"Mr. Lupin!" cried Judge Holmes.

"Maimed wolves still destroy cattle. I'd *kill* the vermin!"

By now the court officers were leading Emily from the witness stand and down the aisle of the courtroom.

"Trap them! Shoot them! Disembowel them!" she shouted back at judge and jury. "And you think because she's called 'Granny' that Jessica Lovett is a sweet old thing? That hussy stole Len Lovett from me. He was my man until she vamped him."

Emily was almost to the doors to the hall, but still she hollered back, "Talk to Red, why don't you? You don't think that whole 'trying to eat Grandma' thing isn't a motive?" She gave a sharp, sudden laugh. "If you pry hard enough, you'll find holes in their alibis so large, you'd declare neither one of them has a leg to stand—"

The courtroom door closed on her last word, and there was blessed silence... until the babble of excited, gossipy voices began swirling through the crowd.

~~~~~

"And how was today's testimony?" Red asked as soon as her grandmother entered their house.

Granny chuckled. "The so-called witnesses for the so-called prosecution are destroying their own case. Mercy, it's like the Jerry Springwood show in there."

Red cocked her head. "Why? What happened?"

Granny explained in detail, making it sound even more outrageous than it was.

When she was done, Red looked worried. "Do you think they can make anything of that cooking at 2am?"

Granny frowned briefly, then repeated what Emily Evans-Smythe had
~~~~~

said as the doors slammed on her, adding, "Maybe we can tell them we cook at all hours because we need a 'leg' up on our competition."

~~~~~

If the crowd in the courtroom was expecting Day Three of the trial to be as raucous as the first two days, they were disappointed. The initial surge of excitement when Little Red was called to the stand was squelched when her testimony didn't go as expected.

"So, Red," Tucker drawled, "can you give us details on just where your grandmother gets the meat for her stuffed fry bread?"

The court audience held their collective breaths, waiting, straining to hear her answer.

"I'm afraid I can't," Red whispered.

"What's that?" Tucker asked.

She cleared her throat. "I can't."

"Can't what?"

"I can't give details on where Granny gets the meat," Red said.

The court audience *ooohed*.

Tucker drew himself up with a wicked grin and faced the jury. "Can't? *Or won't?*"

Now the court audience *aaahed*.

"Objection!" Izzy shouted.

The audience's mumbling grew louder. The wolf section growled. One of the wolf victim's wives stood up. "Liar!" she shrieked.

Judge Holmes banged the gavel. The court clerk, Donald Dormouse, squeaked, "Order! Order!"

Even the jury joined in the fray.

Clerk Dormouse picked up a small megaphone. "Order! Order!"

As the judge banged the gavel for the fifth time, a tremendous CRASH of splintering wood echoed in the courtroom. Everyone's screaming came to a sudden halt. Izzy, who was practically weeping, turned to look at the demolished courthouse doors just as the Huntsman swaggered through them.

~~~~~

About the time the courthouse doors were being chopped down, Detective Sam Hill was working on some closed doors of his own. He hit a dead end with the Squirrel Network, although he suspected the contrary critters weren't being forthcoming. Still, there was no reason they wouldn't share all they knew. How would it benefit them? He must be missing something.

He pushed the intercom button. "Pepper? Will you come in here?"

"Sure thing, Mr. Hill."

Sam sat at his desk, his fingers steepled under his chin. Pepper watched him, her pen poised over her yellow legal pad. Finally, he spoke.

"The Squirrel Network has not uncovered anything. I may have to contact ... her."

Pepper gasped. "Are you sure, Mr. Hill? I mean, are things that desperate?"

"Hmmmmm, maybe not yet, but I want to keep it in mind."

She scribbled on the pad. "I'll have her number ready. Anything else?"

Sam smiled. "How about a nice turkey club?"

~~~~~

"Order! Order in the court!" Clerk Dormouse screeched hoarsely, his megaphone hanging uselessly at his side. "Please!"

No one paid him any heed as the Huntsman strode up the center of the courtroom aisle and took a seat in the front row, directly behind Granny and Izzy.

Judge Holmes banged the gavel once. "I'm going to have to charge you with destruction of public property, sir."

The Huntsman nodded curtly.

"May I ask why you felt it necessary to chop the doors down?" the judge asked.

"They were locked," was all the Huntsman replied.

Judge Holmes leaned toward the clerk. "Why were the doors locked?"

"I don't know, your Honor. I'll look into it."

"Thank you. Now, let's continue." He looked at Tucker. "Do you have any more questions for this witness?"

Tucker strolled over to his table, looked over his shoulder at the Huntsman, then said, "No more questions, your Honor."

Izzy was on her feet and in front of the stand before the judge could ask if she had any questions. Red shifted nervously in her seat.

Izzy smiled at her. "It's okay, Red. Let's try that last question again. About where Granny gets her supplies. Do you know anything about that?"

Red shook her head. "I don't. I'm sorry! I really don't. Granny, well, she doesn't talk about that part of the business."

"And how long has Granny been in business?"

"For as long as I can remember. She's had that food truck since I was a little girl. The only time she hasn't worked was the one time she'd gotten down ill, and I checked in on her, making sure her cottage was clean. Taking her baskets of goodies."

Izzy turned to face the jury. "And when did the attacks on the wolves begin?"

Red was visibly shaken by this question. "I—I, well, the first I heard of them was five weeks ago."

"So, no wolves were attacked until five weeks ago, yet Granny Lovett has been in the food truck business for decades!" She turned back to the judge. "No more questions."

Tucker jumped to his feet. "Re-direct, you Honor?"

The judge nodded.
~~~~~

"Ms. Red, may I ask how long you've been working with your grandmother in the food truck business?"

"Two years," Red answered.

"And you don't know where she gets the meat for her fry bread?"

"No."

"No more questions."

The judge banged the gavel. "Court adjourned until tomorrow at 9am."

~~~~~

Granny, Red, and the Huntsman sat at Granny's kitchen table. Granny had brewed some strong chamomile tea for them and set out a plate of butter cookies.

"I made it look bad, Granny. I'm so sorry!" Red wept. "And I didn't want to implicate Lelan."

The Huntsman, Lelan, reached out and squeezed her hand. "It's fine, my love. I'll talk to Izzy. Get her to put me on the stand. That fleabag shyster does not scare me."

Granny grunted. "That fleabag shyster isn't stupid. And if we have the Squirrel Network, he'll have something. Squirrels aren't the only small animals in the forest that get around. Chipmunks, voles, even skunks. Which, now that I think about it, seems appropriate."

They all laughed. Lelan reached for a cookie. "I'll take the stand tomorrow."

~~~~~

The door debris had been cleared away by the next morning. In its place was a velvet rope and one of the prison guards, a large black bear named Brutus. Those who wanted to enter the courtroom had to have an ID and a darn good reason for being there. Consequently, the court audience was smaller that day.

Izzy called Lelan Huntsman to the stand. She got right to the point.

"Mr. Huntsman, will you please tell the court what you told me last night?"

Lelan sat in the witness seat, leaning on the right arm, exuding assurance, poise, and a bit of élan. "Of course." He turned to face the jury. "*I* supply the meat for Granny Lovett's food truck business."

The wolves in the audience broke into howls of rage. One of the female jurors, an opossum, fainted. Tucker leapt to his feet. "OBJECTION!!!!"

Izzy spoke quickly. "It's a valid question, your Honor, and if you'll allow me to continue, you'll see where I'm going."

"Proceed," said Holmes.

Once the courtroom was again quiet and Ophelia Opossum had been revived, Izzy said, "Can you tell us where you get the meat, Mr. Huntsman?"

His smile oozing complete confidence, Lelan leaned forward, as if that would make his words clearer. "I can tell you where I didn't. Mrs. Evans-Smythe was right about one thing: no butcher in the region has sold Granny Lovett a speck of meat for more than four months."

Once again, the courtroom erupted, and the wolf wife who'd shouted, "Liar!" the day before now screeched, "Yeah, because she used my precious Nero's leg! And since he's, well, a bit on the large side, I'll betcha she got a ton of fry bread outta him."

Another wolf hollered, "She's using *all* our legs."

Judge Holmes hooted loudly and sharply, and everyone fell silent. Then he said in a deadly-serious voice, "If there is one more sound, even a sigh, from anyone in this courtroom, I will clear it of all spectators, and it will remain clear for the duration of the trial. Or I may declare a mistrial for whichever side is responsible for the most chaos. Does everyone understand?"

The complete silence made it clear that everyone did.

"Mr. Huntsman?" Izzy prompted. "Can you clarify your remark?"

His nod was as confident as his smile. "I repeat: *I* provide Granny Lovett's meat. After all, I'm a huntsman. I get her pheasant and quail, duck and grouse, and venison. Lots and lots of venison." He winked at Granny, and she offered him a small, satisfied smile.

The spectators in the court moved their lips as if they wanted to comment, but no one dared utter a peep.

"And can you state categorically that there is no wolf meat in the mixture you provide?"

Lelan's smile resembled a smirk. "Wolf meat? No one would eat that." He paused, then stated, "It's got an unpleasant, game-y aftertaste."

Someone shouted, "Hey!" and was immediately shushed by several other spectators.

Izzy's smile was as satisfied as Granny's. "No more questions."

Looking like he wished he didn't need to say it, Judge Holmes asked, "Any questions, Mr. Lupin?"

Tucker stepped forward with a satisfied smile of his own. "Mr. Huntsman, are you prepared to swear that Granny Lovett's Forest Fry Bread is a mixture of what you just mentioned?"

Lelan nodded. "Pheasant, grouse, duck, quail, and venison."

Tucker's narrowed eyes glittered. "Lots and lots of venison?"

"Objection," Izzy said. "Mr. Lupin is badgering the witness."

"Sustained." Holmes sighed. "Mr. Lupin..."

Once again, Tucker bowed low. "But it does contain only those ingredients?"

Lelan hesitated for just a moment, then nodded.

"I'm sorry, can you speak that aloud? For the record?"

"Yes."

"You realize what it would imply if meats other than pheasant, grouse, duck, quail, and venison are found in the fry bread?"

Lelan's confidence seemed to waver for a moment, but he sat up straighter and declared, "Yes, I do."

Tucker nodded to the judge. "No more questions. And I ask for a recess to await the results of the tests my side has done on the composition of Granny Lovett's Forest Fry Bread."

Judge Holmes agreed to the recess at the same time the courtroom erupted in a clamor of howls and shrieks, so whether his promise of clearing the courtroom for good would prove true remained to be seen.

~~~~~

Since it was Chukhpelek who summoned Izzy and not the other way around, she assumed he had news for her and burst into his office exclaiming, "Please, tell me it's something good. Did you hear Lupin is testing the meat? Sure, I know it will turn out okay for Granny but—"

Chukhpelek overrode her. "I got two things to tell you and you're not going to like either one."

Izzy gulped and waited for Chuck to continue.

He took a deep breath. "This is particularly bad, considering it comes so soon after his testimony. Early this morning, Sydney Squirrel was found unconscious outside his nest. His left hind leg had been cut off."

Izzy gasped. "Why the poor little..." She stopped, looking deep into Chukhpelek's eyes. Warily, she asked, "Wait, you said two things?"

He nodded. "This afternoon, Sigmund Squirrel was found in the woods just outside town. Missing *his* left hind leg."

Izzy pressed her paws to her lips. "That's awful, but... I don't understand... I mean... I don't even recognize his name let alone what it might mean for my client."

"Maybe nothing," Chuck said, and she felt a moment of relief. Then he added, "But maybe everything. Sigmund's the squirrel who collected the fry bread samples for Tucker Lupin."

~~~~~

Sam Hill said one thing to Pepper Mink. "It's time."

Pepper said one thing in reply. "I'll call her."

A minute later, she buzzed Sam. "Ms. Rizzo-Hill on line two."

He took a deep breath, pasted a wide smile on his face, and lifted the receiver.

"Hello? Mother?"

~~~~~

Tucker Lupin took the envelope from the courier and shut the door. He ripped it open, scanned it, then chuckled. "Oh, Granny, there's no hiding behind that sweet wrinkly smile now."

~~~~~

Chukhpelek sat with his best Network agents. "Fellas, we gotta do better. Someone or something is after Granny. And Izzy is my friend. I'm not ordering, but I *am* asking for volunteers to go into the east end of the forest."

To his extreme satisfaction, they all raised their paws.

~~~~~

Granny, Red, Lelan, and Izzy sat at the kitchen table. Their coffee had long grown cold, and the plate of molasses cookies sat untouched.

Finally, Izzy spoke. "I'm sure Tucker won't find anything."

Granny shrugged. "I'm sure he won't. I really *don't* put wolf meat in my fry bread."

"And I really don't chop off their legs," Lelan said.

Red said nothing.

~~~~~

Judge Holmes tapped his gavel lightly on his desk while Clerk Dormouse paced back and forth and back and forth on the edge of it. "Will you stop pacing?" the judge snapped.

"I can't help it," Donald squeaked. "I'm so nervous!"

"Yeah, I am, too."

"What do you think the report will say?"

Judge Holmes sighed. "With this case, whoooo knows?"

~~~~~

"What? You never call, you never write. And last Mother's Day? Nothing!"

Sam put a paw over his eyes. "I'm sorry. I get busy. You know how it works."

"You only call when you're stumped on a case. What is it now?"

Sam filled her in. "Can you help?" he asked.

"Why should I? Christmas? A fruit basket. My birthday? Just a card. No cake, no flowers. Your father may as well still be alive!"

"I'm sorry, Mother," Sam said again. A pounding started in the back of his head. "This is a tough case. Toughest one I've seen in years. You're the best detective anywhere. Everyone knows that!"

A little buttering up can't hurt, he thought. And really, his mother *was* the best.

"Buttering me up won't help," his mother retorted. "Your father buttered me up and I married him. Look at how *that* turned out! A lazy slob who relied on me to make ends meet. Card playing, swill drinking bum! I should have known when he showed up half an hour late for our wedding with beer on his breath!"

Sam rubbed his eyes. When Mother got on a roll, it was best to let her go until she ran out of steam. He laid the phone down and doodled on a Post-It note until he couldn't hear her voice anymore.

He picked the phone back up. "I know, Mother. I know. I'm sorry."

There was a momentary silence. "So, how long do I have?"

"Well, it's 3 o'clock now, and the trial starts again tomorrow at 9am. Is
~~~~~

that enough time?"

"For me ... plenty of time!"

~~~~~

The weather on the morning of the fifth day of the trial started off cloudy and sleeting. The coat racks were literally dripping with wet jackets and hats. The court audience was subdued, not wanting to be tossed out of the trial.

Granny and Izzy sat at the defense table. Lelan and Red sat in the seats directly behind them. Tucker Lupin tapped a pencil on the large white envelope in front of him as the jury filed into their seats.

Finally, Judge Holmes, his feathers a bit ruffled, came in.

"All rise! The Honorable Judge Owl-iver Wendell Holmes presiding!" Clerk Dormouse called.

"You may be seated," Judge Holmes said. "Before we start, I'd like to remind the court audience to use restraint in their reactions today or I *will* have you all removed." He glared around the courtroom, then looked at Tucker. "Mr. Lupin?"

Tucker stood, nodded at the jury, then picked up the envelope. "Your Honor, in this envelope, I have the results of the tests run on the meat filling for Granny's fry bread." He pulled the paper out slowly. Then he walked to the bench, gave a copy to Judge Holmes, and went back to his desk.

Izzy blew air out of her nose in frustration.

Tucker picked up his copy. "Hmmmmm ... interesting. Yes, I see pheasant, grouse, duck, quail, and venison, but what's this?" He paused dramatically. "*WOLF MEAT!*"

The uproar in the courtroom could probably have been heard in Northlands, which was a good ten miles away. Howls, screams, cursing filled the air. Two wolf wives jumped out of their seats and lunged toward the front of the court at Granny, whose expression was unreadable.

Brutus and his team of bear guards grabbed them before they could reach her. Clearly, they were ready for this kind of reaction. More security guards arrived; the room couldn't have held one more creature.

"Order! Order!" Judge Holmes called. "If you want to stay, I need order!"

Gradually, the noise quieted, although several wolves made rumbling noises now and then. Tucker gave Izzy a small smile. She glared at him, resisting the urge to stick out her tongue.

"Your Honor," Tucker said in a brisk voice. "With this new evidence, there is no doubt of Granny's guilt. I see no reason for this trial to go on. You have no option other than declaring her *guilty!*"

The court audience howled in agreement.

Judge Holmes lifted the gavel once more, but just then, the newly repaired courtroom doors burst open, and Chukhpelek, followed by five squirrels, marched into the room.
~~~~~

"Your Honor, I'd like to address the court!" Chuck called.

The judge still had the gavel raised. It fell out of his wing, clattering onto the desk. "What now?"

Chuck motioned for his squirrel informants to stay back. He turned to the judge. "May I approach the bench?"

Judge Holmes sighed. "Why not?"

Chuck didn't look at Izzy or Granny as he pushed open the gate and walked to stand in front of the judge. "Your Honor, my Squirrel Network has discovered information that will show Sigmund Squirrel, who had been hired by Tucker Lupin, has a cousin who works at the East End Testing Lab. This cousin, Stephen Squirrel, falsified the test results!"

Again, the court erupted with angry protests.

The judge banged his gavel. "Let me see this information."

Chuck waved over one of the squirrel informants who handed him a thick blue envelope. "In this envelope is a flash drive with the recordings my squirrels made while, um, observing the goings on in the East End Lab."

"Objection!" Tucker shouted. "You can't break into an official building and plant a spy camera!"

"They didn't!"

Everyone gasped and turned. There in the doorway stood Detective Sam Hill. "While the general public *is* allowed to take a tour of the testing lab, the Squirrel Network isn't exactly the general public. They're professionals who can conduct themselves with decorum."

Izzy's ears perked up and she leaned forward eagerly, but Tucker's face twitched.

Sam continued, "Professional investigators, as the court and our esteemed counsel know, *can* record conversations overheard in public, if the persons recorded have no reasonable expectation of privacy. And, unlike police officers, they do not need warrants, which means they can obtain information unavailable to persons in the legal sector."

"Judge Holmes." Tucker tried turning on his silky smile, but it was clear from the way his voice shook that he was rattled. "We all know this, so why allow Mr. Hill to use a fancy spiel to preface an obviously last-minute, unprecedented bid to disrupt this trial—"

"Disrupt? *This* trial?" Judge Holmes blurted, then shook his head, took a deep breath, and said in a quieter voice, "We all also know, Counselor, that a judge can admit whatever evidence he sees fit, if it's both relevant and authentic." He nodded to Donald Dormouse. "Let's see what Mr. Hill brought and discover if it fits both factors."

Quiet whispers fluttered though the courtroom as the flash drive was inserted into the court's video system and a picture flicked to life: Stephen Squirrel, in what was obviously the testing lab's cafeteria, eating stuffed acorn squash as a female squirrel joined him at his table.

Although the video seemed to be filmed from several feet away, the sound and picture quality was clear and showed the wariness in Stephen's eyes when he said, "Sybil." A moment passed. "I'm sorry about your boyfriend's, uh, leg."

"My boyfriend," Sybil's tone had a sardonic twist, "is your cousin, so I can offer the same condolences to you." Now she paused. "But is either one of us really sorry about what happened to Sigmund?"

Stephen looked surprised.

"Number one, please don't pretend the entire forest doesn't know that my boyfriend..." Here, Sybil did angry air quotes. "...cheated on me with Cherie Chipmunk. Number two, doesn't everyone in the forest know Sigmund swindled you out of your family fortune?"

"Hey." Stephen's voice was indignant. "Are you trying to say I maimed the guy?"

"Heck, no, because I just gave a reason *I* could've done it. My point is number three: Sigmund, the sleazeball, cooperated with that wolf, Tucker Lupin, to get the goods on poor Granny Lovett, who was attacked by a wolf, knowing full well that we squirrels are also eaten by wolves. Sigmund, however, is honorable about one thing: his work product. If that test he authorized came back a certain way, you can bet your bottom dollar it was legit." Sybil paused to smile a hard smile. "But *you* took care of that."

Stephen flinched, then looked around nervously.

"Relax. No one's around but our fellow employees and the usual tour group crowd, enjoying our cafeteria food." Sybil leaned closer to him. "One of the benefits of working in the lab office is I see the test results when they come in, and when they're mailed out."

The video quality was clear enough to show Stephen swallowing hard.

Sybil placed her paw on his paw and smiled tenderly. "Stevie, you know I'm sweet on you, and the feeling's mutual, right? You can trust me. *You* changed the test results to show wolf meat in the fry bread mixture, didn't you?"

The surprised snarls erupting in the courtroom drowned out the audio relating Stephen Squirrel's words but couldn't hide the image of his quick grin or his smug nod.

"Your Honor!" Tucker Lupin had to shout over the hubbub. "It should be obvious that Sybil Squirrel was a plant sent to the cafeteria to entrap Stephen Squirrel."

Either Judge Holmes couldn't hear, or he chose not to answer.

Tucker shouted louder. "But even if she wasn't, none of what was revealed clears Granny Lovett of the wolf attacks or, may I add, the squirrel attacks. Unless someone can provide proof that a person besides Jessica Lovett is responsible, you must allow the trial to continue with the evidence provided!"

Izzy jumped up. "Your Honor, with the new evidence provided, I move for a mistrial!"

The court audience shrieked their displeasure.

Clerk Dormouse just shook his head.

"Your Honor," Tucker shouted over the din, "the trial must continue. We must determine who is doing these heinous attacks on wolves! We need someone to provide proof, and do we have that someone? No! Who is that someone?"

Which is the exact moment a female voice boomed out, "*I* am that someone."

A collective gasp filled the courtroom as Josephine Rizzo-Hill advanced up the aisle.

"May I approach the bench, Your Honor?"

The judge waved her forward. "Might as well."

Whispers filled the room as Josephine pushed through the gate.

"*Do you see who that is?*"

"*It's Jo-Jo Rizzo-Hill!*"

"*She's the greatest detective of all time.*"

"*The racoon riddle resolver!*"

"*The champion case cracker!*"

"*She really knows her onions.*"

"*Be quiet! I want to hear!*"

Jo-Jo stood before the judge. "Thank you, Your Honor."

"Objection!" Tucker screamed.

"Overruled," the judge said. "Ms. Rizzo-Hill, it's nice to see you again. I hope you can bring some sense out of this mess."

"I can," Jo-Jo said. "It's nice to see you again, too. Now, let me first clear up who is responsible for the squirrel tainting the test results. That would be Emily Evans-Smythe."

The court audience *ooohed* as Granny chuckled. She leaned to Izzy and whispered, "No surprise there."

Izzy nodded.

"Mrs. Evans-Smythe hired Stephen Squirrel to falsify the test results so Granny would be found guilty of adding wolf meat to her fry bread," Jo-Jo continued. "She hired someone else to maim the squirrel who testified and the one who brought in the meat sample to the lab. All these events would point toward Granny also maiming the wolves."

The court audience *aaahed*.

"You can prove this?" the judge asked.

"Yes, your Honor, and I will," Jo-Jo answered. "But may I go on? As to the maiming of the wolves, I have discovered it was a cassowary."

Everyone exchanged questioning glances.

"Excuse me?" Judge Holmes asked.

"A cassowary," Jo-Jo repeated. "Don't tell me no one knows what this creature is!"

Silence met her question.

Jo-Jo sighed. "Doesn't anyone watch National Geographic anymore?" She rummaged in her purse. "Here's a flash drive—"

"Another one?" the judge interrupted.

Jo-Jo didn't respond but handed the flash drive to Donald. In a few seconds, information blared around the room, teaching all there was to know about the cassowary, complete with full color pictures.

As the video ended, Jo-Jo turned to the jury. "As you see, this six-foot-tall bird can easily rip the leg off a wolf, if it chose to do so."

"Objection!" Tucker shouted. "Speculation!"

Jo-Jo rolled her eyes. "I just happen to have a video of one of the attacks."

Tucker shook his head. "We checked all the security cameras in the forest. There was nothing that showed the attacks."

Jo-Jo pointed her forefinger in the air. "But ... *I* checked the camera that *I* had set up three years ago for the case of Ma Porker and the Wild Warthogs."

Judge Holmes put his head on a wing and waved the other one at Clerk Dormouse. "I should have taken early retirement," he mumbled.

Donald inserted Jo-Jo's second flash drive into the video system. There was a flicker, then the video showed the nighttime forest. The wolves were just heading out on their hunt. As they loped past the camera, the last wolf in the group was tackled by what was clearly a cassowary. They disappeared below the camera. There was crashing and howling, and the tree branches shook. Then the head of the cassowary shot up from below, a wolf's leg in its beak. It ran off into the darkness.

The court audience cried in anger and pain. The bear guards tried to settle them down, but chaos ensued as several wolves ran around the room howling. Some clung to each other. The noise level rose to a thunderous pitch.

BANG!!

One of the security guards fired his gun into the ceiling. Bits of plaster dropped onto the wolves and the floor.

Judge Holmes pounded the gavel until it broke.

Clerk Dormouse shouted into his megaphone, "Order! Order!"

Everyone settled down, breathing hard and gasping.

Tucker slowly stood. "Ms. Rizzo-Hill. Since you seem to have so much information, can you tell us just how a giant six-foot-tall bird from the other side of the world got into our forest?"

That caught everyone's attention.

Jo-Jo smiled. "Please. Just who do you think I am? Of course, I can tell you." She pulled out a newspaper clipping from her purse. "Five weeks ago, a cassowary escaped from the Northlands Forest Zoo." She handed the clipping to the judge who gave it to the clerk who passed it to the jury.

"And you'll have us believe that this animal could come all the way to the east end and our forest on its own?"

"*This animal*," she emphasized, "is an excellent runner, capable of reaching speeds of thirty miles an hour. And zoo animals are *wild* animals. If they get out of their cages, who knows what they'll do or where they'll go?"

"Objection!" Tucker said, wearily. "According to your video, cassowaries do not eat meat."

Jo-Jo held up a paw. "But they *do* attack when threatened. A pack of running wolves could easily have startled it."

There was a buzz of murmurs in the courtroom, and Izzy shouted, "Your Honor, in light of this evidence, it is plain that my client must be declared innocent."

Judge Owl-iver Wendell Holmes banged his broken gavel twice and spoke the following words with more relief than even he could have anticipated. "I declare the case of The Forest Wolf Pack Versus Granny Lovett officially dismissed."

~~~~~

Once again, Granny, Red, and Lelan gathered in Granny's kitchen, but this time they hungrily ate the chocolate chip cookies before them.

"Oh, heavenly days," Granny exclaimed. "I'm glad that's finally over."

"Vindicated," Lelan cried, and they embraced.

"But is it?" Red asked. She hadn't joined the embrace.

They turned to her.

"Over, I mean."

Lelan's brow wrinkled. "My love, I don't..."

Red bit her lip, then blurted, "Isn't your cousin Holter a locksmith? And doesn't he live in Northlands?"

Lelan answered carefully. "Yes, but...?"

"Please tell me you did not ask him to release that cassowary and bring it to the east end."

"Why would I do that?"

Red gave him a pointed look then lifted her skirt to reveal her left leg, which was wooden from below the knee down.

A strained silence filled the room.

Lelan gave a short laugh. "Well, my love, like Jo-Jo said, you never know what wild animals will do. It's not like we can control them."

"*Did* Holter let the cassowary loose? *Did* he bring it here?"

Granny patted Red's hand. "Well, dear ... *if* he did ... I assure you, Lelan had *nothing* to do with it." And Granny lifted her own skirt.

Red sighed and rolled her eyes. "Oh, Granny!"

The End
~~~~~

FACE THE WOLF
Kathleen Bird

Her migraine was only getting worse by the minute, and she'd forgotten her meds at home. Bridget massaged her temple and closed her eyes against the harsh fluorescent lights of the library study room. The other occupants of the room certainly weren't helping either.

This is why I hate group projects, she thought with a quiet groan that no one else heard over their arguing.

"We should focus on the classics like *Pride & Prejudice*. That's been retold a million times!"

"Why would I want to do a project about a girly book like that? It's all kisses and swooning."

"That's not exactly true…"

"Shut your mouth, dork!"

"Hey, don't talk to him like that!"

"Enough," Bridget said in a voice so low it was almost a growl. She opened her eyes and glared at each of her groupmates with a vengeance. "Will someone just pick something already so we can make a plan? Some of us have better things to do than spend their whole night in the campus library."

"I second that motion," said a brunette with sleepy eyes. "There's a warm bed calling my name right about now." She leaned her head on her boyfriend's shoulder to emphasize the point, and he shook his head with a quiet laugh. Drema was the only one able to get a laugh out of that guy. Most of the time, Julius was a real stick in the mud. He always seemed to be focused on whatever grander story was playing out in his head rather than whatever was happening right in front of him.

"Okay then. Bridget, do you have any suggestions?" Annaliese flicked her bangs out of her eyes before she started perusing a printout in front of her. "We're supposed to look for allusions from classic stories in modern cinematography. Since my Jane Austen suggestion is out, what other choices do we want to look at?" She tugged at the ends of her short blond hair while she considered their options.

"What about looking at some familiar fairytales? Some of those Grimm ones can get pretty dark, so they should be sufficiently *manly*," Bridget said with just a hint of sarcasm as her gaze shot daggers at her ex-boyfriend, Luke. He grinned at her in response, revealing a row full of perfectly white teeth. He'd shown up late to their meeting and had been forced to take the last seat available, which just happened to be next to her. If he had a higher IQ than a third grader, she might have thought he'd planned it that way.

"Who's afraid of the big bad wolf?" he said in a slightly menacing sing-song that sent shivers down her spine.

Definitely don't regret breaking up with this jerk.

"That's actually not from a fairytale," a soft masculine voice interrupted. "The story of the *Three Little Pigs* is more like a nursery rhyme or something."

"Stay out of this, dork," Luke snapped.

"Is that the only insult you know?" Bridget said as she smacked him on the arm. "Lay off him, okay?" She glanced at the young man on the other side of her who was staring intently at the blank notebook in front of him. Hunter wasn't exactly her type, but she did have to admit he was pretty nice-looking. He had straight brown hair cut in a shag haircut with bangs that swooped over his equally brown eyes. It was a little out of style, but it wasn't like she cared about that kind of thing. *He is a bit of a dork though*, she thought half-heartedly.

"Can we stop the drama for a minute and discuss Bridget's idea?" Annaliese said firmly. She seemed to have appointed herself the leader of their little group, and Bridget had no intention of contending that idea. "I like the fairytale idea. There's a lot of ways we could take that."

"We could analyze one modern adaptation that has a lot of fairytale references in it, like *Once Upon a Time* or something. That would allow for a wide variety of allusion examples," Julius said thoughtfully. Drema nodded in agreement. Not only were the two of them dating, but they had all the same classes. Bridget wouldn't be surprised to find out they'd been partners on several projects.

"What about *Into the Woods*? The musical's been around for a while, and the movie adaptation was pretty good," Hunter said as he finally lifted his head to meet the eyes of the rest of the group.

"Leave it to the music nerd to suggest a musical," Luke muttered.

Bridget rolled her eyes and ignored his comment. It was true she wasn't much of a musical person herself, but that didn't make it a bad idea. Hunter was in a band with Annaliese's boyfriend, so it did make sense that would be his cup of tea. Earlier in the semester, she'd dropped into a coffee shop where they happened to be playing. Annaliese had told her the lyrics were all original and written by her boyfriend, Taylor. Aside from him, there were a couple other guys in the band including a drummer and Hunter, the guitar player. They were pretty good. Not really her style though.

When did I become such a judgy person? The thought bothered her, and she rubbed her temple again as her migraine returned from its momentary respite. She grabbed her almost empty energy drink and chugged the last few gulps of liquid.

"Those things will kill you if you keep drinking them like that. Or at least give you a major crash when it wears off," Drema said with a look of concern directed at her. "I thought you were a health nut?"

"Just because I'm an athlete doesn't make me a health nut," Bridget said irritably. It was enough that her granny always got on her case about the amount of energy drinks she consumed. She didn't need a fellow classmate getting on her case too.

"Aaannyway," Annaliese interrupted again. "Can we finally agree on something? Personally, I like the *Into the Woods* angle. Maybe we should take it to a vote?"

"Anything to get this over with," Bridget muttered as she dropped her head to the table. The coolness of the laminate wood stopped the aching in her brain for a minute.

"All in favor of doing our literature project on the fairytale allusions in *Into the Woods*, raise your hands," the peppy voice drilling a hole in her brain asked cheerfully.

Bridget lifted her head and squeezed open one of her eyes to see that everyone except Luke had their hand raised. *Finally, meeting adjourned.*

"Well, there we have it. So, this weekend does anyone want to meet up to watch the movie together? You could all come over to my place if you wanted," Annaliese offered.

Bridget knew that Annaliese had her own apartment just a few blocks away from the college. Everyone else in the group lived in the university's dorms, but she lived with her granny at a house on the other side of campus. It was a short walk, but much closer to the college than Annaliese's place. She also knew Granny's house was probably bigger than the other girl's apartment, but she didn't feel like opening her home to strangers.

"I've got a copy of the movie I can bring," Hunter offered.

"We're free Sunday night if that works?" Drema said as she started packing up her things.

The others were shuffling papers and laptops as well, but Bridget felt like she might pass out right here on this table. The thought of having to face the frozen tundra outside wasn't helping her motivation either. *Maybe I could just take a nap here before I head home. What time does the library close anyway?*

"Bridget, you okay?' came a soft-spoken voice and a gentle touch on her arm. She turned to meet Hunter's questioning gaze.

"Hey, lay off her, man," Luke got up quickly, toppling the chair he'd been sitting in as he strode over to shove the other guy.

"He wasn't doing anything, Luke! What is your problem?" she shouted as she stood and shoved him away. Her migraine was screaming at her, and her stomach wasn't too happy that she'd skipped dinner in favor of the energy drink she'd just finished.

"My problem is that nobody touches my girl, you know?"

"I'm not your girl anymore, Luke! We broke up over a month ago. You need to get over it and move on!"

She wasn't short by any means, but still her ex towered over her as he took a step in her direction. The snarling wolf emblem on his black sweatshirt seemed to grow larger than life, and she could feel her heart beating faster and faster as he got closer.

"We'll see about that," Luke said eerily, leaning into her face and sneering at her with those iridescent pearly whites of his.

"I think that's enough," said a stern voice accompanied by a body stepping in between them. Julius's normally passive face looked angry, and he firmly placed himself in front of Bridget protectively. "Unless you'd like to move this issue to another location?"

"Did you just ask me if I wanna take this outside, loser?"

"Luke, just stop! Just leave. Don't make this a big deal."

"This isn't over, Bridget," Luke said with one last glare at both Julius and Hunter. Then he shoved open the study room door and stomped out.

She hated to admit how fast her heart was beating. Bridget clutched at her chest and hoped the energy drink was to blame for this more than her fear. *I'm not afraid of him. He's just a jerk.* At least, that was what she told herself.

"Are you okay, Bridget? That was…"

She heard the uncertainty in Annaliese's voice without needing to turn around and face her. She was sure they were all staring at her except for Julius, who was still watching the door to make sure Luke didn't return for a second round.

Just take a deep breath and show them you're not afraid. Bridget pasted a smile on before she turned her back to the door and faced the rest of her groupmates. "That's Luke for you. He's a little much sometimes. Totally did the right thing dumping him," she said with a half-hearted chuckle as she tugged at the sleeve of her sweatshirt. Her head was pounding, and her nerves were getting to her, but she wasn't going to give him the satisfaction of letting everyone else in on that fact.

Drema took a step toward her hesitantly and then paused. "Can I, can I give you a hug?"

"Uh, sure," Bridget said with a shrug. Then suddenly she was enveloped in surprisingly strong arms pulling her close enough that she could feel Drema's heart beating a far steadier rhythm than hers. *This is nice*, she admitted to herself silently. She even managed to return the hug with a weak one of her own. After a moment though, she pulled away. Couldn't risk any tears escaping within sight of these strangers.

"So, um, I guess we were talking about meeting up on Sunday? I think we can safely say that Luke won't be joining us," she said awkwardly.

"I'll ask the professor to reassign him to another group," Julius said as he walked over to the table and pulled out his laptop to do just that.

"Just forget it," Bridget said with a dismissive wave of her hand. "He was never going to help anyway. He just showed up to the meeting to mess with me. He's on an athletic scholarship not an academic one, so he won't care if he bombs a few classes."

Her hand was shaking, so she shoved it into the front pocket of her sweatshirt. Drema raised an eyebrow and glanced at her boyfriend, who gave some sort of non-verbal signal she didn't catch. "Why don't you eat something, Bridget?"

"Yeah," Annaliese jumped in and motioned to the assorted baked goods sprawled out on the table. "With all this cold weather lately, I've been baking up a storm just to keep my apartment warm. Eat something and then feel free to take whatever you want home."

Bridget couldn't argue with logic like that, and her stomach grumbled in agreement. She snagged a strawberry cream cheese Danish and took a tentative bite. It was sweet and tangy and delicious. The perfect distraction from Luke's nonsense.

"Those are my favorite too," Hunter said quietly as he grabbed one for himself as well. He looked a little shaken, and she felt bad that he'd gotten pulled into her mess.

Just then, the door burst open, and they all tensed up as they looked toward the unexpected intruder. But it was only Taylor, balancing two trays of coffee cups stacked on top of each other in one hand and his white cane in the other. He was beaming as he turned his head from side to side in sightless observation of the room, but he frowned at the silence that greeted him. "Did I interrupt something?"

"Hey, come on in, Taylor," Annaliese said hurriedly. She added a brief description of the layout of the room and who was here to fill in the blanks as he tapped his white cane in front of him before fully entering the room. He slid the trays onto the table and then turned in the direction of Annaliese's voice.

"Wasn't there supposed to be one more of you? I brought the usual for everybody except the newcomers, so I just grabbed a couple extra black coffees. You'll have to grab your own cups since I have no idea which is which," he said with a grin. "There's a chai tea, a caramel macchiato, a double shot of espresso, and a peppermint mocha latte."

Hunter, Drema, and Julius all snagged their respective coffees after examining the labels while Annaliese picked up the chai tea. "One of those black coffees is for you, Bridget, if you want it," she motioned with her free hand. "Taylor, the other one is up for grabs. One of our group members ditched us. Don't ask," she added when she saw his puzzled look. "Have you met Bridget yet?"

"Hi," Bridget said, uncertain what to say. Taylor turned his head toward her voice and stuck out his free hand. She shook it and smiled at the strength in his grip. "Thanks for the coffee, but I think I'll pass. There's already enough caffeine running through my veins that I might combust."

"You really should lay off those energy drinks," Drema said gently.

Bridget shrugged and started collecting her things again. "So, um, somebody text me with the details for Sunday, okay?"

"Are you gonna be okay by yourself?" Hunter said, surprising her with the concern in his tone.

He cares a lot for someone he doesn't even know. Maybe that's just the type of person he is.

He shoved his papers into his satchel before slinging it over his shoulder as he continued speaking. "I can walk you home, if you want?"

"That's really not necessary, Hunter."

"It's no trouble, really," he insisted as he picked up his guitar case in one hand and his coffee in the other. His voice was a little stronger now that he seemed to have recovered from the shock of Luke's actions earlier. He even offered her a hesitant smile that made her chuckle at its sweet, lopsided nature.

"It's probably a good idea, Bridget." She heard Julius's input before turning to give him a look that said he should stay out of it. He ignored her silent protest. "Luke could be waiting for you to leave the library before he accosts you again."

Both Drema and Annaliese nodded their agreement while Taylor took a sip from one of the unclaimed coffee cups.

She shivered at the thought that Luke might be waiting outside, hoping to catch her alone, but she also hated the thought of looking weak in front of these people who seemed to have it a lot more together than she did. Bridget was on an athletic scholarship for cross-country, just like Luke, and academia had always been a bit of a struggle for her. The only way to stand up to the bullies of her youth had been to ignore them and not show any sign of weakness. *Old habits die hard,* she pondered as she looked around the room at all of the concerned faces staring back at her. "I swear," she said through gritted teeth. "I'll be fine."

"Famous last words," Drema muttered as she took a sip of coffee. Annaliese gave her a reproachful look before turning her attention back to Bridget.

"At least take some of these pastries with you. There's no way I can eat all of them! Didn't you mention you live with your grandma?"

"Yeah," Bridget admitted, letting some of the tension release as she smiled. "Granny does have quite the sweet tooth. She'll love some of these." She took a few moments to select an assortment of baked goods while Annaliese packaged them up into the Tupperware she'd brought. Once they were safely stored in her backpack, Bridget headed toward the door again.

Much to her chagrin, Hunter was right behind her, almost tripping over the backs of her sneakers in his haste. "I needed to head out anyway, so I can at least walk you across campus. My dorm is on the far side, so I promise it's not even out of the way."

She bit back the sarcastic reply she wanted to say and instead muttered, "Fine. Whatever you want, I guess." But secretly she was relieved as she pulled open the glass doors of the library and greeted the darkness outside.

The campus wasn't a large one, but it would still take a few minutes to cross over to where Hunter's dorm building presumably was. Her granny's house lay on the other side of the walking trails that meandered around the far side of the campus. During the summer, it was a great place to clear her head and enjoy nature, but during the winter months, it was pretty much deserted. Especially since there were no lights in most of the area. Maintenance never seemed to be able to catch up with the burnt-out bulbs for whatever reason, and so the college advised avoiding the area at night due to stalkers or other unsavory types who could potentially hang out there.

But for now, they walked along the lighted pathways that led to Hunter's dorm. She shoved her hands into her sweatshirt pocket, wishing that she'd listened to Granny and put on a coat before leaving this morning. During the day, she'd been able to muscle through the cold as she ran from class to class; but now that the sun had set, it was hard to keep from shivering.

"Aren't you cold?"

And it was especially hard to stay warm if someone else pointed out how cold she should be. *Thanks, Captain Obvious.* She pulled her hood up to at least protect her ears and fumbled with her ponytail in an attempt to tuck it inside her hood so that strands of long black hair didn't spill out chaotically on either side of her head. "No, I'm fine."

"You say that a lot," Hunter said casually. She glared at him, but he wasn't looking at her. His attention was on scanning the path in front of them while keeping a tight grip on the guitar case in his hand. He only paused in his observations long enough to drink the last of his coffee before chucking the paper cup into a trashcan as they passed by.

"Nice shot," she said, choosing to ignore his previous comment. "Ever think about joining the basketball team?"

He laughed, and she smiled at the sound. It was a nice laugh, a lot louder and more confident than his usual speaking voice. "Not a chance! I've got two left feet when it comes to any kind of sport. Think I'll stick with my musical endeavors."

She nodded, uncertain how to keep the conversation alive. They walked in silence, crunching through the snow that remained on the path. Maintenance had shoveled, but the wind had blown some of the drifts over, and snowflakes speckled the sidewalks in an ever-deepening layer. *They'll need to shovel again in the morning.* Bridget sighed and watched the little puff of hot air blow upward and to the left as the wind swept it away.

"What got you into cross-country?" Hunter finally said. Apparently, he'd grown tired of the silence.

"Um, I don't know. I like running, I guess."

"Must have been pretty good to get a scholarship."

She shrugged. "Yeah, I did okay in high school. Granny couldn't afford college for me, so I had to get a scholarship somehow. Wasn't happening with my grades."

"Same here. I wanted to get a music scholarship, but I wasn't good enough at the traditional music stuff. Should have spent more time on the piano, I guess! I just liked the guitar better."

Bridget nodded as if she understood, but she had no clue about musical instruments. "Nice you found something you liked," she finally said in response, hoping that was an appropriate answer to his story.

"Yeah! I think everybody should be passionate about what they do with their life, you know? Helps you be more successful and whatnot."

"Sure, I guess," she muttered. Other than running cross-country, she wasn't much good at anything. She'd been hoping that college would give her some other options, but right now it just seemed like a constant reminder of everything she was bad at. *Maybe I'll drop out next semester and get a job.*

"Well, this is my stop. Are you sure you don't want me to walk you the rest of the way home?" His eyes were as gentle as his question, and for a moment she hesitated. It would be nice to not have to walk the rest of the way in the dark, alone.

But she shrugged off the momentary sentimentality and said, "Nah, I'm sure Luke is long gone by now. It's too cold to hang around waiting to jump somebody. Besides, if you walk me home then you'll have to walk back home in the dark by yourself."

"I wouldn't mind," he said softly, dropping his gaze to the ground as he shuffled his feet and disrupted the footprints he'd already made in the snow.

Bridget paused and gave him another hard look. *What is it with this guy?* She probably should let it go, but now she was curious. "Why do you care? You were concerned about me back in the study room and now here. I don't even know you."

He lifted his head and looked her straight in the eyes as he said, "Everyone should have someone who cares. And well, you seem like kind of a loner. I thought...maybe I could be your person." His confidence faltered, and his face turned as red as her sweatshirt. "I mean, your person who cares about you, looks out for you...not in a creepy way or thing. Just because people aren't really meant to be alone, you know?"

She smiled wistfully at the innocence of his statement. "Thanks for the offer, but I'm kind of a lone wolf myself. Not sure I need a 'carer'."

Hunter frowned, and she almost laughed at the serious expression on his face. "I think you're wrong. Everyone needs someone."

"Guess we'll just agree to disagree," she said as she took a couple steps away toward the nature trail. "But thanks again for the offer. I'll see you around?"

"For sure," he said as his shoulders drooped. "Sunday at Annaliese's, right?"

"Yeah, Sunday at Annaliese's," she said with a wave before turning her back on him. She didn't want to see his disappointed expression any longer nor feel the ache in her chest that whispered he might be right.

I don't need anybody. Just me and Granny like it's always been. I'll be fine.

She squared her shoulders and marched into the mini-forest that separated her from home. Normally, she'd enjoy wandering along the meandering paths, but since nothing was cleared after the recent snowstorm she'd just cut through directly. Bridget had a pretty good sense of direction that told her the house would be a fairly straight shot from this point as long as she angled to the right a little. After a couple steps in the correct direction, she tripped over a tree root that almost sent her sprawling.

"Guess I need a little light after all," she muttered as her cold fingers struggled to pull her phone out of her back pocket. A swipe and a click and she had her phone flashlight illuminating a couple feet in front of her. "That'll make this easier." It felt a little silly talking to herself, but it also felt comforting, given the darkness that was otherwise totally enveloping her.

She could only imagine the picture someone could paint of her right now: Dark and eerie forest with a blanket of snow covering the ground, and one lone female figure clad in bright red sweats and matching sweatshirt. Normally, Bridget would have avoided the brightly colored workout clothes, but it was laundry day. The only option left had been her matching cross-country sweat outfit. It even had the school's mascot, the same snarling wolf Luke had on his sweatshirt earlier, printed on the front with her last name in bold black letters across the back.

Taking a deep breath, she plunged once more into the darkness of the forest. An owl hooted somewhere above her, and she hurried a little faster toward the warm home she knew was waiting for her. There weren't a lot of other sounds in the forest, and the silence was unsettling. If she'd been any sort of singer, she'd be tempted to hum a tune just to break it up.

Her thoughts drifted back to Hunter and his strange offer. *What kind of guy offers to care about someone? That's such a weird thing to say.* It made her feel like a little kid, and she hated that feeling. *Granted, he meant it in a nice way. He didn't mean anything bad by it. Hunter's just apparently a nice guy.* She shoved her free hand back in her pocket as she swept her phone back and forth to see the way in front of her. A smile spread across her face as she remembered his embarrassment at his own proclamation. It was cute and slightly endearing. She couldn't ever remember a guy being sweet like that toward her. Luke had certainly never been like that.

She ducked her head as she came across a low hanging branch and focused on not dropping her phone as she maneuvered through the obstacle. *See? I'm fine. I can take care of myself. No need for anyone to take care of me.*

Bridget paused in her tracks as she realized her backpack had caught on one of the branches, and she groaned at the sudden irony of her thoughts. If there were someone here, they could easily unhook her bag from whatever was catching it. Instead, she wiggled a little, trying to free it without further effort.

"Great," she muttered as she struggled to slip her arms out of the straps. Once free, she turned around and shone her light at the bag, now dangling from the tree while she stared at it. It wasn't hard to pull it loose now that she could see the issue, but it was still frustrating. "At least no one was here to see that."

She pulled her bag back into its proper place on her back and continued making her way through the forest. It was easy to see when she crossed over a place that normally contained a sidewalk since the obstacles suddenly cleared away. *Hopefully, there won't be any more problems, and I can get home in one piece.* After the night she'd had, she was definitely going to eat a few more of the pastries in her bag before handing them over to Granny. Normally she would be more health-conscious, other than the energy drinks, but it was off season now. She could afford to cheat a little.

"Hey," she said out loud as she came to a sudden stop, "my headache's finally gone! Guess all I needed was a little fresh air, or maybe the caffeine is kicking in." Bridget smiled and resumed her walking with a bit more spring in her step. *Maybe I really should lay off those energy drinks.* She considered that thought further as she broke free from the trees and emerged in Granny's backyard. The two of them had talked about putting in a fence a few years back, but the neighborhood was relatively safe, especially since their primary neighbor was the college campus itself.

Bridget put away her phone and stomped her way around to the front of the house. Granny always left the porch light on when she knew her granddaughter would be coming home late, so she didn't have any trouble getting the door open.

"Granny," she called as she pushed the door open and entered the hallway that branched off to the living room on the left and the kitchen on the right. She dropped her backpack on the floor quickly and started pulling at her damp sleeves. The stairs were directly in front of her, and she hollered up them as she shrugged out of her sweatshirt and hung it on the proper hook on the wall. "You really should lock the door even if I'm not home yet! I've got a key, you know."

She was wearing a tank top underneath her sweatshirt, which was a little chilly with the door still open, so she quickly slammed it shut. Granny was particular about no shoes in the house, so Bridget pulled her tennis shoes off and left them in a snowy, dripping pile near the welcome mat. The hardwood floors were cold, but she'd left her slippers upstairs so socks would have to do.

Something smelled good, and it was coming from the kitchen. When Bridget came home this late, her granny usually left something on the stove for her to reheat. Tonight, it smelled like chili, which was perfect considering how much she was shivering. She turned left to go into the kitchen as she continued shouting at the other house's occupant.

"Granny? You asleep? It's not even 10 o'clock yet! I know I promised I'd be home earlier, but I had this group project that ran late and…"

Her words froze, as did her whole body when she saw who was leaning against her kitchen counter. Luke's height meant that he had to duck a little to avoid hitting the light that hung from the middle of the ceiling, but he was no less menacing than he had looked a short while ago as he towered over her at the library. He'd been stirring the chili on the stove, and he flicked the burner off when he saw her enter.

"Come in, come in, sweetie. Granny's been waiting for you," he said as he took a few steps toward her. He was wearing one of her granny's aprons, which he slowly removed and set on the counter. Luke's brown eyes were round like saucers, and his smile was stretched wide across his face like it might explode from keeping his teeth locked up inside.

I'm not afraid, she tried to tell herself. But her body disagreed.

Bridget started backing up slowly toward the opening leading back to the hallway. "What did you do to my granny?"

"Not a thing, not a thing," he intoned calmly. "She's upstairs just taking a little nap. A sleeping pill in your tea will do that to you." He smiled again, and she wanted to launch herself at him in retaliation. But her body felt heavy, and she blinked rapidly to try to clear her vision. She clutched at her chest in an attempt to calm her frantic heartbeat. *Is this what a panic attack feels like?*

"You drugged Granny? How did you even get in here?"

"She invited me in, of course," Luke replied smoothly as he continued approaching her. She was maintaining the distance between them for the moment, but she had a feeling that wasn't going to last long. "Said any friends of her dear Bridget were welcome. Even offered me a cup of tea! Sweet lady, really. Asked me to keep an eye on dinner while she popped upstairs for a bit."

"What do you want, Luke?" she said slowly, trying to sound more confident than she really felt. Her mouth was dry, and her heart was pounding. Her feet felt sluggish as they continued moving backward away from the intruder.

"You, of course," he said, closing the gap between them and shoving her into the wall before she could escape into the hallway. She struggled, but he held her wrists firmly and pressed himself so close she could barely breathe, let alone scream. "Don't worry. Granny won't be coming down to interrupt us. I locked her in with a chair."

He paused, his voice shifting to something accusatory instead of the placating tone he'd been using so far. "You hurt me earlier, you know? When you told me you weren't my girl anymore? You shouldn't have told a lie like that."

"It wasn't a lie," she choked out, forcing herself to keep looking him in the eye while she struggled to pull away. "We're done, Luke."

"How can we be done?" he shouted at her, and she finally turned her face away with a whimper. "You and I, we understand each other. Who else can understand you like I do? I know everything about you, and we have so much in common, Bridget. Nobody likes us. We're not good at anything, except running. Running we're really good at. Always running. Running away from the people who don't understand us."

"Please, Luke," she whispered, furious at the tremor in her voice. "Please let me go."

"You have to promise," he shouted, banging her wrists against the wall to emphasize his words as she let out a strangled cry of pain. His hands felt like blazing hot irons on her cold skin, and she tried not to think about how close he was as he continued yelling. "You have to promise we'll be together!"

"Fine! We'll be together! Just let go of me!"

"I don't believe you," he screamed as he leaned closer into her face. Luke took in a deep breath as he buried his face in her hair. She wriggled and whimpered like a baby, but he only tightened his grip on her.

"Please, Luke. Please, just let me go. I won't tell anyone what happened, and we—we can be together just like I said." Bridget was failing miserably at putting on a brave front, and now she was desperate to say anything that would get her out of this situation. She'd figure out what to do about him when he wasn't literally breathing down her neck.

He ignored her, instead breathing in the scent of her hair for a few precious seconds. "You smell so good," he whispered. "I just want to eat you up."

Now, she was crying.

Suddenly, the weight of her ex-boyfriend lifted off her, and he dropped down to crouch on the floor, holding the side of his head. When he pulled his hand away, there was blood on the fingertips.

"You!" he growled.

She whirled around to see Hunter panting beside her as he wielded his guitar case like a weapon. Luke attempted to stumble to his feet again, but Hunter was already swinging his instrument at him once more with enough force to knock the other young man backward into the counter before he collapsed on the floor and stopped moving.

Bridget slid down the wall and tried to control her shaking arms. She was still crying, and she didn't even care how embarrassing that was.

"Hey, hey, are you okay?" Hunter said as he knelt down in front of her. He'd finally dropped the guitar case on the floor next to Luke and was now fully focused on her.

"I—I—I ..." she stuttered as she struggled to get words out. He was being so careful not to touch her, instead hovering visibly and awkwardly uncertain what to do with his hands. It was almost comical. "What are you doing here?"

"I swear I'm not a stalker!" Hunter held his hands up in surrender. That broke the tension, and she finally started laughing until she hiccupped while the tears continued streaming down her face.

"Hunter, seriously. What are you doing here? How did you get in the house?"

He pointed at the door as he said quickly, "You left it unlocked, I swear!"

"I believe you," she said with a laugh. "I was a little distracted when I came in." Bridget looked over at her ex's body, which was lying very still on the floor. "Is he...dead?"

"Oh, geez, I hope not!" Hunter said as he hurried over to take the unconscious young man's pulse. "Yeah, he's fine. Do you have your phone? We should probably call 9-1-1 now."

"We need to check on Granny!" she said as she attempted to stand, but her legs were too weak to support her. *I really shouldn't have skipped dinner.* Hunter motioned for her to stop trying, and she let her body slide back down to its seated position.

"Where is she? I'll check on her. You call 9-1-1."

"Upstairs in the bedroom on the right." He was gone before she finished giving directions, and that left her to find her phone, which luckily was still tucked away in her back pocket.

Bridget explained the situation as calmly as she could to the 9-1-1 operator, who assured her that help would be on the way soon and asked her to stay on the line. She felt awkward sitting on the floor staring at her unconscious ex-boyfriend who'd attacked her in her own home while another young man, who was practically a stranger, looked after her granny. But it felt like a fittingly strange ending to an equally strange evening.

"She's breathing normally, best I can tell, so I'm hoping she's okay," Hunter called out as he came back down the stairs. "How long on the paramedics?"

"Soon," she said, lifting the phone away from her ear slightly so she wasn't shouting at the operator. Bridget felt an unexpected sense of relief as Hunter came and sat back down beside her on the floor.

"Sorry I followed you home. I know that probably comes off really stalkerish. But that guy just gave me all the bad vibes," he said as he stuck a thumb in Luke's direction. "I followed your footprints through the nature trail and noticed an extra set of prints when you got to the yard. I figured you weren't expecting guests, so I wanted to make sure everything was okay inside."

"Oh," she said simply. If she'd been uncertain what to say before, she was at an utter loss now. "Nice weapon by the way."

"Yeah," he said with a chuckle. "Little music fun fact: Did you know that sometimes people refer to a guitar as an axe?"

She shook her head but couldn't find the appropriate words to respond.

"Well, I didn't have a real axe, so I had to use what I had," Hunter said with that lopsided grin of his beaming at her.

Her emotions were threatening to bubble over in a way she really didn't want to experience right at this moment, but it seemed her body had other ideas. She was shaking, and she wrapped her arms around herself to try to stop the unwelcome movement.

"Bridget?"

She couldn't look at him. Couldn't look at Luke on the floor. She couldn't see anything through the waterfall that was erupting from both her eyes. Sobs wracked her body, and she dropped the phone she'd been holding in one hand. Dimly, she was aware of the 9-1-1 operator shouting at her to make sure she was okay, but she just couldn't handle any of it anymore. She couldn't do anything but fall apart like the weak little terrified girl in need of rescuing that she apparently was.

Hunter was saying something to the operator, assuring her that everything was okay and that he'd stay on the line with her instead. She lifted her drooping head to notice that he was leaving her alone again.

"Don't leave me!" she shrieked, shoving herself to her feet in one swift movement as she awkwardly chased him out of the room and crashed into him in the hallway. Hunter still held her phone in one hand, and he was holding out her red sweatshirt in his other hand. She blushed as she snatched the garment and shoved it over her head, appreciating the sudden increase in warmth.

Moving the phone away from his ear slightly to make it clear that he was speaking to her, he asked, "Do you have a blanket somewhere? You're in shock. On TV they always wrap a blanket around people in shock."

She nodded and pointed at the living room, then followed him on stockinged feet as he grabbed the knitted blanket off the couch and tossed it at her. Bridget gratefully wrapped it around herself before collapsing on the aforementioned couch.

"Hunter?"

"Yeah," he said as he hesitantly sat down beside her.

"Thank you. For — for caring."

He smiled that cute lopsided smile again, and she felt her heart do a little flip. "You're welcome, Bridget." For a moment, he was distracted as the 9-1-1 operator spoke to him before he finally ended the call and handed her phone back to her. "The ambulance is here. We'd better go let them in."

She shuffled to the door but froze in the entryway. Hunter took a step toward her and held out his hand. "You don't have to do this alone, okay? And letting someone care about you doesn't make you weak."

Her eyes popped open even wider than they already were. *It's like he read my mind.* She took another look at his extended hand before taking a step forward and gently placing her hand in his. "How did you know that's how I felt?"

He smiled and pushed open the door. "Because I've been there. Then someone took the time to care for me…and that made all the difference. No one should ever have to face the wolf alone."

Bridget returned his smile as they stepped through the door together to face the sirens and flashing lights that awaited them outside her granny's house.

The End

THE WAYS OF A WOLF
Lindsi McIntyre

"The man and the wolf always appear at the same time. Remember that, child."

"Yes, Granny Anne."

Grey eyes, weathered by nearly a century of life, peered out beneath pure white eyebrows and watched the girl flit about the cottage, her tightly curled, fire red hair flowing out behind her like a riding cloak. Anne huffed at her granddaughter's almost dismissive tone. *Children. Don't know how to show respect nowadays. Then again, Rhiannon isn't exactly a child anymore…*

It seemed just yesterday that the girl had rushed in the front door carrying all the fog of the celts with her, hauling a basket filled to the brim with goodies that was half as big as her, begging for stories. Now, the little redheaded whirlwind nearly towered over Anne, and carried herself like a young lady. The old basket she unpacked upon the small table in the center of the cottage had become almost as worn as Anne.

Rhiannon no longer squealed with joy over the thought of a day spent with her grandmother. There was no more begging for tales of fairies and witches. Time was a fickle thing. Anne leaned forward in her sparsely cushioned chair and rubbed at the ache that had settled deep in her left knee.

Time was a fickle thing, indeed.

"The man will saunter into the village as if he owns the place," Anne went on, ignoring Rhiannon's disinterest. "He'll be holding his shoulders high, all confidence and surety, he will. Searching. Hunting. His smile will steal the hearts of many a lass. But ye mustn't let him fool ye, Rhiannon."

"Yes, Granny Anne."

"That same night, I swear ye, it'll be that self same night, the wolf will howl from beneath the skeleton branches of the old trees of the dead forest."

"But the forest isn't dead anymore, Granny Anne."

"Hush now. It'll be dead again. It's them that kills it. The wolves. Sends all that's good in it hiding away. The man will stalk the village while the wolf hides in the shadows. Watching. Waiting. He has to bide his time, ye ken. Till he's turned enough of the villagers into his kind. Only then, when all the hunters are gone, will he reveal his true nature. Once there's no turning back."

Rhiannon set the last fresh cabbage upon the table and threw the small cloth over the bread she'd baked for an old woman too stiff in the joints to knead it for herself. "Oh, Granny Anne. I dislike those old ghost stories, I do." She turned, flashing the bright dimpled smile that she knew would always get her own way across. Her eyes lit in the familiar mischievous way for the first time since she'd arrived. "I much prefer the lovely stories you tell. The ones about true love conquering all. Won't ye tell me one of those instead? The one about the stolen away princess, and the braw young highlander that whisks in to save her from her captors. That's me favorite, it is."

Anne huffed. "Stories of love and light are all well an' good, lass. But it's the darker tales that teach us the most, they do."

"Ach, please Granny. Just the one story?"

Anne grouched a bit more in the good-natured way that was her hard earned right as one who had lived so very many years before she finally acquiesced to Rhiannon's request, as both women knew she would do.

As the young woman settled in beside the fire and as the old told her story, a cold autumn wind kicked up outside their small cozy haven, carrying an unusually high number of the blood red leaves off the branches of the trees of the nearby forest. And something else. Something dark and sinister came in on the wind.

If Anne had known all that icy wind had carried, she would have insisted Rhiannon listen more attentively to the story of the wolf. Before it was too late.

~~~~~

"My, but it be a windy night."

Anne didn't know to whom she spoke. Only that the sound of her voice offered some comfort from the seclusion of her declining mobility. Oh, how she missed the days when she could leap clear over fallen logs and ford across even the widest rivers. She would settle for being able to walk to the village in a reasonable amount of time. She didn't have any delusions as to her place in their little corner of the world. There were no more friends to visit. No more mentors to learn from. But some time spent freely with the young ones never went amiss. So few ever came to visit her, busy as they were with their own lives. And rightly so.

That was the natural way of things. The good way.

Anne almost always believed that.

Even getting settled in bed proved challenging, but she managed it. As long as she could manage the basics, she wouldn't grouse about time gone by too much. Of the people she wouldn't get to see again this side of heaven. It was the good Lord's business how and when His children were called home. And Anne would do her best to honor His will in seeing her outlive all the others as best she could, while she still could.

Sleep softened the edge of her mind. It slipped into her muscles and stole away the pain that had become an everyday part of her life. Perhaps tomorrow she would make the effort to visit the village. Perhaps she'd stay
~~~~~

for a night or two at her daughter Saoirse's home. Just a night or two. Just to see how they were all getting on—

A howl cut through the screaming wind rushing over her little cottage. Anne sat up far quicker than her aged body usually would have allowed. Her heart took a perilous dip, and then thundered into a race against itself where the prize would surely be her death.

What was that sound? Surely, she had imagined it. There hadn't been a wolf in Abershire since—

Another howl robbed Anne of the small hope she fostered that she'd misheard the portent carried on the wind. A wolf. In Abershire. The first the forest had seen in nigh on seventy years. The cold creeping in at the edges of the room seeped into her bones. Anne laid back down and pulled the thick wool blankets up past her chin as she had as a child all those nights ago. When she'd first heard a wolf's bitter howl. When Father had heard her plea and come in to comfort her, not knowing how much he'd have to give to see the monster gone. It was happening again. Only this time, Father and the others weren't there to hunt the beast out of the village.

It was now up to Anne to see the creature vanquished.

~~~~~

The road to the village grew longer every day. Least, that was what it felt like to an old woman whose joints had decided many years past to stop being useful. Anne let out a curse as her left leg wobbled and nearly sent her into a nasty tumble. Her wrinkled hands barely managed to hold on to the thick, hip-high walking stick she depended on to provide her with mobility. Once she'd recovered, Anne sent up a quick prayer for forgiveness of her crude language. Luckily no one was around to see her little misstep, in either body or word.

The path past the forest to the village stretched out across the moor, empty and barren save for the leaves that patterned the dark brown earth with reds, oranges, and yellows. To her left stood the forest, its branches dark and swaying in the gentle southeast wind. The colorful foliage that had managed to withstand the cruel storm the night before rustled softly in what was left of the gale. To the right, fields of bright green clover rolled over the hills of Abershire. In the distance, atop one such hill, a few white spots indicated the presence of sheep grazing happily on the fattening plant life. Anne saw no sign of a shepherd. Likely the lad had grown cold in the autumn air and had left to warm up. That wouldn't do. They'd grown complacent in the years since the last wolf had sunk its fangs into their little home. She would have to remind them all what happened to sheep left unprotected in a world where monsters roamed.

Anne put her head down and forced herself onward. She wouldn't have much time to warn the others. The beast might already have made his move. Mingling with the locals, gaining their trust, setting his traps. If only she could walk a wee bit faster.
~~~~~

Much like weeds, once a wolf had set its roots in a place, it was harder to remove.

Finally, Anne spotted a few grey pillars of smoke rising in the distance. After several yards more of awkward shuffling along with her cane, the small thatch and peat-covered homes of the villagers appeared scattered across the fields. Further on, the homes grew closer together, closer to the road, until they were directly beside it in a neat row and were joined by larger buildings. These served as places of commerce. A butcher. A blacksmith. The haberdashery and cobbler in one. Everything people might need in their day-to-day lives.

The street was bustling now as the villagers went about their business, becoming more chaotic with every yard closer to the village square that Anne traveled. There a woman carried an empty basket on one hip and a squalling babe on the other. Over yon, a man hauled a load of hay on his back. A group of children chased each other to and fro, darting in and out of people's way and garnering more than a few shouted demands to cease their play from the irritated adults they nearly bowled over.

But it was the well centered in the middle of the square outside the large wood cabin, which served as their meeting hall, that caught Anne's eye. A well made of grey and black stones. A well where Rhiannon stood clutched in the hands of a handsome stranger, her red curls bouncing happily in the wind.

A handsome and sharp-eyed stranger.

"Wolf!"

~~~~~

Rhiannon hauled on the rope until the bucket filled with water was suspended at waist level from the crossbeam support where the pulley had been installed. It swung slightly at the end of the line, its precious cargo dribbling off the sides and bottom. With a huff she wrapped the loose end of the rope around the wooden stop set into the stones of the well with her right hand and kept a firm hold of the tight end with her left, lest she lose her load to the dark chasm of the well. The thirst she'd stopped at the well to quench had tripled from the effort of pulling up the water. But as Rhiannon dipped her hands into the chill, clear water and brought the sweet liquid to her lips, she relished her hard-won victory.

All the best things came with a little hard work.

Water leaked from her fingers and spilled down her chin. It soaked her sleeve and splattered onto the front of her dress, leaving dark marks where it landed. The wind blew, sending a chill through her. Perhaps she should have waited for that sip until she was back home after all. She hadn't taken the weather into account when she'd decided to grab a drink. Mother would scold her for hours if she came home soaked to the bone. *You never think things through, Rhiannon.* Rhiannon sighed. Best take the long way home so her dress would have ample chance to dry.
~~~~~

"Hello."

Rhiannon jumped and spun around to find a stranger standing startlingly close behind her. He'd somehow approached without making a sound and something deep inside instinctively recoiled, but her fear soon dissipated at the sweet tilt of his head when he smiled.

"Ach, I didn't mean to frighten ye, lass. I was only hoping I might be able to convince ye to share some of that wit' me." He pointed to the bucket she still clutched in her left hand.

"Oh. Of course." Her words came out in an embarrassed rush at her uncharitable reaction to him. "Help yerself." Rhiannon stepped to the side, expecting him to take the bucket in hand so she could step away.

Instead, he crowded close to lean over the bucket and dip both hands in at the same time for a sizable drink. If it had been any of the men from the village, Rhiannon would have suspected he'd trapped her apurpose with the unspoken fact that should she let go of the bucket and step away it would fall, thereby depriving him of the offered refreshment. She was familiar with their antics. But it was uncharitable to have such a thought about a stranger. Perhaps he just wasn't aware of the propriety of standing so very close to an unfamiliar woman. Some men were raised without the knowledge of such delicate proprieties.

Seeing as she was stuck, as it were, Rhiannon took the opportunity to study the stranger. He was a foot or so taller than her and broad of shoulder. His clothing was good quality and finely tailored, not something she'd usually see in the village. His hair was a deep black color and cut fashionably. Again, unusual for a place where most men spent their days out in the fields planting or guarding over their animals. His nose was thin but not unpleasant, his chin strong, and his lips full. And the eyes he turned her way had a slight green tinge deep beneath the more prominent brown.

Rhiannon blushed. She'd been caught looking. The smile that exposed his perfect white teeth, including two slightly overlarge canines, proved he'd noticed. "I greatly appreciate yer generosity, lass."

Dark spots stained the front of his shirt, reminding her that she looked similarly wild and completely unladylike. "Oh. Well. That is, it's nothing, sir." Rhiannon's movements were uncertain and choppy. Mayhap that was why the bucket chose to slip from the wall of the well and nearly drag her into its watery depths before she could think to let go.

"Ach, careful now," said the stranger as he quickly grabbed her round the waist so she wouldn't fall.

His hands warmed her sides in their strong embrace. His vibrant gaze captured hers. Feeling dazed, Rhiannon let her burden slip from her fingertips as heat like a fire flooded her body. Somewhere out of focus, the bucket hit the water at the bottom of the well, but she almost didn't notice past the strange rush going through her head. She'd never reacted this way to a man in all her eighteen years. His smile grew, as if he could sense the effect he had on her.

"Wolf!"

Rhiannon jumped away from the stranger. "Granny Anne? Ye near done scared me t' death, ye did!" Her aged grandmother limped across the street, her stooped body shuffling behind the old knobbed branch she used to get around. She had obviously walked all the way into the village. A sizable task for an old woman. "What're ye doing here? And all by yerself. If ye had wanted to come to the village, I would have brought ye on the wagon, I would. Ye must be fair exhausted."

"Never mind that, child."

Rhiannon bristled at the form of address. For some unknown reason, she didn't want the stranger to think of her thus.

"Get away from that man. Now."

"What?" Granny Anne's words slapped her like the cold wind. "Granny!" Rhiannon lowered her voice. "Tis very rude to say such a thing."

"Away. Away!" The old woman shooed at the stranger with her walking stick as she forced her way in between them.

Rhiannon's face burned anew. "We weren't doing anything wrong."

"Hush, child." Granny Anne brandished her stick in the man's face. "Away with ye, foul creature. I ken what ye are."

"Oh, aye." The man smiled good-naturedly. Though, there was a spark in his eye that spoke of taking insult. But who wouldn't at such a greeting? "And what would that be, old one?"

"A wolf." Granny practically spit. "A vile, flesh eating—"

"Granny! That's enough!" Rhiannon took her grandmother's arm in hand. She had never known the old woman to be so rude. And now, to be so to such a dashing stranger…"Ye can't speak so. Have you gone mad?"

"Tis not madness. Tis fact, I say. He's a *wolf*. Disguised as a man. They ingratiate themselves into the village pretending to be human and—"

"Ach! That old story again." Rhiannon needed to speak with her mother. It wasn't like Granny Anne to lose touch with reality in such a way. "Yer confused, Granny. Please, stop."

The man cleared his throat. "Perhaps, t'would be best if I go about me business. Seems I'm upsetting yer wee relative."

Granny Anne hissed again, waving her stick at him. Rhiannon wanted to argue. She found she didn't mind the man's presence at all and in fact, would have preferred to see more of it. But she couldn't very well leave her grandmother to fend for herself during whatever fit had taken hold of her. "Aye. Thank ye fer yer understandin'."

There was a flash of something in his eyes. Disapproval? Nay, as he smiled and gave a little bow to show there was no ill will, she realized t'was just disappointment. Perhaps he had wanted more of her presence as well.

Rhiannon bit back her own wave of disappointment as she led Granny Anne away from the well.

"Ye musn't let him fool ye, Rhiannon." Granny Anne wheezed. "He's a beast in disguise. Be wary lass."

"Aye, Granny." Guilt niggled at Rhiannon. She'd never lied to her grandmother before. She just couldn't bear to upset her further. For the truth was, Rhiannon planned to seek the man out, if for no other reason than to apologize for the old woman's baseless accusations, the very next chance she got. And perhaps, just perhaps, mind, she could see if her lifelong wish for true love might lay within his lovely brown eyes.

~~~~~

Stories.

They all thought they were just stories. Ghost tales told around the fire to pass the time. Anne was the only one left who knew the truth. It had been too long since the last attack. And because of that, no one could recognize the monster in their midst. No one could see the disaster forming on the horizon.

Anne latched her eyes upon the creature who even now had found a new eligible young lady to tempt with his lies. At her side, Rhiannon let out a disgruntled sigh. No doubt the starry-eyed lass had fallen for his charm. The beast was already sinking its teeth in.

Anne huffed. What could she do? The end of her walking stick dug deep into the dark, densely packed earth of the village square as she allowed Rhiannon to guide her back the way she had come. Even if she were whole, hale and in the prime of her youth, she wouldn't have been able to defeat the creature. Not alone. There was no hope for a nearly crippled old woman to succeed where a team of braw highlanders armed to the teeth had almost failed.

A hunter was what they needed now.

"What is it, Granny? Why have ye stopped?"

"The post. Quickly, now. I need to send a letter."

"The post? Nay. Yer cold down to yer bones. I'll take ye home. We can send it later."

Anne dug her heels in against her granddaughter's goodwill. "Now. It must be now." She didn't have the time to sit beside her daughter's fireplace and be coddled. T'was the time for action. "I must send a letter."

Rhiannon sighed and turned them both toward the stage building. "T'will cost a pretty penny to buy the paper there," she muttered. "Ye know how Killian can't resist upping the price when ye buy from him directly."

"It matters not. Tis an emergency." For Anne had struck on an idea. She might not be able to kill the wolf, but she knew someone who made a living in that very business. A man who had been there at the beginning and had helped to slay the wolf that had nearly killed her father. He had turned the skills he'd learned that night and on many others into a craft. He made a living at it now.

And they sore could use a hunter.
~~~~~

Anne only hoped he wouldn't be too late.

Time was a fickle thing.

~~~~~

The ewe cried out pitifully as her pain-filled gaze swung to Rhiannon as if begging for relief.

"Hang in there, lass," Rhiannon murmured to the poor overtaxed creature as she cradled its head. In the next stall she could hear her father speaking to another ewe in a similar state. Bleats of pain near filled the barn to bursting. Their entire flock had begun to lamb early.

The cries in the next stall turned to a mournful sound. Her father cursed and something struck the wall. Rhiannon fought to keep her tears at bay. They'd lost another one. Their family had been fighting for days to stop the deaths of the precious lambs, but it seemed as if it would all be for naught. They were simply too small to survive.

Her father stomped into the stall, face red and fists clenched. He saw the tears gathering behind her lashes and turned away to compose himself. "How is she doing, lass?" he asked, still facing the wall.

Rhiannon forced the lump out of her throat with a cough. "Not well, Da. I think she'll lose her babe as well." Her voice cracked, but she managed to hold back the sobs that yearned to be released.

He took a deep breath and then sighed, his broad shoulders drooping in a way she'd never seen before. When he faced Rhiannon, the kindness in his eyes, eyes that had always been a source of comfort, broke through her defenses and her control. The tears poured out no matter how hard she tried to stop them.

"Ah don't cry, lass." His long stride brought him to her side. "Tis the way of things sometimes." He knelt beside her in the hay.

"But it's never happened afore, Da." She sniffed.

"Nay, not in your life, nor mine." He scratched at the thick beard covering his jaw. "But I've heard tell of a time back when yer Granny was a wee girl...Aye..." His eyes narrowed. "Yer Granny told me the story once or twice when I was a lad."

Rhiannon ran her hand over the ewe's neck as another contraction began. "Was it a sickness? Did she know how to stop it?"

"Nay, not a sickness." He looked toward the door of the stall as if he were trying to see what lay beyond the safety of the barn. "A threat. An unknown danger had been lurking close by. The ewes became distressed by the smell of it on the air and it triggered the premature births. Though they didn't ken the cause at the time, ye see. They had to learn the hard way what the sheep could sense on instinct alone."

A sharp wind blew against the barn. Icy fingers slipped in through the boards and sent a shiver racing down Rhiannon's spine. Or perhaps, it was the sudden tense look that had overtaken her father's face. "But what kind of threat could cause enough panic to result in *this*?"
~~~~~

He opened his mouth to respond when a loud *bang* ripped through the barn. Rhiannon screamed at the sudden noise. Air rushed through the open door of the stall, carrying the smell of dead leaves and heather.

"Sorry. Sorry," a familiar voice called from outside the stall. Mother huffed and groaned somewhere out of sight. "The wind is blowing so hard I near flew away. Ripped the door right out of me hands, it did."

There was a thud. The air ceased blowing into the barn. Mother appeared at the door of the stall. Her eyes took in the sight of Rhiannon holding the ewe and grew sad.

"I see there hasn't been much change."

"Nay, not much," Da replied. "We've lost another three. This is the last one." In that moment the ewe began to thrash as a new and violent wave of contractions hit. Each of them set to work trying to calm her down, but it was no use. Minutes later, the little lamb was born.

Dead.

All three humans watched the ewe sniff at her lifeless baby and cry over its loss.

"Our flock is going to be small next year," Mother said softly.

Da nodded. "Aye. We'll have to make it up the year after. Nothing to be done about it now." He tapped Rhiannon on the shoulder. "Up ye go lass. Off to rest with ye. I'll take over cleaning up and settling her in."

Rhiannon reluctantly stood. Her legs ached as she moved. She'd been sitting with the ewe for hours and her muscles did not appreciate being in that position for such a long time. Her father started preparing to bury the lost lamb as Rhiannon joined her mother at the door.

Mother's eyes were filled with love and concern. "Whist, ye look worn through and through." The older woman wrapped her arms around Rhiannon's shoulders and pulled her close.

Rhiannon leaned into the embrace. "We all are. But at least the worst of it is over—"

A dreadful sound cut through the walls of the barn from the field outside. Both women jumped a clear inch off the ground.

"Glories from above, what was *that*?" Mother asked.

Da was up in a flash. Rhiannon and her mother practically dove to get out of his way as he barreled past them. "It's the sheep," he called back. "Stay inside."

Rhiannon followed her mother out the door of the barn despite her father's order. The sheep had never made *that* sound before. It was like they were screaming. Her family raced across the field that made up their farm. Something had driven the sheep far out to pasture while they'd been distracted by the ewes. The huddle of fluff pressed in on itself as the beasties tried to stand as close together as possible for protection. All twenty-something black noses were turned toward a pile of torn wool and shredded flesh. A pool of red spread out across the clover.

"Oh, no," she murmured.

"Heaven help us," her mother said.

Father's eyes scanned the area, searching for the culprit. Rhiannon followed his line of sight until they both spotted a grey blur just as it disappeared into the nearby forest. It seemed the ewes had been right to be afraid after all.

~~~~~

"Are ye sure tis a good idea to go after it?" Mother rung her hands as Da settled the quiver full of razor-sharp, iron-tipped arrows over one shoulder and slung his bow across the other.

"There's no choice," he replied. "I have to warn the others of the danger. Any creature brave enough to come into our fields in the middle of the day would snatch a child as quickly as a sheep. If we can kill it 'fore it strikes again, we'll all sleep easier at night." He paused by the front door of their cottage where her mother waited anxiously. He leaned down and kissed her forehead tenderly. Rhiannon looked away from the private moment. What would it be like, to have a love like her parents?

"Aye. Yer right on that, Cathal."

Rhiannon looked back in time to see her mother tweak at her father's ear.

"But ye be careful, ye hear me?" she continued.

He smiled. "Course I will. Can't be missing out on yer famous haggis come dinner time."

She rolled her eyes. "Ach, right. That's the reason."

Da sent Rhiannon a wink as a final goodbye and walked out into the blustering wind.

Rhiannon bit her lip. "He'll be safe enough won't he, Mother? The others will be with him once he reaches the O'Neils' place."

Mother stared after him, her profile troubled. Wind whipped mercilessly at her braid and the loose strands of hair it had already ripped from her ribbons, but she seemed not to take note. Rhiannon got the distinct impression that the older woman was watching until she couldn't anymore. Rhiannon knew just when her father walked out of sight, the moment her mother stopped her vigil and turned to her. "Aye. He'll be fine."

If her mother's certainty sounded forced, neither woman acknowledged it. Neither could say for sure how much danger lurked beyond the trees of the forest. Nothing like what they'd seen that day had happened before in either of their lifetimes.

Something had killed and eaten one of their flock.

It seemed impossible. They were too far away from the mountains for a lion to have done it. And there hadn't been any wild dogs in the area for years. The grey blur they'd seen running into the forest had been big. Much bigger than a dog and not the right color for a lion.

Mother seemed to shake off the dread that had settled over their little
~~~~~

home. "Well. We've work to do, lass. And we best get to it."

The next hour was spent sorting out the stalls and their temporary inhabitants. It was harder without Da to help, but they managed well enough under the circumstances. Mother had taken over burying the stillborn lambs while Rhiannon got the ewes tucked in and resting. Fresh hay, clean water, and sealed doors saw them safely tucked away. Rhiannon made sure the door to the barn was barred tight against whatever stalked their land.

Rhiannon leaned against the outer wall of the barn with a sigh. She couldn't remember a time when she'd been so tired. Days on end of tension, fear, and wakefulness had left her drained. The loss of the lambs lay heavy on her heart. The births were always her favorite part of spring. It would be far too quiet without them bandying about on their shaky legs once winter had passed. The wind continued to rage, but Rhiannon was happy to face it if it meant a few moments alone to catch a breath.

Gravel shuffled to her left and a shadow loomed over her. Rhiannon jumped away with a cry that was snatched by the wind.

"Whist, easy now. I didn't mean to startle ye."

"You!" Rhiannon felt her face heat even as the chilled air seeped in clear to her toes. It was the stranger. The man from the well.

"Whatever are ye doing here of all places?"

His wide smile and strong shoulders seemed impervious to the wind that threatened to knock her off her feet. "Would ye believe it if I said I came to find *you*?" He waggled his brows in a mischievous manner.

Rhiannon couldn't help but laugh. "Not one bit, I won't." It must be a good sign if he could make her laugh so easily. Her cheeks grew warmer.

He sighed overlong. "Ah well. Ye'd have found me out then. Truth is," he sent her a chagrined look, "I've gotten myself a wee bit lost." He ran a hand through his thick black hair. "I only meant to do a wee bit o' exploring, but after a while, all of the fields started looking the same…" He chuckled and gave a self-deprecating shrug. "I've been wandering around for hours. When I saw yer barn, I figured I'd swallow my pride and ask for some assistance."

"Ach 'tis good ye did," she replied. "We've had a terrible trouble here. 'Tisn't safe to be out alone."

"Ye don't say?" His eyes widened. "I'm especially glad I spotted this place, then. What's happened?"

Rhiannon motioned for him to follow. "One of our sheep was killed."

"Thieves of some kind?"

"Nay. An animal. But we didn't get a good look at it."

His shoulders relaxed. "I'm sorry fer yer loss. But at least it isn't a band of roving marauders. Most animals can be scared off."

"Aye, well, it was big, whatever it was. Fast too. Best not to be caught off guard out in the open alone, at any rate." She shoved her curls out of her face and shivered. The cold air was taking its toll. She wanted to go inside but didn't want to leave him out on his own. Voices carried to her during a break in the wind. "Ach. That'll be the men come back from the search. I wonder if they caught up to it? Let's go see. If not, I have a notion one of them will be sent into the village to spread word of what happened. Ye can go back with them."

"Aye, tis a brilliant idea." His smile made her blush anew. "Safety in numbers, and all that."

Rhiannon fell into step beside him as they made their way out into the field. What were the odds he'd have stumbled onto *her* farm out of all the farms in the area? It must be fate.

~~~~~

A huddle of bodies dotted the nearby hillside as Anne made her way toward her daughter's family farm. Nearly a sennight had passed since her last trek into the hub of their little community and her body was not pleased. But it had to be done. Until the wolf was vanquished, no one would be safe. Vigilance was key to defeating the monster that had slipped into their lives. And it seemed she'd already missed some crucial happenings whilst her old bones had been recovering from a simple walk.

None of them seemed to notice her presence as she drew near, too focused on whatever lay on the ground before them. Anne huffed up to the men. "What is it? What's happened?"

Her son-in-law, Cathal, startled at her side. "Ah. Granny. Where did ye come from?"

"I sprung out the ground. Where do ye think I came from, lad? Now, answer me question."

"It's like ye warned. Something's attacked the sheep."

"Not something. A wolf."

The men exchanged a look. Aye, none of them believed her. They hadn't when she'd first warned them a sennight ago and they wouldn't now, after the death of a single sheep. But if she couldn't convince them…

"It's true, I tell ye. 'Tis. If the creature isna' caught and killed at once, t'will only grow bolder. Afore long t'will be sneaking in through yer front doors and snatchin' yer babes out from under yer very own roofs."

"Ach, easy, Granny. Easy now." Cathal gingerly placed one of his large hands on her shoulder as if he were afraid the touch would crumble her. "Yer goin' ta overtax yerself again. Saoirse will have me hide if I allow that ta happen."

"Fah," Anne replied, wishing she could throw his arm away to show her ire, but settling for a quick thrust of her walking stick into the soft clover and heather of the field. "There's no time. Ye must charge after the beast. Ye must kill it, else all will be lost."

"Whist, we tried," said one of the other men. "We even found its tracks."
~~~~~

"Aye. Massive things too."

"Hush." Cathal cut the men off. "Ye'll upset her again." His eyes shifted to Anne's and he flinched as she glared up at him.

"Hiding the truth is how we lose, Cathal. Lies are where the monster thrives."

"Da. Granny!" Anne turned to face Rhiannon. The younger woman broke into a run as she spotted her grandmother. "What're *ye* doing here? Ye could hardly move for days the last time."

But it wasn't her granddaughter's disapproving frown that sent Anne's heart skittering to a stop. It was the droll smile and casual saunter of the man who followed her that had the old woman clutching the girl and dragging her into the center of the band of armed villagers at her back. "Arm yerselves. The beast is amongst us!"

"Ach, Granny." Rhiannon pulled her arm away.

Cathal's eyes narrowed at the young man. "Who're ye then? And what're ye doing here?"

The wolf stopped with a few yards between himself and the group of men holding deadly weapons. His teeth flashed with a warm smile that would have fooled most anyone. Anne was *not* most anyone. She flashed her own teeth in response. A look of disgust. Rhiannon stepped in front of her and sent both of her elders a pleading look. As if begging not to be embarrassed.

"Da. This is…" Rhiannon's cheeks stained as red as her hair. She sent the man a half-pleading, half-humiliated look.

He took a step forward. "Me name's Niall. Niall Ferguson. And I stumbled onta yer land much by mistake, I'm embarrassed ta say. I'm new to the area and got a wee bit turned round whilst explorin'. Just in time it seems." His eyes fell onto the shredded livestock at their feet as if he weren't the very creature that had wrought the deed. "I've heard ye had trouble with some sort of predator."

"Some sort of predator," Anne mocked. She brandished her walking stick, ready for a fight. "Ye know just as well what did this, wolf. I won't let ye have yer way here. Mark my words."

"Granny!"

Cathal cleared his throat. "We have had some trouble."

"Bah," Anne said. She shot her son-in-law a withering look. "Beware Cathal. Letting the beast fool ye will only embolden him."

Rhiannon spun on her. "Stop. Just stop. Niall hasn't done a thing wrong. It's a blessing he found his way here. It may well have saved his life if whatever did this," she waved at the corpse, "had come across him."

Anne shook her head. "Ye don't understand—"

"Yes, I do. You're the one whose gone off to the land of fairies—"

"Rhiannon, that's enough!" Cathal rubbed his forehead, clearly vexed. The other men shifted uncomfortably, unsettled by the bickering women.

Cathal sighed and narrowed his eyes in a meaningful way at his daughter. "Ye musn't speak to yer elders so, lass."

"But, Da." Rhiannon's eyes filled with sorrow as they shifted between the wolf and Anne. "She's being so rude," she muttered.

Cathal lowered his voice as if he could hide his words from her old ears. "She's merely distressed is all. I told ye before. Yer Granny has a history with such things. We must be patient with her."

Anne nearly brandished her stick at him but decided it best not to. She needed allies, and he already thought she was loony. Off to the land of fairies *indeed*.

One of the men cleared his throat. "Tis gettin' late. I still have stock out that need to be bedded down. And it'd be best, me thinks, to stick close to home at night. Least until we can kill whatever's done this."

"Da." Rhiannon clutched her fists close to her chest and turned to her father. "Can Niall stay the night? Tis too late for him to be travelin' so far under such circumstances."

To his credit, Cathal eyed the younger man like a predator then, though it was clear he considered him more of the human kind. "Well..."

"Absolutely not," Anne cut in. "To turn a blind eye to the threat is one thing. To store it in yer own house overnight is another thing altogether."

Rhiannon looked like she wanted to tell *Anne* that she weren't welcome but held her tongue. Being an elder had some perks to it at any rate.

"Ye can stay with me," another of the men cut in. "Me and the missus live alone." He gave Cathal a nod of understanding. "And I've plans to travel inta' the village on the morrow. I can take ye with me."

The wolf shot a brief glance at Rhiannon as if waiting for her to argue. When she didn't, he turned away from her decisively and gave a nod. "I'd be much appreciative of yer hospitality." The wolf didn't spare Rhiannon another glance as the group of men dispersed.

Anne could tell the snub burned her granddaughter. And knew it had been intentional. There was more than one way to lure in prey.

Her granddaughter watched after the wolf mournfully as if in a trance. Though it was no magic that held her captive. Only an innocent and naive maiden's infatuation.

Cathal dropped his hand on her shoulder, breaking the spell. "Come on, then. Sure, yer mother's worried. We should head in and set her mind at ease."

Rhiannon turned toward the house in a huff, being sure to ignore Anne as she did. Cathal frowned apologetically and then followed. Anne watched them go before casting another glare toward the shrinking silhouette of the creature who had taken human form.

She'd managed to keep the wolf from their door. But for how long?

Anne looked down at what was left of the sheep. It wasn't a coincidence that the first attack had been at Cathal's family farm. Or that the beast had chosen to hide its true form by cozying up to Rhiannon. It was after the girl as sure as anything.

With a grunt Anne turned and slowly made her way across the field. Cathal and Rhiannon had stopped. Her son-in-law with the well-meaning, if insulting look of a long suffering youngster in the face of a deranged old woman. Her granddaughter with arms crossed and an angry pout planted firmly on her face. They still didn't believe her. And it seemed unlikely they would before the attacks began in earnest.

For Anne did not know where or when the beast would strike next, but she knew one thing more surely than the ache in her bones. Things were about to get much, much worse.

And she was powerless to stop it.

~~~~~

The village was quiet despite the sun shining brightly. Rhiannon spotted only a few familiar faces going about their daily tasks. Even the blacksmith was closed. Where was everyone? More importantly, where was Niall?

She had hoped to catch him before he'd gone back to the village, but the morning's chores had dragged on for forever. By the time she'd gotten away, he'd already left with their neighbor, forcing her to wait even longer to find him until she could get permission to make the walk in herself.

No other sheep had been attacked during the night, proving her grandmother *wrong* about Niall. If he'd somehow been responsible for the dead sheep, why wouldn't he strike again with such a good excuse to stay close to their livestock? But of course, she'd been wrong. A wolf shaped like a man was just a fanciful tale. Rhiannon felt a twinge of concern that her grandmother's mind had deteriorated so rapidly since the last time she'd visited the far off cottage in the woods.

But she was far more concerned with finding the man whom the old woman had insulted so unjustly and apologize before the damage to their relationship was irreversible. Rhiannon's face burned. Not that there *was* a relationship. Just that, she hoped there could be…

She shook the thought away. First, she had to beg forgiveness for her elderly matriarch.

Rhiannon searched the village until the sound of laughter drew her toward the inn at the far end of the square. Smoke poured from the chimney top. Light glowed from within despite the time of day. The proprietress, Mrs. O'Haggerty, must think she'd be making back the money she spent on the wax for candles. Shouts and cheers seeped out through the edges of the door and front windows, as if to confirm her estimation. Rhiannon pushed the door open to find nearly the whole village gathered in the large dining room. The door closed behind her, sealing out the frost bitten wind and covering her with the warmth of the roaring fireplace.

People mingled and laughed with one another, drinking and eating, as
~~~~~

if it were a holiday and not the middle of an average day meant for work. Rhiannon's normal sense of order and duty was eclipsed by the excitement flowing through the room. He had to be there. Her eyes scanned the crowd. Sure enough, there he was, sitting in the middle of the room at the table reserved for high-ranking members of the village or high paying travelers. Niall. The surge of happiness seeing him brought quickly soured as Rhiannon recognized the people huddled closest around him—most of whom were young, eligible women of the area.

An unpleasant heat settled into Rhiannon's chest as she watched one of them clutch Niall's arm and lean into him with her bosom pressed against his bicep. Fiona was wasting no time trying to stake her claim on the handsome newcomer. Orla leaned against him from the other side, not to be outdone. From across the table, Doirean leaned in with a look that played at casual interest but managed to showcase her profile to perfection. No mistake about it, all three of the young ladies had set their caps for Niall.

Rhiannon braced herself and forded through the crowd until she reached the table.

"Ah, here she is," Niall said as he caught sight of her. His gaze was edged with disgust. "We were just talking about ye and that crazy ol' grandmother of yers."

Rhiannon stiffened.

"Aye," Fiona tittered. "We heard all about her ranting."

"Poor Niall got quite the welcome to the village thanks to *yer* family," cut in Doireann.

"That ol' Anne seems to have taken a turn for the worse," Angus the blacksmith guffawed.

"Granny didn't mean any harm."

"Granny didn't mean any harm," Niall repeated in a tone of mockery before taking a swig of the ale sitting on the table.

"I came to apologize—"

"Oh aye, let's hear it then. Let's hear yer excuses and be done with it."

He was mocking her. And she was embarrassing herself in front of nearly everyone, trying to be kind to the man. The heat of the room seemed to settle atop her lungs. Or maybe it was the pressure of her rising fury.

Rhiannon pulled in a deep breath past the weight of it. "I don't have any excuses. I only wanted to apologize for any hurt feelings that we might have caused ye the other day. Sorry ta trouble ye. I've said my piece. Now, I'll be on my way." She tried to ignore the chittering laughter at her back as she made her way back to the door and the blessed chill of outside. She battled against the wind, grateful for the vent to her anger.

What a boorish, judgmental, loathsome—To think she'd ever fancied the man. The lump in her chest moved into her throat. Aye, she'd fancied him. But not anymore. She swiped at the single tear that slid down her cheek, bold enough to mark her a liar. *Not* anymore.

"Ach, watch it."

Rhiannon stopped her mad dash down the inn's front steps. "Ah, I'm so sorry Ian. I—I didn't see ye there."

Ian Crowley looked up into Rhiannon's face from the lower step and his smile faded slightly. "Ye all right, Rhia? Ye look upset."

Rhiannon shook off her anger. It wasn't Ian's fault. And it had been forever since she'd seen her childhood friend. Not since his wedding back in spring. "Aye, Ian. I'm perfectly fine." She joined him on the bottom step. "How're ye? And Mathilda?"

"We're doing just cheery, thanks fer askin'." His infectious grin drove away the last of Rhiannon's sour mood. Would she ever find the kind of love that lit up Ian's eyes any time someone mentioned his wife? "I've just popped inta town for some supplies but Ol' Angus isna at the smithy."

"Aye." She snorted. "He's in there, right proper drunk. Not sure how much work ye can get out of him today."

Laughter poured into the street as someone walked out of the inn, interrupting their conversation. Rhiannon glanced back and froze. Niall. She stiffened. What did he want?

Niall's eyes took in the scene at the bottom of the stairs. "Rhiannon. Why did ye leave so soon?"

She scoffed. "Why would I stay? I don't find much worth in being used for other people's amusement."

Ian looked between the two of them with a frown. "Are ye all right, Rhia?"

"Ach, aye." Rhiannon waved. "No need to worry, Ian. I'll be fine."

The two men eyed each other as if sizing the other up. The brief look Niall sent her during the process was filled with jealousy. A thrill went through Rhiannon. Perhaps she hadn't been a total fool after all if he could feel jealous of her speaking to another man.

"Don't let me hold ye up, Ian. I know ye have work ta get done," she said, wondering what Niall would say once he was gone.

"Very well. Take care, Rhia."

Rhiannon waited until he was gone before turning to stare down Niall. "Well, what is it?"

"I came ta call ye back." His smile was charming and her anger was instantly disarmed. "Ye didn't take all that joking seriously, did ye? We were just having some fun."

"At my expense."

"Nay. Yer just being too sensitive. Ye have ta admit, yer granny's actions are rather off the cuff." He shook his head sadly. "I didn't realize the other women would be so quick to join in. Ah. I should have, though." He tilted his chin down and looked up at her simultaneously in a way that sent a flutter through her chest. "Of course they'd get jealous, seeing ye join in on the fun." His voice dropped to a whisper. "Ye have ta know yer the prettiest girl around."

Rhiannon blushed. *Jealous*? Well. He thought they should be jealous of her. Prettiest girl around? The heat in her face grew.

His smile deepened, and he held out a hand to her. "Come back inside with me?"

Rhiannon took his hand and let him pull her back up the stairs.

~~~~~

Rhiannon slowed her steps deliberately as she neared the village. She didn't want to seem too overeager to spend the day with Niall, but it had been all she could think about through the night.

It had been over a fortnight since she and Niall had started spending more time together. He'd officially asked her Da if he could pursue her only a sennight into their time. Da had seemed somewhat reluctant, but that was to be expected from a father allowing his only child to court, wasn't it? Or perhaps he was only expressing the fear that seemed to weigh heavily on everyone's heart. Each passing day, more and more sheep were found slaughtered by whatever predator haunted their little farms. No one seemed able to stop it.

Niall was perfect. Funny, charming, beloved by all. Rhiannon frowned as she rounded the corner of the inn and the center of the square came into view where she spotted Niall and Fiona clearly deep in conversation with one another. And standing quite intimately at that. Perhaps he was a little *too* beloved by all.

Awkwardly Rhiannon approached the two, expecting—hoping—he'd turn to address her in such a way that Fiona would get the hint that she shouldn't be speaking to him in such a way. Instead, he continued to laugh, and *flirt*, with Fiona. Right in front of Rhiannon. He even let Fiona touch his arm as they carried on as if Rhiannon weren't even there. After a moment, Fiona cast her an odd look. As if Rhiannon was the one who shouldn't have been there. Then, Niall blessedly looked her way and smiled.

"Oh, Rhiannon. Lovely day, isn't it?"

Rhiannon blinked at him in surprise.

He didn't wait for her to respond. "Thank ye for the chat, Fiona. I'll be seeing ye around."

Fiona glared at Rhiannon. A clear message she was not pleased to have her conversation interrupted. Then she sashayed off with one last smile for Niall.

"What was that?" Rhiannon asked.

He frowned down at her. "What was what?"

"That?" She waved after Fiona. "Ye ignored me. And acted like ye weren't even expecting to meet me even though yer the one who invited me ta spend the day with ye."

He scoffed humorously. "No, I didn't."

She blinked up at him. "Yes. Ye did." She deepened her voice in a
~~~~~

mockery of his. "Oh, Rhiannon. Lovely day, isn't it?" She slammed her hands on her hips. "How is that something ye say to the woman ye've invited to—"

"What's wrong with asking ye if it's a lovely day? Ye sound as daft as yer granny."

Rhiannon flinched.

He shook his head. "Yer oversensitivity is becoming insufferable."

The wind picked up and carried a long strand of her curls into his face. He sputtered obnoxiously in response and shooed it away as if it were a fly.

"Ach, yer hair. Why do ye insist on letting it be such a mess? A lady ought to be a bit more orderly." His eyes narrowed at her brightly colored dress. Her favorite dress. The one she usually reserved for Sunday mass because of how special it was. "And that dress. I'm certain to get a headache if I have to spend the day looking at that bright color under the sunlight." He spun away with a snort. "Perhaps a walk with ye today isn't the best idea?" He left before she could respond.

Rhiannon reeled as if struck. He was suddenly so cruel. So uncaring. What had she done wrong?

She lifted a hand to brush her hair out of her face. It could stand to be a bit tidier. She eyed her dress. And perhaps, perhaps it was a strange color for a walking dress. Tears burned her eyelids as Rhiannon turned back for home. Shame weighed her head down and despair dragged at her steps. If only she hadn't challenged him. Made him angry. Dressed in a way he didn't like. Then he would have walked with her. Then he wouldn't be heading off to God knew where. Probably to continue his conversation with Fiona.

Would he end their courtship so soon?

Rhiannon shook her head violently. She'd make sure the next time he saw her, there was nothing short of a perfect lady in her place. Then he'd see they were meant to be together.

~~~~~

Saoirse watched her daughter move through her nightly chores with a weight in her step that the mother had never seen before. Rhiannon's bright red curls had been tucked into a tight braid and trapped beneath a light blue kerchief. Rhiannon had hated braids and anything that tied her hair down ever since she was a wee tot at Saoirse's knee. It had been vexing back then but she'd grown to love seeing her daughter's curls bouncing happily with her every flamboyant motion.

Now, even her movements were subdued. She didn't need any special mother's magick to know something was wrong. Saoirse was trying to find the right words to broach the subject when Rhiannon turned to address her.

"Mother. Could I use some of the cloth ye bought the other day? I'd like to make a new dress."

Saoirse blinked. "The brown cloth. The one I bought to make yer Da
~~~~~

new trousers."

Rhiannon bit her lower lip and looked close to tears. "I know ye've need of it, but I'll go in to get more. And do extra work around the farm to make it up to ye."

"That's not what—" Saoirse huffed. "I don't care about the need for it, lass. But why would ye want to make a new dress out of that brown? Ye've already got so many lovely colorful dresses that ye enjoy so much."

"Oh, please, Mother." The tears spilled over. "I need it to be brown. Brown and ladylike."

Saoirse's frowned deepened. "Is this because of that young man—"

The front door slammed against the wall, eliciting a scream from both women. Howling wind rushed into their little home, stealing in seconds what warmth the fireplace had generated over the hours as Cathal stalked in.

"Cathal. What in heaven's name—"

The serious look he sent her filled Saoirse with dread.

"Fiona McKinley's been attacked by the creature," he said. "She's dead."

~~~~~

A violent knock shook the thick wooden door of Anne's cottage against the bar set across it. Anne flinched in her rocker as a shot of fear bolted through her aged heart. Could it be the wolf? With a grunt, she pulled herself to her feet, not bothering to keep the woolen blankets she'd piled on her lap from falling to the floor. If the beast had come to kill her, the attack would leave the place far from tidy, so there was no need to worry about a few blankets scattered about.

Anne crept to the window and shoved aside the heavy curtain an inch so she could peer into the falling night beyond the glass. A man stood outside her door, bundled tightly against the early winter air. He seemed taller than the wolf's human form had been, but she couldn't be sure it wasn't that very monster standing on her stoop.

If it were, Anne wasn't sure the bar across the length of the door or thick paned glass would be enough to keep it out.

"Who be ye? And why disturb an old woman so late?" she called.

His eyes shifted to the glass, but she still couldn't see his face. "Me name's Faolan O'Keefe. Ye wrote fer me ta come."

"I did no such thing," she replied.

"Aye, ye did. Ye wrote ta me grandfather, who can no longer answer such summons. Honor would not allow me to ignore such a plea on his behalf. I've come for the hunt."

Anne hesitated. It was possible that the wolf had intercepted her letter and knew the surname of the man she was expecting and why she'd sent for him. "What was yer grandfather's name?" *That* the wolf would have no way of knowing.
~~~~~

"Bowen," he replied.

"Ah." Anne muttered to herself as she bustled toward the door. She opened it to the disapproving frown of a young man in his early twenties.

"That was very foolish," he said.

Anne glared up at him. "What?"

He stepped past her and walked into her home, surveying the room as if he expected a wolf to leap out from behind her rocking chair. "If ye ever have reason to doubt who's standing outside yer door, ye need to err on the side of caution. Leave nothing ta chance."

Anne snorted and shoved the door closed once more. "Ye would rather I left ye out in the cold?"

He sent her an apologetic smile. "I would rather ye stay alive. Ye assumed I was telling the truth because I gave ye my grandfather's name, but that might have been information the wolf learned while assimilating with the people in the area. Are ye absolutely certain no one remembers the name of the man who saved yer village all those years ago? It might be something that stuck in an unlikely place. Wolves are cunning and dig deep when they get their teeth in a place. He won't have stopped until he uncovers every secret the people here have to use against them in whatever way he can."

Anne studied him a moment and then gave him a serious nod. "Aye. Ye have a very good point. I should've thought of that." She shuffled back toward her chair.

"Tis a simple mistake," he began to say.

"Ye were doing such a good job of not patronizing me a second ago." Anne groaned as she sat heavily in her chair. Then she gave him the hard look she gave all misbehaving youngsters. "Don't start now."

He studied her a moment and then his smile turned from comforting to admiration. "Yes, ma'am."

Anne pulled her blankets up from the floor slowly, cursing how the weight of them troubled her hands. Faolan waited a moment, then came to her aide, settling the heavy wool over her legs. As he did, Anne studied him. He was a handsome young man, even with the scar that ran from the top of his left ear all the way to his chin. "Faolan. Yer mother must have had a sense of humor."

"'Twas my father's choice," he replied with a smile as he stepped away from her chair. "And aye. He found it quite humorous to give me a name that means *little wolf*. Sometimes I wonder if mayhap he hoped it would confuse the beasts I hunted." He laughed. "Or at the very least, enrage them."

"Well, I hope he was also good at the hunt." Anne scowled. "The beast has grown bold and may already be plotting to expand his territory."

Faolan sobered. "Aye. He was the best in the business. Taught me everything I know. Which he learned directly from my grandfather. Only reason he isn't here himself is because he was injured during a hunt a few years back and never fully recovered." The young man straightened to his full height and stared hard into Anne's eyes. "I have no plans to let him down on this mission."

Anne leaned back, letting her chair rock slowly beneath her. "It's all happened just as before. First came the howl. Then the stranger was seen in the village. Then the sheep. And now he's moved on ta killing any woman he can find out alone. Soon he'll try to sway other men of the village into transforming into his kind."

"Aye, Grandfather's told me the story of his first encounter. And it's always much the same, though occasionally, they'll turn the men before attacking the women." Faolan rubbed the end of the scar at his jawline where his otherwise tightly cut beard left a slight gap. "Ye know who 'tis then. The beast?"

"Ach aye." She glared. "Ye'll know him as soon as ye lay eyes on him. He has the stink of the wolf about him in every way. No one who's seen a wolf before would be able ta mistake 'im."

Faolan nodded. "In that case, I'll head back ta the village inn for the night—"

"Nonsense, ye'll stay here," Anne insisted, sending him a look that would tolerate no argument if he intended to give her one. "The wolf may have followed ye here. Better to err on the side of caution. Leave nothing ta chance." She smiled. "Isn't that what ye said?"

He returned the smile. "Aye. In that case, I'd be much appreciative of the hospitality. I'll bed down on the floor by the fire."

She gave a nod. "Meanwhile, I'd like ta hear yer plans for moving forward."

Faolan settled on the bench by the table, and as Anne listened to him explain how he planned to get the villagers on his side, she felt her confidence growing. He certainly sounded like he knew what he was doing, and he'd brought his weapons with him, a clear sign he was always prepared for the fight, whenever it might come.

Finally, they had what they needed to turn the tide against the creature.

~~~~~

Rhiannon's steps were heavy as she made her way down the forest path to her grandmother's house. She didn't want to visit Granny. Partly because she was still angry with the older woman for the role she'd played in the misunderstanding of Rhiannon's and Niall's early relationship.

But mostly because of the deep-seated disquiet she felt over what Niall was doing when she wasn't around. Fiona, God rest her soul, wasn't the only woman she'd caught Niall flirting with. Despite their understanding, he still insisted on being "friendly" with other women, even at her expense.

Rhiannon didn't know how to make him understand that his actions were hurting her, so she'd gotten used to trying to go with him everywhere,
~~~~~

just to be safe. A trip all the way into the forest made that impossible. And she just couldn't stop thinking about Niall and Orla leaning into each other like they had been the day before.

She picked up her pace. The sooner she delivered the basket of food to her grandmother, the sooner she could be back. Then everything would be fine.

A howl ripped through the air and echoed through the trees. Rhiannon froze, her blood running cold despite the layers of wool bundling her from head to foot. That sound had plagued their homes for months, but she'd never heard it from so close before. A stick snapped somewhere behind her. The *creature*. It had found her.

Rhiannon bolted with a scream, sprinting as if the devil himself were after her. From the crash and snarls at her back, that seemed likely. The trees drew in closer as she neared her grandmother's house, but so did the sound of the monster closing in. Rhiannon spotted the familiar grey rock building through the thick trunks. The door stood open, as if waiting to pull her to safety. A hot breath warmed the back of her legs as the creature snarled. She wasn't going to make it.

A man stepped out from behind a tree up ahead with a bow nocked and drawn. His eyes were hard with command.

"Get down!"

Rhiannon dove forward, crashing into the unforgiving earth as the man let his arrow fly. It sliced through the air to her right and struck something. The creature gave a cry of pain tinged with rage. The man had another arrow nocked and ready, but the beast tore off back the way it had come, as if sensing its demise.

The man gave chase, practically leaping over Rhiannon as he went. She turned over to watch him disappear into the trees. A shuffle brought her attention back to where Granny Anne hauled herself over the uneven terrain on her walking stick.

"Are ye all right, child?"

Tears slipped down Rhiannon's face as the fear from the past few moments settled into relief. "Ach, Granny Anne. I was so afeared."

"I know, lass. But yer all right now." Anne tried to pull her granddaughter to her feet, but Rhiannon did most of the work. "Come, we must see this through. No more lives can be lost."

Rhiannon sniffed away her tears. Her grandmother was right. If the man with the bow could stop the monster, their village would finally have peace again.

And she *so* wanted to feel peace again.

~~~~~

Anne let Rhiannon lead her down the path toward the village.

A strangled cry echoed down the path from up ahead. "Help."

"Niall?"
~~~~~

Anne tried to grab her granddaughter. "Rhiannon. No!"

But the girl brushed her off and sprinted down the path toward the voice before Anne could stop her.

Anne did her best to run after the girl, but it was a pathetic attempt. Up ahead, two men stood in the path, one backed against a tree, the other with bow and arrow drawn for the kill.

"What're ye doing?" Rhiannon cried.

"Rhiannon," the wolf said. "Thank the heavens ye've come. Get this madman away from me."

"Stand back, lass," Faolan said.

Rhiannon jumped between the two men. "Stop this at once. What's wrong with ye?"

"Tis not what ye think," Faolan replied.

"Tell him to drop his bow, Granny," Rhiannon said, her eyes pleading for Anne's help.

Anne huffed and dug her stick into the ground. "Get out of the way, lass."

"Yer mad." She looked from Anne to Faolan. "Yer both mad."

"Get out of the way, daft woman," Faolan growled.

"Or what? Ye'll shoot me?"

"Aye, Rhiannon," Niall said. "He's crazed. He's already shot at me once. He's going ta kill me."

"No, he won't." Rhiannon glared up at the hunter, brave as a bear protecting her cub while the wolf cowered behind her skirts. "We're leaving." She turned her body to grab the wolf's arm but kept her eyes focused on Faolan.

Which was why she missed the smug, knowing smile the wolf shot at the hunter.

Anne watched them go, knowing she wasn't the only one they'd have trouble convincing. "Well. I hope yer better at speaking ta men than ye are at speaking ta women."

Faolan didn't respond as he watched Rhiannon lead the limping wolf away. "I'm going ta follow them back to the village. Make sure he doesn't try ta attack her again."

Anne nodded. "Go. Don't let him out of yer sight. Please."

He shot Anne a grim smile and then set out after the two.

~~~~~

The group of men exchanged a look that proved Faolan was *not* better at talking to men than he was to women. He ran a hand over his chin absentmindedly. It was dark outside, and the inn was nearly abandoned for the night. He'd decided to begin searching for allies immediately while keeping an eye on the stairs the wolf had run up after Faolan had entered the inn. He'd found a group of men already discussing the recent slayings and hoped he could sway them to his side.
~~~~~

Laying out the facts wasn't working. It usually didn't. People didn't want to believe they could be fooled so easily. Once the wolf had a foot in the door, getting people to acknowledge what he was became all the harder.

It was time to try a different tactic.

He focused on one man in particular. A large man named Cathal with bright red, curly hair Faolan had to assume he'd given his daughter. Something Faolan had overheard that day after he'd watched Rhiannon leave the wolf at the inn was about to come in handy.

"Are ye defending him because ye believe the tale unlikely? Or because yer daughter is courting him?"

Cathal's eyes narrowed but it was Angus, the blacksmith who answered. "Cathal wouldn't have anything to worry about there. Niall's already courting me Doireann."

"What?" All the men at the table flinched as Cathal rounded on Angus. Even the big blacksmith seemed loath to address the anger building on the man's face. "What do ye mean by that, Angus?"

Angus did his best to return the man's stare. "I mean that Niall asked me fer permission to court Doireann not more than two days ago."

Cathal's skin turned the same shade as his hair and his nostril's flared. "He asked me over a month back to court Rhiannon. They've been spending many days together ever since."

Angus sputtered, his face twisting into rage. "Why, that no good — He's been lying to our girls?"

"I might kill him just for that," Cathal said.

"Agreed," Angus grunted.

Finally, a chink in the wolf's charisma. A weakness in the armor made of humans he'd formed around himself. Faolan leaned into it. "In that case, we can take out two birds with one arrow, if ye catch me meaning. We'll have Doireann ask this Niall out for a meeting in the forest. We'll name the time and place. If he shows," Faolan nodded to Cathal. "ye'll know for certain he's been playing with yer daughter's affections. And if I'm correct, we'll also prove the creature doing all of the killing and the man you think is Niall are one and the same. We either catch a wolf dressed as a man or a man who acts like a wolf."

Cathal studied him, but Faolan refused to back down. This was far too important. Finally, the older man replied, "Aye. But ye'll keep yer weapons sheathed. Dallying with young lassies isn't a criminal offense." He sneered. "Though I don't plan on letting him off the hook with just a warning, I won't have him killed unjustly. And once we prove yer daft theory about him being a wolf wrong, ye'll leave our village fer good. We don't need yer kind of crazy spreading."

Faolan hesitated only a moment before he shrugged. He didn't like the thought of a young woman being so close to danger and having his bow unnocked, but it couldn't be helped. This Doireann was already in the wolf's sights. Exposing the beast was worth the risk. "Agreed. If there's no wolf, there's no need for me to stay anyways."

Besides, it wouldn't come to that. The creature would unwittingly show its true nature, and these men wouldn't stop him from killing it once it did.

Faolan took a long drink of ale to hide his grim smile.

Sometimes all it took to take down a wolf was to expose its lies.

It wasn't always that easy, but it was the way that Faolan found to be the most satisfying.

~~~~

Faolan crouched behind a large oak tree, waiting for his prey.

To his right several yards away, Cathal hid behind a boulder that was almost too small to conceal the man. A half dozen others were likewise scattered nearby, with enough space between each that nothing could pass through unseen. The trap was set. Out in the open, Doireann stood waiting for Niall to arrive.

Footsteps signaled his approach. He stepped out of the tree line with a smile that exposed his overlarge incisors.

Doireann bounced happily. "I knew ye'd come." She shot a quick look to where her father was hiding. "I knew ye wouldn't go be with..." She hesitated as if realizing it might be insensitive to say such a thing while the father of the other woman she was talking about was hidden nearby. "Well. Anyone else."

"Of course I'd pick ye, my sweet," the wolf replied.

Cathal's body grew rigid with anger. He made a move as if to stand.

"Ye looked so tasty when I saw ye waiting to speak to me this morn at the inn. I couldn't resist coming out here for a taste."

Cathal froze, his eyes growing wide with horror as the face of the man he thought of as Niall started to transform into the vicious visage of a fanged beast. Faolan was up on his feet with his arrow nocked before anyone else could move.

Finally, the hideous change in her would-be lover's face registered to the young woman. It lunged for her throat as her scream echoed through the trees. But Faolan's arrow intervened, knocking the beast away with a howl of pain, its steel tip buried deep into his shoulder.

Faolan and Cathal charged forward. Faolan tried to get another arrow off. But the wolf, ever cunning, dove to place the screaming woman between himself and the hunter. The other men broke out of their shock and piled into the clearing, their assorted weapons now drawn.

Seeing the inevitable loss for what it was, the wolf ran with inhuman speed into the forest, out of the line of fire. Faolan cursed his luck. If the wolf hadn't moved at just the right moment to attack the girl, the first arrow would have struck his heart. He'd missed and now it was injured, desperate, and on the loose.
~~~~

"He's headed toward Cathal's place."

Faolan whipped his head round to face the older man.

Cathal's face paled and then he sprinted toward his home. "Rhiannon!"

~~~~~

Rhiannon kneaded bread at the table while her mother peeled potatoes at her side.

"Mother."

"Hmmm."

"Do ye think I'm pretty?"

Her mother's knife stopped flying over the spinning spud in her hand as she looked at Rhiannon with surprise. "Of course ye are. How could ye even think to ask that?" Rhiannon shrugged. Her mother huffed. "It's that man again, isn't it?

"No, Mother."

"Why I ought to—"

The door slammed against the wall. Both women jumped to their feet.

"Niall?" Rhiannon cried. "Ye scared the life out of us." Then she spotted the arrow in his shoulder. "What's happened?"

He charged into the room, his eyes narrowing on Rhiannon. "That lunatic that was with yer grandmother attacked me. Again. And yer father was there with him."

"What?"

Rhiannon looked at her mother, who seemed just as surprised.

"I need ye, Rhiannon. I need ye to come with me while I flee. Before they can catch up and finish the job."

"Nonsense," her mother said. "There has to be some kind of mistake. I'll speak to Cathal—"

"There's no time," he shouted, his eyes sending hateful daggers at her mother. Then they shifted to Rhiannon, eliciting a flinch. "Ye love me, don't ye?"

"Ye—yes. But—"

"But nothing." He stalked toward her. "Ye have to come with me. Now."

"No." Her mother moved around the table, placing herself between the two younger people. "She isn't going anywhere."

"Get out of my way." In a blink, Niall grabbed Rhiannon's mother and threw her across the room. The older woman's head struck the floor with a thud.

"Mother!" Rhiannon tried to go to her, but Niall leapt at her. They both fell to the ground. Rhiannon stared up in terror at the twisted face of the man she thought she loved. His jaw grew long and narrow. His teeth grew sharp. His eyes shifted into that of an animal. "Ye said ye loved me," he said. "Now it's time ye proved it."
~~~~~

Rhiannon screamed as his teeth sank into her shoulder.

~~~~~

It had been days since the wolf had attacked Rhiannon and Saoirse, and while Anne's daughter had suffered a bad crack to the skull, her granddaughter was still missing. Anne had insisted on joining the search party, despite Faolan's warnings that she wouldn't like what she would find. She had to try. She'd failed to stop the monster from striking. She had to at least see his death through to the end.

The day after the attack, Faolan spotted two sets of tracks in the forest.

"He's turned her," he had said. His gaze filled with pity and regret. Anne had ignored it. She couldn't falter. If Rhainnon was a wolf…

"Do ye know of any way to save her?" she'd asked, knowing the answer.

"There have been rumors. But they seemed to be fanciful fairy tales." He scratched his jaw, then shook his head sadly. "Only a natural born wolf can pose as a human. As far as I know, a turned beast can't ever be human again. I'm sorry."

She'd sighed, and though her body had trembled with despair, her voice had been steady. "Ye must do what must be done. Don't falter."

He had nodded.

They were close now. Close to wherever the beast had chosen to hide out. Cathal reluctantly carried Anne on his back so they could keep up with the hunter. The other men, some fathers and husbands who had also lost loved ones to the monster, had joined them.

It was time to end it.

Suddenly, a grey shape dove out of the trees and knocked Faolan off his feet. Hunter and wolf grappled across the leaf-covered soil in a whirl of teeth and steel, fighting for the killing blow. Cathal quickly knelt to let Anne off his back and jumped in to help. The old woman stumbled back a step when a red blur leapt onto Cathal to save her mate.

Anne's eyes filled with tears as she watched her son-in-law throw the red wolf off him and draw his sword. His eyes grew pained as he looked between the she-wolf and Anne.

"It can't be."

The she-wolf attacked again. Cathal, torn by his emotions, hesitated long enough for her to take a chunk out of his arm with her thrashing claws.

"Rhiannon!" Anne called.

The she-wolf hesitated. The sharp slit of the pupils inside her big green eyes softened into a human-like circle and swung from the injured man before her to Anne, uncertain, pained.

Anne inched toward her. "Rhiannon. Please. Listen to me. This isn't who ye are."

"Anne, look out," Faolan cried. The grey wolf had abandoned his attack on the hunter, perhaps sensing his hold on Rhiannon weakening. He
~~~~~

charged toward Anne with deadly intent. Faolan scrambled to reclaim the bow he'd lost in the struggle.

He wouldn't make it in time.

Anne braced to feel the wolf's jaw around her throat, but the she-wolf flew forward to intercept him. The wolves fought viciously, teeth and claws tearing at each other, staining the ground with their blood. The she-wolf, smaller than her opponent, was no match for her grey counterpart. He pinned her down, his fang-filled jaw opened wide to rip out her throat.

"Stop!" Anne and Cathal yelled uselessly from the sidelines .

In the end, an arrow proved far more effective.

Faolan's aim was steady and true. The steel tip buried itself deep into the wolf's right eye. He froze and then fell to the earth, dead.

Anne nearly collapsed with relief as the she-wolf got to her feet. Faolan nocked another arrow and drew it back, ready to make true on his promise to Anne.

"No!"

Faolan shot her a frown, which she ignored. She knew the risk. And her granddaughter was worth it. Anne inched forward once more. The she-wolf looked up at her mournfully.

"Rhiannon. Please, lass. Come back ta us. Come home." She reached out her hand.

And a very human hand reached back and slipped into her weathered palm.

Fur and claws faded into skin. Sharp teeth turned into chattering human incisors. And her beloved granddaughter's face reappeared from beneath the harsh visage of the beast as the wolf faded away.

"Granny." Tears filled her brilliant green eyes. "I want ta go home."

"Rhiannon!" Cathal fell to his knees beside his daughter and pulled her into his embrace.

"Well. I'll be." Faolan shook his head. "The fairy stories said the voice of true love could free a turned person of the curse." He shot Anne a look of irritation. "That shouldn't have worked." Then he smiled. "But, 'tis very glad I am it did."

Anne merely held her family close and wept.

~~~~~

Anne leaned back in her rocking chair, letting the warm sunshine settle into her skin and seep down into her core. The day was balmy and clear, as whatever storm had followed the wolf into their lives had dissipated as soon as it was slain. The sky was the soft blue of early fall and even though the air was crisp, it lacked the bite it had before.

"Hold steady now." Cathal's shouted order carried on the gentle breeze from the nearby hillside. Angus and several others grunted beneath the weight of a grey stone they'd hoisted overhead as her son-in-law helped ease it into place on top of the slowly growing wall. A pile of grey rock and
~~~~~

stone lay in the field beside their construction site. The remnants of Anne's old cottage.

Things seemed to be coming along nicely. Soon her little home would be back together in its new place, closer to the village. Cathal had suggested it. Inspired, perhaps, by Anne's early warnings and the knowledge of the lives that could have been saved had those warnings not gone unheeded. In fact, the entire village seemed determined to prevent another disaster. They'd taken to asking Anne to tell her stories to the children whenever she could spare time in the hopes that her tales could prepare them for future threats.

The general sense of awareness was a balm to Anne's mind. She no longer had to carry the burden of protector alone. A laugh drew her gaze to the path leading up the hill.

Rhiannon walked beside Faolan with a gaggle of the village children skipping along before them like a herd of sheep. Rhiannon's red curls blew free in the breeze while the skirt of her brightly colored dress danced around her ankles. Her smile came just a bit more naturally now than it had in recent days.

After some convincing, Faolan had agreed to stick around and share some tricks for hunting wolves with the men of the village. Rhiannon had insisted on joining in the discussions, determined, it seemed, to be ready should another wolf ever dare darken their door.

And perhaps there was a bit more growing behind their two smiles as they talked, though neither were willing to move too quickly away from friendship born of a mutual respect.

Anne sighed and settled back to enjoy the sunlight once more as she awaited her little class. Such relationships shouldn't ever be rushed. And while Anne knew better than most how fickle time could be, she was certain they would find happiness eventually.

When it was all said and done, Anne had to agree with Rhiannon. Fairytales with happy endings were far better than ghost stories.

The End

A CACTUS AMONG WOLVES
Yvonne McArthur

"Ready, kids?" Grandma Brumby asked, catching a whiff of wintergreen as she tucked her purse into the sidecar of her vintage Royal Enfield motorcycle.

"Yup!" Miriel chimed, popping the end of her string cheese in her mouth, then gripping the edge of the sidecar with both hands. Grandma Brumby caught the four-year-old's elbow and gave her a lift, noting something fuzzy on Miriel's feet as she scrambled inside — bunny slippers. They poked out beneath her unicorn dress. Well. That was an oversight.

"Put your goggles on, my little cheese monster."

Miriel giggled and did as asked.

Eight-year-old Nico graced her with one of his sunburst grins and squeezed behind his sister. It was a tight fit thanks to his backpack, which was an enormous, rain-proof, camouflaged affair that contained their picnic lunch, an assortment of scientific equipment, Nerf guns, and decorated bandages. For a fee, he also carried sweaters, snacks, and explosives for his two sisters.

Nico adjusted his goggles, which plastered portions of his brown hair to his head, clicked his combat-grade rain boots together, and gave her a thumbs up.

That only left Zara, the oldest at ten, a sparky-eyed sewing and chemistry savant. She waited on the sidewalk, sharing carrot sticks with the guinea pig that perched on her shoulder. Today, she wore a crimson romper she'd sewn herself — not that the color surprised Grandma Brumby. Crimson was Zara's dye of choice these days.

Grandma Brumby had loved that color in her teenage years, too, so much so that her piano teacher had called her his "Little Red Tune." But banish thoughts of *him*. He'd have no part in today.

She put on her goggles, then hefted her leg over the leather seat of the motorcycle and slid — wobbling — into place. Old age. Bah. It roared down on her like a snorting bull with furious red eyes and steaming breath. In the first pass, it had bleached her hair. In the second, it'd turned her face into a thin-skinned bag of wrinkles. Now, it aimed to steal her balance, too. Well, she'd face it head-on without flinching 'til it killed her. Which it would. But whatever. She had bigger fish to fry.

Bigger fish, at the moment, meant an idyllic motorcycle ride, a delicious picnic, and a tromp in the woods with her grandchildren. She'd been looking forward to this outing all month.

Zara stowed her guinea pig in the front of her romper, snapped her goggles into place, and hopped onto the motorcycle, tucking her hands against Grandma Brumby's waist.

And they were off! Nearly.

Grandma Brumby turned the key and pressed the starter button, relishing the roar of the engine. And then, just as she was about to pull out, a scrawny, curly-topped, bespectacled man stepped in front of the motorcycle. He held a notebook and pencil, both of which he flapped at her with a pleading expression. Poking precariously out of one pocket was a minuscule potted succulent. She knew where he'd gotten that.

Terence, Grandma Brumby thought wrathfully, *up to his usual meddling*.

"Rose Brumbaugh?" the reporter called over the noise, shoving his glasses more firmly onto his face. "I'm Levi Tupp from *The Sun*. A word?"

Bah! She jabbed the kill switch and lifted her goggles so he could see her glare. "What?"

He nodded as if to thank her for snapping at him. "Nice rig." He motioned at the motorcycle, but the gesture turned into a wave directed at her grandchildren. "I have a Katana 650 myself." Then he cleared his throat. "Are you the founder of the Society of Badass Grandmas?"

A Katana. Nice. That merited an ounce of civility. "Yes."

"Can I ask you a few questions?"

Grandma Brumby squeezed the handlebars. "You've been talking to Terence Cooper."

The reporter raised his eyebrows, then glanced at the succulent sticking out of his pocket and smiled in chagrin. "A dead giveaway, isn't it?"

"Mhm. He's given me several." No need to mention that he only gave *her* cacti. No pretty jade plants for Rose Brumbaugh. Nope. Only poky, spiky, spiny, metaphorical cacti. Humph. If she hadn't needed both her arms to steady the motorcycle—or herself on the motorcycle—she'd have crossed them. Or put them on her hips. Too bad she'd turned the engine off. It would've been fun to rev it menacingly. "As you just pointed out, the Society is named The Society of Badass *Grandmas*, not grandpas, not grandparents. *Grandmas*."

The reporter nodded, scratching behind his ear with his pencil. "So your objection to the appeal spearheaded by Terence Cooper is purely based on the name?"

Zara shifted to peer around her shoulder. Right. Be civil. Grandma Brumby ground her teeth together, then pointed at the tranquil cobbled streets and the flower baskets hanging in the surrounding windows. "You see this town? Looks pretty calm, right? Safe? Well, it wasn't always like that. We had kids selling drugs, making out, sneaking off into the night. Terrible stuff. So what did I do? Well, I thought about what resources we were underutilizing. One of those resources is ladies in their older years who suffer from insomnia and care a great deal about keeping their grandkids safe. They're familiar with fear, darkness, and people who've gone astray. And they need a reason to get out of bed, keep exercising, keep eating, and keep taking their five trillion pills. We needed a reason to keep living. And not just living, but living well. Walking, trotting, staying fit, doing resistance training, reading the news, reading crime reports, using our gray matter. So, we got together and started patrolling. For two years, we've been the eyes and ears of the police, keeping the neighborhoods safe. And now, suddenly, the old *men* decide they want in on it?"

"Ah." The reporter nodded sagely. "You don't want to share the spotlight."

"That. Is. Not. It." Grandma Brumby's chest tightened. She shouldn't have agreed to this interview. She should have… What? Run the man over? Blast Terence Cooper to the bowels of a septic pit.

The reporter twiddled his pencil in his fingers and shrugged. "Aren't the elderly men as much of an underutilized resource as the elderly women? Don't they need as much of a reason to get out of bed and keep living? A way to contribute to society?"

"No."

The reporter raised his eyebrows. "Why not?"

"Because—" Grandma Brumby snapped her mouth shut, yanked her goggles back over her eyes, punched the ignition, and revved the engine.

The reporter hopped nimbly aside as she roared past him, out of town, and onto the scenic highway that led to the state wilderness area. Angry tears puddled in the bottom of her goggles, and she knew she was driving much faster than was prudent. Zara's arms cinched around her waist. One hand patted her side a couple of times, serving as an anchoring reminder that she was fine. A glance at the sidecar showed Nico and Miriel grinning into the wind.

Breathe. Just breathe. She would put it all behind her now. The reporter, the Society, and Terence Cooper. Grandma Brumby unclenched her jaw, reminding herself of the delightful picnic and woodland exploration ahead. Everything else could wait.

She could withstand the backlash and accusations that would greet her return as long as no one knew her true reason for refusing to admit male members to the Society. But that reporter had nearly gotten it out of her— the one thing she could never say out loud. The thing that would undress her in public and dredge up the past she'd worked so hard to bury.

Men can't be trusted.

She *couldn't* let them in. She couldn't let them close. And yes, she was a cactus.

~~~~~

"Look!" shouted Miriel, squishing into the mud of a forest pool in
~~~~~

bunny slippers that would never again be white. "There are squiggles in the water!"

"Tadpoles," said Zara, around the wintergreen mint tucked into one cheek. She plopped her guinea pig beside the pool. "Do you eat tadpoles, Titus?"

Nico fished a jar from his backpack, which was much lighter now that they'd eaten their picnic lunch. "Let's collect some." Then he cocked his head, listening. "What's that?"

"Oooo, it's a pretty doggy!" Miriel pointed at a beautiful Irish Setter bounding through the trees toward them, barking merrily. Following in its wake came a strapping ginger-haired teen and an elderly man. The elderly man was bowed, but in an elastic way, as if he could still zing off arrows. Perhaps it was the jutting eyebrows that gave this impression, for they sprang like lightning from above his eyes or, more likely, it was his spry, long-limbed gait that ate up the distance with ease.

Heat rushed through Grandma Brumby's body and set her face on fire. *What* was Terence Cooper doing here?

"Hello Rose," he said as he approached, not showing the least surprise at finding her and her grandkids in the middle of the woods. "It's a beautiful day for a romp, isn't it? This is my grandson, Dean."

The grandson flashed a grin at Zara, then lunged forward and caught his dog by the collar before it got a mouthful of guinea pig. "Whoops! This is Rosso."

Zara installed Titus on her shoulder and eyed Dean. A sly smile quirked her lips. "How do you feel about explosives?"

He glanced, puzzled, between Zara and his grandfather.

"Zara loves blowing things up," Nico said, digging a package from his backpack and tossing it to Zara. "Shall we find an old log?"

"Stay where I can see you," Grandma Brumby warned. "And leave the animals here. No, Miriel, come sit on this rock with me and eat some cheese."

In two eye blinks, Grandma Brumby found herself all alone with a four-year-old, an Irish setter, a guinea pig, and her arch nemesis.

"Terence." She eased the word between her teeth.

He smiled, winced, and sat on a nearby boulder, stretching his legs before him. Then, of all the galling things, he ignored her completely and addressed her granddaughter. "Nice to see you, Miriel. What cheese phase are you on?"

"String." She proffered a shy grin. "I tried seven…. Seventeen different ones this week, and Ms. Frog's is the best. Want some?" She held out a whitish lump covered in dirty fingerprints.

Terence took it and popped it in his mouth. "Exquisite. Mrs. Who's?"

"Frontmongue," Grandma Brumby supplied. "No cacti today?"

He spread his hands. "None. I am woefully unprepared."

Grandma Brumby bit the inside of her cheek, then nearly fell off the rock as an earth-shattering BOOM slammed through the trees.

Terence put a hand to his chest. "Good God. Are they still in one piece?"

Hoots and laughter emerged from the distant trees. Yes, it seemed they were.

Miriel shrieked in excitement, squirmed off the rock, and ran, stumbling, in their direction. The Irish setter whined and stuck his head under Terence's knee.

Leaves pattered from the trees, the wind blew, and tadpoles squiggled in the pond. Grandma Brumby couldn't think of a single civil thing to say.

Terence winced again, then patted the setter on the head. "Well, I guess we'll continue our ramble."

She watched him tramp around the pool, then hopped to her feet, grabbing a tree when she wobbled. "Terence!"

He paused, perhaps at the acid in her tone, before turning to face her, his expression wary but unsurprised *again* — the snipe.

"Why?" she hissed. "Why the constant needling? Endangering the Society? Turning a reporter loose on me?"

Sorrow softened his features. "Perhaps someday I can explain it to you." He took a few more steps, then swiveled toward her, swinging his arms back and forth. His spine popped audibly, and he winked. "There's a special beauty to cacti, you know. I'm quite fond of them, prickles and all."

She waited until he got out of earshot before letting loose several choice epithets. Afterward, she apologized to the guinea pig.

~~~~~

"Goggles on, everyone?" Grandma Brumby hollered over the roar of the motorcycle engine.

All three grandkids chimed, "Yes!" And so they were off.

Trees blurred past, the seat vibrated beneath her, and Grandma Brumby's grip on the handlebars made her bones creak in protest. Too tight. Tightness everywhere. In her chest, in her throat, in her tear ducts. Blast that man. Why did he get to her, so?

She took the next curve a hair too sharp and hair too fast. *Concentrate!*

Then something roared up her flank. Multiple somethings. A thundering pack of motorcycles flashed by. She caught glimpses of helmets emblazoned with snarling wolves.

Startled, she jerked to the right, and the sidecar's nose rose, threatening to lift the front wheel off the ground. Grandma Brumby tried to correct for it, braked hard, fishtailed, hit the bank of the corner, and tipped into the ditch.

~~~~~

The first things she noticed when she came to were the smell and taste of dirt, a crushing pain in her ankle, trees swaying overhead, and the sound of someone sobbing.

"Zara!" She barely got the words out. "Nico! Miriel!"

"Grandma!" Zara's face appeared in front of hers, anxious, dusty, and apparently unharmed. "Are you all right? Your ankle's stuck under the bike. We can't get it off."

That hardly mattered. She groped around her. "Nico? Miriel?"

"Here, Grandma, we're here. We're all right."

Small hands patted her shoulders and arms. She caught one of them. "You aren't hurt?"

"Well, we're skinned up pretty good. Cut my elbow, see? That was terrifying!" Nico grinned. Then his mouth drooped. "Miriel's up on the bank, crying. She knocked her head when we went over and has some scrapes, but she's okay. Just shocked, mostly."

Grandma Brumby squeezed her eyes closed.

A roar grew in her ears. Engines. The motorcycles returning. The image of the snarling wolves on their helmets flashed into her mind and, with it, a deep-rooted terror. She inhaled with a gasp and seized Zara's wrist. "Into the woods, all of you! Get Mr. Terence! Now! Don't let them see you!"

Zara's eyes went wide. Then her face disappeared from view. Dirt rained on Grandma Brumby's shoulders as three sets of feet scrambled up the bank. She panted for air while spots swirled at the edge of her vision, memory warping reality. *Oh no. Not now. Breathe. Just breathe.*

But she couldn't breathe. She was sixteen and pressed against the floor under a suffocating weight, the piano stool bruising her leg as she kicked uselessly, tears streaming down her cheeks.

Suddenly, the weight lifted, and she opened tear-blurred eyes to see several figures hauling her Royal Enfield off of her and out of the ditch. Someone crouched by her side — a young, craggy face peered into hers with concern.

"Are you... a predator?" She wheezed.

His eyes flicked to the helmet-wearing figures on the road, then back. He took her hand. "No, ma'am. I'm a Wolf Rider. And a grandson. We'll get you out of here."

She squeezed his hand and felt him squeeze back. "Just... wait for... Terence. He's coming." She hoped.

~~~~~

Grandma Brumby bit back a curse as Terence's pickup hit a bump, jarring her ankle. A flotilla of motorcycles drove ahead and behind. One of the Wolf Riders rode her banged-up Royal Enfield for her.

Feels like I'm in a hearse.

"I'm sorry." Terence glanced at her, then back at the road. "We'll have you to the hospital in no time."

Just what she wanted to do with her afternoon. Grandma Brumby turned to the window, a shiver in her bones. Her grandkids, Dean, and the
~~~~~

animals were in the back, patched up with iodine, and under strict orders to keep their buttocks planted on the pickup bed. Thank goodness they were all right. It could have been so much worse. What if they'd died?

She let out a ragged breath. Would she ever drive again? And if she did, would Sophie and Gerard let her take the kids? Would she trust herself with them? Would the kids trust her?

The wobble was inside her now, deep down in the place she used to feel secure.

Terence thrummed his fingers against the steering wheel, drawing her attention. "There's a tree that grows in Central America that's covered in thorns when it's young. Ceiba Pentandra, it's called. But as it grows, the trunk smooths and thickens into a towering pillar leading up to branches, leaves, and sky."

Grandma Brumby stared at him. Couldn't he leave off about thorns for one spare minute?

"You were wounded, Rose," he said softly. A sheen of sweat glossed Terence's face, and his hair was mussed and askew. Something in his tone made her pulse skip.

She clenched her hands against the tears. "I know I'm wounded! I have a broken ankle and five dozen bruises and scrapes!"

He nodded, his expression kind. "I just mean," he said, eyes on the road, hands shifting gears with ease. "You're strong, Rose, a strong full-grown tree. You won't be bowled over or hacked down. You aren't the sapling you were when the thorns might have done some good."

She *knew* that. Didn't she? On some level. And yet, somehow, hearing it from Terence made the wobble inside her feel different, less threatening — more like an invitation to plant her feet on firmer ground. How… oddly refreshing.

She crossed her arms. "Don't think sweet-talking me will change my mind about the Society."

His grin had the same effect on her as a splash of tequila in black tea.

~~~~~

"I told you, I'm fine," Grandma Brumby said, using her body to bar the small opening in her front door and keep her daughter and son-in-law from barging in from the front porch. "Thanks for dropping me off, and you know I love you, but I'm tired and need to rest. So shoo!"

She clicked the door shut, then threw the bolt just to be sure. Cool, welcome house. Quiet. She rested her head against the wall and breathed deeply of the calm. Then she swiveled awkwardly and glared at the contraption before her. A walker. How humiliating.

The doctor had insisted she didn't have enough strength and balance for crutches.

"He's doing us a public service," her son-in-law Gerard had teased. "You with crutches would be a menace."
~~~~~

Grandma Brumby gripped her walker and stumped across her compact house, heading for the tiny sunroom at the back. The glassed-in space held her coziest armchair and dozens of potted cacti. The room smelled faintly of soil. Fresh air floated in through an open pane near the roof.

She eased her walker into the room, pausing before one of the small tables she'd picked up to house some of her plants. Gingerly, she touched the spiny protrusions with the tip of her finger — angel wings cactus, bishop's cap, monkey tail, barrel cactus, blue columnar cactus, rat's tail, silver ball, and a rare moon cactus.

Beautiful, each one in its own way. The poky bits were part of what made them so.

She'd needed her thorns and spines, too, after *him*. They had protected her and helped her feel a tad safer when Sophie was born, when she'd become a mother and seen wolves everywhere. They'd given her the gumption to study a correspondence course and move far away.

But Terence had a point. She wasn't that girl anymore. Whether cactus or ceiba tree, perhaps she could afford to be a little less prickly.

Grandma Brumby positioned herself in front of her armchair and sank into a warm slant of afternoon light.

After a long, deliciously quiet interval, the light faded, and darkness swathed her. Grandma Brumby switched on the fairy lights. The sight of her plants hammered the point home.

Bah. *Fine.* Grandma Brumby took a deep breath, picked up the phone, and dialed.

"Terence," she said when he answered, "Why don't you come over tomorrow, and we'll discuss this appeal business? Yes, all right. And I'll be a lot less inclined to smack you with my crutches" — no need for him to know she didn't have any — "if you bring lunch…. Yes, noon sounds good."

She hung up the phone and then smirked at her audience of cacti. "What are you looking at me like that for? Not even you are 100% bristles."

~~~~~

Three days later, Zara hopped onto Grandma Brumby's porch with a fistful of permanent markers. "Can I draw a goblin on your cast?"

"And I'll do a rainstorm." Nico thunked up the steps behind her with Miriel in tow.

Grandma Brumby laughed, noting that all of their scrapes and bruises looked markedly better. "What about you, Miriel? What'll you draw?"

"Squiggles."

The sound of someone clearing their throat drew her eye to the street. A scrawny, curly-topped man adjusted his glasses and waved at her.

"You may sit." Grandma Brumby indicated the rocking chair beside her.

The reporter toppled up the stairs and into the rocker. He pulled a pad
~~~~~

of paper from his pocket and snatched a pencil from behind his ear.

Her grandkids eyed him askance, then clustered around her cast, conferring in quiet voices and popping the tops off markers with their teeth.

"So…" he said, "you have an update?"

Grandma Brumby nodded. "Terence will found the Society of Badass Grandpas. Assuming all the ladies in the Society of Badass Grandmas are in agreement, we'll be partner organizations from the start."

The reporter scratched a few things on his pad of paper. "When is the vote?"

"End of the month."

He glanced up. "It sounds like you've made your peace with Mr. Cooper. Care to elaborate on your change of heart?"

Grandma Brumby settled deep in her rocking chair, enjoying the smell of grass and markers and the low hum of her grandchildren's voices. How to explain a change involving gifts of cacti, ceiba tree facts, woodland explorations, Wolf Riders, and a broken ankle?

"Not particularly, no. If you'll excuse me, I have grandchildren to entertain."

"Right." The reporter coughed, thanked her, then made his way off the steps. He paused halfway down. "Nice succulent, by the way." He gestured toward a miniature pot on her windowsill.

"Mhm. Swing by and show me your motorcycle sometime."

The reporter nodded and ambled away.

"It is a neat plant," Nico said, peering up from his rendition of a hurricane. "Did Mr. Terence give it to you?"

"He did."

Zara smiled slyly, then bent carefully over her goblin troupe. Grandma Brumby's face warmed.

"Oooo, can I see it?" Miriel asked, hopping up.

"Gently," Grandma Brumby said, showing Miriel how to run her finger over the zebra plant's spiky leaves. Small white nodules ridged each green spear.

Miriel giggled. "I like the bumps."

"Me too," said Grandma Brumby. "Me too."

The End

KELLI AND KIRMIZI
Michelle Houston

Life isn't fair.

I think that is why I like the original fairy tales and despise the new ones. In the original stories, Snow White is sold, Rapunzel is pregnant from rape, and Red Riding Hood is eaten. Horrible things happen, but not because they are horrible people. It was not their fault.

In the new fairy tales, the old truths have been sugar-spun into happiness and light. The good characters get a happily-ever-after and the evil characters have horrible endings. The moral is if your life is good, you must be good. If your life is bad, you must be evil.

What a horrible thing to teach impressionable children.

~~~~~

I first became aware of how unfair the world is when I noticed how people treated me and my cousin, Kirmizi, differently.

Kirmizi is actually my double cousin. Her mother is my father's sister, and her father is my mother's brother. That might sound like the start of a fairy tale, but it isn't uncommon in rural towns. Especially considering that my father's family immigrated from Turkey, so they had dark, sultry looks and exotic accents. They could date whomever they wanted. My mother's family, with their Scandinavian roots, were considered the local beauties with their blue eyes and golden hair.

Even though our parents look alike, Mizi and I are opposites. Where she has silky blond hair and clear blue eyes, I have frizzy brown hair and dark eyes with deep shadows. Where she has a warm and clear complexion, mine is so pale it is almost white, which makes my enormous bushy eyebrows stand out all the more. And where Mizi has a heart-shaped face that perfectly fits her features, I have a long oval face that makes my ears and eyes look too big. And that doesn't even start to cover my nose, which is large for any face.

In short, Mizi is beautiful and I am ugly.

That didn't matter at first. Mizi and I were best friends as preschoolers, spending all of our time together. Every morning, we were both dropped off at Grandma's house, because she watched us until our parents got off from work. We built pillow forts, baked brownies, and planned for our futures — we were going to be movie stars, get rich, travel the world, become astronauts, and raise our kids together in the same house. Grandma treated us the same. She would even take a picture of us together to send to the missionaries she supported overseas. I never felt like I was less, or that Mizi
~~~~~

was more, when I was at Grandma's house.

But as soon as school started and I met new children, it became apparent they agreed with the new fairy tales, which declared that ugly was evil. The first day of kindergarten was a nightmare. No one would talk to me or play with me. They would run away whenever I came near. I learned to stay on the fringes and disappear so that they wouldn't tease me. In contrast, Mizi was instantly a favorite, with all the other kids basking in her beauty.

I was never asked to share a treat. Never invited on the see-saw. Never picked for a team until the absolute last.

If I had believed the new fairy tales were true, I would have only seen a path into despair.

Even my name seemed destined to push me in a certain direction. But my family always pushed back.

There was the time at Christmas when Great-Uncle Demir collected the children into the living room for games and stories, temporarily adopting all of us. A short and stout man with wild hair, he told us his childhood fairy tales with different voices and sounds to make them come alive.

We heard about The Rose-Beauty and The Silent Princess, two Turkish tales that had Mizi and me loudly declaring how we would never have acted so stupidly. Great-Uncle Demir chuckled and demanded to know how we would have acted in America's Red Riding Hood, which he proceeded to tell us with shrieks and growls. After we dissected that story, with its foibles and its strengths, he gathered us up in a huge hug.

"Kirmizi, my dear, you are named 'red' like in that fairy tale. You are vibrant and beautiful, like the poppies in the fields back in Turkey."

"What about me, Uncle?" I pulled on his white beard gently, wanting his attention. "What does my name mean?"

He smiled fondly at me and smoothed down my frizzy hair. "Kelli, my love, you were not named for anything from the homeland, but for your mother's grandmother. I am told she was a woman of kindness and faith."

I pouted. "But I want something from the homeland," I whined.

"Hmmmm. Well, your name does sound very much like killi, the wolf."

Mizi hooted with glee and bounced on his knee. "Wolf! Kelli, I'm the girl and you are the wolf in the story!"

My lips began to tremble. I didn't want to be the villain in a fairy tale.

Great-Uncle Demir saw my look and leaned down to whisper in my ear. "Remember, my little killi Kelli, you can write your own tale. And also remember, wolves are known for their loyalty, strength, and fearlessness. Make those traits your own."

Then he tossed both of us in the air, inducing giggles all around, before he called for a game of indoor tag, to the annoyance of my father.

Another moment that sticks in my mind was my seventh birthday party. I invited all the girls in my grade and a few came over. We watched *Tangled*, and at the end I announced (along with all of the other girls) that I wanted to be Rapunzel. Mari told me I couldn't. I was too ugly. I had to be Gothel instead.

I fled.

My father found me sobbing in the bathroom. "I don't want to be evil! I want to be Rapunzel! I want to be pretty like Mizi!"

"My Kelli-yavrum," he rumbled, pulling me onto his lap as he settled onto the cold tile floor. His beard brushed the top of my head as his arms enfolded me in safety. "You are not Rapunzel, you are not Gothel, you are not a fairy tale story. You are Kelli and you are wonderful."

"It's not fair!" I whined through my tears.

"No, it's not fair. Life isn't fair. But it is good." When I glared at him skeptically through my puffy eyes, he continued. "Think about all the good things you have. Parents who love you. A best friend in Mizi. A warm house and food and safety." I knew this was important to him. I had heard a few stories of what they had escaped from when they fled the political violence in Turkey. "You have a chance to be whatever you want to be. Thank God for those things." He pulled away and looked at me, his dark eyes shining into mine, his love into my tears. His warm hands gripped my shoulders, giving me his strength. "You don't need to be like Mizi."

I thought about his words a lot. As a seven-year-old I still wanted to look like Mizi. But at least I didn't *need* to be like her.

The next week at school Mizi found Mari on the playground and attacked her, yelling at her for daring to hurt me. She had to be pulled off of Mari and got suspended for two days. My mom baked Mizi a dozen of her favorite cookies.

~~~~~

So I learned that life would hurt me, but it wasn't my fault. I learned that my role wasn't predefined by other people's impressions, or names, or the stories told in any culture. That who you are was more than what people see on the outside. I learned I could be kind, loyal, and fearless.

And that sometimes, life was simply unfair.

That saying was a comfort. When I followed the advice of my parents — smile, be polite, bring cookies, the other kids will like you — and it didn't work, I knew it wasn't my fault.

It wasn't always easy to remember. But I tried to fight the lies of modern fairy tales by carrying the truths my family gave me from their love and faith.

I would need those truths the rest of my life.

Because unfairness intruded again and again.

~~~~~

School got harder as we got older. Mizi became aware of social strata and where we both fell on the ladder of popularity. At first, it bothered her, but then it influenced her.

She stopped saving a seat for me at lunch. I would see her laughing with her new friends. At least I knew Grandma's house was still a refuge where we would play together without interference from social pressures.

But one week when I was sick and staying at Grandma's instead of going to school, that changed.

It was sixth grade, when I was too young to be on my own but old enough that my mom felt comfortable leaving me in the care of Grandma while I was sick.

I was miserable, with a runny nose, sore throat, and a fever. Grandma had dressed me in some old PJs and snuggled me into her guest bed, covered with her puffy down patchwork comforter. I was just drifting off to sleep when I heard the door downstairs shut, indicating that Mizi had come in after school.

Sometime later a giggle woke me up.

"My, what big ears you have, Grandma."

I cracked an eye open to see Mizi standing in the doorway, holding a tray with warm soup that Grandma must have sent up. She was grinning from ear to ear.

Go away, I thought grumpily. I felt horrible and wanted to be left alone.

She came closer, her smile and eyes bright as she tried to tease me into a better mood. "And what big eyes you have, Grandma."

"Shut up," I growled at her. But due to my sore throat, the words came out garbled.

Mizi giggled again. "And what big teeth you have, Grandma."

That really hurt. My teeth were the only normal, non-ugly part of my face.

I grabbed the first thing my hand found on the bedside table and flung it at her, wanting to make her leave. Unfortunately, it was a heavy stone paperweight. It clipped her shoulder, knocking her down and sending the tray crashing to the floor.

"You're awful," she cried, clutching her shoulder. Grandma rushed upstairs and surveyed the mess, displeasure on her face. She got a cold pack for Mizi and more medicine for me. She threw towels on the carpet to sop up the spilt soup.

Throughout the activity, guilt raged through me. I wondered if there was some truth to the new fairy tales after all. Maybe I was the evil, deranged wolf of legends and not the strong, fearless wolf of Great-Uncle Demir.

I tried apologizing to Mizi and Grandma. Grandma readily forgave me, once again coating me in her love. But Mizi wouldn't listen to me. It was only after her bruise faded, and I had brought over numerous cookies, that our relationship slowly thawed back to acceptance. But she still wouldn't sit with me at school.

~~~~~

Then elementary school progressed to high school and hormones rushed through all of us, changing our minds and our bodies. One thing didn't change. I was still avoided and Mizi was still popular, all because of our looks. I was as friendly as I could be, always volunteering and saying 'hi' to acquaintances, but it was the rare individual who was willing to look past my looks and miserable reputation to be my friend.

Mizi avoided me in the hallways. She got friends to drive her home so we didn't see each other on the bus. Saturdays she was too busy with her other friends to see me and Sundays she maneuvered to sit on the opposite side of the church pew from me. There was never time for sleepovers or confidences anymore. A conversation with her felt like chipping through a glacier — I made no progress and was left chilled.

In my loneliness, I poured myself into my studies. Mizi had always been able to get A's in class by just listening, while I usually slid by with Bs and Cs. But now my grades climbed to the top of the class. I got honors and received awards. For the first time during family gatherings, the adults praised me as much as Mizi.

I tried to draw Mizi back into my life, to overcome the barriers that modern lies had worked between us. But I was never successful.

Once when Grandma was sick and Mizi didn't have an excuse to avoid me, I convinced her to walk to Grandma's, to bring her favorite soup that she had taught us to make. We strolled for a while just listening to the birds and enjoying the late spring weather. I broke the silence to tell her of a book I had read about CRISPR and gene therapy, which I found fascinating. I got to the part where a change in one part of the DNA could change a person's traits when Mizi coldly said "boring" and wandered off the path into the park. She started picking wildflowers but quickly moved on to the planted beds.

"Mizi," I hissed. "Those aren't yours! You could get in trouble!"

She grimaced back at me, still looking beautiful despite having rolled out of bed that morning to come with me. "Nonsense, it is a public park. I'm part of the public. And Grandma loves peonies."

I fussed at her, but she refused to go further, protesting she had to bring something to Grandma, too. Eventually I left, letting her slowly accumulate a bundle of flowers while I brought the soup to Grandma. It was only as I was leaving that Mizi finally showed up with the bouquet at the door. Grandma gushed over the flowers as I squeezed past them, causing Mizi to throw a smirk at me. I muttered, "I hope the park doesn't miss them," loud enough for Grandma to hear as I hurried away from the house.

I never knew what Grandma did with that information.

But the next day I found what Mizi did.

At school the kids usually ignored me, flocking around either the popular kids like Mizi or huddling in their own little cliques. That day
~~~~~

people started calling me "Killi" instead of Kelli and making growling noises. By the end of the day, I was totally spooked and went to my parents for help.

Though Mizi denied everything, someone spread the news that "killi" is Turkish for wolf. Along with my looks, it was enough to make me the wolf-girl for the rest of the year.

I cried most nights, lamenting how unfair life was.

But I didn't give up. I wasn't who the school claimed I was. I concentrated on the plans I had for the future. Meanwhile, Mizi was getting more and more sucked into a story of her own telling.

I found out her plans during a wedding we were required to attend. I asked her what college she was going to. I had a scholarship to the best state university and was very excited about my new possibilities. Mizi shocked me when she casually said she wasn't going to college. She was going to marry someone rich and tour the world.

I tried to talk her out of it, saying she could marry after going to college. But Mizi wasn't interested. "That's too much work for nothing," she said. She flipped her silky hair over her shoulder and flashed me her heart-rending smile. "I already have Carleton Smith interested in me. He's rich enough to take me around the world for a honeymoon."

I protested more, pointing out how Carleton almost failed school and had been suspended at least once. Mizi didn't care. "I know you have to work," she said, eyeing my large nose and unkempt hair as she smoothed her dress over her curvy hips, "but I have other options. I'm going to travel to places I have dreamed about for years."

After that, I didn't see Mizi for a long time.

She ended up marrying Micheal Hunt, the second son of the lumber magnate Daniel Hunt. She did indeed go around the world, multiple times, which she chronicled on her social media sites. Her pictures always featured gorgeous backgrounds, exciting adventures, or famous celebrities. And she always wore red in some fashion.

It was her signature color, her calling card. It might be cherry red shoes or a deep maroon red hat or a Christmas-red dress. But somewhere on her person there was always red.

What was missing was her husband.

Almost the only time I saw them together on social media was when they were promoting his dad's lumber companies.

I'm sure if Mizi was asked, she would have said she was living a happily-ever-after straight out of a modern fairy tale, traveling the world without a care.

By correlation, I should have been miserable in an evil ending from those same tales.

Instead, I thrived at college.

No one knew me, so I was able to ditch the wolf-girl label. I also started straightening my hair, tweezing my eyebrows, and wearing foundation. I discovered designer eyeglasses changed the look of both my eyes and face. I was never pretty, but I could now pass for normal.

It was an incredible experience.

Even better, I worked part time in the lab of one of the top researchers of rare genetic disorders. It was his influence that convinced me to get a medical degree and specialize in genetics.

I had good friends, a wonderful career, and a supportive family. I had so many blessings, I forgot about fairy tales and unfairness.

~~~~~

Mizi came back into my life two years after I started practicing medical genetics.

We were both at her baby brother's wedding. Robert was marrying a local reporter named Holly. They matched each other well. Robert's love of jokes was a wonderful foil for her serious nature, and he loved to make her roll her eyes when he told a particularly bad pun.

Mizi's mother had put us both at the same table during the dinner. I wasn't sure if I was excited about talking to Mizi after all this time, or dreading seeing someone who had been avoiding me for years.

We started off with small talk: the weather, how bad traffic was to get to the wedding, how happy Robert and Holly looked. I mentioned that Holly was wanting to get pregnant right away, since they planned on having several children and were already in their early thirties. A wistful look quickly passed on Mizi's face, before she forced a smile and said she was going to spoil their kids. It reminded me of how much she loved children when we were younger.

"Mizi," I hesitantly offered, "if you and Micheal are having trouble getting pregnant, I know several specialists who might be able to help you."

Mizi's red lips twisted into a cold smile. "Thank you, but that's not necessary. Micheal is adamant that we do not have kids."

"Why?" I wondered aloud, without really expecting an answer.

Mizi picked up a fork and toyed with her salad. She shrugged carelessly. "It has to do with his dad's company. The family doesn't want to dilute the inheritance, so Micheal gets all the money he wants now on the condition that he does not have heirs."

I gaped at her. "That's crazy! Like, medieval crazy!'

She shrugged again. "Micheal doesn't mind, since he really doesn't like kids anyway."

"But you do!"

She looked up from her plate, sadness leaking from her eyes for the first time. "But I knew that was a condition when I married him. At the time, it didn't seem as important as...."

She didn't finish, but mentally I could hear her younger self say "...marrying a rich husband." In the background Whitney Houston's *I Want*
~~~~~

to Dance with Somebody played.

I didn't know what to say. I could see she was hurting, but at the same time there was a huge gulf that time had created between us.

"You looked like you were having a great time in India on Facebook," I offered. "The Valley of the Flowers was especially beautiful." I absently stirred the soup in front of me.

Her eyes lit up. She grabbed onto the distraction. "Yes, it was. And though everyone raves about the Taj Mahal, I actually enjoyed the Red Fort better. There was something sad but elegant about it."

She looked at me nervously and twisted her napkin into a ring. "And congratulations on your paper in *Lancet*."

I gaped at her, the soup completely forgotten. "How do you know about that?"

Her timid smile reached out to me. "I have a search that brings up anything with your name." She glanced at the mangled napkin in her hands. "I hope you don't mind. It made me feel more connected with you and my family."

I was at a loss of what to say. I thought Mizi wanted to avoid me.

"Why didn't you respond to any of the Christmas cards I sent?" In my shock, the question blurted out of my mouth. Every year I mailed cards to all the people I knew, even Grandma, who didn't recognize me anymore due to dementia. I had never once heard back from Mizi.

The cold Mizi slipped back on. She nonchalantly replied, "I didn't see them at first. Micheal and I get tons of cards every year from famous people and we were much too busy at the beginning of our marriage to go through them all."

She looked away, distant and haughty. But then she seemed to wilt, shrinking back into herself and into my world. She turned to me with her timid smile again. "Once I figured out you were sending them, I didn't know what to do. It had been so many years. And what could I say? That I had been to various places and seen various people, but it would have meant nothing to you. I was so embarrassed." She looked down at her plate. Her final whisper was barely audible. "But I looked for your cards every year after that. They were the highlight of my holiday."

I sat back, stunned. "I guess I should keep sending you cards." The words slipped from my lips.

We both stared at each other a moment, then burst into giggles together.

We spent the rest of the wedding catching up with surface details. Neither kids nor husbands were mentioned again.

~~~~~

I saw Mizi more frequently after that. Every few months, when she was passing from one side of the U.S. to another, she would drop by for lunch or a quick shopping trip.
~~~~~

It didn't quite feel like our old friendship. There was still a wall between us, built of subjects that Mizi refused to discuss. But I enjoyed what I could, thankful that we had reconnected at least a little bit.

Mizi started sending me Christmas cards in all seasons. I got one in March, three in April, and two more in May. They were in various languages, from whatever location she happened to be roaming through. I responded by writing little notes to her, just giving her a joke or inspiration or a message passed on from a family member.

She asked me to travel with her. It sounded like fun, but I had no extra time. My career was taking off. I had seminars to give, grants to write, conferences to attend. And on top of all that, I had my normal responsibilities as a doctor. I told her I'd save up vacation time and go in a few years.

Then one day Mizi called and said she would be in town the next day. She asked if she could spend the night with me.

Surprised but pleased, I told her "of course." Maybe another piece of the wall between us was coming down.

It didn't take long to vacuum and clean my small bungalow. As I was changing the sheets in my extra bedroom, I tried to see it through Mizi's eyes. I loved the soft grey walls and flowered window curtains, the patchwork quilt on the bed, and the lampshade painted by a local artist. The small dresser was a garage sale find, naturally distressed, and the decorative rocks sitting on top of it were ones I found while out walking. It was not Mizi's world, but I hoped it would make her feel a little more welcome in mine.

I greeted Mizi at the door with a hug. She looked beautiful, as always, with a little extra weight making her curves even more pronounced. But her eyes held worry, or maybe it was sadness. I could tell she was stressed.

I chatted about family news while preparing a chicken pot pie for dinner in my small kitchen, hoping Mizi would tell me what was wrong. But she was as silent as her high school self.

We ate in awkward silence. After dinner, I got her to talk about the new car she bought by mentioning my old one, which would need seat covers soon. She told me about a new painting she had commissioned, and where she wanted to vacation next. Her usual question about me joining her was met with my usual answer about needing more time. During the entire conversation, I could hear anxiety simmering under her words.

"All right, out with it," I demanded once the dishes were done and I put the last fork in the dishwasher. "What is bugging you?"

Mizi wiped the counter one more time. "Is it that obvious?"

"I know you, Mizi. It is to me."

She sighed and leaned against the Formica countertop, staring at the floor. "I'm pregnant." Her voice was small, a mixture of joy and mourning.

"That's great!" I moved to hug her but stopped myself. I couldn't understand why she wasn't happy.

"Not really. I'm not supposed to get pregnant. I messed up." She wrapped her arms around her middle.

I frowned. "According to whom?"

She pushed away from the counter and crossed to the table, sitting down with her usual elegance. Then her face crumpled and tears started to fall. "Micheal. If he finds out, he'll make me get an abortion."

I sat down by her, taking her hand. "Mizi, he can't make you get an abortion."

She sobbed. "He did last time. But I don't want this baby to die too."

"Mizi," I repeated, "he can't *make* you do this. You can tell him no."

She shook her head, looking at the floor, not me. "I can't do that. It's in the prenup I signed. If I have a baby, he will disown and divorce me." She dropped her face into her hands. "I'll lose everything."

I took a deep breath. It was hard for me to relate, having never been dependent on someone else. But I could try. "It is still possible. It might be hard, but your family would help. You could still keep the baby."

She raised tear-filled eyes to me. "Kelli, I can't divorce him. We love each other!"

I patted her soothingly. "Mizi, love doesn't force another person. Love is there to support and affirm, not coerce."

She swatted my hand away. "What would you know? You've never been in love." She tried to sound aggressive, but grief and loss swirled through the anger in her voice.

I pushed away the hurt that bloomed in my heart and filled my voice with gentleness. "I have seen many loving marriages, and I love and am loved. And I know none of them involve forcing the other person into a bad decision."

"Well, I love Micheal! I can't leave him!" Her strident voice struck out at me, once again coming from the cold Mizi.

Silence stretched out. I wasn't sure what to say.

She crumbled again, tears streaming from her beautiful eyes. She appealed to me with a tremble in her words. "Please help me have this baby without him finding out!"

"What?" I couldn't believe what I was hearing. "I don't think that's possible."

She sniffled, reaching for a tissue from the sideboard next to the window. "Yes, it is, I have it all worked out. I'm four months now. He just left for a trip and won't be home for five months. If I can stay here, no one will see me. And I have extra pics saved up that I can periodically put on Facebook so he won't suspect."

"That's crazy."

She shook her head. "No, it's not. The main thing is I can't go home or the staff will see me. But I travel all the time, so they are used to me being gone. Micheal doesn't pay much attention to me when he's away, so he won't notice I'm using pics from places I have already been. And if he does, I can just say I liked them so much I went back."

I tried to use logic to dissuade her. "But five months from now is when you will deliver. You will still look pregnant."

She grimaced. "I thought I could induce two weeks early, then tell Micheal I've got a bad cold and you are nursing me when he gets back. That will give me another month to regain my figure. And I'll tell him I put on weight and am working on losing it."

I stared at her and repeated, "That is the craziest thing I've ever heard."

She grabbed my hand and squeezed. "Please, Kelli, please? I don't want to lose Micheal or this baby. It's the only way!"

I sighed. "I still don't think it will work, but yes, you are welcome to stay as my guest for five months. I'll be in and out a lot with work. I won't be able to entertain you."

She beamed through her tears. Even with red eyes and a runny nose she still looked radiant. "That's no problem! I wouldn't be able to go out with you anyway, since I need to hide the baby." She hesitated a moment, then plowed forward. "And would you adopt the baby?"

I don't even remember the rest of the conversation, just that no matter how she asked, I said no. I couldn't be a single mom. I didn't have family close by to help me. I had med school loans to pay off. I was already exhausted many nights.

No, no and no. I could not do it. She would have to give the baby to an adoption agency.

Mizi's argument was that if anyone else adopted the baby, she would never know how he/she was doing because it would have to be a closed adoption. The baby could never know who the biological parents were, or Micheal might find out.

"You want your cake and eat it too," I said bitterly, worn down with her asking and the unfairness of it all.

"No, if that were the case, I'd be able to raise the baby myself. As it is, even if you do adopt the child, I'll never see their first step, get their first hug, hear them call me mommy. At best I'll be a friendly, distant aunt." She sniffed. "I am trying to have my cake and smell the fragrance, but that is all I'll ever have." She looked incredibly sad.

I didn't feel sorry for her. She could always keep the baby and force Micheal to deal with it.

But that phrase stuck with me. "Call me mommy." It rattled around in my head as I tried to get to sleep, as I took a shower, as I made breakfast in the morning.

What would it be like to have a toddler call me mommy?

And then two weeks later I saw the ultrasound. How is it possible for a grainy, indistinct photo to look cute?

I told myself I couldn't afford to be a single mom. Nanny prices were sky-high, and that didn't include formula and diapers. I couldn't afford the time off. I couldn't afford the extra drain on my energy.

I tried to push the idea of adoption out of my mind.

Then one day Mizi called me over, excited. She was quite big by then and the worn borrowed dress she was wearing seemed to swallow her whole body as she lounged on the couch. I sat down beside her. She grabbed my hand and held it to her belly. I looked at her, puzzled, as she beamed at me.

Then I felt the flutter of a kick.

I was a goner. I knew I would adopt Mizi's baby girl.

I held out for two more weeks, as I tried to talk myself out of it, but I knew in my heart she was mine.

I was going to be a mommy.

~~~~

I laughed more in those next two months than in the previous six years. It was like we were little children again, playing together. Though instead of baking cookies, we made salads and soups. Instead of building forts, we painted and decorated a nursery. Instead of planning our futures together, we popped corn and watched movies and enjoyed just being in the present.

Mizi had a perfect pregnancy with no complications. She gave birth with a midwife to a beautiful seven-pound six-ounce little girl. We named her Melinda Mergan.

The first week after birth, Mizi was a mess. Her breasts hurt from not feeding, her hormones were all over the place, and she was already grieving the loss of leaving behind her little girl. She cried all the time, and there was nothing I could do for her.

Mizi was still crying when she left. She covered Melinda with kisses before putting her in my arms and hugging me tight. "Thank you," she fiercely whispered. Then she turned and got on the train without looking back.

A week later, her first Facebook post appeared. She was in Switzerland, smiling at the camera with the Alps looming over her shoulder and a broad red sash belted tightly around her waist. A short note said she had been sick, which was why she hadn't posted, but was back and looking forward to a great year!

I wondered if Micheal ever bothered to look at her posts. If he ever worried about her "being sick."

I wondered if Mizi would still consider herself in a modern fairy tale.

~~~~

The wail startled me awake, my head pounding. I sighed and swung my legs over the side of the bed, blearily noting it was 4 a.m., and I had gotten only two hours of sleep.

It felt like residency again, only worse, since there were no days off.

As the crying resounded in my ears, I hurried to the kitchen to get a bottle warmed in the microwave.

I tested it on my wrist. Still a tiny bit cool, but that was better than too warm.

I scurried to the nursery, calling "I'm coming, I'm coming."

Little Melinda was laying on her back, fists pummeling the air as her cute little face screwed up in displeasure. Part of my brain wondered how so much volume could come from such tiny lungs.

"Shhh, shhh, I'm here." I carefully picked her up and went to the rocker.

The cries stopped when the bottle touched her mouth. She eagerly sucked down the formula.

I sighed again as I tried to push my headache away. In another hour my alarm would tell me it was time to get ready for a full day of work. I had to drop Melinda off at a sitter's house, along with a hefty check to cover the month. The amount I was saving had dropped to zero.

I certainly wouldn't be retiring early. Or going on any vacations to exotic places. Or even finishing my latest article in time for the next conference.

In an attempt to keep my eyes open, I pulled up Facebook on my phone, tucking the bottle under my chin so that Melinda could keep feeding. Mizi's latest adventure stared back at me. The warm waters of the Caribbean shimmered while she splashed along a beach in a red bathing suit. Alone.

The sucking stopped and I put Melinda on my shoulder to burp. Warm milk dribbled down my back. I suppressed a shiver. I hated that part.

I laid her back in the crib, making sure she was swaddled tight.

Exhaustion pulled on me, my head pounded, and I smelled of spit-up.

But as I watched the little face peacefully sleep, I couldn't help but remember what Dad had taught me, how he repeatedly told me I wasn't living in a fairy tale. I glanced at Mizi's picture again.

Truly, life isn't fair.

I have *so many* blessings.

The End

WOLVES AMONG THE LAMBS
Deborah Cullins Smith

Mary held her breath as the suave businesswoman in a pinstriped business suit sat on the loveseat and spoke with her mother. The "chance of a lifetime," she was saying. "Unusually gifted." Those were the key words. Mary waited for all of her mother's excuses to start rolling.

"We just moved here."

"But it's a school night."

"We really feel Mary should finish school before she pursues her music."

"There's still so much to do. We haven't even finished unpacking yet."

With every excuse, the woman smoothed her manicured hands over her short, slim skirt and adroitly brushed away the words.

"We're only in town for a few more hours. If I don't get a quick video of Mary now, I just don't know when I'll get back to this area again. This is the chance of a lifetime. You might be throwing away her future, Mrs. Mannering." She smiled that same disarming smile and Mary's stomach lurched.

Why did she suddenly think of the words from the old fairy tale? *"The better to eat you with, my dear."* Had to be those perfectly aligned teeth.

"Please, Mama." Mary stepped forward, sensing the moment was right. "Pleeeeeeeease."

Her mother sighed. "Do you have homework?"

"Finished in study hall," she said quickly.

"I want her home by six o'clock," she told the woman. "I'm trusting you with my only precious daughter, and I'm not very happy about it. I can assure you, my husband will be even more unhappy. So she needs to be home before he gets off work."

Candy Jones rose to her feet and pressed a simple ivory business card into Mrs. Mannering's hand. "We'll be at the Hampton Inn. That's where all our equipment is located. And I can have her back here much earlier than six. No problem."

Mary squealed and jumped up and down, clapping her hands.

"Let's go, Mary," Ms. Jones said, placing a firm hand on her shoulder.

"Wait! I'll need my guitar," she said, turning to head for the staircase.

"No need. We have instruments at the studio," she said, gripping the girl's shoulder a little tighter. "In the room. We've set up a makeshift studio in one of the rooms," she explained when she saw a puzzled look on the mother's face.

"But I do better with my own!" Mary felt a sudden panic. She needed to return to her room!

"You'd better go, if you're going, Mary," said her mother, drawing her into a close hug and away from Ms. Jones' grasp. Mrs. Mannering held her daughter at arm's length and eyed her with a tilt of her head. "Oh, I wish we had time to do more with your hair. Let me fix your barrette."

"We'll be doing her hair before the video—" Ms. Jones was beginning to show signs of impatience.

"It'll only take a moment," Mrs. Mannering said smoothly. She unclasped the barrette, frowned at the clasp that had momentarily twisted sideways, then reattached it in her daughter's chestnut curls. "There. You are beautiful, my Mary-berry."

Tears stung Mary's eyes at the use of the familiar nickname. *Good luck,* Mrs. Mannering mouthed silently. Mary nodded and she turned to Ms. Jones.

"I'm ready."

"Don't forget your sweater, Mary," her mother said. "It might be chillier before you come home."

Ms. Jones sighed impatiently. But Mary scampered back and tied the sleeves of the bright red sweater around her waist. "Thanks, Mama! You think of everything!"

~~~~~

The car whisked them across town, weaving through traffic at a speed that made Mary grip the leather seats with white knuckles. Ms. Jones sat in the back with Mary, texting on her cell phone while a muscular young man in a chauffeur's uniform slid through the city streets until Mary was completely turned around. When he dipped into an underground parking garage, she finally found her voice.

"Hey! This isn't the Hampton Inn."

"Of course it isn't, dear." Ms. Jones' silvery laugh sounded like the clang of a tin pan. "It's the Hilton."

"But you told Mama we'd be at the Hampton!"

"You must have heard me wrong, Mary," Ms. Jones chided. "I clearly said the Hilton. Now come along. We have a schedule to keep to if I'm going to have you home on time."
~~~~~

As they exited the car, Mary heard the first rumble of thunder in the distance. *Oh no... No tonight. Please, God... Not tonight.* She hated thunderstorms. It would be harder to concentrate on the task at hand if she had to do it during a thunderstorm. Mary gritted her teeth.

"Don't dawdle, Mary," Ms. Jones said. Her fingernails bit into Mary's shoulder and the girl squirmed.

"Need help?" The chauffeur's deep voice rumbled in a vaguely threatening way that made the hair on Mary's arms stand at attention.

"Do I need Lou's help, Mary?" Ms. Jones asked pointedly.

"No," she whispered. She submitted to being pulled through the parking garage to the elevators that led to the street level above.

But they didn't go into the Hilton. They cut down an alley, then another, and ducked behind a dumpster. At an abandoned building two blocks away, Lou unlocked the padlock on a ramshackle door.

"The Hilton didn't like the noise from our instruments, so we had to make some other arrangements for our last few sessions," Ms. Jones said a little too brightly.

Lou hit the lights and Mary blinked as florescent fixtures sprang to life. The darkened areas still made her shiver, but the lit area showed a small stage with an array of instruments and a brightly painted backdrop. To one side was a rack of clothes in various sizes and colors, most very flamboyant, almost gaudy.

"Would you like to pick out a costume for yourself?" Ms. Jones asked, smiling that 'better-to-eat-you-with' smile.

"C-can't I just be myself?" Mary asked, her stomach churning at the sight of the clothes that had obviously been used on other children before her.

"We want you to make a good impressions, don't we?" Ms. Jones said, frowning just a little as if disappointed. "I'm sure you can find something you'd like."

Mary fingered the clothing on the rack. Every item looked like it came from the red light district or a store called Hooker Central.

"My mama would be very unhappy if I wore something like this," she said, throwing as much disapproval into her voice as she dared.

"Well, she won't ever see this video, will she? But the executives who do see it will be the ones who control whether you have a career or not. Think about that, young lady." Ms. Jones' voice had become more strident. "If you don't choose, I'll do it for you."

Mary swallowed hard. Her hands shook as she finally found a flashy emerald dress that was all ruffles and elastic at the neckline. It hung like a blob on the hanger. Maybe this would cover her adequately. Mary was a well-developed girl, and she didn't want to be wearing something she'd find her body parts falling out of on camera!

"Really?" Ms. Jones sighed. "Fine. We'll start with that. But don't be surprised if I pick out your next wardrobe change." She hauled the girl to a small cubicle to the left of the stage. But as Ms. Jones tried to enter with her, Mary balked.

"I prefer to change by myself, Ms. Jones," she said.

Ms. Jones rolled her eyes. "Fine. But hurry along." She slammed the door, leaving Mary alone with the ruffled dress and a heart that hammered in her chest.

Mary looped the hanger over a convenient hook and began unbuttoning her shirt. She untied the sweater and it joined her shirt on the floor. Then she slid out of her jeans and they pooled at her feet. She shivered a moment before she removed the dress from the hanger and stepped into it, slipping it up over her hips. As she wiggled into it and faced the mirror, she gasped. Oh no! She'd heard of dresses like this. Ones that had no hanger appeal, but once they clung to a human body, they transformed into a piece of fabric magic. This one clung to her hips and her breasts and accentuated every curve. Frantically, she tugged at the neckline to draw it upward.

A sharp rap at the door made her gasp. "Hurry up, Mary. We're on the clock here."

"Coming in just a minute." She closed her eyes. *Lord, there is no remedy for this. I'm in Your hands.* Then she remembered her mother's parting gift. Her fingers fumbled for the barrette. They were going to restyle her hair, she remembered Ms. Jones saying. She couldn't let them find the barrette. She started to put the barrette in her jeans. But what if they didn't let her have her own clothes back later? She fingered the barrette—and the little silver disc pressed to the inside of the clasp. But where could she hide it? There was only one place she knew they'd never find it. She took a deep breath.

~~~~~

"I'm ready." She stepped shyly out of the cubicle.

Lou straightened up and whistled. Mary had her arms crossed over her chest. Ms. Jones stared at the girl.

"Well, I guess I underestimated that dress," she said, eyebrows raised. "As well as what you had under the oversized denim shirt and blue jeans. Well done, Mary. That will do very well."

Mary raised one arm to play with her bangs, a gesture she used often when she was nervous. It also served to hide her face, and she wanted to
~~~~~

hide very much right now. Outside, thunder rippled overhead and she jumped, cringing.

"Now, now," Ms. Jones said soothingly. "Nothing to be afraid of. Let's work on your hair and make-up. Hopefully the storm will pass over us by then. I'd hate for thunder to interfere with our sound system."

Ms. Jones sat her before a lighted mirror and brushed back her hair with quick even strokes. "Where's that lovely barrette your mother put in your hair?" she asked.

"I didn't want to lose it, so I put it in my jeans pocket," Mary said. Ms. Jones frowned slightly, then smiled brightly into the mirror. "Good thinking. It's so easy to mislay things around here. And it was such a pretty barrette. So unusual too."

Mary pretended to examine her fingernails, but she saw Ms. Jones nod toward Lou, and he quietly slipped into the dressing room. She bit her lip and waited, hardly daring to breathe. She heard the door shut quietly and watched Lou in the mirror, her head still ducked down as she peered up through her bangs. He shrugged and nodded as if all was as it should be, and she breathed a little easier.

Second hurdle passed.

"You know, I was going to suggest leaving your hair down around your shoulders," Ms. Jones said from behind her. "But I'm beginning to think we should try putting it up. You have such a lovely neck. It's a shame to hide it."

"Oh no! I'm too young…" Mary put some panic in her voice.

"Nonsense, Mary," she said, patting her shoulder. "I told you. Your parents will never see this video. You have nothing to fear. And you are going to look fabulous. Just wait."

For the next thirty minutes, Ms. Jones clucked and fussed over hair and make-up while Mary obediently turned her head, looked up, looked down, parted her lips, blotted, closed her eyes… did whatever she was told to do. When Ms. Jones spun her chair around to once again face the mirror, Mary gasped. She had aged by a good ten years from the fifteen-year-old that had slouched into this chair a half hour ago.

"One last thing," Ms. Jones said, and she grasped the ruffled neckline, pulling it off of Mary's shoulders.

"Nooooo!" Mary cried, her hands grabbing for the fabric and pulling it back up.

"Now, Mary, it's *supposed* to be worn this way. It looks silly way up on your shoulders like that."

"That will interfere with my guitar playing," Mary whined, panic rising in her voice.

"I don't understand you," Ms. Jones said briskly. "Most girls *want* to look more grown-up."

"I want to look more grown-up," Mary retorted, "but I don't want to look cheap." She felt tears prick the corners of her eyes.

"No! No crying. You'll destroy all this make-up." Ms. Jones rolled her eyes. "Fine. You can keep it up higher on the very edge of your shoulders, if that helps. But they can't be all the way up here by your neck. It looks ridiculous."

Mary swallowed hard and nodded. She noticed Lou in the mirror. He stood back a little way, but he was smiling. Ms. Jones turned away from her and waved for him to take over. He stopped beside her long enough to grip her arm gently. Mary overheard him say, "Take it easy, Candy. She's an innocent. You know how much that's worth. Her folks have never let her outta' their sight before."

Mary couldn't hear what Candy replied, and for the moment she felt grateful for that little reprieve.

Lou smiled and held out his hand toward her. "Let's find you a guitar, sweetheart."

They had a half dozen electric guitars, but those were not Mary's style at all. Finally, Lou located an old wooden guitar of no particular value in the back of the pile. It was a nondescript instrument, but the tonal quality was good and it only took a few minutes for Mary to tune the strings. The pure silk of that first G note, then E-minor, sent a quiver through Mary. It wasn't her own instrument, but it would do.

She performed a few folk classics, then a couple she had written herself. But her own music was a little too "religious," Ms. Jones said. They'd keep the tapes, just in case they came in handy, but for the most part, that type of music was not popular among their clientele.

"It's getting late," Mary said. "Shouldn't you be getting me home now?"

"We have plenty of time," Ms. Jones reassured her. "Besides, now we need to get some publicity shots. It'll save time later, if we land you a contract. Just a few head shots and some full body shots for the magazines and websites."

"Not dressed like this!" Mary said, her voice rising. "You said my parents would never see!"

"These are just for the professional sites, Mary," Ms. Jones said. "We can do a costume change for the public stuff if you want to." She sighed and rolled her eyes again. Lou chuckled from behind the camera.

"Now for this one, I want you to put your hands on your hips and turn sideways to the camera. Then tilt your chin up a little. Yes, that's good."

Click. Click. Click.

For each shot, Ms. Jones posed her, manipulating her like a mannequin in a store window, and Lou clicked off three or four shots each time. Finally, they took a break and he strolled over to her.

"Here, sweetheart, take a gander. Look at how great you are on film." He scrolled through the digital frames, and Mary saw herself displayed. She felt her stomach flip flop and swallowed to keep from throwing up.

"I-is that really me?" She tried to make her voice sound impressed. It must have worked. Lou seemed very pleased with himself.

"Of course it's you! You're gonna be a star, and don' you forget it." He patted her on the shoulder, but his hand lingered there a second too long, and Mary fought the urge to jerk away. Her heart started to hammer. Then a bolt of lightning cracked right over the building, and Mary yelped. The lights in the building flickered.

"Okay, that wraps this up," Ms. Jones said with a dry chuckle. "I thought that storm was going to pass us by, but it looks like it's going to land right on top of us. We'd better get going."

"Go get changed, princess," Lou said to her softly.

Mary bolted for the dressing room. With shaking hands, she stripped off the emerald green dress and scrambled into her jeans and her denim shirt. She slipped her arms into the red sweater. Maybe it would help her not to shiver so much. Overhead, the lights flickered again and again, bringing back memories that she needed to keep repressed. She could not allow them to sweep her into an episode. *Not now… Dear Lord, not now.*

She bolted out of the dressing room, but Ms. Jones' voice reproved her.

"The dress, Mary. Where's the dress? Return it to the rack please."

Mary returned and grabbed the garment off the floor, slinging it over the hanger by the silky built-in loops. With shaking hands, she slid it onto the rack with the other dresses. Then Ms. Jones was behind her, tugging at the pins and clips in her hair.

"Might need these later," she explained as she pulled Mary back to the mirrored table. She threw all the accoutrements into a toolbox, while Mary shook out her heavily sprayed curls and finger-combed them as best she could. The hairbrushes were already packed away. Another light had come on in the darker corner of the building, and Mary now saw a large van waiting near a closed roll-up door. Lou was already rolling the rack of clothes over and loading it into the van. Ms. Jones unplugged the lighted mirror and folded it down into the table that had held all of her cosmetics and equipment. Lou came back and hauled away the cases that held her beauty supplies, as she rolled the folded mirror/table over to him to load up as well. She grabbed the portable lights, while Lou disassembled the backdrop. Mary was amazed at how they had completely packed out the entire operation in just moments.

"What are you doing?" she asked.

"I told you," Ms. Jones said over her shoulder. "You were my very last appointment. I stayed just for you, Mary. Now we have to go. We're on a very tight schedule."

Lou packed in the last of the photo equipment, keeping the camera and a small laptop case looped over his shoulder. A low knock made Mary jump. Ms. Jones hurried to the side door and returned with an overweight man. His thinning hair and florid face gave him a piggy look that Mary immediately mistrusted. The look he gave her didn't improve the impression, as he let his gaze wander from head to toe and back again.

"Nice, Candy," he said with a nasty chortle.

"Hands off, Hank," she said with narrowed eyes.

"Van's ready, Hank." Lou tossed him a set of car keys. "You're gassed up and ready to go. See you back at the ranch."

Hank wheezed. "If that's what you wanna call it, buddy boy."

"I'm ready to go home now," Mary said, raising her chin slightly.

"Of course," Ms. Jones said. "We're going to gas up the car and take you home before we head out. And you've been so great, you deserve a treat. How about a milk shake? What flavor do you like?"

Mary shook her head. "Mama would be angry with me if I had a milk shake and spoiled my appetite."

"Oh, just this once? Because you did such a good job?" Ms. Jones did her best to be cajoling, but Mary wasn't taking the bait. "Well, what about a fountain soda at the gas station?"

"Maybe just a bottle of orange juice," Mary said. "One of those glass bottles they keep in the cooler.

Ms. Jones' smile froze in place. "Whatever your heart desires, sweetie."

~~~~~

Lou got out and pumped the gas, then sauntered into the station.

"Sooooo," Mary said, breaking the silence. "How long do you think it will be before we hear anything from these music producers?"

"Oh, not long at all," Ms. Jones said with a tight smile. "You'll be surprised how quickly they'll respond to your tapes."

The door opened and Lou handed Ms. Jones a cup.

"One cappachino, three sugars, two cream." He turned to Mary. "One
~~~~~

orange juice in a glass bottle for the princess." He winked at her before closing the back door and climbing behind the steering wheel to start the car. Mary twisted the cap and heard the satisfying pop of a previously unopened bottle. She took a long drink and sighed as the cold juice slid down her parched throat. One more gulp. She replaced the cap just as she felt the pinch in her left thigh. She jerked as Candy recapped the syringe and slipped it into her purse.

"This could have been so much easier, but you're the one who had to be difficult. *No* milk shake, *no* fountain soda. Oh, no. *You* had to have a *glass* bottle of juice. Well, *princess*, I'm always prepared. And don't you ever forget that."

The edges of her vision blurred to black, then winked out as the traffic whirled around their car. She didn't even have time to scream.

~~~~~

Mary woke to the crack of thunder and a bolt of lightning against the window. She stared around the room, trying to get her bearings. *Where am I? Did our unit deploy? Where's Gunny? Where are Bobby and Nathan? We're under fire! Where are my battle buddies?* She stared down at her denim shirt, which she could dimly see with the next crack of lightning. The rumpled bed smelled sour. She raked her fingers through her bangs, getting the sticky feel of hairspray. Bars were visible on the windows when the lightning struck — a little closer this time.

The warehouse! Candy Jones. Lou. The sting of the hypodermic needle. Mary had expected Candy to try to drug her.

Probably should have accepted the milk shake. She groaned as she rolled to a sitting position on the side of the bed.

Wind threw branches against the building, and Mary cringed. She had no idea whether this was a brick building or a Quonset hut. Could it stand up to a full-out temper tantrum from Mother Nature like the one raging out there tonight? And just where was 'out there'?

Well, mission accomplished. She was inside the operation. She hadn't been sure it would work once they dressed her up. How had they not realized she was older than fifteen?

Greed.

They saw what they wanted to see. A voluptuous fifteen-year-old who would set a pedophile's hair on fire. They saw dollar signs.

Thunder rumbled and the ground shook. Mary rolled to the floor and covered her head with her hands, her body trembling.

God, make it stop!

Lightning cracked right outside the window and a tree fell against the
~~~~~

window, splintering the glass, which rained into the room along with a splatter of icy pellets. Hail pelted the outside walls.

We're taking heavy fire. Sarge, when are the reinforcements coming?

Mary's hands groped for her gun, but it wasn't there. She felt along her pants leg for her knife. She had to find a weapon. But her fatigues were denim and her combat boots were missing.

She screamed in sheer frustration, in rage. In fear.

The door rattled, then the light flickered overhead and Ms. Jones hovered over her.

"You're okay, Mary. It's just a storm. You're okay."

Mary's gaze found the face and reality coalesced around her. *The mission. Focus on the mission.* She forced herself to melt into Ms. Jones' embrace, forced herself to sob like a child.

"Wh-wh-where am I? I want my Mama!"

"I'm sorry we had to do it this way, Mary, but you really gave me no other choice," Ms. Jones said, trying to sound apologetic, but falling short. She sighed. "Most girls are glad to have this opportunity and they come along gladly. But we could see you were going to prove a little more difficult. You'll adjust, but it's going to take a little time."

Lou burst into the room, followed by Hank and a couple of other men. They cursed when they saw the window.

"You're gonna have to move her, Candy," Lou said, pointing to the mess on the far side of the small room. "She can't stay in here. We'll have to board it up until the storm passes, then try to patch it from the outside later."

"I didn't want to put her in with the others —" Candy protested.

"I know," Lou cut in. "But now we don't have any choice. She can't stay in here."

"She's not ready to see —"

"Candy." A tall, gray-haired man in a three-piece suit spoke in a low voice that brooked no arguments. "She. Can't. Stay. In. Here. Move. Her. **Now.**"

The last word shook the room almost as much as the thunder had. Mary could hear Candy's heart hammering, and she looked up to see the woman swallow convulsively.

"Come on, Mary. Let's get you someplace a little warmer," she muttered. Mary stole a quick peek through those convenient bangs and saw the subservient bow of Candy's head. And the look of pure venom in her eyes as she passed the man in the suit.

Yes! Trouble in paradise. I like it.

But more than that, Mary had noted the word 'others.' Her own heart pounded.

I know I'm supposed to praise You in all things, Lord, but I was not thanking You for that thunderstorm. Now I see Your purpose. We had to have a storm to break the window, didn't we? Okay. Thank You for the thunderstorm. But, um, could we stop now please? I really need to keep my feet in this reality, Lord. And PTSD … well, right now it's very inconvenient. Mary amended her first inclination. She'd been with crusty Army grunts too long to be able to keep even her prayers entirely 'ladylike.'

Others. *Please, Lord. Let me find Becca.*

Becca, with her silky blond hair and brilliant blue eyes. She danced like a fairy sprite. Mary's parents wouldn't have been taken in by lies like the ones she and her "Mannering Mother" allowed themselves to fall for. But a music teacher had. She was young and naïve. For a time, they had thought she was in league with the kidnappers, but that was looking less likely. She'd just been foolish. Still, this fiasco had ruined her. No one trusted her with their children now, no matter how much she cried.

Mary forced herself to cling to Ms. Jones. To drag her feet and not race eagerly from door to door. To not appear eager to see the faces in each room along the hallway. Candy paused before the third door on the right and released Mary so she could unlock the door. Mary leaned against the wall, feigning a weakness that was not too far from truth. She glanced up and down the hall. Three doors on each side of the hallway, counting the one she had been in. That left five rooms, possibly filled with children. Or did some of them remain reserved for these men who had swarmed into the room when she screamed? How many children to a room? One? Two? Ten? Why was she kept apart? Was it like Candy said — just until she adapted to the idea of not going home? Then her stomach dropped to her toes. Or was that where they took the children for appointments with 'clients'?

No, surely not. The bedding had smelled sour and stale. They would want something better for a paying customer. Bars on the windows. Perhaps a room for the unbiddable, the unwilling, the uncooperative.

Now she really felt sick.

I knew I was walking into Hell, Lord, but I still wasn't prepared for this. She wanted to pound the wall with her fists. She wanted to grab Candy and use her head to pound the wall. She wanted to grab Candy and just plain pound her face with her fists. She saw one of the men from the room she'd just vacated staring at her, his eyes narrowed intently. He was lean, but muscular, his black sleeveless t-shirt molded to his muscles like a second layer of skin. Snake tattoos coiled around his arms with fangs open to attack.

His icy stare sent a shiver down her spine. Something about this man set off red alert warnings in her head.

He's more dangerous than all the others combined, she thought. *I've got to take him out as soon as possible or he'll stop me from completing my mission. But first I have to find Becca.*

The door swung open and Mary pushed herself away from the wall. Ms. Jones ushered her into the room. Six pairs of frightened eyes darted up toward her, then quickly back down to stare at their knees, which they all had drawn up to their chests. They sat huddled on mattresses on the floor, blankets wrapped around them. Some leaned against each other; others had withdrawn from their fellow captives, curled into corners of their own private torment. They were all around fourteen to fifteen years of age. Too old to be Becca.

No. Wait. Time was playing tricks on her. Becca would have turned fourteen last spring. Eighteen months in the 'sandbox' had shifted reality on her. Her baby sister had been growing up in her absence. She shook her head and looked at the girls again. No blondes. Her heart sank.

"Find a place to sit, Mary," Ms. Jones said, giving her an impatient shove into the room. "We'll be bringing around some supper in a little while." She withdrew and Mary heard the tumblers of the lock as it clicked into place again.

The overhead lights were off, but a small bedside lamp threw dim shadows around the room. Mary let her gaze slide from one girl to another. No one dared to look at her. No one spoke or greeted her. The room vibrated with fear. Mary felt her heart break. She wanted to wrap each girl in a hug and tell them it would all be okay. But she knew that would be the wrong move right now. They weren't ready.

And they would never believe her.

A slim brunette in the corner stirred. She shifted and dull eyes turned to survey the new arrival curiously. Mary's breath caught in her throat. The hair was all wrong, but the eyes… Brilliant blue like the wings of a butterfly. Or like the perfect summer day. A frown creased the brow and the head tilted.

Becca working out the solution to a problem or a particularly difficult math equation. That little tilt and the crease in the brow. Mary crept slowly toward the figure in the corner, and she knelt, then sat, carefully keeping enough distance to not crowd the child.

"You… look…" The child's fingers shook as they rose within inches of tracing the lines of Mary's cheek. Her voice was barely audible.

"Yes, Becca." Tears pricked Mary's eyes. "It's me. Shhhhh…. You have to be quiet though."

The child frowned. "But Mary's hair isn't that dark."

Mary laughed quietly through her tears. "And yours was never brown, little chick-a-dee!" She tenderly reached out and held up a lock of Becca's hair. Becca's eyes widened at the sight of her own hair. Then she looked at Mary more closely, reached out and wrapped a chestnut curl around her finger.

"Mary-berry?"

"Yes. I'm here." Mary opened her arms, and Becca fell into them, and wept.

"How did they get you? Why? They don't want anyone but children." Becca cried softly.

"Shhhh," Mary warned her. "You gotta keep quiet, Becca. I'm going to get you out of here." She whispered urgently. "But you have to help me by holding it together, baby."

"Wh-wh-what do you mean?" Becca raised her face.

Mary drew her head down against her chest again so she could keep their whispers low. "I'll get all of you kids to safety as soon as I can, but I need you to trust me."

"Nobody ever gets away, Mary." Becca's tears left splotches on her denim shirt. "No one."

"Well, baby, that was before your big sister got here," she said grimly. "You rest for now. I've got your six."

"What's that mean?" Becca asked with a giggle.

"I'm watching your back."

"Oh." She snuggled into Mary's arms. "I remember this sweater. Grandma knitted it for you for Christmas."

"That's right, baby," Mary breathed a sigh of relief. *She remembered! Just as we hoped.* A visual cue. She hadn't noticed the barrette, but she had remembered the sweater.

"You're probably just a hallucination, but if you are, I hope I don't wake up from this one. I don't want you to disappear."

"I'm not going to disappear, baby," Mary whispered. "Don't you worry."

~~~~~

When Mary Dalton returned from Iraq, she found her mother in hysterics and her father almost homicidal. Her younger sister, Becca, had been targeted by predators and kidnapped. They had badgered the police, the FBI, even calling their senators and representatives until those esteemed gentlemen started regretfully being "unavailable." They were turned over
~~~~~

to counselors and told that prayer was their last and only option. Their daughter was probably out of the country by now, far from their jurisdiction. Nothing more they could do. *We're so sorry…* Her mother's depression was so deep, they feared for her sanity.

In desperation, Mary sought out some ex-military guys who had taken matters into their own hands. While they still tried to do things in such a way as to bring about convictions, their first and foremost mission was to rescue as many children as possible. Then she called up a few of her buddies. Out of the seven she had counted as her closest friends, three had joined her on this crazy venture. They teamed up with the group who did this regularly, and managed to find the cell they were pretty sure had taken Becca. Becca's picture was up on one of the websites already, and there had been "activity" linked to her profile. While the team had been reluctant to use Mary as the bait, she had proven that she could "dress down" and pass for a young teen.

"We always called her 'Babyface' around the post," Bobby had joked, cuffing her on the arm. "She might as well go for broke."

"We know approximately where their camp is located, but we haven't been able to pin them down precisely," said Allen Brooks, the team leader. "So whatever you do, don't lose this tracking device."

Mary had held the little silver disk in her hand and trembled. That disk could mean life and death for Becca. How would she ever be able to hide it from these evil people once she had fallen into their hands?

Jonas and Nathan had gripped her shoulders, one on each side.

"You can do this, girl," Nathan said gruffly.

"Remember the sandbox, Babyface," Jonas said. "You pulled my butt out of that last firefight when I was locked down in a burning building. I was sure my ticket was about to be punched, but you came blasting through the door like f –" He paused and glanced at Mary's parents, "…like a female Rambo. Saved my life. You can do this too."

"We've got your six, Dalton," Bobby said. "Go get your little sister out."

~~~~~

Mary shifted to speak to the other girls in the room.

"My name is Mary, and I'm here to get my sister out of here. I can get you out too, but only if you follow my instructions to the letter. If you don't want to take that chance, you need to get over in the corner and stay out of the way the best that you can. But if you'll just trust me, I'll get you to safety. You have my word. I'm not a kid. I'm an Army war veteran, combat trained, and I have people coming to help us. We *are* going to get out of here.
~~~~~

Tonight."

The girls stared at her.

"Do you understand me?" They looked at one another then back at her. "Hey! I need you to snap out of it! This is a rescue mission! You need to decide right now. Do you want to come with me, or do you want to ride it out here? Because I'm taking my sister outta' here! You can come along or stay behind."

Becca tugged on her arm. "You can't leave them behind, Mary!"

"*You* are my mission, Becca. I came in here to rescue *you*. And I'm not leaving without you. If they want to come along, fine. But I won't endanger you if they won't do as I tell them to. If they slow us down, or get in the way, they become a liability."

Becca shrank from the hardness in her eyes, and Mary felt like a knife pierced her heart. What had happened to her in all those months of battle? There was a time she would have never considered leaving a child behind. Now she could think only of the mission: her sister. She shook her head. She couldn't think about it now. They had to get out of here.

The doorknob rattled. *The meal!*

Mary motioned for all the girls to move back against the wall and away from the door. Lou shoved open the door with his right hand. He stepped in with a metal tray in his left hand and one balanced precariously on his left forearm. Then he shifted to hold a tray in each hand.

"Dinner, ladies," he announced with a leer.

"Let me help with those trays," Mary said, reaching for the first tray. She took it and handed it off to one of the girls, then reached for the second tray, while straining to see who else was in the hallway.

"Hey, Jacko, hand me the next two trays," he called.

"Just you two guys on supper duty?" Mary asked lightly.

"How many guys do you think it takes to pass out supper trays, little girl?" Lou asked sharply.

Mary took the tray and turned like she was going to hand it off, then she swung back around and smashed the edge of the metal tray into Lou's throat with all her weight behind the thrust. As he bent forward, gasping for air, she rammed her fist into his stomach, then brought her knee up and drove his nose into his face. He hit the floor. In one swift move she straddled his body, twisted his head and broke his neck.

"Hey! What's going on—" Jacko's skinny shape came around the door frame and Mary caught him in the jaw with well-placed right hook. She grabbed a handful of hair and rammed his head into the doorframe, dazing the man, then deposited him beside Lou.

"D-d-do you have to kill him?" Becca asked, her eyes wide. "He never tried to hurt us."

"He can prevent us from escaping," Mary said roughly. "I can't allow that."

"P-please…"

"You have to trust me," she insisted. She snapped the man's neck. With both men down, she returned to Lou's body and searched for a weapon. The only thing she found was a knife, but it was a respectable one, a dagger about twelve inches long.

"Follow me and stay close."

To her surprise, they all got up and followed her out of the room.

"Stay behind me," she whispered.

She heard voices from up ahead.

"Hey, Sean, find out what that commotion was. We don't need those boys getting rowdy back there. Might be those new ones from New York in the back room."

Mary froze. She hesitated. Back room? There were more kids. Should she try to free them too or just get Becca out? No, Becca was her target. If she could get Becca to safety, then she could come back in with the team to rescue the rest of the kids. But she was getting Becca out first!

A figure loomed at the end of the hallway. It was the man who had given her such an intent stare! The one that set off such red alerts in her. This must be Sean. She tensed up, waiting for the attack. His eyes narrowed. Suddenly gunfire erupted outside. Hank burst in from the opposite end of the hallway.

"What the—" His expletive never left his mouth.

Sean's gun raised.

Mary screamed at the girls, "**Down!**"

Hank's blood splattered all over the walls of the hallway. Sean ran toward Mary while tossing a spare gun at her. She caught it in mid-air and swung it around to point it at him.

"FBI undercover," he said tersely, pointing his own gun toward the ceiling. "Hey, would I have given you a gun if I meant to hurt you? I assume that's your friends out there?"

"How do I know you're really FBI?" Mary asked, the gun rock steady in her hand.

Then a flash bomb shook the house, and Mary fell against the wall, once again in the clutches of a PTSD flashback.

"Snap out of it!" the agent said, shaking her arm urgently. "We've got to get these kids out of here now. Let's go!" He propelled Mary and the girls past Hank's body and toward the back door.

"H-how did you know?" Mary asked.

"Well, I knew you weren't a fifteen-year-old kid." He snorted. "Just as well they showed up when they did, because Candy's been showing the boss your videos. I think he's been having some doubts about it too. You're blowing a two-year operation. Thanks a lot."

"Sorry 'bout that," she mumbled, her arm tightly around Becca.

"Hold here for a minute and let me check ahead." Sean disappeared around the corner.

Suddenly Candy grabbed Mary's arm from behind. "Just where do you think you're going?"

Mary brought her left elbow up and caught Candy in the mouth hard. She fell back against the wall. Mary swung the gun in her right hand around and shot four times at close range—right through the heart. Candy slid down the wall, her eyes vacant. She was dead before she hit the floor.

Sean burst around back into the hallway, gun drawn. His eyebrows raised when he saw Candy's body, but he shrugged and said, "Let's go," herding the girls out the back door. Mary held Becca close as they ran for the cover of one of the outbuildings.

"Hold it right there!" voices rang out around them.

Sean's hands went up, gun pointed to the sky. "FBI."

"Mary, you okay?"

"Bobby!" Mary's knees wobbled. "There are more boys in the back room. I heard them talking. And this guy has been undercover for two years. He can tell you the whole layout."

"But you got your sister?"

"Yeah, this is Becca. I got her."

"Oorah." He bumped fists with her, as he eyed the FBI agent. "I assume you can prove what you're claiming, mister."

"Yeah, I'll give you everything you need to check me out. But let's get those kids out of harm's way first. Okay? Mary only got one roomful. There are four other rooms, and they're all occupied.

Allen Brooks trotted over to their group. "Hey, Georgia, get these girls squared away. Blankets, water bottles, and get them loaded on the choppers. You're safe now, girls. I promise you. We're gonna get you out of here and back to a hospital. From there, we'll start contacting your parents. You'll need to work with our counselors for a while. Your folks will get to be with you though. So don't worry. The worst is over."

He turned to Mary. "Nice work, Sgt. Dalton. We followed that tracker right to you. How did you manage to keep it on you?"

Mary smirked. "Swallowed it, sir."

Allen blinked. "Come again?"

"I was afraid they were going to find it. Ms. Mannering fixed it to my barrette, but I was afraid they'd find it. They would have too. But I managed to swallow it in the dressing room. That was the only way I could think of that they wouldn't find it and take it off of me, especially if they drugged me. Which they did, by the way."

She waited a beat, then added, "I can probably get it back to you in a day or two."

"No thanks." Allen laughed. "I think we'll just write that one off as a loss." He walked back to his troops, still shaking his head and laughing.

Mary saw the gray-haired man in the business suit being led away in handcuffs, one of the few to survive the raid on the compound. Most of the others had died in the raid, which was fine by her.

Room by room, they pulled out the children, shaken, crying, frightened by the gunfire. Some still new to the process and belligerent, some beaten and cowed by the abuse they'd suffered. Allen's team was gentle as they herded the children aboard the choppers.

"Just where are we?" Mary asked.

"Middle of nowhere, Arkansas." Bobby laughed. "They must have really dosed you, Babyface!"

"Shut up!" She gave him a playful shove. "Wakin' up from that stuff was not fun, I'm tellin' ya. And wakin' up to a thunderstorm was really bad."

"Ouch." Jonas winced.

"A thunderstorm?" Georgia asked. She was cradling one of the younger girls in her arms and rocking her to sleep. Her curly blond hair looked at odds with her fatigues. Mary wondered if she'd ever even pulled service time. Maybe she'd just been a civilian for a long time.

"PTSD," Mary said. "Thunderstorms can sound an awful lot like a firefight sometimes. And even the lightning can mimic bomb bursts. We're told it lessens with time, but we all just got back from Afghanistan a few months ago. This was bad timing from Mother Nature to throw a temper tantrum."

"Yeah, we were with Air Rescue. So we were pretty much in the thick of things most of the time. In and out of hot spots. Pulling people out of bad situations. That's why this mission was right up our alley."

"We could use a few more good people on our team, you know," Allen said. "You all did good work tonight. You ever want to sign on, you just let me know."

"How do you do it?" Mary asked. "I mean … to go in after a whole bunch of kids like that."

"You had trouble changing focus from one child to a lot of children, didn't you?" he said, nodding. "I get it. It's the military mindset. You went in to save your sister. That was the mission, and that's what gave you focus. It's the way they train you. We come at it from a different perspective."

Mary nodded and waited for him to continue.

Allen studied her for a moment. Not everyone was ready to hear this, but she was. He could tell. She knew he was studying her, and he had seen what he needed to see.

"We're based more on a Biblical standard. We're like the shepherds in the Bible. The shepherds look after the sheep. They tend them, watch over them, see to their needs, make sure they're fed and watered. As parents, that's what we're supposed to do for our children. And most parents do try. But there are wolves out there in the world, and they are devious and cunning. You've just seen it for yourself. They're out to destroy the most innocent lambs in our society. So we've accepted the role of shepherd to go and seek out the lost lambs to return them to their homes. And if we can destroy a few wolves along the way, we'll gladly do that too. But mostly we're focused on saving the lambs. All the lambs. That's what shepherds do. We didn't mind that you had one particular lamb to find. We figured we'd just tag along and grab up all the other lambs while we were at it. We'd had Derek Bristol in our sights for a long time. This is the first time we've actually caught him in the act."

"That's the guy in the three-piece suit?" Mary asked.

"Yep. He's pretty high level."

"Gave me the creeps."

"We'd heard a lot about your friend, Sean Caster, too. That was a deep cover he had going on. We had him pegged as a really bad dude." Allen shook his head. "Never would have guessed he was a fed."

"Then he checked out?" Bobby asked.

"Yeah. He's solid. And he's back to his office duty as soon as he clears all the debriefings they're gonna put him through. His undercover days are over. In fact, the feebies will probably be contacting you for a statement too, just for the record. His real name is John Henderson. He said it was going to feel weird to actually shave and cut his hair again. He hasn't worn it short in two years."

Mary digested that in silence. Two years. She had hated wearing a disguise for just a few days. What would it be like to go undercover for two years? To have to act like a bad guy for that long? That took dedication.

"Yeah, he's interested in our operation too. That surprised me." Allen shook his head. "I'd have thought he'd be ready for his nice clean desk, and a suit and tie again. But I think the idea of saving these kids has sort of gotten under his skin over the past couple of years." They locked gazes. "Babyface, you may have accomplished a lot more than you ever imagined you would."

"Hey now, that's a name for her battle buddies," Nathan protested.

"No, it's okay," Mary said, patting his arm. "I think our circle just got a little wider."

"Welcome home, Mary Dalton," Allen said softly.

Mary smiled as Becca nestled deeper into her embrace and slept peacefully.

The End

THE CURSE
Angela R. Watts

ONE

The wolf lurked in the woods—the perimeter surrounding the village of Teer.

He was cursed.

And he was my best friend.

I pulled my bag over my shoulder, taking one last look over the small, one-bedroom cabin. The village of Teer was small, and defenseless. Now, with sickness breaking out, we would need medicine and a healer from the south.

And if I had to send for a healer and medicine anyway, I decided I would do so—at the same time I would try to end the curse for Luis.

Tucking my grandmother snugly into the trundle bed, I slipped into the cool night, feeling the hilt of the dagger at my side to strengthen my resolve. The full moon hung high overhead. Teer sat silently—everyone was inside their homes, since no one was allowed out after dark because of the wolf's roaming.

Still, I had to do something—for Luis, and for my grandmother. She was all I had left.

And Luis?

I couldn't lose him either.

I set off into the forest that surrounded Teer, footsteps silent.

The wolf's howls echoed from afar.

~~~~~

One hundred years ago, wolves had hunted on the mountains of Kuzec, and had been led by a mighty wolf shifter.

The legend went that once the leader died, one hundred years ago, the curse would pass down to a villager of Teer.

Then, one man would turn into a wolf, never to return. He would spend his days terrorizing the mountains. Legend said this curse remained out of vengeance, so that the hunters who had killed the leader would pay in the future for their deed.

That future had arrived.

Now, the new wolf hunted anyone who left Teer past nightfall.

And the wolf was my childhood best friend—Luis.

He had vanished one night without a trace, and the following full
~~~~~

moon, the wolf had returned to the woods. His howls had carried over the villages like a horrific plea.

In the following week, a local hunter disappeared.

Then a boy from the mill.

Neither had returned, and no bodies had been found in the woods come daylight.

Tonight, somehow, I would reach the healer, and find a cure for Luis. Then I would bring back medicine for the villagers.

It sounded simple, in theory.

In reality, I had no idea if the rumored cure for the curse would work. But what did I have to lose?

Nothing.

Except my life, and I didn't really mind losing it if it meant I might save the others.

I hurried through the woods, heart hammering in my throat. My old, tattered cloak snagged on a few thorn bushes, but I pressed on, trying to keep my breathing quiet. I wasn't sure how fast a wolf shifter could run, or find me, but I was already half a mile from the village.

Things were starting to look up.

Maybe I could reach the other village, Mirstone, for a healer before Luis found me and gobbled me up.

My boots thumped lightly on the dirt path. It narrowed as I took a shortcut—a small path that went off the main road and crossed a narrow creek. Luis and I had taken it all the time to travel to the other village. It saved time and energy. Tonight, I had to make every second count.

The creek whispered softly in the night. Water danced and rippled, shimmering under the white moon. I took a slow breath. Luis and I had visited this creek countless times. We had grown up wading in the waters, fishing in the depths, and dreaming together on the mossy shore.

If I failed him, it was over. He would die a shifter, living his final years as a ravenous wolf.

More howls echoed in the distance.

It wasn't his fault that his ancestor was the old leader.

It wasn't his fault that the curse had taken him.

He didn't deserve any of it.

I had to fix everything—for him, for Grandma, and for the village.

I jumped over the creek using the polished stones that Luis and I had used to make a mini bridge so many years ago. Water splashed slightly as my left boot slipped and hit the water, but I reached the shore successfully, and hurried on.

Still, I moved too quickly.

My boot caught a tree root.

I fell, catching myself with my arms. I gasped in pain but bit my lip just as quickly.

The howling in the distance stopped.

Tensing, I stumbled up and back onto the path. My breath formed little white clouds in the cold night.

Just keep moving.

I have to reach the village first.

I picked up the pace, practically jogging along the narrow, dirt path, trying to avoid roots and rocks. A lone owl hooted in the trees above me, and I tried not to think about what else lay in the shadows around me.

Why had Luis's howling stopped?

Where was he?

My gut twisted.

Had he found something to eat? Was he hurt? No, probably not hurt.

Pushing my fears aside, I broke into a run. The bag on my back bounced, and my cloak ripped on some overhanging branches, but I didn't slow down.

I didn't make it far.

A soft thump hit the ground ahead of me. Something large landed in the center of the path.

I froze in my tracks, breath catching. Blood running cold, I stared at the giant wolf in front of me.

The wolf growled but didn't move. His thick, black fur stood on end. His gleaming eyes didn't look away from mine.

I couldn't move.

Should I run?

I didn't stand a chance. He would kill me before I made it three feet.

Licking my chapped lips, I fumbled for words. "Luis… wait."

The wolf growled again.

Was it Luis? I had never really thought about that. What if he wasn't sentient, and didn't remember anything?

How was I supposed to escape him, and then use the cure—which I prayed existed—on him, if he didn't remember me?

"I'm finding you a cure—and I'm bringing medicine back to the village. A-a lot of people are sick." I choked the words out. Would he listen to me?

The wolf took a step forward. Saliva dripped from his sharp teeth, which he bared slowly.

Flinching, I yanked the dagger from its sheath on my side. "Stay back, Luis! Let me go through!"

But was I speaking to Luis?

Probably not. Friends didn't eat friends.

The wolf snarled and lunged forward. I let out a weak shriek, ducking slightly, and stabbed the wolf's chest. I wasn't aiming for the heart, and prayed I didn't accidentally hit it. The wolf stumbled sideways, growling, and I took off.

I ran as fast as I could—but the wolf didn't follow.

As I staggered through briars and bushes off the beaten path, a lone, aggrieved howl echoed from behind me.

~~~~~

By the second mile, I figured Luis had not followed me, and I limped along in the forest. I was almost there—I just had to keep going.

I moved back onto the beaten path, trying to keep my wits about me. Even if Luis wasn't in the wolf mentally—if I gave him a cure, would he return? I had to try. I couldn't just let him succumb to the curse.

Pain flared in my chest at the idea of losing Luis.

And what if there was no cure for him?

I would gather the medicine for my grandmother and village—but I would forsake Luis.

Sweat pouring down my temples, despite the cool temperature, I resolved that even if this healer had no cure, even if they told me there was no cure, I would spend the rest of my life finding one, if that was what it took to bring Luis back.

TWO

The village was asleep.

I crept to the edge of the tiny villageand knocked on the door of the healer's cabin. Within moments, the man opened the door, frowning at me.

"Teer needs medicine," I said. "A few of them have a fever. It's only affecting the elderly."

The healer's eyebrows shot up. "Teer? You made it past the wolf?"

I nodded. "Is there any medicine I can bring back? I have payment now."

Rubbing his beard, the young healer stepped back into the cabin. "Of course, of course, but… but it is not safe to return to the village during the night—"

"I must. My grandma is very ill," I said tightly. "I can't risk her dying alone in the night."

The healer gathered some small, glass bottles from a cabinet. I didn't enter the cabin, worried I might infect it, but he left the door open. "Very well, but are you armed?"

"I… have a dagger. But I don't wish to harm the wolf," I said weakly.

"A dagger? Is it silver? A cursed shifter will hardly flinch at a dagger," the healer scoffed.

I paused. I hadn't known that. Then why had Luis fallen back like he had?

"Fire is a better option," the healer said, shoving the tinctures into his black doctor bag. "I'll light a torch."

"I can pay for the torch, also," I said.
~~~~~

The healer grunted, shouldering his bag. He grabbed a torch from the wall and lit it, careful not to set anything else in the tiny, cozy cabin on fire. "I'm coming with you."

"W-what?" I tensed. "But I could be contagious—"

"I'm a healer, remember?"

I gulped. "Then... then is there something for the wolf?"

He paused, glancing at me curiously. "Come again?"

"The wolf—if there was a cure, we could give it to him, and save lives," I explained. "It's your job, isn't it? To save lives? If we fix the wolf, then no one else has to die."

The healer studied me, then glanced around the cabin, mumbling to himself. "A cure... A cure for a curse? I do not know if there is such a thing."

"A remedy? Herbs? Something?" I insisted.

"It is a curse born of revenge and bloodlust," the healer said softly.

"But there is a physical form that can surrender to a physical cure, is there not?" I pleaded. "Can we try *nothing*?"

The healer sighed, grabbing a small box on a dusty shelf. He blew it off, and opened it, saying, "This is a blade of silver..."

"I am not going to kill the wolf!" I growled.

"No, no," he said quickly, "listen. When I was young, my grandfather told me that, a hundred years ago, many curses could be broken by a bond stronger than that of hatred. Perhaps, if you kill the wolf form, and do so out of compassion, rather than hate, the curse could then be broken—but," he exclaimed, "it is merely an idea! It might kill both forms, for good."

I stepped onto the threshold. "A-all right."

He pulled a silver dagger from the box and handed it to me. "You know this wolf shifter?" he asked, voice solemn. "Did you see him tonight?"

I hesitated. Should I lie? Would the healer leave if he knew I had, indeed, seen the wolf? Or would he grow more defensive and violent? Should I tell him that Luis was my friend? Would it even matter? "I have seen the wolf," I said. "But... but the man that received the curse is my friend. His name is Luis."

With a nod, the healer sighed. "Come along." He stepped out of the cabin and closed the door. "Lead the way. What's your name?"

I gulped, stepping toward the tree line. "Caron."

"I'm Zeb." The healer followed me into the forest, holding the torch out, though the moon already lit up most of the way under the sparse trees. When the trees thickened, the torch would be a godsend.

"T-thank you for coming. I really don't know if it's a good idea, though." I didn't want him eaten. I didn't want anyone eaten.

"Teer is a part of my territory to provide for," Zeb said simply. "It is my job. I'm only shocked you managed to reach me."

I glanced at the silver dagger in my hand, gulping. "I think he let me pass. But... but it might have been luck. I don't... I don't know if Luis is still in there, or not, but I have to try to save him."

"Hmm." Zeb mused. "Anyway, how long has the sickness been in the village?"

"Only since yesterday," I said meekly. "Grandma is one of the sickest. I... I couldn't wait any longer to get help."

"I am sure you caught it in time." Zeb nodded as we walked. "It is a fever?"

"Yes. S-she doesn't seem to be in pain, but she's very weak," I said. "I've never seen her so weak."

"Well, I've heard of a similar problem across the mountains. The people healed well with treatment, so I am sure your grandmother will be fine, along with the others."

I gulped, falling silent. I prayed so.

~~~~~

A mile into the forest, snow began to fall. It drifted slowly around us, but we plodded along the path, picking up our pace. Zeb glanced over. "We're not much further, yes?"

"Halfway there," I whispered.

In the distance, but not too far off, we heard one lone howl.

My insides clenched.

Zeb kept the torch held high, and it cast a warm glow on the darkening forest. The moon vanished, covered in thick clouds. Snow began sticking on the path and bare trees.

I kept close to Zeb, gripping the silver dagger tightly.

"You know Luis well?" Zeb asked.

"He and I have been best friends since childhood," I said, voice small. "W-we always knew it was possible that he might take the curse but... well, truthfully, we stopped believing the legend was even real when we grew up."

"Aye." Zeb sighed. "Well, if anyone can break the curse with the rumored option, it would be you. Don't lose hope yet."

The howl came again.

We walked in silence until we reached the creek. Snow clustered on the bank. I gulped hard, steeling myself. "Those rocks are stable to use for crossing," I said, "I don't think they're frozen over."

"I'll go first." Zeb handed me the torch. He gingerly stepped onto the big stones, and tested them out briefly before saying, "We should be safe."

We crossed the creek, and Zeb took the torch back. "Is this shortcut one you use often?"

"Aye."

"Interesting. I'll have to remember it." He glanced toward the path. "Hmm."

"The howling stopped," I whispered.

"He must be close." Zeb started off again. We tried to move quickly.
~~~~~

The cold air bit my face, and I pulled my red cloak over my head, trying to ward off the snow.

We barely made it one hundred yards before something went *whoosh* in the trees to my right. A stick—a big one—snapped.

"Luis?" I tensed, lifting the silver dagger slightly.

Zeb looked back, lifting the torch to peer into the forest.

Empty.

A growl from our right.

Something shuffled.

Zeb whirled with the torch again.

Too late.

The wolf pounced. Darkness shrouded my vision, and heaviness slammed my chest. I hit the forest floor.

"Caron!" Zeb swore.

The wolf pinned me down, growling and snapping his teeth above me—but he glowered at Zeb.

"Luis! He's helping!" I tried moving my arms, but couldn't,

The wolf snarled, lifting one paw from my shoulder, beginning his advance toward Zeb.

Panic rising, I mustered what strength I had left in my shaky arms and shoved the silver dagger into the wolf's belly. It wasn't his heart—had I missed, or did I just not have the courage to risk the wolf's life and Luis's, like the rumor said?

The wolf howled, jerking backward.

I sat up, holding the bloodied dagger up. "Luis! Please!"

The wolf snapped his jaws and lunged again—this time, straight into the dagger I held. The blade pierced his fur and skin, lodging into his heart.

A shriek escaped me.

Zeb reached over and pulled me away. I was too frozen to move.

The wolf shook his head once, then collapsed on the forest floor. Snow stuck to his thick, dark fur, and Zeb's torchlight illuminated his face. He snarled in pain and went still.

The wolf's blood oozed onto the dirt.

Another cry tore from my throat, and I rushed forward, grabbing the wolf's head. "Luis! No! Why did you do that? I wasn't trying to—"

"Caron—" Zeb started.

The wolf went limp in my grasp. Tears burned my eyes. "I shouldn't have believed the rumor!" What else could I have tried?

"I can carry the wolf back to the village. If it works—" Zeb began again, but before he could finish, the wolf moved.

My breath lodged in my throat. I froze.

The wolf flinched again. In a moment, the wolf's body shifted, and Luis returned—he was naked, and bruised, and had a bleeding wound over his heart, but the wound was slowly healing.

"L-Luis!" I cried, quickly yanking off my cloak and covering him with it. "You're alive! He's alive! He's cold—we need to carry him back!"

Zeb handed me the torch. "Here. Guide us." He lifted Luis up and tossed him over his shoulders. "Look—the wound is already healed."

I glanced at the freshly formed scar over Luis's heart. "I-it worked…" Shaking my head, I quickly led Zeb down the path.

THREE

When we reached the village, a small group of the men had rallied near the mill. Their torches blazed in the snowy night, and one called out, upon seeing us stagger from the trees, "She's there!"

Zeb carried Luis, sighing.

I led him to my cabin, calling to the group of men, "I'm fine! I got the healer, and medicine!"

"Is that Luis? Is he dead?" another shouted. "Is he human again?"

"One thing at a time, gentlemen!" Zeb returned.

I opened the door to my cabin. Zeb placed Luis on my empty bed, and then he turned to Grandma's bed. She slept, her face red in the light of the lantern hanging nearby.

Zeb shook snow off his coat, then opened his bag, and checked Grandma over. While he did that, I put a few blankets over Luis. I couldn't fathom how he was alive, or how the curse had stopped, or how the wound had healed—but all that mattered was that he was back, and I had gotten Grandma help.

Zeb sighed. "Her vitals are strong. This medicine should help her recover." He administered a small dose from a bottle, then glanced over. "I'll tend to the others and explain what happened. You stay here and warm up." With that, the healer took his bag, and went out, shutting the door behind him.

I checked on Grandma, giving her a kiss on the forehead, and sat beside Luis's bed. He slept soundly, though he was still pale. But the bruises had vanished, too. I tucked him in tightly. "It'll be all right," I whispered. "Just rest."

I watched the snow fall outside of the tiny, glass window. Zeb would help the sick, and he sounded hopeful that it was just a fever, and nothing too serious.

Sinking forward, I fell asleep against Luis's bed.

~~~~~

When dawn broke and light peeked through the window, I shifted slightly, then my hand hit something soft and warm.

Frowning, I lifted my head.

Luis lay still but grinned a little when he saw me.

I jumped up and threw my arms around him in a tight hug. "Idiot!" I
~~~~~

said. "You scared me so bad—why did you do that? What were you thinking? Why—"

"Easy!" Luis grunted, patting my shoulder. I pulled back.

"Are you hurt?" I asked.

"Just sore." He shook his head.

"Why did you..." I dropped my gaze.

Luis looked past me, sighing a little. "Your grandma would skin me alive if she heard me, but it looks like she's asleep, so..." He sat up a bit more. "I didn't kill anyone, Caron. I watched the man and boy leave—but I did not kill anyone. Still... I... it was growing difficult to not want to hunt... and it would be better if I were dead, than dangerous. But I didn't... intend to make you kill me. I wasn't thinking properly. I'm sorry."

My blood ran cold. "I... I see." I sat down again. "Well, the healer said the... the only idea he had heard of ending the curse was killing the wolf's form—out of... well, love, I guess. I didn't... think it'd work."

"Guess it did." Luis gave a cheeky smile. "I owe you."

"You can repay me by healing up fast," I snapped. "I've had to chop wood since you left. You know I hate that."

Luis held up his hands. "I shall return to my neighborly duties as quickly as possible, m'lady." But his smile vanished. "Thank you, Caron."

I shrugged off the relief flooding my chest. "You'd do the same for me."

"I would." Luis leaned back, rubbing his face.

"I'd best go check on the others. A few of the elderly are sick, but they should mend fine." I stood once more, grabbing my red cloak from the wall. "Rest."

Luis smirked, and I slipped outside. Snow covered the little village, coating the ground and trees, and I smiled tiredly.

No howls came from the quiet forest.

The wolf was gone, and Luis was home.

The End

DRESS REHEARSAL
Jim Doran

Dee:

Wearing her Juicy Couture velour hoodie, Dee strolled to high school with a northern spring breeze pushing her along. Yes, seniors often went to school in the yoga pants they slept in, but her classmates expected Dee to arrive in style. She hadn't had a chance to wear the black sweatshirt in the brutal Wisconsin winter. The Canadian parka she had for the winter months was so plain—all navy blue and boring.

Most of the people at Grant High School would admire her more if they understood the value of clothing. Her friend Aleesha understood style and art, and she knew how to attract attention to it. And since she and Aleesha were in Mr. Garrett's first-hour Civics class, the hoodie would be perfect. She wanted to soak in that moment and arrive early.

Excited, Dee skipped a few steps toward her destination. When she realized what she was doing, she stopped. What possessed her to skip? How childish, skipping to her classes. She'd rather skip school than skip *to* it.

Or did she?

Dee paused. She could start a trend.

How perfectly retro. If others asked, she'd say skipping was the new walking. What a fantastic idea! Skipping felt right.

Well, why not?

Without giving it another thought, Dee hurried down the street, hopping from foot to foot, with Grant High in her sights.

Aleesha:

"Mom! Come here!" shouted Aleesha.

Her mother shuffled toward the bathroom, much too slow for Aleesha. *Older people take forever!*

Aleesha had her finger near the corner of her eye, the one she hadn't applied eyeliner to yet. "What's this?"

Her mother leaned down and examined her brown skin. "It looks like crow's feet."

She turned her head to study herself in her makeup mirror. "What is 'crow's feet'? Isn't it something you get when you're ancient?"

Her mother hmphed. "I have crow's feet."

123

Aleesha moved her face closer to the mirror. "You know what I mean. First pimples, and now this?"

"We'll figure it out when you get home." Her mother patted her shoulder. "Put some makeup over it. You are going to be late for school…again!"

Aleesha swiveled her head from left to right. The crow's feet were only visible beside one eye. Was that possible? And did it have anything to do with her bones popping when she performed her morning exercises?

Ralph:

Ralph strutted out of his house with a single thought on his mind: late puberty was awesome. This morning, examining himself in the mirror had revealed a major surprise. He had chest hair. Took long enough. This was what it meant to be an adult. He had arrived.

No longer would his family call him *Ralphie*. He was *Ralph* now. Eighteen—ready for the world.

The new growth had nearly distracted him from the other change. The arm exercises he had been doing were paying off; his biceps had rounded off overnight. Yeah, Ralph at five feet, five inches was one of the shortest boys in class. No matter. When his friends saw his physique, their mouths would hang open.

Especially Opal. He'd have to wait until their brief passing between second and third hour. Man-o-man, would she be surprised!

Opal:

The last person Opal wanted to meet this morning was her boyfriend, Ralph. If disaster had a day on the calendar, today was its day. Everything had gone wrong.

What was happening to her? Had her face and body conspired against her overnight and decided to rebel? Opal had tried to use tweezers, but the tiny buggers refused to come out. And the other change! She could hide her body with the Grant High sweatshirt Ralph had given her. She loved his shirt for lounging around the house but not for school. Yet, desperate times called for desperate measures. *And these are desperate times, let me tell you.*

Opal would have to meet Ralph between the second and third hour. They often snuck in a quick kiss. Not today.

She touched the skin above her lips.

Not with this on her face.

Dee:

Of course, Aleesha was late.

Dee had to walk alone to her locker instead of skipping into Grant High with Aleesha. That girl! Dee waited at her locker for her, but Aleesha never showed up. Instead, she strolled to class, a lighter step than normal but not quite skipping.

She passed the office on her way and spied a vase full of orchids on the counter. She turned into the room with wide eyes. The scent of the flowers drew her toward them, and the dazzling whiteness—brilliant as a bridal gown—compelled her to touch them.

"Do you like them?"

Dee jumped. Ms. Freybush had emerged from an office, unnoticed. The woman was all smiles.

Dee fondled the flowers as if they were artifacts in a museum. "Yes, I do."

"My boyfriend sent them to me," Ms. Freybush said.

For a moment, Dee was tempted to grab a handful and rush out of the office. What a bizarre thing to think. Instead, she played with the flowers, watching them bob in the water as she ran her hand through them.

"Dee?"

Dee blinked in response.

Ms. Freybush pointed at the clock. "Hurry, or you'll be late."

Opal:

Ralph strolled up to Opal at her locker. Though her nose was level with his forehead, he lifted his chin to give the appearance he was taller. The action was childish, but she loved his immaturity at times.

Before Ralph spoke, Opal lifted her hand in a stopping motion. "Don't ask."

"You have a bandage across your upper lip."

"Actually, it's across my philtrum, not my lip." Opal gritted her teeth. "I looked it up to see if it would start bleeding when I removed the bandage."

"What happened?"

Opal grimaced. "I told you not to ask."

Ralph ran his hand along her shoulder. "I love the shirt."

When he proceeded to move his hand down her arm, she pulled away.

Ralph stepped back. "What the—!"

A few people turned around and stared at them, chuckling at Opal's bandage.

"Shut it!" she hissed.

He leaned forward. "Have you been working out?"

Opal pretended to find something interesting on the floor. "No. Suddenly, I have a few...muscles."

Ralph grinned. "Ain't puberty great?"

Opal didn't think so.

Dee:

Dee arrived at the lunch table first, reserving the other three seats for her friends. It wouldn't do to have Weird Wilma or Karl "Picky nose" Picnuse grab a seat. Karl had been eyeing her in her French IV class. She swore boys took French class just to pick up girls.

Opal arrived first with a bandage sprawled across her lip. She spoke before Dee had the chance. "Please don't be the hundredth person to ask why I have this above my lip."

Dee ran her finger under her nose as if shaving her philtrum. "Were you…?"

Opal whispered, "Plucking."

Dee's eyebrows raised.

Opal waggled her fingers near her lips. "Overnight. Tiny hairs sprouted. I have more than Ralph."

"He's a redhead. It's hard to notice."

Opal pointed at her dark brown tresses. "It's obvious on me."

Ralph walked up behind her and put his hands over her eyes. Opal jumped and then swatted them away. "Not in the mood, Ralph."

He sat down beside her. "Today's not so bad."

"Says you." Aleesha grabbed the seat next to Dee. "Today's a wreck."

Opal grabbed her bottle of water and opened it. "You can say that again."

Dee agreed with Ralph. "Ms. Freybush had some beautiful orchids on her desk this morning. What a pleasant surprise."

Aleesha wrinkled an eyebrow. "Flowers? I didn't know you liked flowers."

Dee never had before. They were fun to paint, but she wasn't what she'd call a flower child. Yet, in third hour, she observed a patch of wildflowers sprouting among melting winter snow and lost all track of time admiring them. She was about to say something in her defense — probably a lost cause with Aleesha's sharp wit — when something in her best friend's hair grabbed her attention. She reached for a stray strand.

"What's this?"

Aleesha reared back. "What's what?"

Opal put a hand to her mouth. "Aleesha. You're going gray!"

"What?"

Aleesha's camera appeared in her hand as rapidly as a magician pulled flowers out of the air. Swinging the camera to reflect herself, she examined her hair. Dee spotted a twin of the gray strand among her black tresses.

"It's not the only one."

"No." Aleesha moaned. "What is happening to me?"

Ralph opened his mouth, but Opal poked him in the ribs.

Dee put her hand on Aleesha's shoulder. "Don't worry. A little dye will return your natural color. You'll see."

Aleesha spouted off the mother of all cussing words. "I hope so. I want to go home and crawl into bed."

"You can't." Dee unwrapped her granola bar. "We have practice tonight."

Aleesha crossed her arms. "I'm wearing my hat, then."

Opal ripped open a packet of crackers. "I haven't memorized all my lines. Let's meet tomorrow instead."

"We perform next week, and I reserved the stage after school." Dee looked around the table. "Come on, guys. You all agreed. I don't want people who can't act on the stage with me. We've been doing the school play since sophomore year. We're going out on a high note."

"*Little Red Riding Hood* is a high note?" Ralph snorted. "Why couldn't we do something good like *Hamilton?*"

Opal nudged him with her shoulder. "The play's a selection of Grimm's fairy tales. And we're helping Dee. It'll be fun."

"The costume better make me look cool." Ralph made a circling motion around his face. "Werewolf, not a kiddie wolf."

Dee rolled her eyes. "You'll look cool, Ralph. Trust me."

Aleesha:

Aleesha groaned as she lifted herself from her bed. She had groaned many mornings, but all in the spirit of awakening. This time, something was off. She wasn't sick, but a pain in her toes flared when her feet hit the cold floor. Aleesha examined her hands. Her fingers were curled inward and knobbier than she remembered. When she flexed them, sparks of pain ran through her joints.

What was this, now? Had she jammed her fingers in her sleep? If she had, wouldn't the pain have awakened her? She didn't need this on top of the lack of energy last night and the restless sleep.

She stepped away from her bed. Normally, she'd do a few sit-ups for energy but not today. Her body was rebelling against her. Ralph had trumpeted the wonders of puberty. She had a message for puberty: *leave me alone.* She had already gone through the hardest part. She didn't want a second round.

Aleesha hobbled across her room. At this rate, she would receive another tardy slip from Mr. Garrett. Not that it mattered, but she wanted to chat with Dee about the play. Dee had been a bit harsh with Heather and Tyson when they refused to relinquish the stage after she and the cast of *Little Red Riding Hood* had arrived. Heather had overheard Dee whispering that Heather had the easiest part of anyone in the cast.

What time was it? Five a.m.! Whaa —

When was the last time she had been awake at five in the morning? These pinpricks of agony kept giving her presents. Oh well, she was awake now and not returning to bed.

Padding down the hallway, she entered the bathroom. She had her fingers in her frizzy hair, shaking the bedhead from her curls. She turned on the light and screamed.

Opal:

Opal pulled on the tweezers, extending the short strand, but it wouldn't break free of her skin. She blinked at her reflection in the mirror. Yes, still there. She had more hair than her older brother after a day of not shaving. Yuck. She had no shaving cream of her own. She had no option other than to borrow her brother's.

Opal, shaving her face at eighteen. Her life was over. Ralph would dump her, and she'd have to run away to the circus as the bearded lady.

Dee's voice rang in her thoughts. "Save the dramatics for the stage, Opal."

Sighing, she left her bathroom and snuck down to her brother's. Thankfully, Opal lived in a three-bathroom house. His bathroom was the most disgusting she'd ever been in. She covered the lower half of her face as she moved through the house, the little bristles prickling her fingers. She was going to puke.

Flicking on the light, Opal extended her left foot's toes onto the disgusting bathroom floor. When she had entered her bathroom, she had only turned on her makeup mirror to examine her skin. In her brother's bathroom, she saw her entire reflection.

Opal gasped.

She leaned forward, grabbed the sink, and studied her shoulders. Were they broader than yesterday?

Ralph:

Ralph smelled coffee brewing downstairs, waking him from a restless sleep. His mother must be awake and getting ready for work. The automatic timer on their Dr. Café machine had broken months ago. She must have started it herself. The pungent aroma irritated his olfactory senses, and Ralph rolled over and grunted.

Funny, he had been drinking coffee for two years and loved the taste of it. But with his recent changes, Ralph preferred something a bit thicker. Say, milk. Mmm…a nice cup of warm milk sounded splendid if he could drag his tired body out of bed. Perhaps he should try the coffee with cream. Or hold the coffee — cream sounded delicious.

Without opening his eyes, Ralph stretched and recalled his dreams from last night. He was in the woods behind his house, running and scratching at trees. He dodged trunks and fallen branches. His feet had more cushion, so he moved across the dead pine needles, thorny weeds, or tiny rocks effortlessly. At times, he wasn't sprinting. He was… What was the word? Loping.

Yeah, he remembered now. Sometimes he was down on all fours, rushing along.

The chilly night hadn't bothered him with his newfound chest hair. And stomach hair. And back hair. He had found bristles everywhere on his body yesterday evening, and a stubble when he went to bed. Awesome!

In the dream, he carried something in his mouth. Whatever it was, it bothered him, and he had ripped into it. Leaving it behind wasn't an option. He had placed a piece of it in his mouth and let it drag along while he skirted, free and fast, through the woods.

What strange things dreams were, huh?

Ralph's eyelids fluttered. The coffee scent wouldn't go away, and the milk beckoned him. He threw off his sheets and placed his feet on the floor. His sweats were still on, but he had taken his shirt off during the night and thrown it somewhere.

He surveyed his room, spotting his shirt. On the floor, his red tee from yesterday lay waiting for him to throw in his laundry bucket. Ralph stood, then bent over. He was more at ease with his shoulders bent forward. Hunched, he grabbed the shirt as he exited his room.

His vision focused near the door and noticed something strange about the T-shirt. Blinking, he held it up. The shirt had been shredded into strips. What had happened to it?

Ralph rolled his tongue around his teeth in thought and recoiled. Reaching into his mouth, he removed two red fibers.

Dee:

Dee pulled down on her hoodie, the frayed hem an inch above her waistline. She had selected it instead of the Juicy Couture, having worn that sweatshirt yesterday. She wanted something familiar; clothes that hugged her in a warm embrace. And this top was as tight as a grandparent's hug.

To her left, Heather had her head down on her desk, snoring. She should jostle her, but why bother? Let her get her rest.

Aleesha was going to be late again, but so what? Dee didn't have anything to show her today. But three minutes before class started, Aleesha strolled in with a sunny expression and a rectangular plastic container, proving Dee wrong. But what caught Dee's eye was the leopard print scarf wrapped around Aleesha's head. *Oh, here it comes! She must have found another gray strand.*

Aleesha opened the container in the front of the class and placed a muffin on Mr. Garrett's desk. He thanked her, calling her "chipper."

Aleesha blushed. "Oh, I was up early so I baked a few goodies."

Baked? Dee nearly fell out of her chair.

Aleesha proceeded down the rows, handing out muffins to surprised seniors and dropping a baked good on sleeping Heather's desk. She sat down at her desk and placed the container under her seat. Reaching across the aisle, she handed Dee a muffin.

"What are you doing?" hissed Dee.

"Where's the Juicy Couture?" Aleesha shot back.

Dee hugged her arms. "I haven't worn this in a while. I thought I'd give it some love."

"A no-brand, red hoodie I haven't seen since ninth grade? It doesn't even fit you."

Dee eyed Aleesha's wrap. "I'm not wearing some relic of a scarf on my head."

Aleesha patted the scarf. "I had to wear it."

"Why?"

Aleesha rubbed her hands together. "I'll tell you later. But you must keep it in the family."

Family. Funny she should use those words. She and Aleesha were friends, but the word "family" seemed right.

Ralph:

Ralph nudged Weird Wilma aside as he strode down the hallway between second and third hour, hurrying to meet Opal. He strutted toward their morning kiss, and he couldn't wait to show her his new mustache and beard. Ralph was now a player!

When he spotted Opal, he suppressed a chuckle. She had a neck gaiter wrapped over her nose, chin, and throat. When he caught her attention, her bushier eyebrows creased. This was not the reaction he had hoped for.

Ralph approached her and stroked his new growth. No, not a full beard by any stretch of the imagination, but noticeable. "What do you think?"

Opal's nose wrinkled. "Shave it!"

"Why?" asked Ralph. "I think it's wicked."

Opal mocked stroking her chin. "I'm not kissing that. Gross!"

Ralph grabbed the end of the neck gaiter and started to lift it. "Well, I don't want to kiss you through this thing either."

Opal snatched the cloth and pulled it down. "Leave it alone. I have a note to keep it on all day. I'm susceptible to the flu."

"All right." He pursed his lips.

She wrinkled her nose. "No kiss. Let's not get each other sick."

Sick? Opal was acting as if she'd get sick if he kissed her. The thought of a quick peck also soured his stomach. "Yeah, fine."

Opal crossed her arms, and Ralph's jaw dropped. He touched her shoulder. "Wow, woman! You've been working out."

Opal stepped away and spoke in a deeper voice. "Stop touching me!"

"What is the matter with you?"

Opal released a deep breath, and the neck scarf fluttered. "Sorry. I'm just sensitive today."

"Ah! Got it." Ralph whispered. "The monthly visit."

Opal pushed him. "You're such a dog!"

While his girlfriend stormed away, Ralph stood alone in the hallway. A few people laughed at him, including Weird Wilma! He wasn't going to take this lying down. He'd show her at lunch.

Dee:

Why was Ben, at the other table, eating candy canes for lunch?

Dee watched as acne-infested Ben chomped down on a candy cane across the lunch aisle. He reached into his backpack and retrieved a cookie wrapped in foil. Swapping bites between the candy cane and the cookie, Ben stopped eating to take a swig from a liter bottle of Coke.

Grant High gets more and more odd.

Opal rushed into the cafeteria, adjusting her neck gaiter. The gossip grapevine broadcasted to "the right people" about Opal's new accouterment. Only certain students wore a mask to school. When someone like Opal wore one, everyone noticed.

Opal selected a space on Dee's side of the table, and Dee shifted over. Opal normally sat across or kattie-corner to her, not next to her. She and Aleesha usually sat on the same side of the table. "What's up, Opal?"

"Not talking about it!" Opal glared at her.

Dee offered her hand. "Does it have to do with the neck scarf? People are noticing." She knew Opal avoided attracting attention to herself.

Opal opened her water bottle. "They're also noticing you dressing in no-brand clothes. And clothes you've outgrown, too."

Dee squirmed and pulled down the hem of her top garment again. "The hoodie felt right when I selected it this morning."

Aleesha emerged from a crowd and walked to their table. She passed by Opal sitting in her seat but didn't comment. Instead, she sat down across from Dee. "Kathy told me she saw you skipping to school today."

Dee beamed. "I'm starting a trend."

"Is it a 'Most bizarro' trend? Because if so, you're nailing it," said Opal.

Aleesha made a gentle swatting motion. "Opal, be nice!"

Dee gaped at her two friends. Two days ago, Aleesha would've voiced the insult and Opal would have defended her. The role reversal was noticeable. "What's with the scarf, Aleesha?"

"A touch of coiffure mismanagement, I fear," answered Aleesha.

After taking a sip of her water bottle, Opal set it down. "Do you mean a bad hair day?"

"Tsk." Aleesha patted her scarf. "Such a juvenile term for it. But I may be a teensy-tiny bit grayer than yesterday."

Tsk? Aleesha never tsked! And teensy-tiny? Dee was about to make a snide remark when Ralph stormed to their table. Dee thought a double-take only happened in movies, but she found herself making that exact motion as her bearded friend approached. A mat of hair covered his head. Even his hairline was lower.

Ralph plopped himself down on the open seat to Aleesha's left. He squinted at Opal. "If you think I'm giving up sitting near to my friends at lunch because of *you*, you're wrong!"

Opal surveyed the lunchroom. "Maybe I'll sit somewhere else."

The single open seat around them was beside Heather, asleep and drooling. Opal grimaced at Heather's growing pool and recoiled. "Or maybe I won't move."

"Children. Children." Aleesha reached into her brown paper bag and rummaged. "I baked cookies. Let's eat and calm down."

Ralph's deep voice answered her. "I'll be nice if Opal will."

Opal slammed her fists on the table and rattled it.

"Anger issues, much?" Dee side-eyed her friend. "Opal! Your shoulders are splitting the seams on your blouse!"

Opal scrunched her shoulders. "This blouse was the largest one I had."

Aleesha placed chocolate chip cookies close to each of their lunches. When Dee received hers, she asked, "You baked these *and* muffins?"

"All in a day's work!" Aleesha brightened, and then her face fell. "I don't know why I did it."

Ralph sniffed the cookie before taking a bite. "Because you're a good friend. Unlike others at this table."

Opal gripped the edge of the table. "Shut it, Wolf. Or I'll make you shut it."

Dee and Aleesha regarded their timid friend. Dee cleared her throat. "Did you just call him 'Wolf,' Opal?"

Opal scratched under her neck gaiter. "No. I said Ralph."

"You definitely said wolf," agreed Aleesha.

"They sound the same." Opal bit her lip. "Let's drop it."

"Next thing you know." Ralph chewed with his mouth open, crumbs falling to the table. "She'll ask to use a real ax in the play."

Opal rubbed her chin. "A real ax would be more believable than the stupid plastic toy we have."

Ralph pawed at his ear as if a mosquito had landed there. "I was kidding! Now she's trying to kill me! I'm not going to be in this play with *her*."

"Stop it!" Dee put her hands between them. "We're all acting strange. Opal, you're turning into a lumberjack."

Opal shrank from the words, but Ralph laughed. Dee turned to him. "And you? What are you becoming? And Aleesha? Baking and a head scarf because she's a little gray?"

Aleesha lifted the scarf to allow the other three a peek. "All gray."

Dee leaned forward. "You are all turning into the characters in the play. You have to stop it."

Aleesha examined Dee's clothes. "The strings on your hoodie are red. Weren't they white originally?"

Dee put her hands on her cheeks. "I decided to change the string color. It's happening to me, too!"

Dee:

"Hey, skipper!"

Dee froze in place. She hadn't realized she had been skipping home from school — the flowers enroute had distracted her. The voice wasn't one of her friends, and she tensed her body to receive the incoming teasing.

A schoolmate, Brenda, rushed up to her. "Are you skipping because you're jazzed about our show?"

Did every drop of blood rush to her face at the same time? "I want to make sure our last performance will be the best."

"Okay." Brenda dug her camera out of her pocket. "The sets are done. Want to see?"

Dee jumped in place in glee, reminded herself she wasn't five years old, and stopped. "Yes!"

Brenda eyed her and then showed her the viewscreen on her mobile device. She thumbed through the images. "*Hansel and Gretel. Sleeping Beauty. Pinocchio.* Speaking of which, I haven't seen Tim in two days. I hope he isn't sick. And here's *Little Red Riding Hood.*"

Dee used her finger to scroll through the scenery. "Those are perfect, Brenda."

"I had help." Brenda put the camera away. "My sister Wilma drew most of it. Why you asked me instead of her, I'll never know. She's a much better artist."

Dee tugged at the collar of her hoodie. "Oh, is she now?"

"Oh, yeah. Wilms built clay sets while drawing them. She calls it a diorama. She created miniature clay figures of all the actors in costume. They resemble you and your friends."

Dee stiffened. "Did she put clothes and hair on them?"

"Oh, yeah!" Brenda said. "Yours has a red cloak, Grandma's all gray, and the huntsman has a beard. The whole deal. I'll take pictures when I go home."

Brenda turned and began to walk away. Dee called after her.

"Brenda, did Wilma mention she tried out for the part of the witch in *Hansel and Gretel*? She made a joke about your grandmother being a real witch."

She shrugged. "Oh, it's no joke. My grandma claims to be a real witch. She's done things…let's say I don't cross her. And Wilms adores her."

Brenda marched away. Dee didn't feel like skipping home anymore.

Opal:

Her mother promised to take her to a dermatologist in the afternoon. No way she was attending school today. She texted a message to the group. "Worse today. 😠 "

Worse for a teenage girl. If she were Ralph, she would be far happier. Taller, broader, more hair on her face than before. Why was this happening to her?

Aleesha texted. "Same. 👻 "

Ralph answered an hour later. "I skipd. @ grove."

Ralph was probably hiding in the trees there, the coward! Opal should go and pull the scoundrel into the wide open, and expose him as the—

Stop, Opal. Just stop.

Fifteen minutes before noon, Dee sent a text. "You left me here, alone. 😨 "

Aleesha texted. "R Hood doesn't change."

Her phone chimed. Dee responded, "Shrunk two inches. 👊 Hoodie fits."

Ouch! How was Opal growing and Dee shrinking?

Dee wrote another text. This one was long, lacked emojis, and summarized an encounter with Brenda, Weird Wilma's sister. After the detailed message, she sent another text with her hypothesis of what was happening.

Unreal, but how could Opal deny it? Nothing else made sense.

Opal wrote. " 💀 But I believe it."

The others all agreed with her. Dee's last text was to meet her at Weird Wilma's house later this afternoon.

Dee:

Dee was the first to Weird Wilma's house, a bi-level with black shutters, a purple door, and a copper weathervane. "Artistic" was what the neighborhood had called it, but Dee wondered if they had it wrong. Perhaps the house reflected the dark inhabitants inside.

Dee mounted the porch. She didn't want to confront the braces-filled mouth and freckled-nose Wilma alone, so she examined the knocker. A golden toad was affixed to the door and the clapper was its tongue. Gross, like Wilma.

She checked her phone for the fifth time when Opal rounded a corner and approached. Opal still had on the neck gaiter, but the scarf failed to disguise her two extra inches of height or broader shoulder width. Her small friend with the slightest build was now the tallest and most muscular. Shoulders back, she marched up to the porch.

Dee pointed at her neck. "That bad?"

Opal blushed but pulled down the neck scarf, revealing a beard and mustache. She replaced the mask over her lower face.

Next, Aleesha came from the other direction. She shuffled along, her body bent. Her scarf was still in place, and wrinkles caused her face to sag. Approaching Weird Wilma's house, she mounted the steps with pain-filled effort.

"Where's Ralph?" asked Dee.

"Who cares?" Opal crossed her arms. "Ring the doorbell."

Aleesha remonstrated, "Opal! Manners! We're still human, at least."

As if on cue, a boy with an auburn shag all over his head half-walked and half-leaped down the street. He was hard to identify, but it had to have been Ralph. He approached the other three and stopped far from the porch. He sniffed. "Maybe, I not be here."

"You're still Ralph." Dee pointed to an empty space beside her. "And our friend. Come here."

Snorting, he leaped onto the porch. Dee and Aleesha took a step away, but Opal moved toward him. "No closer, or you'll regret it."

"You don't scare me, *hunter*."

Dee came between them. "This isn't the two of you." She turned toward the door. "It's her."

She wasn't going to touch a toad's tongue! Ew! She knocked on the wood with her knuckles. A few seconds passed then Weird Wilma answered the door. When she surveyed them all, she grinned.

"Hey, there."

Dee bounced from foot to foot, then forced herself to stop. "You know why we're here."

"I have no idea what you're talking about, *Red*." Weird Wilma's eyes danced with delight behind her eyeglasses.

Ralph crouched down as if ready to pounce. "Undo whatever you did! The spell you threw."

"A spell?" Weird Wilma glared at Ralph through her screen door. "Weren't you the guy who teased me when I said my grandmother was a witch and I was training with her?"

Ralph cowered, reminding Dee of a dog whose owner had scolded it. She pointed at Aleesha's wrinkles and Opal's neck gaiter. "This isn't funny,

Wilma! Soon, one of us will hurt someone or get hurt. Heather fell asleep before she started her car. I had to drive Sleeping Beauty home."

"You've read the story of *Little Red Riding Hood*." Aleesha put her hands on her hips. "We all hurt each other through the story."

Opal mumbled, "Especially me. I don't want to hurt anyone, Wilma. I'm not weird like you."

Weird Wilma flinched when Opal branded her with her familiar moniker. "Well…I never intended for anyone to get hurt. I'll reverse the spell. The effects will be gone in a couple of hours."

"Finally." Opal's muffled voice had a deep timbre.

Weird Wilma stepped back into her house. "I wanted you to realize how it feels to be an outcast. You never include me in anything. You didn't select me for the witch part, and I know why. And asking my sister to create the sets? You knew I'd help her. But you did it to avoid me."

Dee crossed her arms and gulped.

Weird Wilma jerked her thumb at herself. "I have feelings too, you know."

She slammed the door, and the foursome jumped back. They stood there, not speaking, as they gazed at the ugly toad.

Opal broke the silence. "I'm not a bad person."

"Then why do I feel like one?" asked Dee.

Dee:

Weird Wilma was in the audience when Dee and her friends took their bows at the end of the play. They had apologized to her in person at school the day after the confrontation and asked her to attend. They corrected the program to ensure Weird Wilma received credit for the sets along with her sister, and Dee had claimed they wanted her to experience people's reactions when they lifted the curtain.

Weird Wilma was clapping with everyone else and louder than most. Dee held up her hands for silence. The audience quieted down, and she approached a microphone. "Tyson, the spotlight? As we discussed?"

Tyson moved the stage light to shine on Weird Wilma. The girl's mouth dropped open.

Dee gestured to her. "Come here, Wilma."

Dazed, the awkward girl in glasses and braces stumbled to the stage. Dee grabbed her hand and held it up. "We wanted to say a special thank you to our friend, Wilma. She's the best acting coach we could've ever asked for."

The End

THE NIGHT OF THE MINDBENDER
Stoney M. Setzer

Something felt wrong tonight. Marshall Ritch couldn't put his finger on it, but he could feel it. Had he been in wolf mode, his hair would have stood on end.

It didn't help that today was June 20th and would have been his and Lizzie's wedding anniversary. She was on his mind more than usual and dwelling on Lizzie always led to him wonder if she could see him now from Heaven, to wonder what she might think of what he had become since the night of the wreck. That inevitably led to wondering what God thought about it, about him. Such thoughts were always a struggle, and anniversaries were the worst. Even though that played on his mind, it didn't account for his uneasiness.

Part of it, he knew, was his fear of being spotted. The RV had made perfect sense back when Ritch first purchased it. Mobile headquarters had been a solid idea when he was roving throughout the Southeast as a hitman, targeting miscreants beyond the reach of the law to satisfy the hunger of his wolfen side. In those days, he had drifted a lot, and the camper was perfect for that. Usually, he was long gone from an area before the authorities had noticed his handiwork, preventing them from making any connection to the drifter in the RV.

Now that he had been back in Sardis County for a while, Ritch constantly worried about how conspicuous the camper was. Trying to hide it could be a nightmare, and it seemed to get more difficult the longer he lingered here. Tonight, he was parked on a dead-end dirt road on the northeastern corner of the county—relatively less populated, but he could never be one hundred percent certain that he hadn't been noticed. It only made matters worse that tonight he actually needed to be easy to spot for two people—if they could find him, anybody else could.

The knock at the door came right on time—8:20pm, just as the shadows were beginning to get long over the summer day. Ritch opened the door to see two people standing there, a mismatched duo if ever there was one. The lady was in her seventies and seemingly as wide as she was tall. Standing just behind her was a behemoth with patchwork skin, the result of sloppy skin grafting.

"Do you really think it was a good idea for both of you to show up at the same time?" Ritch whispered as he stepped aside to let them enter. His anxiety ratcheted up a notch. *As if we weren't already conspicuous….*

"I have a mother-in-law suite in my basement, and Boyle has been living there," Mrs. Dell replied. "It made more sense for us to arrive together."

"Even if I did have to ride lying in the backseat with a blanket over me," Boyle added. "But how else would I have gotten here without drawing attention? I can't transform like you can. The whole reason I hide out in her basement is that I stand out anywhere else."

"And meeting at my house isn't exactly expedient," Mrs. Dell added. "You can relocate if you need to. I can't."

Ritch waved them off with his maimed right arm. "Fine. Point taken." Logically he knew it made sense, but for some reason it worried him. "Let's get this meeting underway, shall we?"

Even though there should have been no passersby way out here, Ritch turned up his stereo, raising the volume of the yacht rock enough to mask their conversation. He grabbed a store-brand grape soda out of the cooler and offered Mrs. Dell and Boyle their choice between that and bottled water.

"My mission was a success, for the most part," Ritch said as he popped his can open and took a sip. "Huey is dead, and so are the mutated frogs. Sheriff Carter blew up the building and presumably all of Huey's stash of caprinium with it."

Boyle's brow knotted, making his patchwork skin look that much worse. "The sheriff saw you?"

"Yeah, him and his wife."

"Girlfriend," Mrs. Dell corrected. "Dr. Staci Bridges, veterinarian. Give it time, though. Something tells me this won't be a fleeting thing between the two of them. I suspect they'll make your misnomer correct before all is said and done."

"But should we be worried about him seeing Marshall?" Boyle pressed. The level of anxiety he showed seemed out of place for a man of his powerful build. In a weird way, it made Ritch feel better to know that he wasn't the only one feeling uneasy.

"Probably not too much," she said. "Maybe this happened a bit earlier than I would have preferred, but we're all on the same side. They would have seen him eventually. And by now, Carter's seen enough strange things around here for the idea of a werewolf to at least seem plausible to him."

Ritch took another sip. "I wonder how he's doing. I had to pull him out because he hit his head right after the explosion."

"I did my candy-striping duty today and checked up on him," the old lady replied. "He's already discharged, of course. Mild concussion, plus a couple of broken ribs. No permanent damage, but he will be sidelined for a little bit. We'd just better hope nothing big happens while he is out of commission. As my Elwood would say, it would be like having to play a big game without one of our big hitters." She got a wistful look in her eye, reminding Ritch that he wasn't the only one here who had been widowed.

"But doesn't he have deputies? People to fill in for him?" Boyle inquired.

Mrs. Dell chuckled. "Yes, but his deputies all fall into one of two categories. Some are young hotshots aiming for something bigger, like Memphis PD where Sheriff Carter still has some connections. Then you have older types who wanted to leave big city law enforcement for something quieter, like Carter thought he was doing when he ran for sheriff here. Unfortunately, none of them are as experienced with the bizarre as he is, so most of what we deal with would fall beyond the outer limits of their—"

Ritch's body tensed. "Did either of you hear that?"

Boyle looked puzzled. "What, you mean the music?"

"No. Listen!"

When Janus Labs had done their experiments on him, one of the side effects had been enhanced hearing. Listening intently, he heard the sound of a motorcycle engine coming closer…closer…

"I hear it now," Mrs. Dell said. "But who in their right mind would be riding a motorcycle way out here?"

"Maybe a couple out who thinks this dirt road would make a good lover's lane?" Boyle asked.

"On a motorcycle? Before dark?" Ritch looked out the window and saw a single headlight approaching with a plume of dust rising up behind it. His apprehension intensified.

"Wouldn't be the first time a couple has done that." Boyle chuckled.

The headlight stopped a short distance away. "You two keep low for a minute," Ritch directed. "I'll go check it out." He suppressed the urge to transform into werewolf mode before he opened the door. If it was just something as innocuous as Boyle had suggested, that would be a disastrous level of overkill.

Whatever it is, it's not that innocent…

Exiting the RV, he saw the motorcycle sitting maybe fifty yards away. In the last remains of daylight, Ritch saw the rider was a female dressed entirely in red, including the helmet—scarlet, Lizzie would have called it; nothing was simply red in her sight—and the motorcycle's paint job matched its rider's attire perfectly. Clearly someone wasn't too worried about being seen.

The waning sunlight glinted off the pistol she held in her hand. She gunned the engine, and the motorcycle leapt forward like a pouncing tiger, closing the distance rapidly as she took aim.

This is a hit! Live by the sword, die by the sword…

"Take cover!" Ritch shouted as he dove for the ground. A shot rang out as his face hit the dirt. He couldn't hear the bullet strike anything, but he sensed it had come too close for comfort.

The rider was turning for another pass. Who was under that helmet?

Maybe it was somebody connected with Janus Labs—one of Dr. Lockhart's lackeys, out here to avenge either Boyle's liberation or Huey's death or both. Or it could have been someone connected to one of his own hits, a relative who had tracked him down and was here to serve as a blood avenger.

Does it matter? One can kill me just as dead as another...

"Ritch! What's going on?" Boyle shouted from the RV window.

"Stay in there and protect Mrs. Dell!"

The rider charged forward again. Still in a prone position, Ritch rolled aside, trying to distance himself from the RV. He didn't want a stray bullet to find Boyle or Mrs. Dell. Especially not her—she was the brains of their operation.

Gravel pelted Ritch as the rider darted past. Another gunshot pierced the air, again sounding as if it had sailed wide of its mark. *Why does she only shoot while she's moving?* Ritch wondered. *Why not just sit still and aim?*

Seconds later, she slowed to turn around once more. Despite the cloud of dust, the red of her outfit was clearly visible. Red like blood.

"Bring it, Little Red Riding Hood," Ritch growled. "Come on and see what big teeth I have."

While Ritch's transformations were somewhat easier during a full moon, they had never fully hinged on the lunar cycle. The moon was waxing gibbous tonight, but it made no difference. Ritch only had to concentrate for a second or two before the fur, fangs, and claws appeared. His shirt ripped, but his pants remained intact. When he was making a hit, he usually liked to have something with his mark's scent, but in this case it wasn't necessary. The rider's scent already permeated the air.

Wait for it...

As Hood swooped in close, the wolf pounced. The impact toppled the motorcycle and sent both Hood and Ritch sprawling. He recovered quickly, looking around.

No time to waste. I must end this now!

Ritch charged again, slamming into her at full tilt. She didn't have time to brace herself, but she shot her knee up between his legs. He howled in pain, his attack disrupted. Once they hit the ground, he rolled off of her to prevent her from kneeing him again.

Pull it together before she has time to regroup...

Hood had already rolled over and was struggling to her feet. Instead of attacking again, she looked around frantically, searching. She snatched her helmet off, and Ritch stopped cold at the sight of her face.

Lizzie?

She looked exactly as she had the last time Ritch had seen her—chin-length ash-blonde hair, dainty nose, the whole nine yards. Having seen her face, he realized Hood's frame was just like Lizzie's. A mix of heartache and nausea swirled through him.

At last, she spotted her motorcycle and scrambled for it. For just a moment, her back was turned to him. It would have been the perfect time to strike, if only he hadn't seen her face. Now his only thought was to revert to human form, to let her see him…

"Lizzie! It's me, Marshall!" Ritch called as soon as he had transformed enough for his vocal cords to work. "Don't you recognize me? It's me, your husband!"

Hood looked at him, but there was no recognition in her eyes, only terror. Frantically, she put her helmet back on and threw her leg over the bike.

"Lizzie!"

Just then Boyle lumbered out of the RV, banging the door into the side of the camper as he exited. Despite the noise, Hood didn't even glance in that direction. Instead, she revved the engine, keeping her eyes on Ritch. The bike roared as she turned and sped away.

"What happened?" Boyle asked.

Ritch was barely aware of him. "Lizzie!"

~~~~~

"I'm telling you, it was her!" Ritch pounded his good fist on the wall. "Don't you think I'd recognize my own wife if I saw her?"

They were back inside the RV now. Boyle looked out the window frequently, watching like a hawk. Mrs. Dell took a deep breath. "I think you saw somebody who *looked* like your wife, but…"

"Think back to the wreck! Dr. Lockhart took me from the hospital and started experimenting on me, and now look at me!" For emphasis, Ritch transformed his left hand into a werewolf's paw and back again. "Who's to say that he didn't do the same thing to Lizzie, only he's kept her hidden until now?"

"Because Lizzie died in that wreck," Mrs. Dell said gently. "You didn't."

"But what if we only *think* she died? What if she didn't? She had a closed casket funeral because…well, because they said it *had* to be that way. Who's to say she was really in there?" Ritch looked at Boyle. "That National Guard troop you were in…they did all sorts of experiments on you guys, right?"

Boyle chuckled bitterly without turning from the window. "You've seen me, and you have to ask that question?"

"Yeah, yeah, I know. Sorry. But I meant the rest of your troop, too. Were you there voluntarily, or against your will?"

"Very much against our will." Boyle looked downward. "And they did experiments on all of us, with different results and different side effects. Villanueva became an acromegalic and a firestarter. Mays gained the power of telekinesis but lost his eyesight—now there's a messed up combination for you. And Sarge…." He shook his head ruefully.

"And I'll bet that nobody ever came looking for you, right? They
~~~~~

probably put out some kind of a story where your unit was either on a top secret deployment, or they told people that you had all died, or both, or…"

Boyle nodded solemnly. "Nobody ever came looking for us that I know of. I wonder if Kayla…." His voice trailed off. He still looked out the window, only now he seemed to be looking at something a million miles away instead of right outside.

"What did you say?" Mrs. Dell asked.

"Nothing. I mean, I guess they would have had to tell our families something," Boyle said, rubbing his eyes.

Ritch could barely contain himself. "Don't you see, Mrs. Dell? That's the answer! We were both experimented on, but in different locations. There's no telling how many facilities they had. So suppose Lockhart took Lizzie too, but he experimented on her in a different location, and…"

"You're assuming that Lockhart is the only threat we have to worry about here," Mrs. Dell said. "Why exactly do you think that Lockhart has been doing all of this? When we first met, I told you that he was just a cog in a much bigger machine. Same with Huey. But do you think they've been doing all of these experiments just because they didn't have anything better to do?" She leaned in and looked him in the eye. "What do you think happened to *Mr.* Dell?"

Ritch thought about the day he had found Boyle at the ruins of Janus Labs, about his long-distance conversation with Lockhart, and about his words. *A threat is out there — a living nightmare. Our conventional military is powerless against it.* Despite the warm summer night, he felt cold.

"It's possible that Lockhart could be the explanation for why she looked like your wife," Mrs. Dell conceded, "but that's not the *only* explanation. Did she look as if she had aged any?"

"No, but…."

"And if she really is your wife, why would she be trying to kill you?"

Boyle turned from the window and pointed to one of the scars on his neck, where there had once been a pair of bolts. "Lockhart controlled me like a puppet at one point. If he can do it to me, couldn't he do it to somebody else?"

Mrs. Dell nodded. "Yes, he could…if that's really her."

Ritch threw up his hands. "If, if, if! Okay, then. *If* that is her, and *if* Lockhart is controlling her somehow, then I've still got to help her!"

Mrs. Dell bowed her head as if in prayer and was silent for a moment. For an awkward moment, Ritch wasn't sure what to do, but then he finally decided to try praying as well, just on the slim chance that God might still want to listen to him after all he had done. About the time he started, she lifted her head again.

"It seems to me that the only way to find out whether she really is Lizzie or not is to find her," Mrs. Dell sighed.

"That works for me," Ritch said.

"Don't you think that sounds a little risky?" Boyle asked. "If she's trying to kill Marshall, and we find her…."

"She didn't kill me just then," Ritch said confidently. "Once I shifted into werewolf mode, I—"

"Blew the element of surprise." Mrs. Dell rolled her eyes. "Next time she might be ready for that."

Ritch rolled his eyes. "You know, I'm learning to hate it when you have a good point, Mrs. Dell."

She chuckled and patted his good hand. "Just as long as you're listening, how you feel about it is entirely up to you. Do you think you can track her?"

"Without a doubt."

"Then let's start there. Boyle, do you think you can be ready to help him if we do find her?"

"Yes, ma'am."

"All right, Marshall, are you ready?"

"Yes, ma'am." Ritch nodded, although he wondered if he really was. The idea of Lizzie still being alive excited him—what an anniversary surprise that would be—but if it was her, what had she suffered to this point, and could they get through to her? It would almost be easier if Hood was a stranger, but that would mean Lizzie truly was gone.

"One other thing," Mrs. Dell said. "I think we had better pray before we start. No matter which way this goes, we're going to need all the help we can get."

~~~~~

For the first mile or so, Hood's motorcycle tires left a track in the dirt road that was easily seen even in the waning daylight. Ritch drove slowly with the window rolled down, so as not to miss any subtle changes in the scent. Mrs. Dell and Boyle probably couldn't tell much difference, but he could pick up the mixture of exhaust fumes and Hood's perspiration, mingling to tint the air and leave a trail just as strong as the tire tracks.

Lizzie, what did they do to you? Why would they say that you were dead? They never told anybody that I had died. So what would have been so different about you? He couldn't dismiss the possibility that Mrs. Dell might be right, but he desperately hoped she was wrong. Whatever they had done to Lizzie, maybe he could get through to her, somehow…

Please, God, if You can even hear me anymore, if that really is Lizzie, and if there's any chance at all…

Once they got back onto a paved road, Hood's tracks were no longer as visible, but Ritch could still follow her scent. Usually whenever he had to track someone this way, the person was a target, and he worried about not being able to keep the wolf's appetite in check if they did find her. *Maybe she's with Lockhart or whoever is responsible for doing this to her, and I can satisfy the hunger that way,* he thought.
~~~~~

The scent went off to one side, down a road that was paved in only the loosest definition of the term.

"I should have known," Mrs. Dell muttered.

"How's that?"

The old lady's face was grim. "Unless I miss my guess, we're about to pay a visit to an old acquaintance of mine. I won't say she's a friend, just for the truth's sake. But this only strengthens my suspicions."

"You said Lockhart isn't the only threat we have to worry about," Ritch said. "This person, would she have anything to do with the other threat?"

"Quite perceptive, aren't you?" She forced a smile. "Yes, I'm afraid she does. And with that said, we'd better all be ready. She's not from the Other Side, but she has a history with them."

The scent led them another half-mile, to a house sitting on a fair amount of acreage. Since this particular road probably didn't get much more traffic than the dirt road, this place seemed almost hidden. It occurred to Ritch that plenty of things could happen out here without anyone being the wiser—a thought that brought him no comfort at all.

"Do you still have the scent?" Mrs. Dell asked. "Is she here?"

"Yes, ma'am. Very strong. She's around here somewhere." Ritch gripped the steering wheel tightly.

She nodded grimly. "Figures. Park so that my window is facing the house, but don't get out yet, either one of you. Not until it becomes absolutely necessary."

"Until, or unless?" Boyle asked.

"Probably until."

As their headlights fell on the house, a tiny old woman came out of the front door. At first she looked surprised, as anyone might when confronted with the prospect of unexpected visitors at nightfall. In the passenger seat, Mrs. Dell tensed noticeably. "You two can get out if you want to, but let me do all the talking. And be ready for anything."

"Even me?" Boyle asked. "But Ritch looks normal. I don't."

Mrs. Dell smirked. "I promise you that you aren't the weirdest thing she's ever seen. Not by a long shot."

Once they started getting out of the RV, the tiny lady stepped off the porch and scowled. *These two ladies don't like each other very much,* Ritch realized. Mrs. Dell's tension was palpable, but there was something much harder in the other woman's glare. Something outright malevolent. Hate.

"Good evening, Val. How are you?" Mrs. Dell was doing a good imitation of her normal cheerful greeting, but he had been around her long enough to recognize it as just that—an imitation.

"I've been better. What are you doing out here?" Val snarled. Ritch sensed an extra edge to the question, as if it might have carried a deeper implication. Something between the lines that he didn't know enough context to decipher.

"You ain't seen anybody riding around out here on a motorcycle lately, have you?" Mrs. Dell asked.

Ritch knew the look on Val's face all too well. It was the look people got when they had just been caught in something, confronted with something they thought they had hidden. She tried to laugh it off. "Why do you ask? Do I look like I run a biker bar out here?"

"Never can tell with you, Val. You have your hand in so many things. By the way, how has Angela been these days? She hasn't shown her face much around town lately."

Even without knowing the history between the two of them, Ritch saw that she had struck a nerve. Val's face reddened, and she trembled with the exertion of trying to hold herself back. "You've really got some nerve, don't you, Mrs. Dell?"

In the rear of the RV, Boyle cleared his throat. Ritch glanced up at the rearview mirror to see him giving him a pointed look. Time to be ready for anything.

Something in the air shifted. A little breeze had kicked up, but there was more to it than that. The breeze carried something, a scent that Ritch caught immediately but couldn't identify. Nobody else seemed to notice it, but nobody had his augmented sense of smell. Whatever it was, he recognized something wrong about it, something ominous. As if it didn't belong to anything of this world.

Val was about to say something else when another sound interrupted her. It was the roar of a motorcycle engine, distant but getting louder. Moving fast, closing in rapidly.

Val's mouth twisted into a smirk. "Oh, you meant *that* motorcycle?" she asked. "Quite a favor you did coming out here, Mrs. Dell. Not too often the mouse comes right up to the cat."

The single headlight of a motorcycle rocketed around from behind the house. Hood veered sharply, coming straight for them.

"Get down!" Boyle shouted, lunging to protect Mrs. Dell. They both hit the ground and rolled. It looked like a rough landing, but it got Mrs. Dell out of harm's way in the nick of time.

"Lizzie!" Ritch shouted, knowing it was useless. No way she would be able to hear him over the roar of the engine. Even if she could have heard him, it wouldn't have mattered. Lizzie had never been a violent person, and this was out of character for her. Either she was being controlled by someone else like Boyle once had been, or else Mrs. Dell was right about Hood not really being Lizzie.

Val was the only one who hadn't taken cover. Instead, she was laughing her head off as Hood turned around to make another pass.

I could transform, but then Val would know my secret. That wouldn't be good, but if I don't do that, then what?

Hood buzzed them again, going between Ritch and the spot where

Boyle was sheltering Mrs. Dell. No gunfire, not yet. It was as if she was just toying with them, trying to intimidate them before striking—something Ritch never did on any of the hits he performed. Could that be played to their advantage?

Maybe, if I could transform…

Boyle caught his eye. He was moving away from Mrs. Dell, motioning for Ritch to move in the opposite direction. *What does he have in mind?* Ritch thought, trying to keep one eye on Hood as well.

Soon Ritch was in front of Val, Boyle was behind her. With surprising quickness for a man of his girth, Boyle ran up and put one hand on Val's neck from behind. Her eyes rolled back in her head and she slumped, reminding Ritch of a scene from a movie he and Lizzie used to watch together, *The Princess Bride.*

The big man looked Ritch in the eye. "Beast mode?"

"Beast mode." Ritch nodded.

It didn't take much effort on his part. Within seconds, he had morphed into wolf form, just as Hood rocketed toward them again.

She thinks she can toy with us? I've got a game for her. Ritch charged straight at Hood, playing chicken with her. It was an illogical strategy, maybe even crazy, but that was why he chose it—hoping that it was just crazy enough to work.

Hood veered off sooner that Ritch expected. Now she was racing toward the spot where Mrs. Dell still lay on the ground, trying to stay low. Boyle hadn't made his way back over to her because he was moving Val's inert form to the side. The glint of gunmetal flashed in Hood's hand.…

I'm not the real target. Mrs. Dell is! Ritch scrambled to change directions, fighting against his own momentum. He ran toward them, angry at the extra distance he had put between himself and them.

Mrs. Dell must have realized it too, because she was rolling away as best she could. She tumbled down a slope, and Hood's first shot sailed above her. Unfortunately, the slope wasn't very long, and Mrs. Dell hit the bottom quickly. Hood braked, took aim downhill at Mrs. Dell.…

Ritch pounced, biting down on Hood's arm. Screaming, she dropped the pistol. The taste of flesh and blood jibed with the feral nature of the wolf with him, and he fought the urge to feed, just in case it really was Lizzie.…

"Let me go!" Hood yelled. Her voice didn't sound like Lizzie's.

"Hold her, Ritch!" Boyle joined the fray. Hood jerked as he grabbed her from behind. Ritch sank his teeth in deeper, trying to hang on. Boyle fought to put the sleeper hold on her, but her helmet was in the way.

Thrashing, Hood tried to shake off her attackers. She was surprisingly strong, making it difficult for Ritch to keep his footing. Suddenly she jerked backward, slamming the back of her helmet into Boyle's solar plexus. It knocked the wind out of the big man, and he stumbled backward.

With Boyle off of her, she turned all of her force against Ritch. She smacked him in the forehead with her free hand. The blow staggered him, forcing him to release his bite. Pushing him off, she ran.

Ritch recovered quickly and bolted after her. Mrs. Dell was no longer at the bottom of the slope, thank God. Hood stooped down to grab her pistol, giving Ritch an opportunity. He pounced on her, and they both rolled down the hill.

As soon as they reached the bottom, Ritch scrambled to his feet. The barrel roll had dislodged Hood's helmet, doing what Boyle could not. Seizing his chance, Ritch kicked the helmet as far away from her as he could.

"You don't give up, do you?" Hood snarled with Lizzie's mouth.

"Not until you do," Ritch growled, letting his mouth change enough to permit him to speak.

"Kayla? Is that you?" Boyle's voice. He stood at the top of the hill, looking down at them. Joy flashed across his face for a moment, but it quickly gave way to horror. "Don't tell me that they got you too!"

She looked back at him with revulsion. "Who are you?"

"It's me, Dallas!" Boyle started down the hill, his arms outstretched. "I know you don't recognize me because of my face, but it's me! Baby, what have they done to you?"

Ritch looked back and forth from Hood to Boyle. How was it possible that they both saw different women when they looked at Hood?

We're in Sardis County, that's how it's possible.

"Kayla, it's me!" Boyle pleaded.

Inspiration came to Ritch. Looking right at Hood, he allowed himself to become more human. "Lizzie, I forgot how pretty your blonde hair looks in the morning sun."

Boyle did a double take. "Blonde? Her hair is pink, not blonde!"

Hood looked frantically from Ritch to Boyle and back. Her demeanor was that of a cornered animal, looking for escape. "Pink hair? Really?" Ritch asked.

"She's in a rock band," Boyle answered. "Plays a mean bass. Where's Mrs. Dell?"

"I'm over here," Mrs. Dell replied, stepping out from behind some bushes. Ritch and Boyle looked her way for just a moment, but that was all the diversion that Hood needed. She rushed toward Mrs. Dell, growling in animalistic fury.

Boyle ran after Hood, but instead of tackling her, he grabbed her by one arm and spun her around. "Kayla, what are you doing?" he pleaded.

"Get your filthy hands off of me, you dirty ape!" Hood yelled. Ritch still saw Lizzie's face, but it was twisted into an expression unlike anything she had ever shown during their years together.

A few yards away, Mrs. Dell was frozen in her tracks. "Elwood? Is that you?"

Ritch's jaw dropped. "Wait a minute! You see a *man*?"

Moving with the speed of a striking snake, Hood stomped on the instep of Boyle's foot. As he howled in pain, she thrust the heel of her free hand into his chin. Boyle was dazed just long enough to loosen his grip, and Hood jerked her arm free. She scrambled away, searching frantically for something—her pistol, no doubt. Reaching into the front of her jacket, she produced another pistol, more like a derringer. "Hands up!" she demanded as she swept it from one side to the other.

The three of them obediently reached for the sky. "Kayla! What are you doing?" Boyle asked.

Ritch shook his head. "I don't know who that is, but it's not your Kayla—or my Lizzie." *Even though she looks just like Lizzie....*

"So all three of us see different people," Mrs. Dell mused. "I see my late husband, you see your late wife...."

"Yeah, and Boyle says he sees some pink-haired chick." Ritch shook his head. "Not making that up."

"Kayla is my fiancee, thank you very much," Boyle retorted. "Or at least she was before my unit got abducted. Hopefully she hasn't given up on me coming home yet, but if she could see me now, who knows?"

"Can the three of you not shut up for one minute?" Hood snapped. Everything about her body language signaled desperation.

"You're the one who needs to be quiet," Mrs. Dell said, her tone confident and authoritative. "Gentlemen, what we have here is a mindbender."

"Mindbender? Ain't that the name of a roller coaster at an amusement park back home in Georgia?" Boyle remarked.

Ritch shook his head. "Yeah, it is, but...." His voice trailed off as he watched Hood intently. Even though she was holding a gun on them, she seemed shaky and vulnerable. All of his instincts told him to look for an opportunity to strike, but he couldn't. Despite what he knew, he still saw Lizzie's face.

"Mindbenders come from the Other Side," Mrs. Dell explained. "They can read minds, discern who someone else most wants to see. Then they project that image into the other person's mind so that they see who they want to see."

"Like I want to see Lizzie again," Ritch said solemnly. It didn't make the illusion go away, but it did make the image of his late wife seem less real to him. "That's how we all saw different people when we looked at..."

"So what's this mindbender doing here, then?" Boyle asked.

"Because of their ability to appear as anyone, they make very effective assassins," Mrs. Dell replied. "And I assume that's why you're here?"

"Yeah, that's right, Grandma!" Hood barked. "And you're the one I'm here to kill!"

Mrs. Dell was noticeably more composed than the mindbender was. "Yeah, it's the caprinium from the Other Side that gives her this ability."

She tilted her head ever so slightly toward her companions. "You know, the stuff that Dr. Lockhart and his team used when they experimented on the two of you. What made you two what you are today."

Lockhart. The name resonated in his mind, in his heart. Fury coursed through him. All of his suffering was because of Lockhart....

"Go ahead, Grandma. Get it all out now," Hood said. Now that she was focused more on Mrs. Dell, her intended target, she seemed to be slowly gathering herself. "Last chance you're ever gonna get."

Mrs. Dell ignored her. "Ritch, Boyle, don't you two wish that Lockhart was here right now to see how much trouble he has caused you?"

Just then, Lizzie's face was gone. In spite of Hood's feminine shape, her face was now that of one Dr. Kelvin Lockhart. Thinning gray hair, beady eyes behind thick glasses, and emaciated cheeks. The fury within Ritch kicked up a notch....

"Do you see what I see?" Boyle asked, but it was almost a musical voice, like imitating an old song.

"Let's go," Ritch said just before fully switching back to wolf mode.

Hood still looked like Lockhart to them as they charged at her. Panicked, she pulled the trigger, but her shot went wide. She didn't get another opportunity to shoot.

~~~~~

When they came back up the hill, Val was nowhere to be seen. They looked everywhere and found no trace of her. Mrs. Dell didn't seem the least bit surprised.

"That thing, that mindbender...it wasn't entirely human, was it?" Ritch asked as they got back into the RV.

"No, not entirely," Mrs. Dell said. "It was from the Other Side. I can't fully explain it, but that thing was as much inhuman as it was human." She raised an eyebrow at him. "Why do you ask?"

Ritch grabbed a grape soda and held it between his legs so that he could open it with his good hand. "I've been thinking a lot lately about what I've become—about what I've done since this happened. Sometimes I just wonder what Lizzie would think about me if she could see me now—or what God must think of me."

Boyle said nothing but looked on intently. Judging from the look on his face, similar questions must have gone through his mind at some point.

Mrs. Dell pondered the question for a moment. "How do you think Lizzie would have felt if you had been a soldier who had killed enemy soldiers in wartime, defending our country? Protecting the innocent?"

"I suppose she would have been all right with that," Ritch replied. Boyle nodded in agreement.

Mrs. Dell put her hand on his shoulder. "As far as I'm concerned, you're like a soldier, only in this case you've been defending our entire world from a completely different kind of enemy. And in the past, I know
~~~~~

you have struck against those who have committed extreme wickedness and protected innocent people in the process. Haven't you?"

"Yes, ma'am, I suppose so." He thought about all the wicked people he had eliminated in the past—drug dealers, child abusers, human traffickers. All people who might have continued ruining lives had he not intervened.

"This time, it was an assassin, and you saved my life in the process. Does that help you any?"

"Somewhat." Ritch shook his head. "I can't believe that there's something out there that could get into my head like that. Lizzie had been on my mind before you showed up...."

"And Kayla's been on my mind for a while too. I was one hundred percent convinced that she *was* Kayla."

"You see what I mean about Lockhart not being the only thing that we have to worry about?" Mrs. Dell asked.

"So now what are we supposed to do?" Boyle asked.

"I think we had better be ready," Mrs. Dell said. "Tonight proves that the Other Side does not rest. They still have designs on our world."

"And somebody wanted to kill you because you knew," Ritch said. "We've got to be ready, no matter what."

The End

WOODLAND CRAVINGS
Rachel A. Greco

The wolf was always hungry. The hunger was as persistent as a shadow and as tenacious as the trumpet vines climbing the trees, ripping him apart until he would soon only be a ravenous appetite.

The hunger was the predator, he its prey.

No matter how many rabbits, deer, or foxes he devoured, the emptiness remained, a hollow hole demanding to be filled.

For some reason, the wolf knew that the only thing that could end this relentless hunger was the young woman walking along the path. She smelled like summer evenings and tenderness.

But he could never get close to her. The cloak she wore, the color of a slit throat, seared his eyes, and he had to flee, shame and desperation teasing him like the girl's delicious scent.

The girl didn't give chase, never even saw him. Her eyes were always on the path before her. Where it led, the wolf didn't care. He only cared about filling this cavern inside him.

~~~~~

It felt almost like blasphemy to admit, even to herself, that Laurel didn't want to walk into the forest to see her grandmother. Once, the jaunt had been the highlight of her week. The two would chat over her mother's fresh-baked apple stack cake or buttermilk biscuits while sipping pine-needle tea.

Then her grandmother would show her the latest cat blanket she'd stitched or Laurel would help her weed the tomatoes or flowers, laughing at her grandmother's terrible jokes.

But ever since her grandmother's sickness, she hadn't been the same. Her grandmother's laughter had dried up, her temper shortening.

Laurel glanced at the painting of her grandmother and her great-aunt Agnes that hung over the dining room table. Grandmother Gladys smiled, her blue eyes wrinkled in laughter at some secret joke, hair escaping her bun. A pang of longing for the happy grandmother shot through Laurel.

Gladys's sister, Agnes, though similar in features, scowled, as if she couldn't believe her sister dared smile for the painter.

Grandmother had stopped talking about her sister after some kind of falling out a few years ago.

"Here you are, Laurel." Her mother rolled into the dining room in her wheelchair and dumped some biscuits into a basket on the table. She
~~~~~

handed the basket to Laurel. "Maybe these will make Mother feel better."

The rolls smelled buttery, golden, and magical. Laurel wanted to shove one into her mouth, but instead closed the cloth over the biscuits to hold in the heat for as long as possible.

"You've been baking your healing herbs into these treats for weeks now, and nothing has changed," Laurel told her mother. Although Grandmother was no longer sick, the illness had warped her like time mottled the skin with wrinkles and spots. Except these changes were worse because they were inside her.

Laurel glanced at her grandmother's portrait again, hungry for the days when her grandmother laughed quicker and smiled easier.

"These are baked with a new concoction." Mother nodded at a jar of purple powder on the kitchen counter. "Chrysanthemums and asters I picked from our garden under that full moon two nights ago."

Laurel looked down at the biscuits. Thankfully, they weren't purple, but she'd eaten enough of her mother's magical treats to know they always tasted delicious, no matter what bizarre ingredients her mother put into them or what color they were.

She didn't have high hopes for this latest experiment, but judging by the way her mother caressed the jar of purple powder and the way her gaze lingered on the basket,, she did. So Laurel kept her mouth shut.

She grabbed the red cloak hanging by the door that Grandmother had given her two weeks ago to protect her from wolves. She didn't understand why Grandmother had just recently become concerned about them; they'd never roamed these mountains before that Laurel knew about, but Grandmother was apt to become as fiery as a dragon these days when her requests were denied, so Laurel put it on.

As she did, she told her mother, "When I get home, I'll finish mending the table." Because her father had died when Laurel had only been five, and her mother had been paralyzed from the waist down since Laurel had been a little girl — unable to get to her concoctions in time — most chores fell on Laurel's shoulders. She didn't mind; they made her feel useful and took her mind off the changes in Grandmother.

"No need to rush." Mother waved her hand. "It's still standing, which is all that matters." She wheeled over and handed Laurel the basket. "I'll have soup ready when you return."

Before Laurel walked out the door, Mother gave her daily mandate: "And stay on the path."

The basket lowered in Laurel's hands as guilt dropped stones into her stomach. She had never told Mother about the weeks she'd wandered off the path to indulge in long conversations with a young man. Another kind of hunger, deep and simmering and needy, bubbled to the surface, but she clamped a lid on it. She had no time to dwell on such fantasies.

With the cloak draped over her shoulders, and the basket of magical treats on her arm, Laurel journeyed through town, its stone buildings rosy-red with the late afternoon May sunshine.

"Give my regards to your Grandmother," Whitaker, the watchmaker, said as she passed the clock tower.

"I will," Laurel lied. Grandmother didn't care about anyone's regards anymore, and the illness had taken much of her memory. The first time she'd been well enough to hear and understand her granddaughter, Laurel had given their neighbor's regards, and Grandmother had said, "She can keep her regards, and I'll keep these." She'd grabbed a blueberry muffin and stuffed most of it into her mouth.

Laurel was the only one who knew how much the illness had taken from her grandmother. Not even Mother knew, for then Laurel would have to explain how she had skipped visiting Grandmother for three entire weeks.

Laurel could already see the disappointment and shock filling her mother's face—a sword she didn't want to fall on yet. So she buried her secret deep inside where she buried her cravings for those too-short afternoons spent with a man who had butterfly-soft blue eyes and scratched hands that were somehow both rough and gentle. She threw some dirt on the image. Good daughters and granddaughters didn't chase after their own desires at the expense of those who needed them.

As soon as Laurel stepped into the woods, the bluebirds and sparrows stopped singing. A fog swirled around the trees, and though late spring had settled on the forest south of town with a warm embrace, leaves unfurling and wildflowers blossoming, here it felt like winter. The trees flung naked, white branches into the air, and the ground was carpeted in pine needles and mushrooms.

This was the other reason Laurel no longer enjoyed her jaunts into the forest. The woods weren't her woods anymore; they belonged to some shadowy coldness, lost in a deep slumber, and Laurel didn't know how to wake them.

She kept her gaze forward, trying to ignore the way the wind moaned through the trees, as if crying out her name—a wordless plea for help. There was nothing she could do. Besides, the last time she had helped someone, she had strayed off the path and lost her grandmother.

Laurel's feet stumbled at the place where she'd gone off the path over a month ago. That day, a yell, like someone in the grip of pain, had yanked her to a stop. Without even thinking, she'd stepped off the path toward the sound. Laurel could excuse this behavior—any decent person would have rushed to help someone after such an anguished cry.

She'd come upon a man doubled over, swear words flying out of his mouth.

"What's wrong?" Laurel had asked.

The man looked up, his dark blue eyes open and honest like a child's and as soft as butterfly wings, but his face twisted as he cradled his hand. "I was an idiot and hammered my own thumb. I think I broke it."

It hadn't even occurred to Laurel to be afraid of the man. He had a need, and she could fix it. She had been taking care of her mother and grandmother all her life, so it was natural to step close and examine the man's thumb, then create a splint for it out of bark and twine.

The man, who introduced himself as Hunter, had been replacing a window on his new cabin when he injured his hand. He'd only lived out here a few months after escaping his drunken father in town.

His honest expression wasn't the only trusting thing about him, and he poured out words like a flooded river, as if he'd just been waiting for someone to talk to. He seemed to need Laurel more than her grandmother with his swollen, purple thumb and the loneliness that gushed out as he told her about his father, his newly built house in the forest, and the peace he had found in the woods.

No, Laurel didn't blame herself for helping Hunter that day. But she did blame herself for staying, for giving him the treats that had been baked with love and magic for her grandmother.

And she unquestionably was to blame for returning to Hunter's house the next day and the next for three weeks instead of visiting Grandmother. Laurel had let Hunter's booming laugh and quiet dreams force the thought of Grandmother to the back of her head. It had just felt so good, like a warm bath on a cold evening, to do something solely for herself.

And it was so easy to be with Hunter; both of them had experienced the ripping loss of something vital at a young age—Hunter's mother had died after giving birth to him, and she had lost her father to the mines.

Laurel taught Hunter the names of the trees, birds, and mushrooms, and he drank it all in with that easy, childish innocence, asking so many questions that they never stayed on one topic for long.

She had let the current of happiness carry her away from her other responsibilities until the guilt from lying to her mother every week built a wall and dammed up the current of warmth.

One day, she left Hunter with only a weak excuse and farewell, and had found Grandmother sweaty, pale, and moaning, in the throes of a sickness that was not kind to the elderly. Laurel had rushed home and returned with a potion from her mother.

Laurel visited Grandmother every day that week until night brushed the trees with its cool breath. Her mother also needed her and didn't like Laurel staying in the woods at night, or she would have slept there.

At the end of five days, when she returned with a healing cake from her mother, Grandmother had been sitting up on the couch. Grumpy, confused, and with more wrinkles after battling the sickness, but at least she was healed physically.

Laurel hadn't seen Hunter since she left him that day, and she longed to step off the path now and see if he had finished his house. If the pine cones she'd made into a wreath still hung on his front door.

She had stopped by once on her way to Grandmother's house to explain about her illness. He hadn't been home, so she'd left a note. He had never responded to her, and Laurel was too much of a coward to visit him and be rejected in person, so she hadn't tried to visit him again. But she still volunteered every day to fetch the mail, and her heart mewled for her to step off the path now and walk the short distance to his house.

But her grandmother needed her. Shutting the door on her own dreams and the longing coiling inside, Laurel turned away from the path that led to Hunter's house.

"It took you long enough," Grandmother said from where she sat on the couch knitting an orange mitten. Laurel hoped it wasn't for her; she loathed the confines of mittens and preferred to stuff her hands into her pockets. Another thing that Grandmother had forgotten, unless the mittens were for Mother.

"Sorry, Grandmother." Laurel swallowed the sharp retort she wanted to say. These days, in Grandmother's presence, she swallowed more than she spoke.

Grandmother huffed and grabbed one of the biscuits from the basket placed on the table near her.

Laurel sat across from her in her customary spot, a well-loved armchair that smelled of wood smoke and memories, and drew her cloak closer. It felt like the fog had followed her inside, and the fireplace was cold and empty.

"Would you like me to build a fire?" Laurel fell easily into the role of taking care of others, a role she wore more comfortably than this heavy cloak.

Grandmother shook her head. "I'm fine. Here, have some tea." She poured a cup of steaming, amber-colored liquid and handed it to Laurel.

The brew smelled of pine and lemon—one of Laurel's favorite mixtures. At least Grandmother remembered that. She took a sip, letting the familiar flavors warm her and melt some of her cold thoughts.

"I don't understand why you insist on living out here all by yourself, Grandmother. It would be so much easier to take care of you if you lived in town with Mother and me."

Grandmother rummaged around in the basket for another biscuit. "As you get older and can do less and less, you treasure your independence more and more." She stuffed one of the biscuits into her mouth.

Laurel averted her eyes; her grandmother's eating habits had become disgusting since the illness.

"The dishes need washing, and the kitchen needs sweeping," Grandmother said with her mouth full. "If you wouldn't mind," she tacked on as an afterthought

An aching for the old days sighed out of Laurel. Once, she and Grandmother had talked for hours about the boys in Laurel's class, her mother's latest concoctions, and the animals that had visited Grandmother's part of the forest. Then Laurel would help her with her chores as repayment for the tea, attention, and good conversation.

Now Grandmother seemed to measure her worth more for how many chores she could accomplish than as her granddaughter. How could sickness change someone so completely? Perhaps Grandmother blamed Laurel for leaving her alone for so long, though she had never mentioned it and didn't usually hold grudges.

Laurel set down her empty tea cup, removed her cloak, and walked through the sitting room to the kitchen. Dirty cups, plates, and bowls lay in piles on the counter. She expected the mess, but it still made her nose wrinkle in disgust. Fog pushed against the window over the door that led to the forest as if trying to come inside.

She shouldered past the temptation to flee out the back door to Hunter's house where she was valued for herself. Where she could exist outside the needs of others, where she could just breathe and be.

But Laurel now knew the cost of such a decision, and she wasn't willing to pay it.

Instead, she grabbed a bucket and filled it with dirty dishes. Her grandmother used the stream behind the cottage for drinking and washing. It murmured condolences to Laurel as she came near. The only plant that was blooming was the flame azalea that Laurel and her grandmother had planted three springs ago. The golden-red blooms were so shockingly bright against the surrounding dreary brown and white landscape, like little candle flames, that Laurel dropped the bucket of dishes.

Her grandmother—the one who had taught her how to sew, pointed out the birds in the forest, took her mushroom hunting, listened to her talk about nothing for hours—felt so close, as if she was standing beside her.

Laurel glanced around, but, of course, didn't see her. Just the ever-present fog, the too-white and bare branches, and the eternal sighing of the creek.

The burning glow of the azaleas drew Laurel closer. She touched them as Grandmother barked at her for leaving the door open—such a harsh difference from the delicate, bright blooms, from how Grandmother used to be.

Then, the question struck again. How could sickness have changed her grandmother from a person as bright as these blooms to someone as cold and dreary as the fog slinking through the forest?

Laurel's thoughts turned to someone else who would better match that harshness—a scowling, harsh-angled face that she'd seen in a portrait that morning.

Her heart pressing too close to her chest, Laurel spun and darted into the kitchen. A clump of azaleas that she didn't remember picking dangled from her hand.

She stopped behind the woman in the chair who had resumed knitting, the basket in front of her now only containing one biscuit.

"You're not my grandmother." Laurel's voice came out surprisingly strong, considering how the world seemed to tilt around her. "You're her sister, my great-aunt Agnes." It was obvious to her now, when she'd compared her grandmother to the woman in the painting without sickness skewing her view.

Silence as brittle and near to breaking as ice stretched between them, then, "I'm actually surprised it took you this long to find out. You visited Gladys so much."

Laurel stepped around the sofa so she could see the imposter better. Now that she knew there were differences, she could see them clearly. Agnes's eyes lacked her grandmother's laugh lines, and more frown lines twisted from her mouth. The sharp angles Laurel had attributed to her grandmother's sickness were just the hard planes of the woman's natural expression.

She should have realized it sooner. Her mistakes and guilt at straying off the path and leaving Grandmother for so long had been like wearing weak glasses that had blurred her vision.

"What have you done to her? Where's my grandmother?" The azalea petals crushed in Laurel's hand.

"Your precious grandmother is dead. I killed her one night when you were gone, when she was weak from the sickness. I got enough information from her though to learn enough to fool you. Then it wasn't hard to pretend to be ill until you brought plenty of those magical cakes." She licked her lips, but kept her gaze on the mitten she knitted, as if Laurel wasn't worth her attention.

Laurel closed her eyes. Grandmother dead, and her home and woods overtaken by this terrible hag. But Laurel had a hand in it too, for if she had been here the whole time, perhaps the hag wouldn't have dared kill…the thought faltered in her mind. She couldn't think it.

"Don't blame yourself," Agnes said as if she knew what Laurel was thinking, and Laurel opened her eyes again. "If you had been here, I would have killed you and gotten the cakes directly from your mother. This was easier, and I didn't even have to do any cleaning." A sly, slick smile slipped onto her mouth. It didn't seem to belong, as if her face had been created only to shape frowns.

Laurel was still trying to accept that her grandmother would never again tell her to wipe her feet on the doormat, never share another cake with her, never knit her another sweater. It was an uphill battle, and her mind kept stumbling to make sense of the loss. It would have been kinder for both of them if the sickness had killed her grandmother.

"You killed your own sister? Why?" Laurel clutched the azalea petals to her chest as if it was her grandmother's hand.

Agnes still didn't look up at Laurel. "I grew weary of being alone and reading Gladys's letters, before she stopped corresponding, about how wonderful it was to have a grandchild like you.

"What happened between you?"

The woman took a sip of tea, then continued knitting. "Two years ago, Gladys realized I was still dabbling in dark magic. She refused to give me any of your mother's treats or the recipes, and when I replied a little nastily, she cut off our correspondence.

"But thankfully, you've been able to give me both of the things I wanted." Agnes glanced up, her gaze haunted with a hunger that had nothing to do with food and everything to do with a deeper, greedy longing.

Laurel took a step backward, recognizing the expression from her own reflection.

"When I found your precious grandmother's house and saw that you'd left for the day, I took my chance. As I was about to do the spell, that boy had to poke his nose in my business, but I took care of him too. Then, I got all the information I could—"

Laurel stopped listening. Her mind had finally grasped that her grandmother was gone, stuck on the image of her form still and unmoving, killed by her own sister. All Laurel saw beyond that was fog and despair—spewing from this woman.

The fog threatened to slither inside her, blocking out all sunshine and warmth. But Laurel wouldn't let it; she couldn't. She had to protect her mother; she wouldn't let this woman reach out a greedy hand to her too. Laurel had to leave this place tainted by the hag, had to make sure her mother was all right, and finally tell her the truth.

Acting out of habit, Laurel grabbed the basket. Inching her way backward, her hand fumbled for the doorknob behind her, not willing to turn her back on Agnes.

The woman's eyes narrowed, as if sensing her prey was about to escape. "If you tell your mother about any of this, I'll make her life miserable. I have ways of finding out."

"I thought you needed her to make the treats?" Laurel's voice trembled like leaves in a winter wind.

"Yes, but I could still cause her pain. And I don't need you anymore. Having a granddaughter isn't as lovely as I thought it'd be." Agnes twisted her knitting needle, and it flashed in the candlelight, now a dagger.

Laurel grasped the doorknob and slipped outside as the hag stood, dagger poised to throw. She sprinted down the path into the fog, thinking only about how to protect her mother from such a monster.

She didn't see the shape until it was right in front of her.

A wolf materialized out of the fog, its fur just as thick and white. Its black eyes stared at her with desperate hunger.

Too late, Laurel realized she wasn't wearing her cloak.

The wolf lunged for her throat.

~~~~~

The wolf had waited outside the cottage until the girl exited. When she came out without her cloak, he wanted to howl his glee at the sky. Finally, he could end this agony.

Distracted by hunger, he let himself be seen by his prey—a foolish mistake. Her bud-green eyes tugged at something in him, like a dream he couldn't remember, from before the craving had taken over. But then, it was gone, devoured by the ever-present hunger, and he could control himself no longer. He leapt at the girl.

At the last moment, he realized the delicious smell was stronger in the basket. He shifted toward it, running into the girl and knocking her over.

All the wolf cared about was eating the thing that had fallen out of the basket. It smelled of new beginnings and sweet daylight. He gobbled up the treat.

The desperate appetite that had reached into every waking moment, demanding more, vanished.

At first, a different, smaller emptiness took its place, for he wasn't sure what to do or who he was now that his obsession had disappeared.

Then, a warmth as gentle and unhurried as spring crept through him.

~~~~~

Laurel was still alive. She hurt and coughed too much to be dead. Dirt choked her, and the world spun. She stopped rolling and breathed deep, wondering if these would be her last breaths, sure the wolf would return for another attempt.

When she could breathe without choking on dirt and didn't hear any darting paws or snarls, she sat up.

Hunter, covered in ragged, filthy clothes, sat beside her mother's basket, staring at his hands as if he'd never seen them before.

"Hunter?" Laurel's voice sounded as if it was still clogged with dirt and grass. She spat then swallowed, looking around for the wolf. "We have to get out of here. There was a wolf—"

"I know." His butterfly-wing blue eyes met hers. "It was me."

Laurel could only stare at him, wondering if he'd just said the bizarre thing that she thought he had.

Hunter swallowed, as if fortifying himself. "A few weeks after you left me, I went to visit your grandmother." His gaze flicked to her face and away, and she read the words that he didn't say—'hoping to see you.' "There were two women talking inside. One of the women opened the door, yelled some words at me that I didn't understand, and threw some kind of powder at my face. And then I was a wolf."

He looked at his hands as if reassuring himself that they were not paws. "I'd forgotten about it, even who I was, until just now, when I ate that biscuit."

Laurel's great-aunt had probably thought he'd heard and seen too much, though it sounded like Hunter had no idea one of them was about to kill the other. Laurel wanted to pull him tight for a hug, to let the warmth of her touch wash away the nightmare. She had lost her grandmother, but Hunter had lost himself.

He stood, his gaze assessing her dirty, torn trousers and shirt. "Are you all right? I'm so sorry that I lunged at you." He glanced away as if too ashamed to look her in the eyes. But he held out a hand to her.

Laurel grasped it, and the three freckles on the back that she had counted while he'd hammered a shutter seemed to ground her.

Hunter didn't let go of her hand, which was fine with her. It was the only normal, familiar thing that had happened to her today, and she clung to it as if his touch could keep her from sinking into the fog of the witch's words.

"I'm fine." Physically at least. It would take her a long time to heal, if ever, from learning that her sweet, silly grandmother had been murdered by her own sister. And that Agnes had turned Hunter into a wolf that had almost eaten her. Laurel didn't know what to do with that knowledge, so she thrust it away. At least they were alive and both human. For now.

"Let's walk while we talk." Laurel tugged Hunter down the path. There was no sign of the hag behind them, but Laurel wanted to put as much distance between them as they could. She wanted that interloper out of Grandmother's house and this foul fog out of the forest, but she would settle for distance until they came up with a plan.

With his free hand, Hunter handed her the basket and asked, "What were you running from?"

"My great-aunt Agnes. She killed my grandmother." Laurel stumbled at the words, and Hunter kept her from falling. "She's probably the one who turned you into a wolf."

"Why would she do that to her sister?"

"Because she had no heart. And, supposedly, she was tired of being lonely and wanted the treats my mother bakes." Laurel knew her mother's treats were special, but because she had grown up eating and helping bake them, some of the extraordinariness had worn off. She couldn't fathom why anyone would kill someone for them. Yes, they could keep someone younger for a long time, but not forever. They weren't worth murder.

"But to do that to her own sister?" Hunter muttered.

Laurel thought of the haunted shadows in Agnes's eyes. "Her envy of her sister and desire for these treats poisoned her."

"They are pretty tasty." Hunter eyed the empty basket and smacked his lips. "They're the ones that heal people? The ones you brought me that first day at my house?"

In explaining why she had been in the forest the day of their first meeting, Laurel had mentioned the healing properties of her mother's treats. "Not only that. They can also keep people young. Not forever," she added as Hunter's eyebrows shot into his curly black hair. "They can slow aging, depending on how much wood sorrel my mother is able to find and how many dreams she's able to put into the dough."

"Dreams?" Hunter blinked in confusion.

"I don't understand how the magic part works. You'll have to ask her."

After a few steps, Hunter asked, "If people found out that the treats your mother baked could do that, you would both be rich."

Laurel shook her head. She too had once wondered why they had to keep that property of the treats a secret. Until her mother had explained it to her. "Probably just dead."

She had spent enough time with Hunter to know that he would never share this secret; all he wanted was a peaceful life in the forest.

"So what happened in there?" Hunter's question nudged her back to the imposter in Grandmother's house. Laurel didn't want to return to that place of darkness,, but Hunter deserved to know who the lady was who had cursed him. So, she told him, her voice coming out like a scared rabbit, hopping through her words.

When she'd finished, Hunter gripped her hand more tightly. He didn't speak. What words could heal such a wound?

After a while, Hunter said, "I'm glad the hunger I felt as a wolf was just for your mother's treats." His lips curved up, but there was an apology in his eyes, which was ridiculous. He had nothing to apologize for; his attack had been the witch's fault. "They are pretty delicious."

Hunter's laugh was a river that carried Laurel's thoughts to afternoons spent holding nails for him and teasing him about his aim. She let the cleansing sound wash away the worries about her mother.

"I'm glad you didn't eat me," she told him.

"Me too." His tone lightened. "You probably would have gotten stuck in my teeth."

Now a laugh—raw and rough, but still a laugh—erupted from Laurel. "I would probably have caused you all kinds of indigestion."

They took a few more steps in a comfortable silence.

"What are we going to do now?" Hunter's question swept all the lightness out of her.

"We can't let that witch stay in my grandmother's house." Disgust sharpened her voice into iron. "And we can't let her taint the forest anymore with her presence." Laurel gestured at the fog. The ache from missing the rustling, vibrant leaves of the forest made her stomach throb.

Hunter said nothing, and Laurel was thankful for his small gift of quiet that let her decide what to do since it was her family that had been destroyed by the witch.

After a few minutes, a loose sketch of a plan formed in Laurel's mind. "The witch isn't the only one who has magic. My mother does too. We can use that to our advantage."

She explained her idea, and Hunter shook his head. "I'll be the one to go inside. You've already risked yourself enough today.".."

Objections rose like a pack of wolves: it was *her* grandmother who had been killed, Hunter shouldn't have the witch's blood on his hands, but fiercest of all, she didn't want him to get hurt or turned into a wolf again. Watching that would probably rip her up worse than learning of her grandmother's death.

Did that make her a terrible granddaughter? Shame blew a cold breath through her. But Laurel reminded herself that she had had years with her grandmother, and her death had loomed like winter — coming closer all the time. Inevitable.

She didn't want to lose Hunter after just learning what his hands felt like in hers and how his gaze was her safe haven, even if she had closed the door on him and any dreams of a future together. But his death wouldn't just be a closing door, it would be a disappearing door with no hope of reappearing. And it would be her fault.

As if he saw the conflict warring in her expression, Hunter stopped their progress on the path. He met her gaze with his butterfly-soft one, his hands gentle, yet firm on her arms.

"You don't have to take care of everyone all the time, Laurel. Let someone take care of you for once. It will give you the strength to keep caring for others. Please let me do this one thing for you. Let me show you how much I care about you." His gaze warmed her like fire.

Beneath such a tender look that saw into her deepest parts, Laurel felt bare and exposed. But also seen. Loved. "I—" No other words came. Just tears as she leaned into his familiar smell — wood smoke and pine sap.

She couldn't remember someone actually asking her what she wanted or offering to carry her burden. It slid like a saddle off a weary horse's back. Who would she be with room to be herself? To run after the things that filled her up instead of those that drained her? The door to her dreams cracked open, full of possibilities.

"I'm sorry," she murmured at the ground. "It's just…no one's ever offered to do that for me."

Hunter grasped her jaw and angled his eyes on hers. "Never apologize for crying."

Laurel nodded.

"We'll figure out how to share our burdens together." The statement was crammed with promises and hopes, pushing the door open even wider.

The problem of the witch almost seemed like a bad dream, something they could easily deal with together.

They stopped at Hunter's house so he could grab some cleaner clothes and shoes. Laurel waited on the fog-shrouded path, not yet ready to see his house and open her heart to all those memories and mistakes. She had to stay focused on getting that woman out of her grandmother's house, out of their forest.

Soon Hunter rejoined her, clad in loose trousers and a blue shirt that made his eyes burn blue. Laurel clutched her hands so she wouldn't pull him in for a kiss. Maybe, hopefully, there would be time for that later. Days and years.

When they reached her cottage in town, Laurel asked Hunter to wait outside in her mother's garden. She didn't want to explain him yet.

"Mother, I'm home," Laurel called as she set the empty basket on the table in the dining room.

"Oh, good. I just made some leek and onion soup for dinner. How's your grandmother?" Mother wheeled into sight through the kitchen door, her hair in a messy bun, flour splattered on her apron.

Laurel had never been good at lying to her mother, and it always chewed her up until she confessed. Besides, she needed her mother's help, so she settled on a half-truth. "Not well. I'm going to take her more treats. Can you make one of your illusion cakes?"

Her mother frowned. Illusion cakes were tricky to make and hardly ever needed. "What for?"

Laurel scrambled for some kind of plausible explanation. "Grandmother keeps going on about her wrinkles and spots. She's never liked them," that was true enough, "and an illusion cake might calm her down. Or at least give her something else to think about."

Her mother's green-speckled gaze flitted over Laurel's face as if searching for a lie. Laurel couldn't tell if her mother believed her or not as she wheeled back into the kitchen.

"Very well, but as you know, it's one of my more complicated recipes, so it will take a while, and I will need your help."

"Of course." Laurel took her apron off the hook and entered the well-lit, organized kitchen.

Her mother began opening jars, and Laurel grabbed ingredients from the shelves her mother couldn't reach and helped chop them. When her mother wasn't looking, she added a few more slices of ginger, a flower found on the coast, and a pinch of her own hair to make the recipe stronger. Hunter was quite a bit larger than her grandmother, and the recipe would need something of Laurel to work.

Thankfully her mother didn't ask her any more questions, but she also didn't hum or chatter like she often did while they baked. But Laurel couldn't worry about whether her mother believed her or not; all her thoughts were tangled up in their plan.

~~~~~

"I have them." In the garden, Laurel handed the basket filled with
~~~~~

warm ginger cakes to Hunter. The setting sun streaked his dark curls with a golden glow.

"Those look and smell wonderful." Hunter gazed at the cakes as if he wanted to fall into their spicy, nutty deliciousness.

Laurel grabbed his hand and pulled him back into the forest. "Well, you'll have to wait. The magic will only last a few minutes after you eat one."

They stopped at a clump of rhododendron bushes that grew outside Grandmother's cottage. Laurel didn't want to take the risk of the hag overhearing or seeing them. This close to the cottage, anger at the woman's betrayal bubbled hot and furious inside her.

Laurel gave Hunter one of the illusion cakes. "Eat it right before you enter so its effects will last as long as possible."

Hunter stared at the treat then at her, a sliver of doubt in the twist of his lips. "You're sure this will work?"

Laurel nodded. "I put a piece of myself in the dough so that the witch will see the right illusion."

Hunter's lips twitched as if not sure whether to laugh or ask more questions. Instead, he shrugged. "It should taste delicious then."

The possibility that Laurel could lose him today too rolled over her , crushing her lungs.

"Are you sure you don't want me to?" she managed to get out.

"I'm sure." He clasped her fingers with his free hand. "Let me do this for you, Laurel. Please. It's the least I can do."

"I haven't done anything for you."

Hunter shook his head at her, like she was a silly child. "Nothing but put a splint on my hand, help me fetch and carry wood, clean my house and make it look like more than a shack, teach me about the creatures that share this forest, and fill my lonely days with laughter. That's all."

"But you did those things, well, some of them, for me too," Laurel protested.

"I definitely didn't help you with your chores." Hunter winked at her, then his expression firmed. "That's what love is, Laurel. A partnership, a sharing of burdens. I hope we can learn to do it together."

"Me too." The whisper was a sigh, a longing, a nudging at the door to her dreams.

Hunter leaned forward. His kiss was as sweet as wild honey and as fleeting as spring rain. Laurel longed for more, but they had to uproot the evil invading this place.

"I'll see you soon," Hunter murmured hot and fervent against her face, then he disappeared into the fog, thickest around the cottage.

Laurel couldn't just stand around waiting, not knowing what was happening to him. She crept behind the rhododendrons and leaned against a silver birch to peek through the fog toward the lights in Grandmother's house. She could just make out a shape by the front door.

Hunter ate the cake, then paused for a moment while he morphed into her. What an odd sensation to see herself this way. Her dress needed to be mended in the back, and her hair needed a good brushing. Then he—as her—entered the cottage.

Laurel snuck up to the door and pressed her ear against it, the thundering of her heart making it difficult to hear.

"You came back? Do you *want* to die?" Surprise raised the impostor's voice. Good. She hadn't known they were coming, and she believed, for now, that Hunter was her.

"No. I want to know what you did with my grandmother's body so I can lay her to rest." Hunter's voice was a little rougher than hers, but hopefully the hag wouldn't notice the difference.

A step creaked on the wooden floor. Probably Hunter moving closer to Agnes, though Laurel couldn't be sure. She wished she could see, but there were no windows her height, and she couldn't risk being seen.

"You don't need to worry about that," the hag said. "Although I had more envy than love for my sister, I did bury her."

Another step as Hunter neared his prey. Or was it the witch nearing *her* prey?

"You know, I didn't know my granddaughter very well, but I do recall that she was quite a bit shorter than you. And her eyes were not blue."

Laurel's stomach fell to the floor. She and Mother must not have made the illusion strong enough, or the witch's own twisted magic must have been able to see through her mother's.

Laurel pressed her hand against the door, but before she could open it, there was quick movement, then a shout.

The door flew open at Laurel's push.

The witch's finger was pointed, her blotchy face glowing with triumph. The expression caused panic to rise up like floodwaters in Laurel, threatening to drown her.

Hunter was nowhere to be seen.

Then, a squeaking sound, and Laurel glanced at the table where the witch was pointing. A squirrel stood there, chattering away, its tail flicking back and forth.

"Hunter." Laurel rushed to him, but the squirrel darted away, apparently not recognizing her. Loss sheared through her, then anger bubbled up in the empty spot. Laurel wouldn't let this woman take anything from her again.

She picked up a fire poker from the fireplace and swung it at the hag.

The woman darted away, holding her hands up. "Now, now, dearie. You wouldn't want to hurt an old woman, would you?"

Laurel very much wanted to hurt *this* old woman who had caused her so much agony in such a short amount of time. She wasn't a killer, but to take care of those she loved, this witch had to die.

With a cry rising out of the depths of her pain, Laurel swung the poker again.

But the witch had taken advantage of Laurel's brief hesitation to dart away, faster than was natural for an old woman.

Something cold and sharp burned Laurel's throat.

The witch's voice, hard as frost, filled her ear. "You've caused me enough trouble. I think it's time you joined your grandmother." The cold edge of the dagger dug into Laurel's throat, and she sent a quiet apology to Hunter and her mother for failing them.

"Take your hands off my daughter." The voice was as firm and even as an iron-forged blade.

The witch whirled Laurel around to face the door. In the entrance was her mother, sitting on their neighbor's horse. A rope around her waist bound her to the saddle. The horse shook its head as if annoyed that its rider had taken it through such a narrow opening.

"Mother?" Laurel didn't know her mother could ride, especially because she was paralyzed.

"Elaine?" Agnes asked, her tone as surprised as Laurel's.

"Let's stop the games." Laurel's mother lowered the reins. "You're here for my magic, not for anyone else."

"Well, to be precise," the witch said, her arm tightening around Laurel's middle. "I'm here for your baked treats. They make me feel so good, as if I could live another sixty years."

Laurel's mother's expression soured. "You killed my mother, didn't you?"

"Had to be done, I'm afraid. Now, promise to give me more of those treats, the kind that let you live longer, and I'll let your daughter go free."

Mother scowled down at Agnes, then reached into a saddlebag. She threw a muffin at the witch. Agnes let go of Laurel to catch it, and she darted away from the witch toward the center of the room.

The witch ate the muffin in two bites. Laurel watched for the familiar signs of wrinkles disappearing, her white hair darkening.

Instead, her hair turned green. Leaves shot out of her head as the witch grew. She screamed and tried to take steps toward the kitchen, but her legs became roots, her torso a trunk.

Within minutes, the witch had turned into an elegant maple tree, trunk rooted into the floor, the summer-green leaves nearly touching the ceiling. The leaves rustled though none of the windows were open.

"It was less messy than killing her," Laurel's mother said, gazing at her handiwork with the hint of a smile.

But Laurel only had thoughts for the man in the corner. The hag's transformation must have broken the spell over him. Laurel threw herself at him. He clasped her close, his wood smoke and pine sap smell faint, but his hands firm and familiar.

"I'm all right," he murmured against her hair. "I just can't believe she turned me into a squirrel. Much more humiliating than a wolf."

Laurel didn't know whether she wanted to laugh or cry, so she did both, the floodwaters of terror receding, leaving relief in their wake.

"And who is this, Laurel?"

Oh, right. They weren't alone. Her cheeks on fire, Laurel untangled herself from Hunter and faced the door. Her mother still sat astride the horse, which took in all the excitement as if it was just another day on the farm. It looked almost bored as it cocked its back leg.

Her mother, however, though she still wore her flour-dusted apron, looked like a queen, her cheeks red and her hawk-brown eyes fierce. A magical baking queen.

Laurel couldn't meet the gaze that demanded the truth from her. "This is Hunter. I met him in the forest. He recently built a house there." She let go of the walls she'd built to keep her shame and secrets hidden, and it all surged out. "This mess is my fault. I went to Hunter's house instead of Grandmother's for weeks. If I hadn't left her alone, the witch probably wouldn't have dared to kill her. None of this would have happened."

"It is not your fault." Her mother's butcher knife-sharp voice cut through Laurel's self-pity. "It was that foul woman's fault. Ever since she learned of my powers from your grandmother, she craved them for herself. That's why your grandmother moved out here by herself, to try to separate herself from us, to protect us in case Agnes came for my baked goods ."

Her voice dropped, like a gentle hand urging Laurel to look at her. She did. "You have your grandmother's desire to protect, to take care of others. A gift. But your grandmother and I have taken advantage of it over the years."

Laurel opened her mouth to protest, but her mother raised a hand, stopping her. "No, it's true. I have let you help me and your grandmother, asked you to, knowing that you enjoyed it, but forgetting that you would want your own life too. That you might want more than baking treats or visiting your grandmother." Her attention drifted to Hunter. "It's natural that you would want your own life. Your own dreams." She glanced back at Laurel, her expression an apology. "I'm sorry for not realizing that sooner."

Laurel took a step toward her. "But I still want to help you."

"You can." Her mother's voice softened to the almost-croon she used when Laurel had nightmares as a child. "You can have both. It doesn't need to be either/or.

"But you can't live in the forest." The door to Laurel's dreams slammed shut.

"I don't have to live in the forest," Hunter said.

Laurel turned to him. She believed the earnestness in his face, that he would give up the safety and peace he'd found in the woods to return to town with her, but she didn't want to ask him to do that. To give up all the hard work he'd done on his house.

"You know, when people tell me that I can't do something, I often want to prove them wrong," Laurel's mother said, her mouth twitching. She took in the cottage with its new tree. "It *is* more peaceful out here. And you two could sell my baked goods for me in town."

Laurel couldn't think of any objections. The door was wide open, beckoning her to step inside.

The End

CRIMSON SPY
Jessica Noelle

Once upon a time —

"Bella, you can't start a true story like that!" My sister leans over the first line — the only line — I've written.

"Lottie, how else would you have me start it?" My laughter echoes joyously through the cottage in the middle of the woods, a sharp contrast from the screams of terror, of pain, from three lunar cycles ago.

From the moment when I almost lost my big sister.

But she's here beside me now, and her next words make me laugh harder.

"You start with the facts! Once, there was a girl with a red cloak. She *always* wore the red cloak." Lottie spreads her hands as she talks, her green eyes bright.

Green eyes, not the piercing yellow they had been three lunar cycles ago.

"All right, all right," I agree with my sister, if only to humor her. "I suppose I should start over. After all, how many people have our story wrong?"

Lottie snorts. "Way too many. I can't believe the bard got the facts so wrong!" She darts over to give me a quick hummingbird peck on the cheek before grabbing her navy-blue cloak and a basket. "You write, Bells! I'll go pick some apples from the grove." She leaves with a jaunty wave, and tears of happiness prick my eyes.

We've come so far since *the incident.*

Healing, Grandmere says, comes in many forms. A steaming mug of tea rests next to my phial of ink, and, remembering Grandmere's encouragement to step into the light, I take a single sip of it, the warm honey notes bleeding through the rose-flavored elixir.

Lottie says once upon a time won't work? Then how's this?

~~~~~

Smoke curled up toward the sky as hungry flames licked the insides of the building. Ash coated my lungs, and I sucked in another wheezing breath as I stepped closer to the blistering heat.

"Mama!" The scream tore from my throat, frantic and pleading, but everywhere I turned, in every once-familiar area of my home, I saw only flames leaping higher.

The kitchen where I last saw my father three years ago — before he left us for the sea — was gone. Only a half-burned table leg reassured me that I
~~~~~

was indeed staring at the remains of my family's kitchen.

Our bedroom — Lottie's and mine — would be in the back, but with the fire still raging across my home, I knew I might as well kiss all my old manuscripts goodbye. And what would Lottie say about losing her knitting supplies? The dragon she had been working on for a sick little girl three towns over?

"Mama!" I shouted again, my gaze falling on the metal trunk that we always kept under the living room rocker. Its lid was open, and the fire licked the edges of the box.

No.

I drew up my cloak, covering my mouth and nose, and prepared to launch myself into the flames, but a hand pulled me back from the still-burning building that I once called home — and the iron, magic-proof trunk that held all my family's *secret* gear.

"Bella, are you insane?!" Dorian's voice rang behind me, hoarse from the flames. "Your ma's not here! And no trunk is worth your life!"

"Dorian," I coughed. I couldn't correct him, not when the mission I had just returned from had emphasized the need for secrecy.

Not after my run-in with that blasted sorcerer who could see through my cloak's enchantments.

"Your ma is on an erran', Bella." The blacksmith's son guided me away from the flames and toward one of the sparse green patches of grass — the drought had been raging for months, and all the crops in the village were dying.

Only the ringweed thrived in droughts, allowing this little patch of greenery. Granted, my ash-covered boots marred the scenery, but I managed a nod. "Thank you, Dorian." My words came out more even than they should have, judging by Dorian's odd look, but I barely processed that information at the time.

My crimson cloak hummed with energy, and the inner seam that hid all the runes shifted, each stitch unraveling even as I brushed against them. Thread sang beneath my fingers, oblivious to my touch, and a single glance I dared to take showed me the silver thread glowing and shifting, like the sea my father abandoned us for, before stopping and solidifying like a pit of sinking sand.

"Bella, anything I can do for ya?" Dorian's voice was soft, and I realized he had been trying to talk to me for several minutes.

Yet there I was, lost in my own head. A few townspeople milled around the remains of my home, soaking the grass around the flames, yet no one tried to douse the fire.

What was the point?

Everything of value was gone, including the house. I fingered my cloak again. "Dorian, might I borrow Filip?" His father's horse might give me the speed to reach Grandmere's house before my sister so I could give them the news together.

After all, it wasn't every day we lost a safehouse.

"Can't. Filip's in the field with Farmer Milligan today," Dorian told me, a frown on his face. "But why would ya need my da's horse?"

"My grandmere needs to know, as does Lottie. She traveled a few towns over to help one of the sick children and agreed to visit Grandmere first." The lie fell easily off my lips, years of practice making it sound as true as could be. I glanced at my cloak's inseam again, studying the runes.

This fire was no accident.

No.

No, no, no.

How could this fire be intentional?

How could one of our enemies have found us?

Because if this fire was arson…then whoever set it knew the truth about my family.

They knew that we were not simply a baker's family struggling to make ends meet.

That my mother's errands were more than just delivering loaves of bread.

That my sister, for all her love of children, scarcely saw them and spent her days instead in taverns and trees, listening and bartering for information.

That my grandmother was more than just a kindly old lady in the woods.

No, whoever lit this fire knew my family's secret occupation, knew of the mission the royals gave our ancestors centuries ago.

"It's all right, Dorian, really." I stumbled over my words. "I have to go, have to tell Grandmere and Lottie." I forced my feet to move, but my boots felt heavy despite being made of soft leather.

I felt heavy, exhausted from the escapades of the previous week, yet I still found myself running over the recent encounter with the sorcerer.

But I defeated him. My cloak had protected me, just as Grandmere had promised, and I had delivered the sorcerer to the king.

So who could have done this?

Had a villager found out?

A knight or noble?

Or could my father's debts have finally caught up with us?

The well-worn forest path opened before me, the setting sun turning the yellow and red leaves to golds and rubies, yet the sight did nothing to calm me. Instead, I was on edge, each bird's chirp grating on my nerves and every chipmunk's chitter burning against my ears.

Trembling, I sank down against a trunk, tucking my cloak closer around me.

No.

I couldn't freeze up, not now. I couldn't.

The mission—the mission *had* to come first.

Grandmere had to know that someone was after us.

Someone was after us.

Someone knew who we were.

Knew what we did.

Knew who I was.

I pulled in a deep, shuddering breath, forcing myself through the calming techniques Mama had taught me after Father left.

Step one: Assess the situation.

We were in trouble. Someone knew who we were, knew that we were spies for the king.

Someone knew, and they wanted us scared or dead, probably both.

Step two: Assess your options.

I could say nothing and let them catch up with my family.

I could stay here, frozen in terror, and let my family suffer because I did nothing.

Or I could act and make my way to the Matron's—to Grandmere's—house.

Of course I had to pick the third option.

I had to get to Grandmere's house, to our primary base of operations, and I had to warn her and Lottie. Then, we could get a message to Mama.

I could do this.

I can do this.

I forced myself to my feet, wrapping my hands around my cloak, leaning into its comforting weight. The brocaded fabric was thick, sturdy against my nails, just as it always had been.

Was the sun setting? Yes.

But I knew these woods just as well as any of its inhabitants, and reaching Grandmere's house was just as simple as following this path, going over a river, and traveling to the heart of the forest.

After brushing my cloak off and spinning once to make sure my plain brown dress hadn't picked up any stray leaves, I started moving, fingering the branches that swept low and avoiding the spider webs where I knew they were.

But the forest always shifted, and a few minutes later, I shrieked as I walked into a spider web.

I'm fine.

I can do this.

I took another deep breath, pausing to listen as the owls hooted a warning.

"Hello?" My voice was steady even as my heart thundered in my chest. "Who's there?"

"Bells?" My sister's voice came through the trees, ragged and pained.

"Lottie?"

No answer.

My chest tightened, the lingering smoke tickling the back of my throat.

"Lottie? Where are you?" I whirled around, but the starlight filtering through the depths of the forest wasn't enough to reveal my sister to me.

"Lottie!" My voice took on a desperate, pleading tone. Where was she? Where was my sister?

And why had she sounded distressed, like she had after she had broken her ankle when she was thirteen and I was twelve?

"I'm right here." My big sister's voice was aloe on a sunburn to me, but her hug was even sweeter. She was four inches taller than me, just tall enough for me to be able to bury my head into her shoulder.

A sob shuddered through me. "Oh, Lottie, you scared me."

"I'm okay," Lottie said breathlessly. "Bells, it's okay."

"Grandmere—" I began, but Lottie shushed me. I looked up at my sister, but her navy-blue cloak enveloped her face in shadows.

"Bells, it's okay," she repeated. "I just sprained my ankle going through the river and dropped my basket. No big deal."

"But your basket has evidence for the Matron in it," I whispered. "How—"

"It can wait till morning," Lottie interrupted me, her voice tightening. "Let's just go to Grandmere's house, okay?"

I paused, pulling away from my sister and fiddling with my cloak. *The mission came first.* That was what Mama always had told us, even if the mission was what had driven Father away.

Even if the mission felt like it was crushing my soul on some days.

But Lottie? Lottie had always supported that. She would never leave her basket behind, not unless she was more hurt than she said and just didn't want to worry me.

I always was the worrier.

"I'll go get the basket," I told Lottie, my voice trembling. "You go to Grandmere's, and I'll meet you there."

"Bells—"

"It's okay, Lottie," I said, using Lottie's own words against her. "The mission, remember? We have a duty, and I can help. Please, Lots, let me help."

Lottie hesitated, but in the splintered starlight, I saw her nod, and I leaned onto my tiptoes, pecking her cheek. "Love you, Lots." I told her, and she laughed, ruffling my braids.

"I'll be safe," I reassured her, twirling away before she could say anything else.

Faintly, I heard her say, "Love you too, Bells." The forest swept her words away as I jogged toward the river and avoided the rocks that dappled moonlight danced over. The burbling noise told me the river had decreased since I last saw it, revealing more of its rocky bed. Dead fish littered the rocks, the putrid smell making me gag. No wonder Lottie had tripped.

Still, the basket was near the center of the once-raging-river-turned-rippling-brook, and I slipped my boots and stockings off, wading into the warm water until I could reach the basket, the riverbed's mud slimy beneath my toes.

The basket was easy to grab, and a look inside revealed flowers. Pink-tipped begonias, purple hyacinths, sweet-smelling lavender stalks, and orange snapdragons filled the basket to the brim.

Flowers…why did Lottie always have to use the flower codes? Why couldn't she just use the rune code I actually understood and remembered?

Lavender meant distrust, so maybe Lottie had been trying to say that someone knew our secret and not to trust anyone?

She would explain it all to Grandmere and me in the morning, I knew, but that didn't stop me from trying to unravel the mystery of the flowers.

Yet despite wracking my brain for answers, I couldn't remember any more of the code, so I went to Grandmere's cottage—the Matron's house—humming a lullaby my mother used to sing when Lottie and I were still children.

Because eighteen was no longer a child—but I hadn't been a child for years.

I hadn't been a child since my father left and the mission fully consumed my family.

The crescent moon hung midway in the sky by the time I reached Grandmere's house, and the windows were lit with candles.

"Matron?" I called, entering my grandmere's house. She always told us to call her that when we had news to report.

A cough came from the bed.

"Grandmere!" I dropped Lottie's basket and approached the bed, my hand still around some of the flowers. but it was Lottie in bed, her eyes closed.

"Lottie, where's Grandmere?"

"Gone." Lottie's voice was a rasp.

"Lots, what's wrong?"

"Lots." Lottie's voice was weak and shaky. "Sorry."

"Lottie, sit up." I sat next to my sister, prying open her eyes and flinching back.

"Lottie, when did your eyes become yellow?" I asked, hands shaking.

"Better to see you with, Bells." Lottie coughed again, but I looked at the kitchen table, where a mug was on its side, tea still leaking out of it.

Lavender meant distrust.

But this was Lottie I was talking about.

My sister, my best friend.

The one person who got me.

My *big* sister, my *protector*.

I leaned closer to my sister again, tucking a lock of her brown hair behind her ear. This time, I hid my flinch as I took in her too-large, pointed ears.

Lottie had always had round ears, like me. We were completely and totally human. That was why the king had trusted us.

"And your ears?"

Begonias meant beware, I recalled.

Beware the sister you said hi to.

Beware the family you embraced.

My chest tightened as Lottie answered, "Better to hear you with."

"Oh, Lots," I sighed, pressing a hand against her forehead, searching for a nonexistent fever. Searching for some way to quell my growing fears. She grasped my hand in her…hairy hand?

My sister didn't have hairy hands.

My sister was supposed to have four fingers and a thumb.

She didn't have claws.

Why did she have claws?

Who had cursed my sister and where was my grandmere?

It couldn't be the sorcerer. I stopped him —

"Lottie—" I broke off as my sister yawned, her jaw cracking to reveal sharp fangs.

A werewolf curse.

"Lots," I began again. "Who did you meet on the road?"

"No one." Her voice was sad.

Purple hyacinths means sorrow.

She didn't want this, hadn't chosen this, and was under multiple spells. I rubbed the hem of her cloak, noting the rune thread ripped.

No.

"What big teeth you have, Lottie." I whispered, stroking my sister's cheek. A low growl came from the bed, from her.

But I couldn't move, petrified as my cloak fought off an unseen magic caster.

"Better to eat you with." My sister's voice was a low growl, none of the honey-sweetness left, but still, she remained in bed.

"Snapdragons are for deception," I recalled. "Oh Lots." I slipped my hands into my cloak, unsheathing my daggers. "Who's with you?"

"No one."

Another lie.

"Where's Grandmere?"

"The Matron is gone."

And now the true villain decides to show himself.

A scowl twisted across my face, and I turned to face the man who had cursed my sister—

"No, I locked you up. Hand-delivered you to the king myself."

In front of me, a dagger to my Grandmere's throat, was the sorcerer, the very one I had vanquished last week.

His beard was still as long and gray as it had been, falling to his waist, and his eyes glowed purple with magic. A whimper of pain came from the bed, and my sister curled into herself, whispering, "No, no, no."

"Release my sister and Grandmere." I demanded, but my voice shook.

"No." The sorcerer gave me a cruel smile. "Your sister will be cursed to be a wolf by the time the clock strikes midnight, and then, she'll eat both you and your grandmother. The great Matron of the Royal Spies dead by a wolf, the line extinguished, and the king no wiser."

"Why?"

I had to do something, had to save my family.

My sister writhed in pain, moaning as she fought off the spell, but her cloak had been stripped of its magic.

Anything she had to fight off the spell was gone.

And what could I do?

Grandmere's eyes met mine, and then…. she smiled. A soft smile, the kind my mother used to give before Father left.

This sorcerer — his reasons lay in the fact that all he believed in was *his* mission.

Just like Mama.

Just like we all had.

The Royal Spies, Grandmere the Matron and Mama the Heir.

Lottie and I meant to follow in their footsteps.

But my sister was *here* now and *hurting*.

Even as anxiety clawed into my throat, that was all I could think, and Grandmere was smiling like she *knew* I could save the day, but how could I?

How could I when I didn't even believe in the mission?

When I didn't want to spend every day telling tall tales and spreading lies just to gain half-truths to bring back to the king?

I had never stopped a war, and only inconvenienced a few bad people. And yes, while that felt nice, the meager bit of justice wasn't why I stayed.

No, I stayed for *Lottie.*

Not for Mama, who never smiled.

Not for Grandmere, who had said we could leave if we so wished.

Not out of spite for my father, who had abandoned *Lottie* and *me* alongside Mama.

I stayed for my big sister, my protector…and now I couldn't even protect her.

Tears pricked my eyes, and for once, I let them fall, half a plan forming.

The mission was irrelevant.

What mattered was my family, my sister.

"It doesn't matter why you're doing this, does it?" My voice was thick with my tears. "You're doing this for some... some mission, but you're hurting my sister."

My fingers trembled as I unlaced my cloak. "So instead, you're going to transfer the curse to me."

"No." Lottie's voice was barely a whisper. "No, Bells, no."

"No." The sorcerer laughed, still cruel, but I draped my cloak over my sister, and its magic seeped out of me and into her, burrowing itself deeper than the curse.

"I love you, Lots," I told my sister, and the sorcerer fell back when I lunged at him, twisting his staff and shooting a bolt of electricity. My grandmere fell, hitting the ground, and a cracking noise came when her hip hit the stones, but my mind was white with pain.

When my vision cleared, the sorcerer was looming over me.

"You will pay," he hissed. "If your sister will not be the hand by which I destroy the Royal Spies, I will use you instead."

"No." I whispered, bracing my hands against the cold stone. "No, you will not hurt my family." I raised my voice, stumbling to my feet and grasping the sorcerer's staff, but he held fast, letting out another bolt of lightning.

A scream tore from my lips and tears leaked from my eyes.

But I didn't let go.

I couldn't.

Not with my family on the line.

Not with *Lottie* on the line.

I tightened my grip on the staff, wrenching it from the sorcerer's hands and slamming it to the ground.

With a burst of rainbow-colored light, the orb at the top shattered, driving a shard straight into my stomach. As I stumbled to the floor, blood pooling from the wound, I was dimly aware of Lottie forcing herself to her feet, swaying before she decked the sorcerer in the face, sending him tumbling to the ground.

The taste of iron filled my mouth and spots of black danced across my vision, but Lottie's warm hands — now bare of fur — stroked my hair back.

"Bells." A soft, broken plea.

"Love you, Lots," I rasped, giving into the darkness.

~~~~~

"Bells." Lottie's soft voice woke me up, and I winced as pain flooded my senses, my stomach aching like I had been stabbed.

*Oh wait. I **was** stabbed.*

"Lots," I wheezed. "Wha' happened?"

"Your stomach got shredded by the orb. There's some intense scarring, but Bells, you saved me, saved us."

"I did?"
~~~~~

"And I told Mama that we are out of the business. Grandmere supported me."

"Grandmere?" My mind felt like fog.

"Broken hip, but nothing she won't recover from. We're in her cottage—the old Matron one. We're safe, Bells."

"We are?"

"Yeah." Lottie nodded, her green eyes bright.

I don't think I had ever loved those green eyes so much.

~~~~~

And now, with the ink drying, I think that's still true. My sister is safe. *I'm* safe.

So, as you've read, I'm Bella…but most people know me as Little Red Riding Hood, the foolish girl who trusted a big, bad wolf.

But that story? That's just a fairy tale.

It's not the truth.

And take it from me—this is *my* story, after all—when I say that the big bad wolf isn't always big or bad.

So yes, once there was a girl with a red cloak. Except, it wasn't just a cloak—it was magic.

And once, there was a girl who went to her grandmother's house. But not to deliver food.

And once there was a forest filled with flowers—there still is. The difference lies in the meaning of the flowers, a warning for a sister.

Once, there was a fairytale about a girl in a red hood, but it forgot that love can overcome fear and allow villains to be conquered.

The End
~~~~~

RED WOLF
An Enchanted Castle Archives Story
Michelle L. Levigne

"All I'm saying is that it's suspicious timing, with Ambrose away for a few months on that diplomatic mission," Zared said, as he and his wife, Ashlyn reached the second-floor landing of the castle's central grand staircase. They turned to head down to the first floor and paused when they came face-to-face with their daughter, 'Na, coming up from the ground floor.

She halted, one foot raised to start up the flight of stairs between them. "*Now* what's happened?"

"Nothing new," her mother said with a sigh.

"It's the werewolves again," Zared said.

"Is that better or worse than the vampires acting up?" She sighed and stepped back to settle on the banister and wait for her parents to join her. "What are the werewolves doing now? They're not starting up again about the wolf mask being a royal treasure, and trying to arrange another marriage alliance, are they?" 'Na shuddered. "You'd think after what Ambrose and I went through with the Dripmorians, proving true love's kiss really works, all those diplomatic marriage brokers would give up!"

"You'd think," her mother agreed with a sigh. She and Zared reached the ground floor, and she looped an arm through her daughter's to tug her off the banister. "Actually, I have been dreaming about that wretched mask. And there are tales of a foreign wolf running through the forest."

There were more than a dozen masks in the most secure vault of the enchanted castle, all with the power to grant the wearer of the mask the traits and skills and personality of the animals they portrayed. Ashlyn had more than lived up to the reputation and expectations of the Beastly Beauty during her furious rampage, wearing those masks. Some had come near to taking her over permanently so she wouldn't have been able to remove them if she had wanted to—and in her bereaved fury, sometimes she hadn't wanted to. It had taken Fang the half-vampire bunny and Eyesallova the magic mirror and some friendly enchanted statues in the garden to separate her from the masks several times.

Fortunately, Zared had come to the enchanted castle on his own quest for freedom and healing at just the right time, and they had worked together to free each other.

The wolf mask had been Ashlyn's favorite, and the most cooperative, allowing her freedom of will when she wore it. She had earned the loyalty and admiration of the werewolves she had brought to find sanctuary in the enchanted forest while she wore that mask. They had made her an honorary member of their tribe.

Unfortunately, that meant Zared had to prove he was worthy to be her mate. The rarity of female births among the werewolves had contributed to nearly igniting a war, in the effort to decide 'Na's future mate, when she was born. More than a dozen prophecies about the lost heir to the queen of the werewolves mentioned that mask. Far too many members of the werewolf tribe tried to twist the words of those prophecies to make Ashlyn and then 'Na the fulfillment. A delegation came from the tribe every summer at solstice to request that the wolf mask be brought out, in the hopes it was turning from silver to red, a sign that the queen was returning. 'Na both dreaded and looked forward to the yearly visits, because as long as the mask stayed silver, she was free to run and hunt with her friends among the werewolves without fearing a new campaign to win her as a mate.

In the past, whenever 'Na suspected a new courtship competition was about to launch among the young males, she simply brewed a new batch of perfume with tiger musk, to fend off any heavy-breathing suitor who might try to approach her when she was out in the forest. Having passed her tricky seventeenth birthday, she feared the pressure would increase from more quarters. She seriously considered settling in and refusing to leave the castle until Ambrose came back, strengthening the magical boundaries imposed by true love's kiss.

Could she really count on that protection, though? When it came to magic and the enchanted castle, far too many rules were twisted and knotted completely out of shape and beyond all predicting.

'Na and her parents headed across the grand entryway for the nearest door into the castle library. Time to check several of the maps that monitored activity in the enchanted forest.

The thud-clump of iron feet on the stone central staircase made all three stop short. For a moment, 'Na didn't understand what she heard. It sounded like a suit of armor, but the suits of armor hadn't walked in years. They had in a sense fallen asleep, once the castle had been anchored and the enchanted forest rejoined the normal stream of time. When occasion demanded, the suits of armor awoke, but those tended to be dire circumstances.

She turned to her parents. Ashlyn pulled her shoulders back and turned to look up the staircase. Her eyes widened, then her expression turned solemn and pale. Zared gripped her shoulder and put himself between the staircase and his wife and daughter.

The figure coming down the stairs was the biggest, blackest, glossiest suit of armor 'Na had ever seen. In fact, she had never seen that particular suit, in all the time she had spent investigating every crevice, tunnel, secret passage and hidden room in the castle. At least ten times *each*. The sight was imposing and impressive, and she would have shivered, but the frilly, glittery little lady's hand mirror the suit held out rather ruined the effect.

"Ah, there you are," Eyesallova called from the mirror. "The werewolves are coming, and Behemoth here reports that the wolf mask is trying to howl."

"That's ... never happened before," Ashlyn said. She took a deep breath. "Has it?"

"No, dear," the mirror said, as she and Behemoth joined them on the main floor. "Despite everything you lost during those months of madness, you would remember if the mask had howled without you inside it."

~~~~~

The leaders of the werewolf tribe stopped in the outer courtyard. Zared, Ashlyn and 'Na came out to meet them, carrying Eyesallova.

The werewolves had to stop because all the castle's suits of armor had awakened and formed a barrier of self-mobile iron in front of the castle's main doors. Not that 'Na thought the armor could really stop the werewolves if they wanted to get in. They were very good at leaping high, and she doubted even an enchanted suit of armor could manage to jump twenty feet high to slap a werewolf out of the air as he soared past.

"The mask calls us," Arrasmus, the oldest werewolf, announced.

That was no surprise to anyone. The reports of the young males being unusually active lately, and strange howls in the forest, had prompted Ashlyn and Zared to fear another courtship campaign launching.

"How?" Zared said.

"We heard a howl in a voice none of us knows. A scent unfamiliar to us, and yet clearly of our kind, dances on the breeze." He limped forward, and with each step his features melted more from grizzled old Human to battle-scarred wolf, his fur bleached by his many years. Yet he stayed upright, shoulders back, so his elegant clothes didn't look ridiculous on his increasingly hairy limbs.

"When did you start to hear the howl?" Eyesallova asked.

'Na muffled a snort of laughter, when the dozen werewolves looked all around, trying to spot the source of the voice. Behemoth came down the steps from the door and held out the mirror. During the half hour between warning of the arrival of the werewolves and coming out into the courtyard, Eyesallova had switched over into a more dignified and much larger traveling mirror, so her eyes and the swirls of magic that substituted for a face were visible. It gave the werewolves something to talk to.

"Just after moonset this morning," Rolf, Arrasmus's nephew and heir, said.

"I thought so. The time matches when the warning charms activated on the portal in Opal Swamp. It jammed open on Vanyltransia."
~~~~~

At the mention of the far distant kingdom, all the werewolves seemed to inhale in unison. 'Na swore any fur showing on their faces bristled. Exceptionally wonky magic at the portal in Opal Swamp meant it didn't open on a regular pattern. Predicting when it would shift to a new kingdom was nearly impossible, thus traffic coming from the four kingdoms accessed through that portal was sporadic. Since traffic practically never came from Vanyltransia, the theory was that a particularly nasty curse anchored in that kingdom made the portal misbehave. According to 'Na's playmates among the werewolves, none of them wanted to go there anyway.

"What do the charms report?" Arrasmus asked, after meeting the gazes of the rest of the delegation.

"All sorts of spells and charms are interfering. The mirrors in the forest can only catch glimpses, and then they lose them again. The best we can tell, three came through from Vanyltransia. A wolf, a girl, and a man. One of them carries a huge silver axe. The axe is heavy with magic that is interfering with the monitoring spells in the forest."

"Wolves don't like axes," a werewolf in the back of the group grumbled.

"Agreed. Common sense says the man has the axe, rather than the girl," Ashlyn said. "Are there signs of any other weapons, Eyesallova?"

"None that we have seen so far," the magic mirror reported. "The axe could be keeping us from seeing any other magic or weapons the man is carrying."

"That alone makes me think he is in the wrong, to some degree. Coming from Vanyltransia complicates things, since werewolves once lived there."

'Na managed not to react. That was news to her. Common sense said whatever drove werewolves out of Vanyltransia was bad enough, shameful enough, for her friends never to mention it. Or maybe their parents had never told them that bit of their history.

"Could there be some werewolves still there, living in hiding?" she asked.

"There has only been silence from that side of the portal for five generations," Rolf finally said. He sighed. "Yes, perhaps our ancient enemies still hunt our distant kin."

"Do you hear the wolf? Is the wolf the prey?" Zared said. "If you hear the girl, then is she werewolf?"

"We have no way to be sure just yet. It is a female's voice, a werewolf's voice, and the scent is female." Rolf frowned.

"The man with the axe could be chasing the girl and the wolf is protecting her," Eyesallova offered.

That seemed to cheer the werewolves. The other option, which Eyesallova was diplomatic enough not to suggest, was that the girl was bait, luring the wolf so the man with the axe could attack. 'Na pitied the werewolves, constantly having to deal with unreasonably high levels of prejudice, thanks to stories told to frighten children into behaving themselves and staying out of trouble.

The castle doors swung open and Zella the librarian came out, struggling to put on her jacket while clutching a traveling pack. She skidded to a stop just before running into the back of Zared.

"Emergency?" 'Na asked.

"Damsel of distress alert," Zella said, letting the traveling pack slide to the ground so she could turn her sleeve right-side out.

"*Of* distress?" Zared said.

"It's a spell we've been playing with," 'Na said. "We've set it up by some of the portals leading into the more repressive kingdoms. The spell triggers when anything female flees here to get away from a male who expects her to be brainless and obedient and helpless. What did the mirror on duty show you?"

"It looks like she came into the forest using an enchanted charm bracelet. Some pretty powerful charms, including one that kept her hidden for several hours after entering, so the alarm didn't go off until the magic of the charms wore out. Then ..." She dug into her traveling pack and pulled out one of her ever-present journals to consult it. "She stumbled right through a kispie nest, but it looks like she did it on purpose. Ignored all the warning signs."

"Ouch." 'Na flinched, and several of the younger werewolves hissed and hunched their shoulders or shuddered.

"Isn't it swarming season right now?" Eyesallova said. "This is going to get complicated. 'Na, dear, haul me back up to my own mirror, would you? I need to focus on this, and that means staying here and sending another monitor mirror with you girls."

"We should probably ride out and gather up what's left of her," Ashlyn said.

"That's the puzzle," Zella said. She walked with 'Na as she went to take Eyesallova from Behemoth. "The charms got her through the nest without any damage. It looks like she was following the wolf, who got through with no trouble. The man chasing her got stung pretty badly, but he's got a huge axe full of magic. He swatted away the kispies so only a third of them got through to him. Some version of an inside-out spell turned some of the kispies around, so they went after the wolf."

"That sounds to me like the wolf was helping the girl, or at least leading her," 'Na said.

"He's cheating," Arrasmus grumbled, as the girls climbed the stairs to go into the castle.

"Woodsmen," another werewolf muttered. "Hate them. Nasty liars. Always accusing us of eating sheep and goats, just so they can drive us farther away. Then they can chop down more forest and put up flimsy little cottages, usually straw and sticks, charmed to look like bricks. Is that any way to live, I ask you?"

"The first step is to find the girl and hear her side of the story, then catch the wolf and the woodsman, and keep them all separated," Zared said.

"As soon as I get a good view of where she is and what's ahead of her," Eyesallova called. By this time, she and the girls had reached the stairs, and the castle doors closed, so they couldn't hear the rest of the conversation outside in the courtyard.

Once they got the traveling mirror back to the mirror room, it was a matter of a few seconds and several flashes of green and blue magic light, and Eyesallova was back in her own tall mirror, able to move around the floor and turn herself. She muttered and the other, smaller magic mirrors on the walls chimed back at her, everyone conferring, sharing what they could see throughout the enchanted forest. Several housekeeping breezes brought in 'Na's riding boots and coat and her traveling bag, kept packed and ready with a journal, pen, and ink, basic healer's kit, and a large assortment of handy charms. By the time 'Na had put on boots and coat, Eyesallova had found the girl, the wolf, and the woodsman. Somewhat. They kept flickering in and out of sight, sometimes even appearing to be two or three different places at the same time.

The good news was that the wolf got free of the kispies. The bad news was that he had put several miles between him and the girl. The worse news was that the woodsman was cutting his way through the trees between him and the girl, who wore a red hooded cloak, making the trees go up in puffs of smoke with every swing of his axe. 'Na considered that cheating, and rather inconsiderate. Quite a few trees in that part of the forest were the homes of dryads, many of them their retirement homes.

Hazel, a palm-sized mirror in a wooden frame, volunteered to go with them, to provide communication with Eyesallova, and to follow the girl's path through the enchanted forest. Getting a lock on her actual location was the tricky part.

"Bother!" Eyesallova cried. Her surface cleared of her usual magical swirls to show a black wolf racing down a narrow ravine that deepened the further he raced. Tiny figures appeared on either side of the ravine, waving what 'Na feared were weapons.

"Oh, no, is that—" She choked. "The hunting game idiots? The ones who save up all their magic for the entire year and expend it creating monsters to chase down and fight hand-to-hand?"

"And the wolf is running straight into their arena."

Eyesallova's surface split, to show the girl in her red cloak, leaping into the Snarl River and racing across it, sending up splashes of magic with every step. That charm bracelet certainly was coming in handy. Still, Eyesallova had said the magic was being used up at a rapid pace. The dark shape of the woodsman appeared far down the bank from where the girl had jumped in. The wolf continued racing down the deepening ravine, the side too steep to climb, heading toward the growing light of the arena where dozens of magic-generated monsters waited for battle.

"We can't save them both," Zella said.

"Silly girl! Send the werewolves after the wolf. You go after the girl. Bring them both back here."

"Right." She raced down the stairs, while 'Na waited for Hazel to finish collecting tracking information from the mirrors that monitored activity in the enchanted forest.

'Na bit back a cry of protest as the images faded from Eyesallova's surface. She wanted to see if the woodsman would leap into the river and try to follow the girl.

"Go! She's almost to the other side, and the Barrens Cliffs are ahead of her," Eyesallova cried.

'Na raced down the stairs. She reached the second-floor landing before it occurred to her that they had a long way to run to get to the Barrens Cliffs. Time was running out faster than water from a shattered pitcher. She thought for two seconds, then reached into the collar of her shirt to tug out her crystal whistle.

"Sorry," she cried, before blowing the whistle.

None of the werewolves reacted, though most of the song of the whistle was outside normal Human hearing range—meaning it was in the range for dogs.

And dragons.

No reaction meant the werewolves had already raced away to save the wolf. Her parents were just coming back into the castle.

"Sorry," she said again. To Zella this time. "Smedley's going to be faster than going to the stables and saddling horses."

Zared and Ashlyn headed for the stairs. "We'll follow you in the mirrors," Ashlyn said.

Smedley appeared as the girls stepped outside. He let out a crooning sort of rumble as he circled three times before settling in the largest portion of the courtyard.

"Uh … problem," Zella said.

While 'Na did indeed have a riding harness for Smedley, which she had been refining over the last several months since the return of her childhood friend, getting it from the tower adjacent to the dragon's lair and putting it on him would take time. The time she had hoped to save by riding him, instead of going to the stables or waiting for the housekeeping breezes to bring the saddled horses to them.

Smedley wriggled, arching his back so his spines rippled. 'Na laughed. The easy communication between her and her dragon friend had been stolen by some nasty magic when she was a child. Still, she understood exactly what he meant now.

"I'm up for it." She stepped up to put one foot on the bent elbow of his foreleg.

"Are you sure?" Zella followed, clutching her travel bag against her chest. "Going up isn't a problem. It's staying up."

Smedley turned his head, fluttering his unfairly long, curly lashes and made a swiping motion with his hind claws. That seemed clear enough for 'Na. Not that she wanted to think for long about what it would be like, sliding out from between his spines and starting to fall, and caught by a swipe of those sharp claws in mid-air. She settled into place and held out a hand to Zella to help her.

Zella swallowed hard and seemed to lose a few degrees of color, but her hands and legs were steady as she climbed up and settled into the slot in the spine ridges two spaces behind 'Na. Smedley tipped his head back, his muscles bunching, and leaped skyward. His wings snapped open with a loud bang as they caught the air.

The dragon circled the enchanted castle once before arrowing out over the forest, heading toward the cliffs. Smedley barely rose above the clouds before he started to descend. 'Na had to close her eyes against the wind battering them to the point of tears. That didn't help her fight the helpless falling sensation, with a hint of spinning. When Smedley's muscles shifted under her and she sensed that he had leveled out, she opened her eyes again. They were full of tears, and bugs or other debris in the air. She didn't dare let go of the spine in front of her, forcing her to turn her head and rub her face against her shoulder to clear her eyes.

The cliffs hurtled toward them. She caught her breath and fought not to yank on the spine and shout for Smedley to slow down before he slammed into them.

"There!" Zella leaned forward, shouting in 'Na's ear, which was good because the shriek of the wind made it hard to hear. She gestured down at the scrub and shattered land at the feet of the cliffs. The red cloak of the fleeing girl was easy to see against the dull greens and muddy browns.

'Na shuddered once, looking down. Her mother had been chased here through a portal, back when the enchanted forest was still disconnected from the rest of the world. Ashlyn had been attacked by magicians from the Purple Sky and injured in the Barrens. The castle had healed her, but the warped magic had nearly taken over her mind and soul while she was feverish. 'Na had never wanted to see this part of the forest, even though she considered it her duty as one of its guardians to know all of it. She hoped the hidden curses in the air around this area wouldn't latch onto them and make this rescue harder.

"See the man, Smedley?" she asked, leaning forward to get closer to his right ear. The dragon rumbled. "Land to put us between him and the girl in the red cloak."

Another rumble, with an upward lilt at the end. Before she could ask, the dragon dropped. 'Na swallowed a scream, and vowed next time, no matter how valuable speed was, she was taking a horse.

Smedley landed with a bump and deep flexing of his legs. A roar erupted from the dark shape hurtling toward them through the shrubs and shattered landscape.

"Where is she?" 'Na slid off Smedley's back on shaking legs, stumbling in her eagerness to turn and look for the girl.

Zella pointed. "Stop! We're here to help you!"

The fleeing girl looked back, still running, and immediately tripped.

This was one of those times 'Na wished Fang the bunny was visiting, but he had been entirely too peaceful since his close encounter with a rejuvenation spell that nearly went too far. The vampire clan hadn't thrown him out in months. Still, 'Na preferred to aim him at that man with the huge axe, rather than Smedley. Despite his size, in some ways he was still a baby, and she doubted his ability to dodge that axe. Anyone who ran holding an axe out in front of himself was either highly skilled, or dangerously self-destructive. Or maybe had a really strong healing spell that acted so rapidly, he was essentially invulnerable. Which gave him a huge advantage over Smedley.

She had no choice.

"Slow him." She pointed at the man who was still at least a quarter mile away. To see the axe that clearly meant it was huge.

Smedley let out an excited rumble and nearly knocked her off her feet with a wide swish of his tail as he turned to face the woodsman.

'Na turned to find the girl. She hadn't continued running now that she was back on her feet, but she didn't move toward them, either. Zella was now halfway between 'Na and the girl.

"I'm Zella, and this is 'Na. We came to help you. We're going to take you back to the castle, where you'll be safe."

"The castle?" The girl's pale face lit up and her eyes glistened like she might suddenly weep. "You're from the enchanted castle?"

"We live there, yes," 'Na said. Until they had some details about this girl and her problem, wisdom said not to give her too much information. Revealing too soon she was the daughter of the lord and lady of the enchanted castle rarely turned out well.

"Who's chasing you?" Zella held out a hand, beckoning the girl closer.

"Basil, the woodsman." She made a disgusted face. "He'll tell you he's my stepfather, but my mother died before he could force her to marry him. Granny makes me call him my stepfather, but if he is, then he shouldn't try to make me marry his son!"

Zella shuddered and looked over her shoulder at 'Na. "She needs our help," they said in unison.

Smedley let out a belch that shook the ground, and before 'Na could turn around, she smelled the sulfur in his breath. She didn't smell burned meat, so Basil hadn't met up with him yet.

More lack of forethought on her part: how were they going to get on Smedley and fly away if he was busy slowing the woodsman?

Answer: find some other way to fly.

Fortunately, 'Na had all the fascinating enchanted forest locations memorized. The truly bizarre ones, where warped, injured magic had been buried or came to rest and couldn't be removed. 'Na sent up a quick, desperate prayer, asking for A'theosius's mercy and an accurate memory. And for the magic thickening the air to be in a cooperative mood.

"This way. Can you run for a little longer?" she asked the girl as she and Zella picked up the pace and caught up with her.

"Just as long as I'm indoors before nightfall." She gave them a brave smile.

"Oh, wonderful," Zella said as 'Na led the way down a barely discernible path. "Let me guess. The rotter cast a curse of some kind on you to slow you down? You turn to stone at nightfall?"

"Not exactly. He doesn't want me to know, but there's a cure at the castle." She tugged her red cloak closer around herself. "He considers it a curse. I think it's … well, I'm not sure what to make of it. Oh, it's complicated!"

"You're in good company." 'Na gestured to the left when the path ahead of them branched three ways. "If you were hoping for magical help from the enchanted castle, you'll get it, but things rarely work out exactly as we want them to. What's your name?"

"Garnet."

Behind them, Smedley let out another roar. This one sounded a little more serious than the last. He didn't sound angry or upset or frightened. Neither did he sound amused. 'Na kept thinking of that huge axe.

"Thank you, A'theosius," 'Na whispered, as the broken landscape opened up before them, revealing a small waterfall splashing and shattering as it hit multiple jagged outcroppings of stone. "Hope you don't mind getting wet for a few minutes."

"He doesn't have his hunting dogs with him," Garnet said.

"Why would — oh, you think we're trying to hide our scent. No." She picked up the pace and led the way up an uneven series of steps among the jumbles of rock. The spray from the waterfall brushed her face. "We need to hold hands," she instructed them once they had stepped behind the waterfall. "Might help to close your eyes."

"We're not going through a portal, are we?" Zella visibly tried not to cringe.

"No. Might be worse. Depends on whether the marshbubbles are in season."

Portal travel made Zella sick to her stomach. It made snatch-as-can trysts with her wizard sweetheart, Zerocs, rather difficult, without some advance planning, and factoring in time for her to recover before meeting up with him.

Zella wrinkled up her nose. "Is this going to stink?"

"I hope not."

All three girls took firm grips on each other's hands and shuffled along the ledge, with water splashing down close enough to spatter them from time to time. She calculated maybe fifteen minutes of creeping along the ledge, then down a series of rough stairsteps to the edge of the Misty Marshes. Enough time to rethink her plan and try to anticipate any complications.

"He doesn't have any kind of tracking charm to help him, does he? Since he doesn't have hunting dogs with him?"

Garnet hunched her shoulders and bowed her head, so her red hood slipped down almost to her eyes.

"What does he have? We need to know, so we can work against it." Zella tugged Garnet's hood back, to reveal her deep red tangle of curls, almost the same hue as her cloak.

"A pelt," Garnet whispered. She blinked hard, visibly fighting tears, and her moon-pale complexion lost what hints of rosy coloring it had held. "A werewolf pelt. It serves him."

"Werewolf ..." 'Na fought a churning in her belly. She imagined one of her werewolf playmates, hunted down, charmed to keep him in wolf shape so someone could take his pelt to power spells. She wanted to hurt someone. Preferably Basil.

What kind of a monster was Garnet's granny, to make her call the horrid man her stepfather, when he hadn't managed to marry her mother?

"We need to get that pelt away from him," Zella said. "At the very least, we need to give it to the werewolves for a proper burial."

"But—" Garnet trembled. "I need to be indoors before night comes. The moon is getting stronger."

"Oh, don't worry, we'll be home long before nightfall." 'Na gestured ahead, to where the waterfall ended. Their journey would get tricky in the Misty Marshes. The unsteady ground and the thick, churning mists would slow the woodsman, at the very least. If they were lucky, he would bumble through and get stuck. Maybe sucked down and taken prisoner by the marshwrigglers.

On the other hand, she rather liked the idea of leading him straight to the enchanted castle, and into the arms of all those awakened suits of armor. And the werewolves. They wouldn't take kindly to him possessing a werewolf pelt.

Still, if he had hurt Smedley, she wanted him to be terrified and humiliated. Getting sucked down into the mud and trapped in a marshwriggler burrow for a few years would be a good start.

They came out from behind the waterfall and started down the natural stairway. The sweet-musky aroma of the Misty Marshes wafted up on a warm breeze to greet them. 'Na took a deep breath, trying to tell by the scent the marshbubble plants' stage of growth. Too soon in the gaseous cycle, and they would have to slog through the marsh as best they could. Too late, and they could suffocate, and the bubbles would be useless.

It smelled like linens, still slightly damp, hanging on the drying line. Her knees threatened to buckle with relief.

"Please, A'theosius," 'Na whispered as they reached the bottom of the stairs. If the All-Maker was going to listen to her prayer, he had better do it fast.

Friar Ipswich had teasingly scolded 'Na, more times than she could count, that A'theosius heard every prayer, and answered every prayer. The problem was that "no" was just as valid an answer as "yes."

"No matter what happens," she whispered, "hold onto each other, and be silent."

Zella squeezed her hand. Hopefully that meant she understood. There was no telling what Garnet was thinking or if she even heard the instructions.

From the angle of the light, they had maybe two hours until sunset. Hopefully, they could fly the rest of the way, which would be much faster than going on foot.

Then again, there was no telling how strong the marshbubble bubbles were at this time of year. She couldn't depend on luck to remain good for them the entire trip. That would be greedy.

Holding tight to Zella's hand, she headed north across the marsh, stepping as lightly as she could. The ground immediately dipped under her boot. She had a brief, awful image in her head of all of them stepping onto the same hummock of floating vegetation and sinking immediately. Holding hands would keep them too close together, but they had to stay together. Especially when—

White swirled down around her from above, immediately blinding her. The other two girls gasped. Garnet started to speak, but Zella hushed her. 'Na kept moving, following her nose, even though the mist now clogged it so she smelled nothing but mud and rotting vegetation. Where was that clean linen smell? She needed to find it. And quickly.

Ten steps. Fifteen. Twenty. Something made a soft splash and she nearly stopped short, braced for the sound of a big man carrying an even bigger axe, tearing through the vegetation to go over his head in the murky water. If A'theosius was kind, the woodsman would hit so heavily he would sink past his knees into the mud and stick there long enough for them to escape.

No sounds of footsteps. Or splashing. Or sinking. Or even breathing. The mist muffled most sounds.

Mist swirled thicker around her face, so she felt as if damp, gossamer cloth brushed her skin. Then cleared. A soap bubble shimmer glistened in the sunlight as the mist spun in circles out of her way.

Thank you, A'theosius.

'Na hurried forward, tugging hard on Zella's hand. No time to waste looking back, urging them to keep up. They had mere heartbeats to get there before that growing bubble of wispy rainbow grew large enough. Too late, and the wall of the bubble might be too strong and stubborn for them to step through. Too soon, and it would be too fragile, and pop. Marshbubbles were truly the most frustrating wonders of twisted, somehow silly magic to ever come from A'theosius's incomprehensible sense of humor.

A gust of cloying-sweet air, thick and sticky with moisture, erupted under her feet and threw her backward against Zella. 'Na let out a yelp, immediately trying to stifle it. Her mouth filled with a thick, sticky, nauseating substance that threatened to choke her. The other two girls let out yelps and choking little gasps. 'Na struggled to get off Zella and onto her hands and knees, all three still holding onto each other.

"Up," her friend whispered.

'Na spat to get the awful taste out of her mouth. It was the scent of marshbubble, concentrated a thousand times.

She went perfectly still, even before she got the sticky gunk out of her eyes.

The swaying underneath her wasn't the shifting of thick vegetation floating on water.

"Oh, oh, oh," Garnet sighed.

Before 'Na hissed for her to be quiet, the other girl fell silent. She sounded awed, not terrified, ready to break out in shrieks. 'Na got one eye open. Everything around them shimmered in rainbow streaks.

"Can you see down?" she whispered as lightly as she could. Moving or even breathing too hard would threaten the stability of the bubble. She had managed to float a handful of times inside a marshbubble, but she had always been alone. She could only imagine how the weight of three girls threatened the bubble. Forget about how one injudicious movement could pop it and send them plummeting down to the marsh. Through the hummocks of vegetation. Just as she hoped the woodsman would go. Or worse, it would pop after they floated up high over dry ground.

"We're a few yards above the tops of the bushes at the edge," Zella responded after several moments.

They had already floated out of the marsh. That was good. Depending on which direction they were floating.

"How do we get down?" Garnet asked, after what felt like an hour, but could only have been a few minutes of floating, tense, waiting silence.

"It will start losing air, thinning in places, and we'll go down slowly. Soon," 'Na added, anticipating her next question.

"Sooner." Zella sounded like she choked on something. She tugged on 'Na's left arm, so she turned her head left. Carefully.

Smedley floated up to hover even with them, maybe a bowshot away. 'Na caught herself before she shouted for him not to get any closer. They had played together in the marsh, going aloft in the bubbles what felt like two lifetimes ago. Did he remember?

Maybe she hoped he didn't remember? Smedley had taken great delight in popping the bubbles when she got one to enclose her.

The dragon floated closer, his mouth hanging open in a big, rather foolish-looking grin. He swished his tail, and the resulting disruption in the breeze made the bubble bob up and down. Zella inhaled sharply and her hand gripping 'Na's arm squeezed.

"What's going on?" Garnet whispered.

"Smedley …" 'Na didn't dare shout, but if she wasn't loud enough, he might come closer. One flick of his tail, wagging in delight, one too-strong flutter of his wings … and the bubble would pop. "Let us fly. Please."

"He's not going to eat us?"

"Smedley is 'Na's friend," Zella said. "He's more likely to try to blow us up higher and make us tumble around." She grinned. "I remember all the stories you told me when we were little. I was so jealous. I wanted a dragon to come live in my tower with me."

"You played with a dragon?" Garnet said.

"When he was small," 'Na said. "Before his fire came in and he sort of lost control. The library got upset and exiled him from the castle."

A giggle escaped the red-haired girl. "Suddenly, my life doesn't seem so odd."

The dragon's happy, open-mouthed grin snapped shut. His eyes turned red. He bowed his head, looking down. The bubble shifted and the rainbows twisted around them. Something slid past 'Na's fingertips as liquid spattered her. She turned in time to see what looked like a crossbow bolt arching upward, out of sight.

She fell.

"Smedley!" she shrieked, spinning and kicking in mid-air, clutching Zella, who held tight to Garnet, who let out a shriek that sounded like a howl.

A dozen yards below them, Smedley streaked downward, wings clutched close to his sides, aiming for a dark figure on the ground, holding something that glittered silver in the sunlight.

The woodsman and his axe. 'Na saw him lowering the crossbow that had been pointing straight at her.

"Smedley!" she cried again.

The dragon twisted in mid-air, changing course so his head snapped upward while his tail whipped downward. He smacked at the man, knocking him backward so he went head over heels, crossbow slamming into a dozen pieces against a tree, axe tumbling in the opposite direction, to bury itself completely in the dirt.

Smedley snagged 'Na with one foreleg, Zella with one hind leg, and Garnet with the other hind leg. All three girls let out gasps, the breath knocked out of them by the sudden stop, and let go of each other. They hung upside down as he raced away, over the tops of the trees.

Definitely, next time 'Na went on a rescue, she was taking a horse.

She was afraid to try to move and learn what bones had broken. She couldn't take more than tiny, gasping, shallow breaths. Not enough to speak and ask if the others were all right. She could see them, blinking, hanging limp, looking as dazed as she felt. That had to be enough.

Just as the enchanted castle came into view, it occurred to her that she was hanging upside down. Maybe that contributed to the inability to think clearly?

"I've warned them we're coming," Hazel said.

'Na nearly burst out laughing. She would have, if she had enough breath. She had forgotten about the mirror. They were lucky she hadn't fallen out of her pouch when they were twisted around and tumbling through the air.

"Who's—that?" Garnet gasped.

"That's Hazel. She's a magic mirror," 'Na explained.

"Really? I've always wanted to meet one, even though Granny says they're dangerous. She says you can't trust anything that doesn't have a body, and that's always watching you, and talking to others about you."

"I do so have a body!" Hazel cried. "Not to be snappish, young lady, but just how many magic mirrors has your granny met, that she can make such an all-encompassing judgment on the species? Yes, there are evil magic mirrors, just like there are evil woodsmen, evil enchanters, evil bakers, evil fishermen … do you understand what I'm saying?"

"Yes." She gasped a few times, sounding like she was trying not to cry. "I'm sorry if I offended you."

"Oh, that's all right. Ignorance is only offensive when it's maintained. If you try to remedy ignorance, then that makes you a better person, and makes the insult a temporary mistake."

'Na decided Hazel had far too much quiet time to think and get philosophical. The more she learned about Garnet's granny, the more she found to dislike.

"Huh, that's interesting," the mirror said as they approached the castle courtyard. "The watchwillow mirrors report that the werewolves got the wolf away from the monster gamers. He did get tossed around and his hind leg chewed on."

"No!" Garnet wailed and twisted as if in pain. Her face had been turning red from hanging upside down, but now it paled again. 'Na tried to gauge the distance to the ground, fearing the girl would wriggle herself free of Smedley's talons, and fall.

"Is the wolf a friend of yours?" Zella asked.

"Was he protecting you or chasing you?" 'Na had to know.

"Oh … it's complicated," Garnet grumbled. Followed by more sniffles. "We both needed to get to the castle. It may be too late. Maybe Basil lied. Maybe Granny lied!"

"Let's wait until we're on the ground and right side up, all right?" 'Na said.

Smedley came in for one of his graceful, circling landings. She reflected that while it was lovely to see while standing on the ground, it certainly felt like the dragon was showing off and wasting time when observed from up here. And upside down. He settled the girls down with bumps and thuds that threatened to knock the breath out of them again. Considering how they could have landed, 'Na thought he had been unusually gentle. She reminded herself to tell him, once the bruises faded so they weren't quite so stiffly painful.

"Lady Ashlyn says to put you in the top floor of the guest tower, to keep you hidden. There are several new visitors to the forest, heading straight here and using magic to send rather rude messages. Imagine, making demands of the lord and lady of the enchanted castle!" Hazel huffed. "That wretched mask is part of it. I overheard a little bit. It's all rather confusing."

"Complicated?" 'Na said, noticing how Garnet flinched and lost a little more color, when Hazel said "mask."

"That old woman has a voice that could shatter mirrors. She's saying all sorts of nasty things about you, Garnet. Claiming you're a hysterical, spoiled brat who would rather lie than breathe."

"That sounds like Granny," Garnet said, and looked like she fought very hard not to cry.

"Don't worry, I'm ready to consider everything she says as a lie," Zella hurried to say.

"Me, too," 'Na said.

"So are your parents," Hazel said. "It's all right, Garnet. We'll help you. That's what the enchanted castle is for. If you can work your way around all the broken, crazy, twisted spells and other bits of magic filling the place."

"Wait …" Garnet stumbled. "Parents?"

"My parents are the lord and lady of the castle," 'Na admitted.

"Your mother … is the Beastly Beauty?" Now she went even more pale.

"That was years ago." 'Na grew even more sure that mask had something to do with all this. "Trust us."

"Absolutely," Hazel said. "Everything will work out. I imagine all of you could do with a long, hot herbal bath and clean clothes, and an even longer nap to get over your little adventure. I know my nerves are shredded to shards, just waiting for the moment that thong on the bag slid open and

I fell out from five hundred feet up in the air."

Smedley let out a series of burping, crooning rumbles.

"Thank you, dear. I know you'd try to catch me, but, well, I am not that large, and your talons are. Once you're all comfy, Garnet, you do need to tell us the whole story, so we can help you. Complicated is what the enchanted castle does best." She let out a silvery chuckle.

'Na made sure to give Smedley a good rubbing and scratching right on the really itchy spots between the scales at the hinge of his jaw, and told him how clever he was and what a good help he was in their rescue. By that time, several housekeeping breezes had guided Zella and Garnet indoors. When she caught up with them in the guest suite, the breezes already had three huge tubs filled with steaming water smelling wonderfully of all sorts of healing, soothing herbs.

Getting Garnet out of her red cloak and hood turned into a minor tug-of-war. She went pale, tears streamed down her cheeks, and she writhed like a snake, trying to twist and turn and hold onto the cloak. The housekeeping breezes, however, had decades of experience dealing with uncooperative guests and relieving them of filthy or ugly clothes. And magical items they had tried to steal from the castle, when it came to that.

'Na found it odd that the moment the hem of the cloak slipped out of her fingers, Garnet stopped shaking and her color improved. She looked dazed for several moments. Then she took a deep breath, sagged a little, and let the breezes help her out of the rest of her clothes.

"I'll be right back. I need to check with Mother," 'Na said, and hurried out of the suite.

She followed the cloak as it floated down the spiraling stairs and out of the guest wing, along the upper level, straight to the mirror room. That confirmed several growing suspicions. She found her mother spreading the cloak out on the flagstones in front of Eyesallova.

"What sort of magic is in that cloak?" she said.

"Well, just off the top of my frame ..." Eyesallova's swirls of color darkened to mostly deep purple. "I fear half the interfering magic is embedded in it."

"Did we just bring an enemy into the gates?"

"No." Ashlyn settled back on her heels, kneeling with the cloak between her and the mirror. "I'm sure the girl is truly in need of our help. Someone inflicted several spells on her, through this cloak. Please, A'theosius, don't let this be another plot of the Esquadliwoak," she added, her voice dropping to a whisper.

'Na shivered. There truly were few things that frightened her mother, after all the battles she had won and challenges she had conquered, before becoming the lady of the enchanted castle. However, the shadowy league of enchanters who wore a different name in every kingdom they infected was one of them. Their signature magic was multiple layers of spells, so deeply rooted and intertwined that untangling and disconnecting them from their victims could take a lifetime.

She told Ashlyn and Eyesallova of the struggle to get the cloak off Garnet, ending with, "I don't suppose we can just burn that wretched thing, so she can never put it on again?"

"Unfortunately, I can see a dozen or so fine threads of inimical magic leading out of it. Probably straight to the girl. Burning the cloak could hurt her." Eyesallova sighed. "The longer we can keep it away from her, the better."

"Let's hope the wolf has some answers," Ashlyn said.

'Na hurried back to the guest suite, to keep an eye on Garnet. She truly did need a long soak to ease some of those bruises from her rough ride. While the girls soaked, the breezes swirled in and out with all sorts of outfits for them to choose from. 'Na found it interesting that Garnet only wanted red clothes. A personal trait, or a side effect of the magic of the cloak? Maybe her enemy had taken advantage of that to trick her into wearing it.

Garnet seemed completely relaxed until she stepped into the sitting room, where a feast waited for the girls. Her smile didn't so much fall off her face as leap off and push her toward the window. She went deathly white and dug her fingers into the windowsill as she stared at the sun. It perched on the horizon and seemed to hesitate there, as if snagged on the trees on the far side of the wide meadow.

"No. Oh no. Please." She turned, her legs starting to fold, and whimpered as she grappled at the windowsill again. "Please, where is my cloak?"

"We're certainly not going to let you go outside," Zella said. "You look like you're about to faint. Are you ill? We should take her to Herbessa to diagnose."

"Why do you need your cloak?" 'Na said.

"It's magic! It stops me …" Whimpering, Garnet let go of the windowsill and slid to her knees. "Please. I don't want to hurt anyone. Where is my cloak?"

'Na headed for the door, and barely stopped in time to avoid being hit by it as it swung open. Garnet's red hooded cloak swirled into the room on a breeze. For a moment she gaped. How could her mother and Eyesallova have untangled the magic woven into the cloak so soon?

Garnet let out a wail like a howl. She leaped across the room and snatched at the cloak, wrapping it around herself. Weeping quietly, she dropped into the closest chair.

Zella widened her eyes, giving 'Na a "do you know what's going on?" look. 'Na could only shrug.

"Thank you. You have no idea how much danger you were in until …" Garnet sniffled, then froze. Sniffed louder. Then caught up folds of the cloak and pressed it to her nose. "This isn't my cloak … is it?"

"Oh, it just smells different because the breezes washed it," 'Na hurried to say. Now she understood. The breezes had created a copy of the cloak.

"Oh." Garnet's color improved slightly. "Thank you. That's very kind." She tried to smile. "It probably was getting rather … aromatic. I wear it all the time. I even sleep in it."

"Why?" Zella said.

"I'm under a curse. I suppose that's the simplest explanation. Granny gave me the cloak to keep me from turning into …" Garnet sighed and shook her head. "I really don't want to frighten you with the details. It's horrid. And rather embarrassing and …" She shrugged.

"So you came here to get help with the curse?"

Garnet nodded and tugged the hood up, half-covering her face, visibly ashamed.

"It's all right. Everybody who comes here has something wrong with them, something they need help to fix." 'Na sat down on the little couch and took hold of Garnet's hand. "I assure you, no matter how awful you think your curse, we've probably studied or seen any number of stories far more embarrassing and complicated. Not to belittle your problem."

"Really?" Garnet whispered.

"Truly," Zella said. "Do you know who placed it on you? Often there are a number of conditions that have to be fulfilled, to break the curse." She stepped over to the table where she had laid out her journals and pens and ink pots.

"'Na, Eyesallova says you're needed at the door," Hazel announced. "An old woman wrapped in magic has just passed the outer gates. She doesn't want her to go any further than the courtyard."

"What is she like?" 'Na asked, watching Garnet.

"She's very hard to see because of all the spells wrapped around her. She's wearing spectacles the better to see things that are hidden, and an ear horn the better to hear thoughts, and false teeth to make her words strong and biting. All the better to weave word spells and confuse everyone."

"Granny," Garnet said, and an angry flush replaced her pallor. "Hazel?" She wiped the tears off her face with the heels of her hands. "Is there a young man with her?"

"Oh, yes. One of those oafs who spend so much time trying to look and move and sound like a hero, he doesn't have any room in his head for anything else, according to Eyesallova."

"Horatio." She raked her hands through her hair, straightening it a little. "My stepbrother."

"Stay here," 'Na said. "I'll deal with them."

"Bring me with you," Hazel said. "Eyesallova has an idea."

"So do I." She picked up the mirror and strode from the room, only pausing long enough to close the door.

'Na closed every door she passed through on her way from the guest tower to the central hub of the castle, and down the main staircase to the entryway. Several times along the way, she asked the housekeeping breezes to spray perfume to cloud her scent trail, and to sweep the floors and brush the carpets to hide her footsteps. Just in case Granny or Horatio tricked their way into the castle and tried to find Garnet.

She had just reached the opening for the staircase on the third floor when her parents came out of the mirror room. Zared carried the cloak. He tossed it to 'Na. She nearly dropped it. The cloth stung for a moment. She had a sense for inimical magic, inherited from her mother.

"Illusion spell, if you please, Hazel," he whispered. "Wait until we've stepped outside, 'Na, then come only as far as the doorway. Be prepared for a battle."

'Na nodded but hesitated to don the cloak, even with this proof her father had the same idea she had. Masquerade as Garnet and trick Granny into revealing her plan.

"They're almost halfway across the courtyard," Hazel whispered. "Don't let them even step foot on the bottom step."

Ashlyn and Zared hurried the last dozen steps. He flung open the big iron-bound plank doors, then they linked arms and went down the steps. 'Na took a deep breath to brace herself, and nearly let it out in a whoosh a moment later as a tickling sort of tingle enveloped her. Hazel's illusion wrapped around her, making her look like Garnet. She flung the cloak around herself and tugged the hood far forward, hiding her face, as she moved up to the doorway of the castle. She stayed hidden in the shadows, waiting until her father signaled her to come forward, but she could see everything.

A wizened old woman covered in dusty-looking black lace approached the steps where Ashlyn and Zared waited. She clutched the musclebound arm of a young man who strutted like the worst kind of stereotyped hero from the most florid book of ballads and fables. Horatio and Granny. 'Na agreed with Eyesallova's assessment. Horatio's eyes had a vacant sort of look, concentrating so hard on looking heroic, he paid no attention to his surroundings.

"Oh, you are too kind, great lord and lady of the castle. Thank you ever so much for your help. I really must apologize. My granddaughter is out of her mind. She's always been a witless little featherhead, with no grasp on reality. Just ignore whatever she's told you. Give her back to me, so I can take her home. You'll do that for a loving old granny, won't you?" She fluttered her eyelashes, which glittered as if they were full of tears.

"Your granddaughter isn't here," Zared said.

"Yes, she is," Horatio said. He sounded rather as if he had a head cold. "Granny's magic says—"

He *oophed* and bent double, at just the right angle to show Granny's elbow moving out of his ribs.

"More accurately," Ashlyn said, "the girl we are sheltering here isn't your granddaughter. It isn't wise to lie within the walls of the enchanted castle." Her tone cooled. "Nor is it wise to try to use spells within our walls, to look where you aren't welcome, and take what isn't yours to claim."

"Oh, but my dear lord and lady, you don't understand." The old woman's voice strained with the effort to sound feeble and ingratiating. Fury sharpened her tones.

"We understand that when the woodsman, Basil, saw a beautiful young woman traveling the forest, waiting for the portal from Vanyltransia to the enchanted forest to open, he wanted to claim her as his own. Except she had a husband, and was about to give birth, so he convinced you to not only use your spells to keep the portal from opening, but masquerade as a midwife, so the young family would trust you."

"Oh, no, where did you hear such ridiculous, nasty stories?" She shuddered, but 'Na tasted the fury in the air and knew that wasn't fear that made the old woman so pale.

"You did your best to break all the magic mirrors, because you knew they were watching you, to stop you from using your magic to rule in your village and the surrounding countryside. You didn't break them all, and they kept quiet and watched you," Zared said. "Your mistake was in unblocking the portal from Vanyltransia, to try to trick Garnet and her brother into helping you claim the wolf mask. That let the mirrors make contact and warn Eyesallova. The mask has been your goal since you realized Garnet's father was a werewolf. The woodsman wanted their mother, and you wanted the werewolf pelt, so you convinced the woodsman to kill him. But he took the pelt, and you've been scheming for years how to trick him into bringing you the mask. You never realized, when the twins' mother grieved so deeply she gave birth too soon, and died of it, that she was a werewolf as well. In fact, considering how the wolf mask howled the moment Garnet stepped through the door, her mother was of the queen's bloodline."

"No! No!" Granny staggered back several steps, still clutching at Horatio, and nearly yanked him off his feet. "I will not be denied! The mask is mine by right—I earned it!" the old woman shrieked.

"You tried to steal it," Ashlyn countered. "That's not the same thing."

"I raised those two filthy brats! I earned it!"

Full night fell in that moment, and all the torches illuminating the castle courtyard lit themselves. They flickered erratically, stirred by a breeze 'Na couldn't feel. Multiple ugly shadows stretched out from Granny and Horatio.

"The girl is mine. Bring her to me!"

The flames flared with a greenish tinge and threatened to go out.

The cloak twisted around 'Na so swiftly she could barely catch her breath before it tightened, binding her arms to her sides. She dropped

Hazel. The hood slid down over her face and shrank so it blinded and muzzled her. What felt like a giant hand wrapped around 'Na and picked her up and turned her upside down. For the second time today.

Hands snagged her ankles. The cloth of the cloak flamed and took on millions of spider fangs, digging into her. A heartbeat later she hit the steps and tumbled down to the gravel paving the courtyard. The cloak lurched and rippled and she had a sensation of being vomited up. 'Na gasped as she rolled out into clean, free air. She blinked dust out of her eyes, to see her father struggling with the cloak. It twisted and wrenched him from side to side, pulling upward, as if a giant invisible hand played a nasty game of tug-of-war with him.

Granny shrieked ugly-sounding foreign words and spat. Greenish-black sparks streamed from her black lace gloves, like a poisonous fountain that died in sour-smelling puffs of steam before they quite touched Zared.

Ashlyn leaped to his side and caught at the hem of the cloak. Sparks shot up from where she touched it. Granny's cries grew even more shrill. She clutched at Horatio, who stared, his mouth falling open, and his eyes growing wider than his mouth.

"Now, 'Na!" Ashlyn cried.

She leaped to her father's other side and grabbed hold of the cloak. Steam erupted from the cloak, and it writhed and twisted and buckled like a stiff gale yanked on it. The sound of tearing cloth filled the air, deafening loud, turning into a scream. The cloth disintegrated in her hands in a breath, so suddenly there was nothing resisting her. She stumbled and then tumbled backward, falling against her father, with Ashlyn landing on top of them both.

"What did you do?" the old woman snarled. "You'll pay—" She stopped with a choked sort of crackling sound as a howl filled the air.

From inside the castle.

Doors banged open as 'Na picked herself up off the steps. She caught movement, black lace, and lunged on her hands and knees to wrap her arms around Granny's legs to stop her. If Eyesallova said that vicious old hag shouldn't get into the castle, then she wasn't getting into the castle. They went down in a snarling, kicking heap. Horatio stood there, his mouth hanging open. In another minute, he was going to start drooling.

A lean, graceful figure covered in red fur leaped from the landing between the second and third floors to the ground floor. She landed on all fours, panting, tongue lolling out of her mouth. Her face had elongated, her limbs had twisted, taking on extra joints, but she was still clearly Garnet.

"Stupid, stupid girl!" Granny shrieked. "You're supposed to give me the mask. You're not supposed to wear it!"

"How did she get the mask?" Ashlyn cried.

The next moment, Zella hurtled down the steps. A black hulking shape followed her, hitting the flagstones of the entryway with a thud that should have shattered them into dust. The shape unfolded, becoming Behemoth.

'Na had the strangest sensation of a big, victorious, rather nasty grin somewhere inside that gleaming black helmet.

"He gave it to her," Zella cried, gesturing from the suit of armor to Garnet, who stayed crouching before the doors, glaring at Granny.

"Garnet?" Horatio choked out. He took two steps and closed his mouth, swallowing hard.

"Don't be so squeamish," Granny snarled. "One good application of true love's kiss, and she'll be fine again. Who knows? You might not even need the cloak to control her, once you're married. And besides, it's only at the full moon and new moon you have to worry—"

"I'm not marrying that!" he shrieked and turned and raced back across the courtyard to the outer gates.

'Na snorted, watching him go. No one had taught him how to run like a hero. His arms pinwheeled and his legs did a funny sort of sideways kick, so he probably put in twice as much effort as he needed to go forward.

"You!" Granny pointed a gnarled, black lace-covered finger at 'Na. "This is all your fault!"

"No, it's yours," Ashlyn said, stepping up and putting herself between the old woman and her daughter. "You're the one who took a werewolf girl and tried to smother her true nature. You should be ashamed!"

"The mask told me everything," Garnet cried, her voice filled with the wind and all the hunting howls of the werewolves of the enchanted forest. "All these years, telling us we were cursed, making us hide, making us ashamed of what we were. You killed my father! You killed my mother! And for what?"

"Stupid girl," Granny growled, and swept her arm out, gesturing at the shreds of the red cloak. They rose up on a foul-smelling wind. "You will obey me." For a moment, 'Na thought they would reweave themselves into the cloak. "Train a dog, it always obeys."

"I'm not a dog," Garnet growled, and leaped, transforming entirely into a massive red she-wolf. She caught Granny's neck in her jaws and rose up on her hind legs, shaking the old woman until there was a loud snap-crack, and she dissolved in a cloud of fizzling, putrid-smelling sparks. The cloak followed a moment later.

Silence filled the courtyard as the top of the moon peered over the castle walls.

~~~~~

By the time the moon reached zenith that night, Arrasmus and the werewolf tribe had returned with Jasper, Garnet's brother. They took a roundabout path returning to the castle to deal with Basil and retrieve the werewolf pelt. Once it was out of his possession, Basil shrank to half his size, losing his massive black beard and equally massive shoulders. He was unable to pick up his magic axe. Werewolves had a strong code of honor,
~~~~~

and those who weren't reluctant to sully their honor by shredding a defenseless man were repulsed by the stench of his fear and the way he kept bursting into tears whenever any of them bared their teeth at him.

They let him go. According to the monitoring mirrors in the enchanted forest, it took him nearly three weeks of wandering to get back to the portal where he had crossed over from Vanyltransia. His heroic son was too terrified to wait for the portal to open to the correct kingdom to take him home. The last anyone heard of him, he was on the far side of the world, performing sideshow feats of strength to earn a living, with no intention of ever coming home.

Arrasmus was delighted to discover that Garnet and Jasper were his long-lost brother Baneweal's children. Rolf, who had fallen in love with Garnet at first sight, was not so delighted to discover they were relatives. Baneweal had left the forest in his youth on a quest to find the lost descendants of their last queen. He had succeeded, winning Sangriloria as his bride. Their journey back to the enchanted forest took long enough for her to become pregnant. They ran afoul of Granny and Basil when they had to wait for the portal from Vanyltransia to the enchanted forest to open.

"Granny knew the legend of the wolf queen's mask, of course," Arrasmus said.

He had most of the tale from Twinkle, the magic mirror, who had hidden her magical nature to keep Granny from enslaving her and overheard everything over her years of waiting. She had only revealed her true nature to Jasper once she overheard Granny and Basil plotting to kill him. They considered him an obstacle in their plan to control Garnet and use her to bring them the queen's mask. Jasper had to flee before he could share the truth with his sister. His only hope was to find the werewolf tribe and beg for their help. He was waiting for the portal to the enchanted forest to open when Garnet fled, with Basil on her trail. He was still getting used to shifting from wolf to human, and frightened his sister when he approached her in wolf shape. The portal opened just in time for her to flee, with wolf and woodsman chasing her.

Garnet told her side of the story. Granny had convinced the twins that their emerging wolf nature was a terrible curse, and the only way to be free of it was to find the wolf queen's mask in the enchanted castle and bring it back for her to destroy. When Jasper fled, Granny told Garnet her brother was seeking the mask, but he would need her help. She wanted Garnet to go on the quest with Horatio. Garnet overheard Basil and Granny plotting how to finally force her to marry Horatio during the quest, thereby ensuring she stayed Granny's slave. She had fled, hoping to find her brother, and never return home.

There were still werewolves, living in hiding in the far northern forests of Vanyltransia, and Garnet's first act as queen was to vow to find those lost ones and bring them to their safe new home in the enchanted forest. First, though, she and Jasper needed to learn the ways of the werewolves, their laws and customs, lore and culture. Garnet needed to establish herself as a worthy queen.

Ashlyn, Zared, 'Na and Zella accompanied Garnet, Jasper, Arrasmus and the werewolf delegation to the tribe's territory to honor the two ceremonies to be performed. The first was to give an honorable funeral to Baneweal's pelt and break the last binding spells that had enslaved a werewolf's inborn magic to another's use. And the second was to welcome the Red Queen home to her people.

Part of the ceremony included bestowing gifts of friendship. 'Na's made the new queen laugh, when she explained what it was, and what it was for.

A bottle of tiger musk perfume.

THE END

MEET THE AUTHORS

Kathleen Bird is the author of the *Adven Trilogy*, a Christian fantasy series, and the *Isles of Miadhra*, a series of steampunk fairytale retellings. She's also the author of an upcoming devotional, *Seen,* and you can find her writings included in a variety of anthologies! She loves traveling and seeing new places, which give her inspiration for her writing; but when she and her husband are not traveling the world, they live in Des Moines, IA. Be sure to check out her website (www.adventrilogy.wordpress.com) and her Instagram (@birdsthewords) for more information about her books and where to find them.

Rosemarie DiCristo loves mysteries (Nancy Drew, Dana Girls, Trixie Belden, and Judy Bolton were childhood faves) but her only attempts at writing them were a failed "first novel" that's banished to a file cabinet, and a currently-being-pitched middle grade boys mystery… until she co-wrote *The Case of the Missing Legs* with Pam Halter. She's delighted that this story is her third to be published in a Ye Olde Dragons anthology, and is proud to have recently published in a Faith Creativity Life anthology and on the Havok, *Every Day Fiction*, and Flash Fiction Magazine websites.

Jim Doran is a genre writer who enjoys transporting his readers to worlds of wonder, mystery, or danger. Whether it's the fairytale hijinks of his *Kingdom Fantasy* series or his offbeat multi-genre short stories, Jim aims to entertain his audience with every word. Jim has published stories in Ye Olde Dragon Book's *Classic Monster* series, multiple Havok anthologies, and online in *Every Day Fiction*. When he's not writing, he's usually enjoying the seasons in Michigan or playing a board game. Learn more about Jim at jimdorantales.com.

Rachel A. Greco dreams of being a dragon but has settled instead for being an author, which is almost as fun. Her YA fantasy duology, *The Gift of Dragons* and *The Hope of Dragons*, is out now. Her short story, *Fairy Light*, won an honorable mention in the Writer's Digest Annual Writing Competition, and another short story, *Heart of a Volcano*, was published by *Leading Edge* magazine. She is currently working on a project about thought-drinking vampires. When not writing, she can be found reading, kayaking, or dancing with elves in the forests of her North Carolina home. Find her and her enchanting worlds at www.rachelagreco.com.

Pam Halter is a children's, middle grade, YA author who lives in Southern New Jersey. While all her girlfriends were reading Nancy Drew in high school, Pam was a Trixie Belden fan. She enjoys reading mysteries, but this was her first attempt at writing one. It's also her first co-writing adventure. Pam had such a blast co-writing with Rosemarie DiCristo, you'll be seeing more joint stories from them! Read more about Pam at www.pamhalter.com. (Editor's Note: Pam is another of our returning authors, and she's been a fantastic part of our Ye Olde Dragon Books Family. She writes amazing fantasy, with a teensy touch of the macabre!)

Michelle Houston enjoys creating new worlds and civilizations and occasionally getting them on paper. She is a Christian, wife, mother, teacher, and scientist, who strives to connect young adults with the wonders found around us. She spends her free time reading everything in sight, going outside as much as possible (to the relief of the dust bunnies inside), and of course, writing. She would love to connect with you at *whichwaywriting.com*, where you can also find her other stories. (Editor's Note: Michelle is also one of our most prolific authors! She has been in almost every anthology since Ye Olde Dragon Books began.)

Michelle Levigne fell into fantastical fiction writing in college and has yet to escape. She has a bunch of useless degrees in theater, English, film/communication, and writing. She writes in science fiction and fantasy, YA, suspense, women's fiction, and sub-genres of romance. Her stories for the Ye Olde Dragon anthologies are part of the Enchanted Castle Archives series. The heroine of the shorts, 'Na (short for Belladonna) is the daughter of the heroes of the novels. Her training includes the Institute for Children's Literature; proofreading at an advertising agency; and working at a community newspaper. She is a tea snob and freelance edits for a living, but only enough to give her time to write. Her newest crime against the literary world is the storytelling podcast, Ye Olde Dragon's Library, which features audio of new books, as well as chats with authors of fantastical fiction. Be afraid… be very afraid. Despite that, please visit her websites: *Mlevigne.com* and *YeOldeDragonBooks.com*, or her blog, *MichelleLevigne.blogspot.com*.

Yvonne McArthur is a freelance writer, developmental editor, and travel blogger. She has spent over a decade honing her writing skills through her young adult fantasy novel, short stories, poems, blogs, and liturgies, and has worked as a ghostwriter for multiple six-figure travel bloggers. Her stories feature spunky characters who take on everything from overly practical parents to teleporting assassins. She's passionate about stories that encourage us to be kinder, more courageous, and more connected humans.

You can find more of her work at her author website, YvonneMcArthur.com, at her niche travel blog, GuateAdventure.com, which helps thousands of people discover Guatemala every month, and in *These Ties We Forge*, an anthology by Twenty Hills Publishing. She lives in the volcano-studded highlands of Guatemala, where she enjoys motorcycle trips with her goggle-wearing canine sidekick, Lily, and adventures, great and small, with her friends and family.

Lindsi McIntyre is a linguaphile from Texas who hopes to use her words, both written and spoken, to bring glory to the Lord Most High. When not writing she can be found within the pages of a good book or watching the latest episode of her favorite TV shows, and drinking way too much tea while doing both. You can check out more of her work on Havok, grab a copy of *Moonlight and Claws*, *Tales from the Tower*, *Who's the Monster* and *Perchance to Dream* anthologies from Ye Olde Dragon books, or the *Wither and Bloom* anthology from Twenty Hills Publishing. You can also look for her award-winning novella *Broken Pieces* at your favorite online bookstore.

Jessica Noelle is a writer, reader, dreamer, and believer who believes that faith, hope, and a good story are some of the most powerful things there are; after all, stories provide hope and healing for Jessica--and she strives to create speculative fiction stories that in turn do the same. Jessica loves Jesus, playing with her dog, and spending time with her family and friends in addition to large cups of piping hot tea and geeking out over books, Marvel, and more! You can find more of her work via Havok Publishing, Owl Hollow Press, *The Sun Still Rises* Anthology, and Ye Olde Dragon Books' *Perchance to Dream* Anthology. You can also find her gushing about her favorite things on her Instagram (@jessicanoellewrites) or on her website (authorjessicanoellewrites.com).

Stoney M. Setzer lives south of Atlanta, GA. He has a beautiful wife, three wonderful children, and one crazy dog, and he is also a diehard Atlanta Braves fan. He has written a trilogy of novels about small-town amateur sleuth Wesley Winter (*Dead of Winter*, *Valley of the Shadow*, and *Day of Reckoning*). He has also written a short story anthology *Zero Hour*, featuring Twilight Zone-like stories with Christian themes. Several of his stories are set in the fictional community of Sardis County, Tennessee, including his story in this anthology. He has also had some of his short stories featured in such publications as *Residential Aliens* and *Havok*. Learn more at www.tinniepress.blogspot.com or on Facebook@ stoneymsetzerofficial.

Deborah Cullins Smith has been writing stories ever since she could hold a pencil, but she came to her actual career in writing rather late in life. In 2019, she published the trilogy, *The Last of the Long-Haired Hippies*, in a rapid-release timed for the 50th anniversary of Woodstock, which she covered in great detail in the second volume. *CWG Press* released *Shroud of Darkness, The Birth of the Storm,* and *Victoria's War* over a four-month period, a culmination of almost twenty years in development. Ms. Cullins Smith's first Mina Harker adventure, *Mina: Warrior in the Shadows* won the 2022 Realm Award for Horror Novel. Her next novel will continue the saga of Billy the Kid, which she began in the anthology *Moonlight and Claws* with the story "Habitations of Violence," and continued in *Who's the Monster?* with the story "Phillippe." Her love of historical research makes these books challenging, as she is devoted to maintaining as much historical accuracy as possible while sliding things sideways to suggest that a few characters might be more than we gave them credit for! (No disrespect intended.)

Angela R. Watts is the bestselling and award-nominated author of The Infidel Books and the Remnant Trilogy. She's been writing stories since she was little, and has over thirty-five works in print, ranging from gritty adult novels to clean children's fiction. Some of her other titles include *A Solstice of Fire and Light, Winter of the Bees,* and *Where Giants Fall* (a fantasy anthology). Angela is a Christian, editor, article writer for magazines and publishers, founder of Speculative Fiction Society, and artist. If she's not working, she's outside looking for bugs. She lives in Tennessee with her family and many pets. You can get in touch with Angela and follow the journey on social media (@angelarwattsauthor) or subscribe to her newsletter at <u>angelarwatts.com</u>